Missing
Persons

STEPHEN WHITE

TIME WARNER
BOOKS

TIME WARNER BOOKS

First published in the United States in 2005 by Dutton,
a member of Penguin Group (USA) Inc.
First published in Great Britain in May 2005
by Time Warner Books

Copyright © 2005 by Stephen White

The moral right of the author has been asserted.

A CIP catalogue record for this book
is available from the British Library.

HARDBACK ISBN 0 316 72788 1
C FORMAT 0 316 72790 3

Typeset by M Rules
Printed and bound in Great Britain by
Clays Ltd, St Ives plc

Time Warner Books
An imprint of
Time Warner Book Group UK
Brettenham House
Lancaster Place
London WC2E 7EN

www.twbg.co.uk

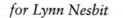

for Lynn Nesbit

. . . Peace is poor reading.
– Thomas Hardy

A girl was missing.
In any other town it would have been local news. Even here,
on any other day, it might have been just local news.
But it wasn't any other town.
It was Boulder.
It wasn't any other day.
It was Christmas.
And a girl was missing.
Again.
God.

1

The fact that I was sitting with Diane behind Hannah Grant's office at 6:30 on a mid-December Thursday evening meant that I'd already lost the argument we'd been having since she yanked me out from behind my desk five minutes earlier. She killed the ignition on her Saab and summed things up for me anyway. 'We can't leave in the morning if we can't reach Hannah. It's that simple.'

She was right.

With only nine shopping days until Christmas, Diane Estevez and I were scheduled to make the short flight over the Rockies to Las Vegas for a weekend professional workshop – Diane, I suspected, was pretending to be much more enamored of EMDR than she really was – and Hannah was generously providing coverage for our clinical psychology practices while we were away. Without coverage, we couldn't go.

Diane had switched our Frontier flight the next day from noon to the cusp of dawn so that she could cram in a few additional hours getting intimate with some dice, and Hannah needed to consent to the slight change in plans. But Hannah – whose adaptive lassoing of her myriad OCD symptoms typically dictated that an unreturned phone call caused her a degree of psychological discomfort equivalent to the physical distress of a sharp stone in her shoe – had failed to return three different messages from Diane since breakfast.

'Is that her car? Do you know what she drives?' I asked. The only other car in the tiny lot was a silver Volkswagen Passat.

'Looks like hers.' Diane offered the comment with a slightly sardonic lilt, and I assumed that she was referring more to the car's pristine condition than to either its make or model. In stark contrast to the spotless Passat, Diane's Saab was covered in the gray-beige film

3

that adheres to virtually every moving vehicle in Colorado after any slushy late fall snowstorm, like the one we'd had the previous weekend.

I stepped out of Diane's car and peered into Hannah's. No clutter on the console. No errant French fries on the floor. No empty Diet Coke can in the cup holder. In fact, the only indication that the vehicle hadn't just been hijacked from a dealer's showroom was a copy of *Elle*, still in its plastic sleeve, on the backseat.

The mailing label on the magazine read 'H. Grant,' and was addressed to the Broadway office. The code in the corner indicated that the subscription would terminate the following April. 'It's hers,' I said.

Diane had joined me beside the Passat. 'Hannah reads *Elle*?'

My own reaction was a little different; I was thinking, *Hannah leaves magazines in her car? Shame!* I said, 'I think you're missing the point. It means she's inside with a patient. She'll return your call when she gets a minute.'

'I don't know about that. I'm getting a feeling,' she said. 'And not a good one.'

'About Hannah?'

'A little, but more about Vegas.' Diane's tone was somber. She took her craps seriously. 'Let's go inside,' she said.

Hannah was a clinical social worker and her therapy practice was in one of the old houses aligned on the side of Broadway closest to the mountains, only a few blocks from the Pearl Street Mall. The cumulative force of more than a decade of migration by psychotherapists had allowed mental-health types to usurp most of that particular urban habitat from sundry lawyers and accountants who had previously set up shop in the houses – some grand, some not – in the row. The uprooted professionals had moved to less charming but eminently more practical spaces in the modern buildings recently erected to fill parking lots a few blocks away on Canyon Boulevard.

The back door of the single-story house was locked. Diane and I followed a flagstone path down the side past a hedge of miniature lilacs that stood naked for winter. We made our way to the front of the building and strolled up a few stairs into a waiting room that had probably been the home's original parlor. On the far side of the lamplit room a thirties-something woman with an astonishing quantity of frizzy hair was sitting on a green velvet settee reading a copy of *Yoga Journal* while munching from a bag of Cheetos. I noted that she checked her wristwatch after she glanced up at us.

I also noted that her fingertips were almost the exact same color as her hair.

'Which office is Hannah's?' I whispered to Diane. I'd never been in the building before. Hannah was one of Diane's close friends; I had no doubt that Diane knew which office she occupied.

'Down that hall on the left. The one on the right is Mary's.'

'Mary' was Mary Black, M.D., a psychiatrist who without benefit of fertility concoctions had given birth to triplet boys only a few weeks before, on Thanksgiving eve. Both Mary's extended maternal adventure and her extended maternity leave were in their earliest stages, which meant that Hannah was without doubt going to be working alone in the building for a while.

Diane stepped down the hall toward the offices. 'Look,' she said.

Stuck into the jamb of Hannah's office door were four folded notes. Two were addressed to 'Hannah,' one was addressed to 'H. Grant,' and one was intended for 'H. G.' Diane picked the one addressed to 'H. Grant.' It appeared to have been written on the back of a page from a daily calendar of unintentionally humorous quotations by the second President Bush.

'What are you doing, Diane?' I blurted. 'Those are probably from patients. You can't read them.'

Without even a microsecond of indecision Diane rejected my protest. 'Of course they're from patients. That's the point,' she said. She glanced at the first note, handed it to me, and said, 'Look, Hannah missed her one o'clock.' Next, she grabbed the paper that was addressed to 'H. G.' 'And see? She missed her four-thirty, too. How come she's missing all her appointments if her car's here? Huh? How the hell do you explain that?'

I didn't know how to explain that.

The other two notes were from patients whose therapist had stood them up earlier in the day. Hannah had apparently been missing her clinical appointments since at least nine o'clock that morning.

The woman with the orange Roseanne Roseannadanna hair appeared behind us in the narrow hallway. Despite the fact that she was balancing on tall, chunky heels, she still had to gaze up at an acute angle to look Diane in the eyes. 'Are you here to see Hannah?' she asked. 'I have a six-fifteen appointment. Every Thursday. She's never late.'

The woman's voice was part annoyed, and part something else. Concern? Fear? I wasn't sure. But her point about Hannah's reliability was well taken. Hannah's obsessiveness was legendary among her friends and colleagues. She was never late.

Never.

I'd begun tasting acid in my throat; I had a bad feeling, too. Though, unlike Diane's, mine had absolutely nothing to do with dice. I tapped lightly on Hannah's office door with my knuckles. My cautious incursion was apparently way too timid for Diane; with an NHL-quality hip-check she moved me aside and grabbed the knob.

The door slid right open.

2

Hannah's classic black patent-leather purse, as un-scuffed as the day it had been crafted, rested on the floor in the middle of the room. It stood up neatly, its arched handles perfectly vertical. But the bag was on the floor.

It shouldn't have been on the floor.

Diane apparently had the exact same reaction I had to the presence of the purse in the middle of the room. But since the distance between her cortex and her mouth was much shorter than mine, she verbalized her conclusion first: 'Hannah would never put her purse there.'

Diane meant on the floor. *Nope.*

In the middle of the room. *Never.*

What was certain was that Hannah had a place for her purse. A specific place. A correct place. I didn't know where she kept it. Probably in a drawer in her desk. Maybe someplace more esoteric, in her filing cabinet under 'P.' But in any circumstance that approached ordinary, she absolutely wouldn't put it on the floor in the middle of the room.

The rest of the office was neat. OCD neat, with one exception: Hannah's coat was tossed carelessly over the top of the desk. I noted the swirled torn paper from an open roll of LifeSavers licking out of one of the coat pockets.

Hannah's 6:15, the woman with the cheddar-colored locks, was trying to peer past us into the office, but she was too short to manage a look over our shoulders. I felt her hand on my back and turned toward her.

I said, 'Hello, I'm Dr. Alan Gregory, one of Ms. Grant's colleagues. Why don't you have a seat in the waiting area while we try to figure out what's going on?' Not overconfident about her emotional stability, I'd adopted a voice that was as comforting as a hot-water bottle wrapped in fleece.

Neither my words nor my tone had the desired effect, though. 'This is *my* time,' the woman protested, tapping the crystal of a garish purple Swatch on her wrist. I detected more than a little pout in her retort, considered the bag of Cheetos, and gave a momentary thought to the clinical regression that Hannah was confronting in her therapy with this woman.

'I know,' I said even more gently. 'I know. But the circumstances today are a little unusual. If you want to leave your name I'll make sure that Ms. Grant gives you a call as soon as we straighten all this out. I'll tell her you were here. I promise.'

She wanted none of it. 'I'll just wait,' she said. 'It is my time. Though I do hope I'm not being charged.'

I sighed, pausing a moment as the woman retraced her steps and resumed her perch on the velvet settee in the waiting room. As she lowered herself to the sofa her fingertips left bright orange imprints on the forest green velvet upholstery. Once I was sure she was settled, I joined Diane inside the doorway to Hannah's office.

I said, 'I think you should go check the bathroom, Diane. Maybe Hannah fell or something.'

'Oh God!' she said. 'Of course. Why didn't I think of that?' She rushed past me and down the hall.

I'm not sure why I did what I did next. Maybe it was because I was standing by myself in the hallway feeling lost and stupid. Maybe it was intuition. Maybe it was because I thought the Cheetos lady might be back and I was looking for a place to hide. I don't really know.

What I did was that I took half a step across the narrow hall and tried the knob on Mary Black's office door. To my surprise I discovered it unlocked. Immediately after I let go of the knob the door began to swing open on its own, as though the old building was listing just the slightest bit in that direction.

One look inside and I knew Hannah was dead.

I knew it because living people's flesh is never that shade of gray and living people can't, or don't, hold the posture that Hannah was in. Her body was splayed backward over a leather cube ottoman, her head only a yard from the edge of the open door. Her legs were spread immodestly, her torso twisted forty-five degrees at her waist. A dark pool stained an area the size of a basketball on the dhurrie rug below her legs. My gut reaction was: blood. But my nose said urine.

Hannah's right arm was bent at the elbow and the thumb of her right hand was hooked in the fabric of the silk blouse near her armpit, as though she'd been thinking about hitchhiking someplace when she died.

Oddly, the left front tail of Hannah's blouse was tucked up under the front of her bra, exposing a few inches of pale abdomen. Why a woman would tuck her blouse up under her bra, I couldn't begin to guess.

Hannah's mouth was open, as were her eyes, and her fine dark hair spilled down, perfectly filling the eight- or nine-inch space that existed between the back of her head and the worn finish of the old pine floor.

I dropped to one knee and touched the smoothly stretched skin on Hannah's neck with the tips of three fingers. I tried not to look into her dark brown eyes but they drew me in like pools of still water. Despite shifting my fingertips a few times I couldn't find a carotid pulse. It didn't matter; the chill of Hannah's flesh on my own had already confirmed to me that I wouldn't.

Hannah had been dead a while. I recalled the four notes that had been stuck in the jamb of her office door, and figured that she had fallen into her current posture sometime that morning. The arithmetic was simple. My watch said 6:45 P.M. Hannah's first known missed appointment had been almost ten hours earlier, at 9 A.M. A brief stint as a coroner's investigator earlier in my career had taught me the usually trivial fact that, after death, human bodies at room temperature yield core temperature at the rate of about one degree an hour. Ten hours meant ten degrees. I guessed that the flesh that my fingers had just touched was probably a good ten degrees cooler than my own.

But I knew it could have been cooler than that, or warmer than that. My experience touching the flesh of dead people was, admittedly, limited. I allowed for the possibility that Hannah had been dead since the night before and I tried to recall how long a body needed to be dead before the stench of death became apparent. Couldn't.

I began inhaling slowly and self-consciously, as though I hadn't already been breathing the air in the room. I thought it tasted stale and sour, but the only foreign odor I detected was that spill of urine.

I knew that medical examiners working to determine time of death also did calculations about flying insects and their eggs and the life cycle of maggots, but I quickly decided that I would leave that entomological arithmetic to them.

I was also self-aware enough to know that I was doing all the distracting contemplating so that I wouldn't be forced to confront the fact that I was unexpectedly alone in an office with a friend's dead body.

Behind me I noted the sound of a toilet flushing, followed by the timbre of water running, the click of a door opening, and the cadence of familiar footsteps down the hall. Diane, apparently forgetting that she and I were not alone, called out, 'Hannah's not there, but I really had to pee.'

I backed out of the room and saw Diane retracing her steps down the hallway from the bathroom. Her eyes caught mine, registering wariness that quickly disintegrated into shock as she digested my expression. I blocked her path and took her into my arms before she could reach the entrance to Mary Black's office. I whispered into her hair, 'Your friend is dead. I'm so, so sorry.'

The sound that came from Diane's throat as she processed my words was plaintive and poignant. Resignation and denial and the first disbelieving chords of grief were all mixed into one long, sad wail.

When I looked up I saw the Cheetos lady standing at the other entrance to the hallway, tears streaming down her face. A bright orange smudge across her cheeks marked the spot where she'd tried to wipe away her grief.

And failed.

3

Neither Diane nor I was going to get home in time for dinner.

It had taken all of my physical strength to keep Diane away from her friend's inert body – I was far from being able to consider it a corpse – and it had taken all my powers of persuasion to get both Diane and the Cheetos lady out of the house while we waited for the police to arrive.

I was staggered by Hannah's death, but my loss was nothing compared to the loss that either Diane or Hannah's patient was feeling. I kept telling myself that I could freak out later.

Diane needed to freak out now.

Outside the house, after I'd called 911 on my cell, I was standing helplessly with Diane on the front walk when she said, 'I don't want to leave Hannah alone. She shouldn't be alone. Let me go in and wait with her. Please. What can it hurt?'

My arm was firmly around her shoulders and I know I whispered replies to her pleadings, but I don't recall exactly what I said. My tight grasp on Diane reinforced my words: I didn't think she should go back inside.

Had Hannah died at home after an illness I would have led Diane to her friend's bedside, not held her back. But Hannah had apparently died in strange circumstances in her colleague's office. Until those circumstances became clear, I knew from my coroner's experience that the environment around Hannah's body should stay uncontaminated.

Three things kept replaying in my brain.

Hannah had been in Mary Black's office, not in her own.
Hannah's purse had been in the middle of her office floor.
Her shirt was pulled up and tucked under her bra.

Why, why, and why?

The lady with the frizzy hair had moved away from Diane and me and taken off her shoes. She was sitting, almost immobile, her chin in her hands, on one of the steps leading up to the wooden porch at the front of the house. Her tears had stopped flowing, her expression a blank mask of shock.

'Are you sure she's dead?' Diane demanded more than once in those first few moments. I explained that I'd felt for a pulse and told her that Hannah's skin was already cold. And then I explained it again.

I didn't say anything about the dark stain of urine.

'She hates being cold,' Diane protested. 'Hannah shouldn't be cold. She doesn't like winter. Maybe a blanket. I could find a blanket. I have one in the car. Raoul makes me keep one in the car in case . . .'

It wasn't easy but I was able to get Diane settled on a kidney-shaped concrete bench that sat amidst some wild grasses beside the front walk about halfway to the street. I stepped a yard away from her, pulled out my cell phone, hit the speed dial and reached Lauren, my wife, who had probably just walked in the door from her job as a prosecutor for Boulder County.

'Hey, it's me. I'm glad you're home.'

'What's wrong?'

She could tell something was.

'Hannah Grant?' I said. 'You remember her?'

'Diane's friend.'

'She was going to cover for us while we were in Vegas. She's dead. We just found her body in her office. We're waiting for the cops.'

'My God. Are you all right?'

'We're okay. Call Raoul, okay? Tell him Diane's going to be late. I don't know how late, but you know how these things go. It's probably going to be a while.' Raoul Estevez was Diane's husband. 'Di-ane's very upset. They were close friends.'

Lauren set her empathy aside for a moment and got down to business. Her business. Cops and courts and lawyers and bad guys. 'Do you and Diane need lawyers?'

'No, nothing like that. Hannah wasn't returning Diane's messages about coverage for our trip. We were concerned. We just walked in and . . . found her body. That's all.'

'You're sure? Don't just say yes. I want you to think before you answer me.'

I thought. 'Yeah, that's all.'

'How did she die?'

'No idea. There was no blood I could see. Could be natural causes, but my gut says not. Her body's in a funny position.' I was still thinking, too, about that black patent-leather purse in the middle of the floor and about the blouse tucked up under the front of her bra. 'Is there any reason a woman would tuck her shirttail up under the front of her bra?' I asked.

'What? The front tail?'

'Yes.'

'No, not that I can think of.'

From the south side of the Pearl Street Mall I heard the piercing intrusion of a siren approaching, fast.

I said, 'The cops are here, babe. I should go.'

'I'll make some calls. Stay in touch. I love you.'

'Me, too,' I said. Diane walked up next to me. I said, 'Lauren's going to call Raoul and let him know what's going on.'

'What is going on?' she asked me. 'Do we know?'

The first of what would become four squad cars rolled up over the curb and then slowly powered up onto the sidewalk, blocking the path. A couple of patrol cops I didn't know jumped out of the car. The look on their faces was either that they didn't believe whatever the dispatcher had told them about why they were rolling to the Broadway address, or that they were hoping the dispatcher had gotten the story wrong. I stepped forward, introduced myself, told them I had called 911, and I explained what we had found inside.

One cop marched to the front door to check out my story. The other one stayed outside with his three witnesses. A minute later a couple of EMTs arrived in their bright, boxy wagon. They too went inside to confirm what I already knew. Everything everyone did, it seemed, was preceded and followed by whispers into radios.

To me it all felt like slow motion. I was thinking: *Somebody is dead. We should hurry.* The reality was, of course, different. The reality was: Somebody was dead. What was the point of hurrying?

More patrol cops arrived in the next few minutes, and after a brief consultation with the two first responders a couple of them strung a perimeter of crime-scene tape that reached all the way to the big trees along the front curb and included the larger houses and yards on each side. Gawking drivers quickly brought traffic to a virtual standstill.

Call it bad luck, call it a side effect of being married to a prosecutor, or of being best friends with a cop, but I'd been around enough crime scenes to know what to expect and wasn't at all surprised that Diane and the Cheetos lady and I were soon separated from one another.

The women were each offered a seat in the back of different squad cars while I was shuttled to the front porch of the elegantly restored Victorian next door. From there I watched the cluster of uniformed cops disperse. Two headed to the back of the house clutching a fat wheel of crime-scene tape. The ones who'd stayed in front were trying to look like they had something important to do, something besides wait. The EMTs waited for something, too.

We were all doing indeterminate time in the wake of unexplained death, a sentence that would endure until the arrival of an unmarked car bringing detectives to the scene.

Part of me wanted to see my friend, Sam Purdy, step out of the detectives' sedan.

That was the selfish part.

The generous part of me hoped that he had the evening off.

4

Sam had the evening off.

As soon as the two detectives who were catching new felony cases on that shift climbed out of their car, I recognized them. One was a buff, square-jawed, tight-eyed man named Jaris Slocum. Over a year before, while I'd been visiting Sam in the detective bureau in the Public Safety Building on 33rd Street, he had introduced me to Slocum as we passed each other in a long hallway. Once we'd paced out of eavesdropping range on our way to lunch somewhere, Sam had added, 'Slocum's kind of an asshole.'

I recognized Slocum's partner, too, though until that moment I hadn't known he was a cop. He was, like me, an avid recreational bicyclist. We ran into each other a few times a year on Boulder's back roads or in the nearby mountain canyons. The previous September we had ended up in an impromptu posse that had done a couple of memorable training climbs together up Four Mile. He was a pleasant, not-too-competitive guy who had legs and lungs that were designed for steep inclines. He was younger than me, stronger than me, and better looking than me. I knew him simply as Darrell.

The two detectives ambled across the sidewalk and checked in with the patrol cop who was manning the log. I watched him point at me seconds before the detectives climbed the slope of the front lawn toward my solitary aerie on the neighboring building's front porch.

Remembering Sam's caution about Slocum, I greeted the bicyclist detective first. 'Hi, Darrell. What a night.' I held out my hand. 'Alan, Alan Gregory. Remember me?' He didn't. 'We climbed Four Mile together a few months back? I see you occasionally when you ride.'

It took Darrell a second but he finally recognized my face. 'Alan?

Yeah, hi. You're, um, part of this?' He waved his left arm in the general direction of Hannah Grant's dead body.

'Unfortunately. I was the one who found her. Hannah. She's a colleague. Was. I'm a psychologist.' The last sentence felt like a complete non sequitur to me. I imagined that it did to Darrell, too. I added, 'Hannah was a social worker.'

'You're the RP?' He caught himself using cop vernacular and added, 'The one who called this in?'

RP. Reporting party. 'Yes.'

Slocum stepped up and took charge. His intrusion had all the subtlety of a belch during grace at Thanksgiving dinner. 'Sit right there, sir. Yes, on those steps behind you. Don't speak with anyone until we're ready to interview you. Do you understand my instructions, sir?'

For some reason – possibly the vice-principal tone in his voice – I found myself questioning the sincerity of his repeated use of 'sir.'

Jaris Slocum either didn't recognize me, which wouldn't have been surprising, or – and this was a more worrisome possibility – had recalled our prior introduction and decided that any friend of Sam Purdy's deserved an additional bolus of hard-ass attitude.

Fifty feet or so away from me a damn good woman lay dead. During traffic lulls I could hear Diane weeping from the backseat of the patrol car where she had been stashed. The Cheetos lady was still looking like she'd just lost her only friend in the world. The sum of those parts? I was in absolutely no mood for any I'm-the-boss-and-you'll-do-what-I-say cop crap from Detective Jaris Slocum.

'And you are?' I said. My tone wasn't exactly a model of I'd-love-to-cooperate-Detective.

Detective Darrell's badge wallet was hanging on his belt for all to see. Slocum's wasn't. Wisely, Darrell chose to answer my question even though it had been addressed to his partner. He was busily trying to douse the lit matches that Slocum and I were slinging at the kindling in each other's pants. To me, he said, 'This is Detective Jaris Slocum. And this is Alan . . . ?'

'Gregory,' I said.

'He and I ride together sometimes,' Darrell explained to Slocum.

'That's nice. Now sit, Alan Gregory. We'll be back to talk to you. Wait for us, understand?'

'I still haven't seen a badge,' I said. I shouldn't have said it. But I did.

Slocum couldn't find his badge wallet. He checked all his pockets, and then he patted them all a second time. Finally, after an exasperated exhale he barked, 'It must be in the car.'

If Slocum had wanted to transport the annoyance that he packed into those few words he would have needed a wheelbarrow, or a tractor-trailer.

'I can wait,' I said. 'Go ahead and get it. I'd like to see some ID. I think that's my right.'

Slocum and I both knew he wasn't about to slink back to his big Ford and fish around for his detective shield at my behest. He gave me an icy blue-eyed stare. 'I said to have a seat.'

I said, 'I'm fine standing.'

He took a step toward me. 'And I said to sit.'

I came so close to saying 'fuck you' that my lower lip actually came together with my bottom teeth.

Darrell sensed what was developing as though he knew either Slocum or me real well. I knew the person he knew real well wasn't me.

'Enough,' he said.

He was talking to both of us.

I had to cool my heels for almost an hour before the detectives got back to me. From what I could see, they'd spent most of the time either singly or together with the Cheetos lady and with Diane. For a while I was perplexed why they didn't go inside the offices and start detecting in there where Hannah and the evidence were, but then I realized they were probably waiting for a search warrant to arrive at the scene.

In the meantime, I was cold and exhausted and hungry and sad and angry and impatient and would have been much more comfortable sitting on the stoop than walking in circles on the front porch.

But I stood. It was a point of honor. Or a badge of stubbornness. One of those things.

The story I had to tell about discovering Hannah's body wasn't complicated and once things had calmed down a little bit between

Slocum and me, it was simple to discern from the detectives' questions that Slocum and Olson – his cop ID had revealed not only bicyclist Darrell's last name, but also a double dose of middle initials, C. and R. – were primarily interested in two specific areas of my narrative.

The first? Why had I decided to reach across the hall and try to open the door to Mary Black's office? I stuck with the truth on that one – I didn't know. I just didn't know. It was one of those things that I had just done.

The truth, however, didn't set me free. One of the detectives – either Darrell Olson playing good cop, or Slocum naturally taking on the role of bad – revisited the question of me opening Mary Black's door at least five times during our relatively brief discussion. They seemed as dissatisfied with my fifth reply as they had been with the first. I told them I wished that I had a better explanation, but I didn't.

The second focus of the detectives' interest was more concerning to me. They wanted to know what I had been doing the rest of the day – minute-by-minute, hour-by-hour – up until the moment Diane dragged me from my office to her Saab to drive to Hannah's office.

'What? You mean from the moment I got out of bed? That early?' I asked in a futile attempt at levity when Slocum pressed me on my day's itinerary for the second or third time.

'Sure,' he replied. 'Assuming you have a witness for that part of your day, too.' His cold eyes weren't smiling at all but his cheekbones had elevated just enough to let me know that he was enjoying whatever temporary advantage he thought he had.

Not for the first time that evening I thought, *God, Sam, you're right. Slocum is an asshole.*

'As a matter of fact, I do have a witness. I want you to be sure to write this name down. Are you ready?'

He glared at me as though he'd rather beat me with a long stick than do what I suggested, but he brought his pen down so that the nib hovered just above the page in his notebook.

Stressing each syllable for his benefit, I said, 'My witness, for this morning's events, is Deputy DA Lauren Crowder of the Boulder County District Attorney's office.' I slowly dictated the ten digits of our home phone number, and then added Lauren's office number for emphasis. 'Give her a call. Please. I'm sure she'll be thrilled to tell you what time her husband crawled out of bed this morning.'

Slocum stopped writing.

Darrell Olson took a step back so that his partner wouldn't spot the smile that was forming on his face.

I said, 'I'm going home now, Detective. I think you know how to reach me if you have any more questions.'

Slocum made a quick move toward me – or at me – but Darrell stepped forward and spoke before his partner could do something he would regret. 'Warrant's here, Jaris. Come on, let's go inside and see what we have.'

I didn't go right home. I found Raoul, Diane's husband, pacing outside the crime-scene tape and filled him in on all that had happened late that afternoon. He was almost too agitated to attend to my words. Raoul Estevez had a roster of relatives who had not survived Franco's reign in Spain, and the sight of his wife squeezed into the back of a squad car being peppered with questions from law enforcement authorities wasn't sitting particularly well with him.

'She is not under arrest?' he demanded, his words causing little cartoonish puffs of steam in the cold air. Although it's his second language – actually, his fourth or fifth – Raoul's English is better than Prince Charles's, but the American legal system still perplexed him at times. English is my only language, isn't in Prince Charles's league, and the American legal system still perplexed me at times, too. Still, since I was the natural-born citizen, I assumed the responsibility of translating the proceedings for Raoul.

'No, they're just questioning her about what happened, what she saw, that's all. She'll be done soon. She didn't see much; I found Hannah's body.'

As if on cue, Slocum, who had not taken his partner's advice about going inside and looking around, hopped out of the cruiser and, I thought, reached in to help Diane from the backseat.

'See?' I turned to Raoul. 'It looks like she's done.'

Diane suddenly yelled, 'Get your goddamn hands off me!'

Raoul's voice grew hard. 'It doesn't look that way to me.'

I turned back to the cruiser. Slocum had Diane completely out of the car and was twisting her ninety degrees so he could shove her face-first up against the rear fender of the black-and-white. Instantly he had her legs spread past shoulder width and in seconds he had her arms behind her back and handcuffs on both her wrists.

I was shocked. 'Don't, Raoul.' I had to stand in my friend's path to keep him from crossing the yellow tape and joining the fray. I planted my feet on the ground and both my hands on Raoul's hard chest. Finally, he stepped back.

Ten seconds later I had Lauren on the phone. 'Get Cozy down here fast. I think Jaris Slocum just arrested Diane for something.'

Lauren said, 'Slocum? God help us, he's such an asshole lately.'

The verdict, it appeared, was unanimous.

5

Cozier Maitlin lived, literally, around the corner.

From my sentry position just outside the crime-scene tape, I spotted Cozy on the sidewalk as he was descending the final steep section of hill that drops down from Maxwell toward Broadway. Despite the crowd of gawkers gathered around the yellow police tape, he wasn't that hard to spot. Cozy stood six-feet-nine.

I checked my watch – no more than seven or eight minutes could have passed since Jaris Slocum had cuffed Diane and shoved her rudely back into the rear seat of the black-and-white.

Pointing toward the corner, I said to Raoul, 'That's the defense attorney Lauren called.'

'That was fast. He's tall.'

'He's good. He helped Lauren with that thing, you know, a few years ago. Hey, Cozy!'

Cozy didn't break stride as he approached, or wave. Maybe he elevated his chin an additional millimeter or two, but that was the only indication that he'd heard me calling his name. He was wearing the same suit I imagined he'd worn to his downtown office that morning – the blue was a navy that shared a lot of DNA with black, and it was lined with the palest of gray pinstripes. His white shirt appeared freshly starched and his black shoes were the shiniest things on the block.

A nice, full-length umbrella or a walking stick would not have been out of place accessorizing his outfit.

We shook hands. 'Good evening, Alan. At least the location is convenient this time. And the weather is delightful for December. No blizzard. I can't tell you how grateful I am for that.'

'Thanks for coming so quickly, Cozy. This is Raoul Estevez. Raoul, Cozier Maitlin.'

'A pleasure, Mr. Estevez. I'm aware of your work.' That was Cozy's way of communicating that he wasn't worried about his fee. 'It is your wife who is being detained?'

'In that car.' Raoul pointed at the squad that was parked at an angle on the lawn in front of the building where Hannah lay dead.

'Do you want to know what happened?' I asked.

'I understand someone died here under suspicious circumstances. Beyond that, not really. If either of you was an intimate of the deceased, please let me offer my condolences,' Cozy said, insincerely. He lifted one of his long legs, stepped over the crime-scene tape, and somehow managed to adopt an even more imperial deportment as he moved out onto the lawn. He paused, turned back to Raoul, and said, 'Give me a moment or two to sort this out. Everything will be fine. It will.' After one more step, Cozy looked back over his shoulder at me. 'Lauren said I'd be speaking with Jaris Slocum. That's true?'

I nodded. I considered the wisdom of editorializing about Detective Slocum's apparent personality flaws, but decided that I didn't need to do anything to inflame the situation any further.

'Slocum is . . . difficult,' Cozy said. He said it in such a way that it sounded more damning than Sam Purdy informing me that Slocum was an asshole, or than Lauren concurring.

'That's been my experience so far this evening,' I replied.

I was feeling a million things. Grief, anger, frustration, fear, even some relief, now that Cozy was there. Still, my anticipation of what was to come next was so sharp that I would have yanked out my wallet and maxed out all my credit cards for a ticket to the production I was about to get to witness for free.

Cozy immediately marched over to the cruiser and confronted the patrol cop assigned to keep watch on Diane, who was continuing to fume in the backseat. Cozy's approach wasn't tentative, and didn't have any excuse-me-please in it. He moved in until he stood toe-to-toe with the cop, a young black man who was about six-two, 210.

Cozy dwarfed him.

Cozy's introductory gambit to the officer consisted of a few words that caused the man to react by trying to step back to create some breathing room. But since the cop was already leaning against the car there was no place for him to go and he had to crane his neck upward

22

to even see Cozy's face. I imagined that the view was like gazing up from below Mt. Rushmore.

The patrol cop listened to Cozy for only another beat or two before he raised his voice and barked, 'Step back, sir! Step *back*! Now! That's a warning!'

The cop's hand gravitated ominously toward his holster.

I held my breath and instinctively grabbed Raoul's arm so he wouldn't do something valiant, and stupid. I'd known him a long time, and knew that Raoul was capable of both.

Cozy, of course, didn't step back an inch. He was daring the cop to get physical with him. And if the young cop preferred to do loud, Cozy could do loud just fine. With volume that matched the patrol cop's do-what-I-say voice and then raised a few decibels for good measure, Cozy announced, 'I am her attorney and I would like to speak with my client, officer. Officer' – Cozy leaned back at his waist so that he could read the cop's name tag – 'Leamer. It's a pleasure to meet you. My client – that is she, by the way, that you are *protecting* – won't, will not, be answering any more of the detectives' questions tonight.'

The volume of that soliloquy drew virtually everyone's attention to the cruiser, including Jaris Slocum's. He was up on the front porch and immediately began a march toward the car with long strides, his hands tightened into fists. Cozy must have felt him coming. He spun away from the patrol cop and greeted Slocum with, 'A pleasure seeing you, as always. Is my client actually in custody, Detective?'

Slocum stopped five feet from Cozy. I don't know why he kept his distance – maybe so that he wasn't close enough to shake Cozy's outstretched hand. Slocum's mouth opened and closed about a centimeter as he tried to process the latest developments: A large, imperial criminal defense attorney had penetrated the perimeter and he seemed to be making speeches for the benefit of the dozens of gathered citizens.

Not good.

'Haven't decided? Is that it? Perhaps I can help,' Cozy taunted. His words were polite, his tone was even doing a clever masquerade as respectful. But everyone, especially Slocum, knew it was a taunt.

Slocum opened his mouth again, but still no words came out. Finally he was able to mutter, 'I'm trying to investigate a suspicious death here.'

23

Cozy's reply was immediate. 'Good for you. As a taxpayer, I applaud your . . . conscientiousness. But that is neither here nor there at the moment, is it? The question at hand is, you see, quite simple.' Cozy leaned over and smiled at Diane in the backseat of the cruiser before returning his attention to Slocum. 'Is my client in custody? Yes or no?'

Cozy's voice carried through the heavy December air as though he were a thespian center stage at the Globe.

'She is not under arrest.'

'Ah, but I didn't ask you that, did I?' He was doing his best to sound like Olivier doing Henry IV. 'I asked you if my client was in your custody – yes, or no.'

I could barely discern Slocum's response. I thought he said, 'For now, she is . . . um, being detained for questioning.'

'I appreciate that clarification. As of now she is officially declining your invitation for further questioning, so I assume, then, that she is free to go.' Cozy leaned over and made quite a show of staring into the backseat of the cruiser. With mock horror he added, 'Has she been handcuffed, Detective Slocum?' He included Jaris's name so that the assembled citizenry would know who was responsible for the travesty. Had he next recited Slocum's badge number – had Slocum been wearing a badge – I would not have been surprised. 'Is that possible? Is she really handcuffed and locked in the backseat of a police cruiser? Are you planning on taking her to the jail and *booking* her?'

'She was not being cooperative.'

Cozy held out his own wrists and used the full power of his baritone. 'Was she? Like my client, I too am planning to be uncooperative if this is the way the Boulder Police Department is choosing to behave toward its law-abiding citizens.'

'Mr. Maitlin,' Slocum implored.

At that moment I actually had just the slightest sympathy for Jaris Slocum. Cozy's performance had gone more than a little over the top.

Cozy ignored Slocum's plea and made a great show of holding out his French-cuffed wrists to see if Slocum would dare put a slightly less elegant pair of cuffs on them. 'Would you like to handcuff me, as well? Is that the current policy of the department when citizens exercise their constitutional prerogatives to grieve silently?'

I could tell that Jaris Slocum would have loved nothing better at that moment than to handcuff Cozier Maitlin, but the presence of fifty or so civilian witnesses served to deter his more primitive impulses.

Darrell Olson's primary role in his detective partnership was, apparently, to sense what was about to go wrong between Slocum and one of Boulder's citizens. Once again, Darrell did his job with aplomb. He rushed up, grabbed Slocum's arm, pulled him closer to the house – and much farther from Cozy – and went nose to nose with him for about half a minute. I couldn't hear a word of their argument but my respect for Darrell C. R. Olson expanded exponentially as he barked whatever he was barking. When the tête-à-tête between the two detectives was over, Slocum climbed the porch and marched into the old house where Hannah lay dead.

Olson returned to Cozy. He used a low voice to address him, modeling for him, hoping to reduce the inflammation. As he spoke he spread his hands in conciliation, palms up, like a don trying to pacify a peer. I couldn't tell what he was saying, but it took him a minute or more to get through it.

Cozy's reply wasn't a whisper; his tone remained floridly oratorical. 'No, Detective. Not in a few minutes. Right now. I want the cuffs off my client and I want her released. Now. There is no point whatsoever in prolonging her agony. She is despairing over her friend's death. I guarantee you that this interview is over for tonight.'

Olson dipped his head a little and spoke again. It was apparent that he was still determined to try to be deferential, to try to lower the temperature of the conflict a little, but that he was also trying not to roll over to Cozy's demands.

Cozy listened to Darrell's continued plea, thought for a moment, and decided that he wanted none of it. He said, 'Now, Detective.' Cozy gestured toward the old house and Jaris Slocum, and in a much lower, tempered voice added, 'That man is your problem, not mine. You have my sympathy, but nothing more. Now, please.'

Olson shook his head, scratched his ear, stuffed his hands in his pockets, and mumbled something to Officer Leamer. Without so much as a nod, the detective walked away from Cozy and the patrol car.

Leamer opened the back door of the cruiser, helped Diane to her

25

feet, and removed the handcuffs from behind her back. The fire in her eyes, if focused, could have ignited candles across the street.

Cozy introduced himself to his client and said something to her so quietly I couldn't discern a word. Diane had fresh tears on her face. She said, 'Thank you, thank you.' Then, as though she'd somehow forgotten, she cried, 'My God, Hannah's dead.'

Raoul said, 'That's it?' Actually, what he said was, *'C'est fini?'*

I said, 'For now.'

6

Diane and I didn't make it to Vegas.

Hannah Grant's ashes were interred the following Tuesday after a sentimental service in one of the downtown churches. I had never before seen so much of Boulder's mental health community present in one place.

I was in a pretty good position to know that the police were flummoxed by the case. The local media was already reporting that the cops had no active leads. Lauren confirmed to me that after a week the investigation was spinning its wheels. My friend Sam Purdy, the Boulder police detective, usually wouldn't talk out of school about important cases with me, but he did roll his eyes when I mentioned Hannah.

That told me a lot.

During one late-night phone conversation he went way out on a limb. 'We got crap,' was what he said.

Lauren swore me to secrecy but revealed that Slocum and Olson had located no witnesses to anything that supported a finding of homicide. No one had seen Hannah leave her south Boulder condo the morning of her death, but she'd arrived at Rallysport Health Club early enough to work out before driving away just before 8:30. The time was almost certain. Two different witnesses recalled an incident in the locker room – Hannah had tripped over another woman's gym bag on the way back from the shower and both women had fallen hard to the floor. The witnesses were confident that they knew what time Hannah had dressed after her workout before heading to her car.

They were confident about one other thing, too. As she fell, Hannah had definitely hit her head on the tile floor. Someone had offered to go get ice. Hannah had declined; she said she was fine and had to get to work.

No one reported seeing her arrive at her office building. The few of Hannah's patients who had shown up for appointments on the day she died and who had voluntarily come forward to speak with the police reported nothing that provided any direction for the investigation.

The detectives weren't able to develop any motive for an assault. Hannah's personal life revealed no promising leads. Her finances were pristine. Her professional record was free of formal complaints.

The cops had no physical evidence that a crime had been committed. Actually, the truth was that they had way too much physical evidence. The little office building was chock-full of fingerprints and trace evidence. Dozens of different patients made their way through the space every week.

Hair, fibers? All the police could want, and more. Apparently Hannah's obsessive-compulsive tendencies had lacunae in the terrain where 'neat' stopped and 'clean' began. For investigators, Hannah's housekeeping weakness created a problem. To use trace evidence to rule in the presence of an intruder in the building, Jaris Slocum and Darrell Olson had to rule out the presence of any and all routine visitors to the building, which meant – minimally – obtaining exemplar prints and DNA samples from all of Hannah's patients and all of Mary Black's patients and from any other routine visitors to the building, including the woman who delivered the mail, the guys from UPS and FedEx, and the various tat-ted and pierced kids who delivered takeout from restaurants on the nearby Pearl Street Mall.

Mary Black, the psychiatrist and mother of three who shared office space with Hannah, declined to make her patient roster available to the police, citing doctor-patient confidentiality. Diane, whom Hannah had entrusted with the clinical responsibility of closing her practice in the event of her death, also declined to make Hannah's patient roster available to the police, citing the same doctor-patient confidentiality issues. When the police pressed the issue, she'd enlisted Cozy Maitlin to run interference for her.

Diane was ambivalent about keeping the information to herself. After what Jaris Slocum had done to her the evening Hannah's body was discovered, Diane wasn't, of course, particularly inclined to cooperate with him. But she was eager to do anything she could to help identify anyone who might have had anything to do with Hannah's death. As far as Hannah's patient roster was concerned, though, Diane had decided that was information to which Slocum wasn't entitled.

Hannah's death officially remained 'suspicious' until the Boulder County coroner issued his report eight days after her death. The medical examiner had identified two discrete blows to Hannah's head, and he identified her cause of death as traumatic head injury resulting in cerebral hemorrhage. He specified the manner of her death as 'undetermined.' The ME's opinion was that the damage inflicted by a flat surface, possibly the tile floor at Rallysport, had not been sufficient to cause Hannah's death. Hannah's death was directly attributable to the second head trauma, origin unknown.

The dual traumas either had been unintentional blows suffered during the fall in the gym the morning she died – one impact caused by the tile floor, one by something else – or had been the result of two blows to her head intentionally inflicted by an assailant. Sam pointedly reminded me that a third possibility existed: One blow had been suffered during the fall at the health club, and the second blow, the fatal one, had been inflicted by an assailant at Hannah's office.

Diane heard the coroner's findings first. Diane always tended to hear gossip first. What source she might have in the medical examiner's office eluded me, but she found me on Friday morning at the office at a moment when we were both between patients and stunned me with the news.

'Somebody may have killed her, Alan. My God, somebody may have killed her. Why would somebody want to kill Hannah?'

I held her while she wept. I'd lost count of how many times I'd held Diane while she wept since Hannah's death. The tears weren't endless, but they were frequent. Diane's grief arrived in short, intense bursts, like the August monsoons. Clear skies before, clear skies after.

I asked myself the same question Diane was asking a dozen times a day for a while after that. *Why would somebody want to kill Hannah?*

I couldn't provide an answer. I used the fact that I couldn't answer it to console myself with the likelihood that Hannah's death had been accidental. Nothing more than a freak reaction to a silly accident in a health club locker room.

29

But the police were left with a buffet of anomalies that they couldn't explain. Why was Hannah's purse on the floor of her office, a place she would never leave it? Why was Hannah's body found in Mary Black's office, a place she had no reason to go? And why was Hannah's blouse tucked up under the front of her bra?

Hanukkah had arrived and Christmas was growing ever closer.

The effort to determine the manner of Hannah's death turned colder along with the weather.

Media interest in the case declined quickly, and Hannah's very public death soon became what, perhaps, it really had been all along – a private tragedy.

7

If you don't happen to be an inveterate shopper in- tent on milking the swollen teat of post-holiday sales – I am not – and if you aren't required to be at work – it was a Sunday, and I wasn't – the day after Christmas is a sleep-in day.

Or maybe – if the snow gods have conspired with the ski gods to dump ten powdery inches of flash-frozen Dom Perignon on the upper reaches of Beaver Creek and one of your wife's friends has generously offered two free holiday season nights at her Bachelor Gulch ski villa – the day after Christmas is most definitely a play day.

Lauren and I had packed our ski stuff and winter clothing and an immense quantity of three-year-old paraphernalia the night before and were out of bed well before dawn in an almost certainly futile attempt to beat the pre-ski traffic that seemed to always clog I-70 West into the Colorado Rockies during the winter months. She was fixing some breakfast for our still-sleeping daughter, Grace; I was loading the car. While I was on a trip into the kitchen to grab a cooler to lug to the garage, Lauren said, 'See that?'

'What?'

She pointed at the tiny kitchen TV, which was tuned to a local channel so we could hear the ski-traffic report. Why? I wasn't sure. If the traffic was awful, we'd take I-70 into the mountains. If the traffic was light, we'd do the same thing. She said, 'That thing at the bottom of the screen.'

I assumed she meant the crawl, the strip of text that I always seemed to be reading when I should be watching the screen and that I never seemed to be reading when news about some important up- date was moving across the screen that I should probably be reading. From the time that crawls first appeared on TV screens, I'd decided that I was genetically incapable of reading the moving words and simultaneously attending to what was happening on the rest of the screen. I'd long ago concluded that I did not possess a twenty-first-century mind.

I lifted the heavy cooler laden with God-knows-what and took a lumbering step toward the door. 'Nope, didn't see it.'

'It said that—'

'We have breaking news from our Boulder bureau,' interrupted one of the morning anchors. With that preamble I turned my attention back toward the TV, but my eyes immediately found the crawl and I couldn't have told you which of the two anchors was speaking. 'Apparently – and details are sketchy – apparently, and this is truly hard to believe, another little girl has disappeared on Christmas night in Boulder. We have a reporter on the way to the scene right now and should have more information momentarily. June?'

June said, 'You're right: This is so hard to believe, that it's happening again. For those of our viewers who aren't familiar with Boulder, it's even the same neighborhood as last time. That was what, eight, nine years ago? We'll get those details for you and we'll be back with more right after a break.'

Lauren said, 'I'm going to check on Grace.'

'I checked her when I got up, sweets. She's fine.'

'So did I. I'm going to check on her anyway.'

She hustled toward Grace's room. I set the cooler on the floor.

Another little girl has disappeared on Christmas night in Boulder.

Lauren was breathless when she tiptoed back into the kitchen. 'Grace is fine,' she said.

'Yes.' I put my arms around her and planted my hands on her ass. Lauren and I were parents of a little girl who hadn't disappeared on Christmas night. Somewhere else in Boulder another pair of parents couldn't say the same.

'Are you catching? You're not catching, right?' I asked. One of Boulder County's prosecutors was always on call for legal emergencies that might require the presence of a representative from the DA's office. Infrequently, that meant that she was called to crime scenes. Like to the location of the disappearance of a girl.

'No, no,' she said, pulling away from my hug. 'I couldn't leave town if I was on call. You know that. Should I wake Grace?' she asked.

'Let me finish loading the car first. We'll both get much more accomplished if she stays asleep until the last possible moment.'

An hour later we were climbing through Mount Vernon Canyon on I-70 into the mountains, sharing the freeway with at least a million other vehicles. Maybe two million other vehicles. Every one of the other vehicles carried skiers or snowboarders who had, like us, crawled out of warm beds before dawn in order to beat the traffic. I searched for irony, knowing it was there somewhere.

In back, secure in her high-tech car seat, Grace was flipping through a fat cardboard book about erudite dogs and talking to herself, while next to me Lauren was flipping through radio stations trying to find the latest news about what was going on with the missing girl back in Boulder. I wasn't really listening to the radio, partly because Grace's almost incomprehensible monologue was too cute to ignore, but mostly because none of the radio reporters seemed to know much about what was happening with this year's missing girl, so they were using their airtime to talk about the other missing girl, the one who had disappeared eight Christmases before.

I'd long before decided that I despised hearing rehashes of that dreadful story.

'It's a teenager. They think she's fourteen,' Lauren summarized for me as the Denver station she was listening to faded away, its signal lost hopelessly in the mountain canyons. 'Her father went to check on her early this morning. She wasn't there. They were going to go skiing today, just like us. We did the exact same thing with Grace.'

I thought, *But at our house Grace was in her bed,* and felt a chill crawl up my spine and goose flesh spread across my shoulders and neck. *What would it be like if she hadn't . . . ?* I tried comforting myself with the fact that it wasn't really as bad as the last time a girl went missing on Christmas night in Boulder. It wasn't.

The last time the girl they couldn't find was only six years old.

The last time a terrifying note was discovered on the stairs.

And I soothed myself with the obvious, the obvious being that six-year-olds don't often run away from home, not for real, and certainly not on Christmas night. I reminded myself that a fourteen-year-old girl might run away.

Fourteen-year-olds do run away. Maybe this girl had just run away. Probably this girl had just run away.

Numerals representing the ages of the two missing girls lined up in front of my eyes as though they were symbols spinning on a slot machine. As the numbers came to rest, I did the math. Today's fourteen-year-old missing girl was the same age – had been born the exact same year – as the tiny blonde who went missing eight years to the day before. If that other little girl had survived, the two children might be classmates, or friends, or sleep-over mates. They might go skiing on Christmas holidays with each other's families.

I felt another chill.

'Their house is only a few blocks away from, you know,' Lauren said. She meant from the other house, the one where the little beauty queen's dead body had been found by her father on the day after Christmas in an unused room in the basement, her head smashed, her neck cruelly cinctured with a homemade garrote.

'Where exactly?'

'On Twelfth, they said.'

Three blocks away. Just three blocks and eight years separated two little girls gone missing on Christmas nights in Boulder.

At that moment we were passing an overhead digital highway sign, the kind that in winter usually cautions motorists of icy and snowpacked conditions ahead. But this one had an even more sobering message – an Amber Alert. All concerned citizens were supposed to be on the lookout for a missing blond-haired, 115-pound, five-foot-six fourteen-year-old. No name was given.

My first reaction? Selfish. I hoped I didn't know her. I hoped she wasn't the daughter of any of my friends, or any of my patients. I wanted to feel the relief of insulation. I wanted her to be a stranger.

'Amber Alert,' I said to Lauren. 'Look.'

She stared in the direction of the highway sign until we passed below it, then turned on her seat and faced our daughter. She said, 'Your parents really love you, Gracie.'

Gracie laughed.

Obliviousness, I thought, *can be a very, very good thing.*

My detective friend, Sam Purdy, told me later on that it was as though a giant warehouse had been surreptitiously constructed nearby when the other case of the missing girl had finally faded into near oblivion and that all the satellite trucks, and all the microwave trucks, and all the flimsy network pop-up tents, and a few hundred cameras and microphones had simply been secreted away so they'd be ready for the next time.

The next time had turned out to be the massacre at Columbine and the time after that had been the Kobe Bryant circus up in Eagle County. After the Kobe invasion, all the equipment had apparently been returned to the secret warehouse to await the next, next, next time the almost-tabloid media would mobilize for a full-scale assault on a Colorado town. That was the only explanation Sam could concoct for how quickly the equipment reappeared on the streets of Boulder on the day after Christmas.

I was determined to miss it all.

By noon on that Boxing Day, Grace was either enjoying or enduring her first day ever in ski school and I was busy chasing Lauren, who was a much better skier than me, and a much, much better powder skier than me, through untracked down on the forest edges of the Golden Eagle run at the top of Beaver Creek.

In Boulder, three thousand feet below us in altitude – based on what Sam would tell me later – the cameras were already in place, the high-tech satellite and microwave trucks were bouncing signals around and through the atmosphere, and producers had already begun choosing locations for the stand-ups the on-air talent would do for that night's news.

Some of the reportorial faces would be familiar from the last time Boulder had endured this invasion. Others were recognizable because of what the country had endured in the intervening years because of the tragedies that had befallen Chandra Levy, or Elizabeth Smart, or Laci Peterson. Or because of the innocent lives ended by the Beltway snipers. Or because of Kobe Bryant and whatever happened at Cordillera. Or because of whatever Michael Jackson was accused of lately. Or because of some other crime du jour.

Or.

In America, there were always plenty of candidates.

As each fresh tragedy was anointed a mega-news event, I'd quickly grown fatigued of the relentless television and newspaper and Internet and magazine coverage afforded, or foisted upon, all the previous victims and all the previous perpetrators, and upon the unsuspecting but apparently ravenous populace.

Somebody had to be watching all this coverage, right?

I suspected that I'd fatigue of this latest criminal/media extravaganza, right in my hometown, even faster. I really was determined to miss it all.

I was. Honestly.

Lauren and I grabbed a late lunch at Spruce Saddle, the big mid-mountain restaurant at Beaver Creek. It wasn't lost on me that I was only a couple of ridge tops away from the elegant resort where Kobe and a young woman had crossed paths, and was within shouting distance of the courthouse where that diseased melodrama played itself out.

Lauren chose a table close to an overhead television so she would immediately know if there were any updates being broadcast about the missing girl in Boulder. I was silently trying to discern whether her acute interest in the case was an indication of parental empathy – or a counterintuitive way to stem the flow of understandable parental dread – or whether it was a more uncomplicated professional prosecutorial curiosity. I was trying to grant her the benefit of the doubt and not even consider the possibility that my wife's interest might be simply voyeuristic. Unsure, I headed for the bathroom. When I returned I spied Lauren folding up her cell phone. I took a chair that left my back to the television.

Which left me facing in the general direction of Cordillera.

'Who'd you call?' I asked.

'The office.'

'Yeah, what did you learn?' I didn't really want to know, and wasn't sure why I'd asked. Probably the same reason that I tried the door on Mary Black's office.

'This is my job. I could be involved later on. I need to . . . you know, whether . . . the girl . . .'

Not too bad, only slightly defensive. 'I know,' I said. I leaned across the table and kissed her lightly on her lips, tasting the waxy gloss of a fresh application of sunblock. 'So, what did you learn?'

I'd done it again; I'd once again asked a question that I didn't really want to know the answer to. I convinced myself that my question was an act of marital generosity: Lauren needed to talk.

'They don't know what they have. But because of what happened last time – you can imagine – they're being extra, extra cautious. They're treating it like a crime scene, even though no one's really sure what it is exactly. The girl's family is cooperating, totally. So far the crime scene techs don't think anything's been unduly contaminated. That's all good, considering.'

She meant, of course, considering what a total mess the crime scene had been the last time. The time with the little blond beauty queen, the one who sang and danced into our homes over and over and over again in her little sexy cowgirl getup.

'What do the police think? Was it an abduction of some kind?'

'Some of what they're seeing says yes, some says no.' She gazed around to see if anyone in the crowded cafeteria was paying attention to our conversation, and she prophylactically lowered her already hushed voice a few additional decibels. 'There hadn't been any threats, and they didn't find a note or anything like that. Nobody's called the family about ransom. There's no evidence of forced entry at the house. But there is some blood.'

'A lot?'

'More than a couple of drops. I'm just telling you what I heard from the office. It's thirdhand, or fourth.'

'Could she have run?'

'It's a possibility, apparently. The cops are trying to track down all her friends, to see what they know. Since the schools are on break, it's complicated. Some of her best friends are out of town.'

'But her family thinks it's possible?'

'I guess. Apparently, the family situation is complicated. The girl has had some emotional issues in the past. I don't have those details.'

I couldn't look my wife in the eye when I asked the next question. With the edge of my hand I moved salt that had been spilled on the table by an earlier diner into one long sodium mogul and pushed it to the side. 'And they checked all the little rooms in the basement that nobody ever goes into?'

That's where the other girl's body had been found eight years before. In a rarely used room in a dingy basement. Her tiny body had

37

been discovered by her distraught father, who had carried it up the stairs for all to see.

'Yeah, twice at least. It's different this time. The circumstances. It sounds like it's a nice house, but it's not huge and fancy like the other one. And it only has a small basement, a partial, like ours; underneath it's mostly crawl space. They checked.'

'Twice?'

'Three times.' She smiled sadly.

'Who's on it?'

'From my office? Andy.'

'From the cops?'

'It's a big team for now. And, yes, it includes Sam and Lucy.'

'Sam won't be happy. It was one of his claims to fame that he never had a thing to do with the other one.'

'I doubt if any of them are happy,' Lauren said. 'There're so many reporters chasing everyone around that they've had to block off the street. You know that all the detectives will be under a microscope.'

Or a microphone. 'Is Jaris Slocum on it?'

She slapped my wrist to shush me. 'Babe, we're on vacation. Let's not go back there.' She held up her cell. 'I want to call and see how Grace is doing in ski school. Am I crazy?'

'You're a mother. You get special dispensation.'

She made the call. Grace, it turned out, was enjoying ski school. I wasn't surprised. As she aged and I got a chance to experience the wonder of really beginning to know her, I was learning that my daughter rolled well with the punches.

Lauren closed up the phone. I asked, 'How's your energy?' That's as close as I would get to finding a safe way to inquire about the current state of Lauren's multiple sclerosis. I knew from experience that on rare good days a couple of hours of skiing was often all that she could manage before her legs began to feel like overcooked asparagus. We'd already done a long drive up to the mountains and spent a couple of energetic hours cutting powder.

For Lauren, that was an awful lot of activity.

'Good, I'm fine. I'll wriggle out of these boots and put my feet up over lunch. That will help.'

Was I convinced? Hardly. 'We can go down the hill and eat if you want. We have all day tomorrow to ski, you know. And Tuesday morning, too. No need to press it today.'

'I'm good, Alan. I want to do the top of Bachelor's Gulch before all the powder is skied off. I love it up there.'

Arguing with her was an option. Prevailing was not. Across the room, the food-court lines were long. I stood. 'You rest, I'll go get you something to eat. What would you like for lunch?'

We drove down the hill to Boulder after a late breakfast two days later, on Tuesday.

The skiing had been a joy, Lauren's atypical stamina on the slopes was a holiday gift, and by late Monday in ski school tiny Grace had managed – for about eleven horizontal feet of a two percent grade – to comport her stubby little legs into something resembling a snow-plow. Lauren and I gladly forked over $24.95 for a DVD that proved our daughter had accomplished the dubious feat.

Midday mountain traffic wasn't bad over Vail Pass, and the Eisenhower Tunnel approach was merely aggravating, not paralyzing. On the eastern side of the Divide I kept my eyes peeled on my rearview mirror for out-of-control big-rig truckers who had already fried the air brakes on their rigs on the highest stretches of the seven percent grades.

Grace and Lauren both slept all the way from Copper Mountain to Golden.

For the forty-eight hours plus we'd been up skiing I had managed to avoid – almost completely – the media saturation coverage about the girl who had disappeared on Christmas night. Lauren had told me a few new things, but with concerted effort on my part I knew almost nothing about what had transpired while we were gone.

And I was proud of it.

But as I-70 bent to follow the final contours of the Front Range, and as the beige winter haze of the Denver metropolitan area became visible in the distance, it was clear that my brief holiday was coming to an end, and I decided, reluctantly, to reenter the real world. I killed the Otis Redding CD and tuned to KOA, a Denver AM station with enough brash watt-power to push its often dubious signal up into the crevices of the Front Range foothills. I didn't have to listen long to hear an update – 'the absolute latest on the tragedy in Boulder' – that informed me that the girl, Mallory Miller, was still missing and that the Boulder Police continued to refer to the event as a 'disappearance,' not a 'kidnapping.'

Fifteen minutes later, as I drove Highway 93 just shy of the entrance to Coal Creek Canyon, Mallory Miller's father – his first name was William – came on the air – LIVE! – with a plea for his daughter to come home, or for whoever had her to release her, or both. Whatever the problem is, he told his daughter, we can solve it.

His plea was poignant, but I didn't hear too much of it. I was distracted by something else: his name.

Gosh, I was thinking, *I once knew a guy in Boulder named Bill Miller.*

8

Details dribbled out the way they inevitably do.

I'd continued to learn a few things from my conversations with Lauren. She wasn't due back in her office until after the first of the year but was staying in touch with her colleagues daily. According to my wife the detectives working the case were apparently split into two camps during those crucial early days: those who believed that Mallory had run away and those who believed that she'd been abducted. Not surprisingly, public opinion was divided along the same fault line.

Lauren's reading of the shifting winds within law enforcement was that the runaway viewpoint was prevailing.

TV and newspapers provided background. Hour after hour of background. Given the paucity of public facts, way too much background. But apparently that was only my opinion. Four thousand reporters and camera people and producers can't be wrong.

Right?

Mallory lived in the Twelfth Street house on the Hill with her father and little brother, Reese, who was twelve years old. The Millers were separated; the children's mother had moved away from Boulder when the children were much younger. The police had been in touch with Mrs. Miller – apparently, and surprisingly, the media had not – and were confident that she could add nothing pertinent to the investigation of her daughter's disappearance.

What was known publicly about the Christmas-night events in the Miller household?

On Christmas evening Mallory had been home by herself. The Miller family had been invited to a holiday dinner at a friend's house, but Mr. Miller and Reese had gone to the celebration alone after

Mallory complained about a stomachache. Mr. Miller had offered to cancel the plans, but she had insisted that they go on without her.

The physical evidence in the Miller home sounded screwy. Although a casement window near the back door was unscreened and unlocked, the family maintained that it had been that way for as long as any of them could remember. The police were not convinced that the rear window had been used to gain entry to the house, and there were no other possible indications of forced entry.

A trail of tiny blood drops ran from Mallory's second-floor bedroom down the stairs. The drops stopped abruptly a few feet from the door that led into the family room/kitchen at the rear of the house. Although DNA testing on the drops was pending, initial examination of the blood indicated that it was probably Mallory's. The upstairs bathroom that Mallory shared with Reese was a mess, and reportedly Reese had told the police that the mess was severe, 'even for her.'

Did the blood drops and the messy bathroom constitute evidence of a struggle? It depended, apparently, on whom you asked.

The record of incoming and outgoing phone calls indicated that Mallory had likely been home from the time her family left for dinner until the last time her father had called to check on her about ten minutes before nine. He had called a total of four times during the few hours that he and his son had been away from their home. Mr. Miller and Reese arrived back home at 9:20 or so.

Mallory had left a note on the kitchen counter thanking Santa Claus for a great Christmas. The note said she'd already gone to bed so that she could be fresh for their ski trip the next day.

In the note, Mallory didn't make mention of her stomachache.

Both Mr. Miller and his son agreed that the note had been written hurriedly. Mallory, known for flowers and hearts flourishes on all her correspondence and many of her school papers, and for generous helpings of XXXs – kisskisskiss – to accompany her signature, had signed the note with a single cursive M instead of her usual florid, all lowercased 'mallory,' or her self-deprecating, ironic, all lowercased 'mall.'

Reese retired to his room, and Mr. Miller closed up the house, turned off the lights on the Christmas tree, and was in bed before ten.

The next morning, Bill Miller went into his daughter's room early – he said 4:30 – because the Millers were planning to drive all

42

the way to Steamboat Springs the next morning and Reese had insisted that he wanted to be in line when the lifts opened to try his new Christmas snowboard in some fresh powder. But Mallory wasn't in her room. Since she hadn't actually made her bed since mounting a brief public-relations campaign to extend her curfew the previous summer, there was no easy way to know if her bed had been slept in.

Her clothes for the ski trip were neatly packed in a duffel on the floor.

Mr. Miller's initial suspicion was that his daughter had snuck out the night before – it wouldn't be the first time – and for some reason hadn't been able to sneak back in before dawn. He guessed she had fallen asleep at a girlfriend's house, and was about to phone her closest buddy, a girl named Kara, when Reese noticed the trail of blood that seemed to start in the hallway between her bedroom and the bathroom they shared.

While Bill Miller was searching for Kara's phone number, it was Reese who called 911.

Mallory's teardrop-shaped backpack, which according to her good friends, Kara and Tammi – they were both more than willing to be interviewed by anyone with a camera – functioned more as a purse than a book-bag, wasn't in the house. Missing along with the backpack were Mallory's cell phone, her wallet, and her school planner. The school planner was important because Mallory apparently used it as an all-purpose notepad. It was where she was most likely to jot down friends' phone numbers, weekend plans, and any musings about current romantic infatuations. The girls also assured police that Mallory kept a diary – they'd both read parts of it, though not recently – but it was never located.

The absence of the school planner and the diary meant that detectives were missing a treasure trove of information about Mallory's current life. The cell phone was crucial because the memory contained the numbers of everyone Mallory considered significant.

The neighbors across the street, the Crandalls, reported that they saw a man 'loitering' on the Millers' sidewalk early that Christmas evening, before the snow had started falling. He was bundled up against the cold, they said, and walked back and forth down the block. They couldn't provide a better description.

An interesting and curious sidelight to the grand scope of media coverage of what was, at face value, nothing more than the case of a likely teenage runaway, was Mr. Miller's refusal to do interviews with any of the national media luminaries who were desperate to do a two-shot with him. He limited his on-camera time to a pair of brief appearances with a local TV reporter, Stephanie Riggs – they'd previously become acquainted on a committee that was organizing a charity run – and to occasional solo stand-ups in the front yard of his home. Each time he professed his love for his daughter and urged her to come home, or at least to call.

If someone out there has her, he'd add, please let her go. Please.

I found that I was admiring his decision not to become a media slut.

I thought he sounded like someone who thought his daughter had run away.

The lead detectives on the case were a couple of senior people that Sam liked. I didn't know either of them. A few other teams were assisting.

Jaris Slocum and Darrell Olson were assigned to interview neighbors.

Another pair of detectives was assigned to put together a detailed time line of events. That pair consisted of Sam Purdy and his partner, Lucy Tanner.

9

Diane had covered my practice while Lauren and Grace and I were up skiing.

Once I'd finished retrieving the dogs from vacation doggie-camp at our neighbor Adrienne's house, and after I'd finished unloading the car and stowing our ski gear, I phoned Diane to let her know that we were home and that I was on the clock. 'We're back from the mountains. You're free to go play. No calls, I hope,' I said.

'No calls. Your patients are always well behaved. How was it?' she asked perfunctorily.

'Perfect – great snow, terrific weather. Too short. You and Raoul have a good Christmas?'

'Yeah, you have a minute?'

'Sure,' I said. I was already wary. Diane's tone was a few degrees too serious. A few as in almost 180. I guessed that we were about to talk, once again, about Hannah, and why someone would want to kill her.

'I need a consultation,' she said.

'Like a clinical consultation?'

'Exactly.'

'Okay.'

'This isn't a casual thing. It's a formal consultation, Alan. You can't tell anyone what I'm about to tell you.'

I was standing in the kitchen and I found myself searching behind me for a stool. Something about Diane's manner screamed that this was going to be one of those why-don't-you-sit-down conversations.

'Of course.'

Yowsa, I was thinking. *What is this about?*

'It's a consultation about a consultation. In a way.'

45

'I'm ready, Diane.'

'Did you know that every once in a while Hannah talked to me about her cases? When she wanted an opinion about something she was a little unsure about, she'd run it by me.'

'I'm not surprised. You're good.'

'I am, but that's not the point. A few days before she died she asked me out for a glass of wine after work. No big deal, we probably did it about once a month.'

'Okay.'

'She had a specific case she wanted to discuss – a kid she'd seen the previous Friday. I didn't know the girl's name at the time, of course. Still don't, not for sure.'

What Diane was describing was far from unusual. Collegial consultations between psychotherapists are often casual, and usually conducted in a way that protects the patient's anonymity.

'Yes?'

'The strange thing – the thing that Hannah wanted my consultation about – was that this kid had come in on her own. Her parents didn't arrange the session. Kid just showed up in her office, sat in the waiting room, and wanted to talk.'

'A walk-in?' I asked. I didn't know a single private-practice psychotherapist in Boulder who saw patients without appointments.

'A walk-in.'

Diane didn't treat adolescents. Occasionally I did. I said, 'Usually a parent makes the contact, and comes to the first session. That should have been a red flag.'

Diane cleared her throat as a way of letting me know that my unfortunate propensity toward platitudes was interfering with her narrative. She added, 'I know that.' Her tone was not only scolding me for being condescending, but was also making clear that even if she didn't eat fois gras she knew what a goose was.

I tried to remember Colorado mental health law. I thought the age threshold when a child could seek treatment without a parent's consent was fifteen, but I wasn't totally certain. I'd have to check.

'How old was the kid?'

Diane answered, 'Fourteen, fifteen – I'm not a hundred percent sure. I'm pretty sure Hannah said "teenager" but . . .' I suddenly guessed where we were going. And I didn't like the road map I was seeing. At all. I feared that Diane was intimating that Hannah Grant had seen Mallory Miller for psychotherapy less than a week before Hannah died, and only two weeks before Mallory had disappeared. I said, 'You're not thinking Hannah's mystery patient was Mallory Miller, are you?'

'Everything fits.'

Other questions began making soft landings in my head like a platoon of paratroopers. Why would Mallory seek treatment without consulting her father? And why with Hannah? Had she made a second appointment? Had Hannah made a diagnosis? Was Mallory fearful? Had Hannah said anything about Mallory thinking of running away?

And the most important question: Is there any way I can avoid hearing any more about this?

But Diane had an agenda that was quite different from insulating me from becoming more complicit, and she had a line of inquiry that I wasn't anticipating. She said, 'I can't tell anybody about this, right? That's what Hannah had wanted my consultation about. I told her that I thought she had to sit on it, had to wait and see what developed with the kid. Now, I want to hear from you if I was right.'

I hesitated while I considered the peculiar circumstances she was describing. While I pondered, Diane filled in the dead air. 'You have the craziest practice within a thousand miles of here. I figured that if you don't know what to do about something like this, then nobody does.'

I ignored the accusation, or compliment, or whatever it was. I said, 'You probably can't tell anybody anything. But it ultimately depends on what the girl told Hannah during the appointment. And on her age. For legal purposes I think you have to assume that right now you're Hannah – you have the same confidentiality responsibilities that she had when she saw the kid. Are you wondering about talking to the police? Is that it?'

'Sure, but I'm wondering about going to Mallory's father, too. I'm sure he'd love to know—'

'You probably can't talk to him. Other than the usual child-abuse exceptions to the privilege, your hands are tied. Even if you were sure it was Mallory – and it doesn't sound like you are – I don't think you could tell anyone about the girl's session.'

Because it was Diane I expected her to argue with me. She didn't. She asked, 'You want to know what she said? Why she was there?'

'To give you any useful guidance, I probably have to.' That was my way of saying, 'No, not really.'

Diane paused before she said, 'I don't really know that much. The girl was depressed about the holidays. And she misses her mom.'

10

Despite its cosmopolitan airs, Boulder is, at its core, a small town. As would likely have occurred in any other small town, it seemed that everyone knew someone who knew someone who had some connection to the missing girl. In the week between that season's Christmas and New Year's celebrations many hours were lost, probably way too many, in informal parlor sessions intended to identify the precise arcs of those degrees of separation.

My friend and neighbor Adrienne, a Boulder urologist, made it clear that one of the key players in the drama – someone connected to the Miller family, or to one of the public faces of the law enforcement team – was one of her patients. I had two biking buddies who had daughters who played on the missing girl's U-15 club soccer team. Lauren's legal assistant's teenage son's best friend used to cut the grass at the missing girl's house.

Like that.

As I'd suspected when I first heard that Mallory's father's first name was Bill, it turned out that I, too, had a tangential tie to the Miller family. It was tangential only because of the passage of time. Years before – I would have to check my records to put a precise number on the question of how many years, but I was guessing somewhere around eight or nine, maybe even ten or eleven – I'd seen the missing girl's parents for a solitary couples therapy session. Just one. Given the time lag since that session, my recall of the intervention was surprisingly clear, probably because of how disheartening my clinical appraisal was at the time.

Mr. Miller had dragged his reluctant wife in for the evaluation. It had been clear to me from the moment the introductions started that Mrs. Miller did not want to be in my office. Her demeanor had

49

reminded me of a child who would gladly promise never, ever to eat candy again if she could only avoid the dentist's drill *this* time. All that was absent was a foot stomp.

My clinical antennae were further tuned by her appearance. Any professional who has spent enough hours with people suffering acute mental illness would have recognized that Mrs. Miller's physical appearance was just the slightest bit off. Her hair, her makeup, her clothes – everything was just a degree or two away from ordinary. My session with the Millers was on a lovely Indian summer September day, and Mrs. Miller came dressed in a wool suit, carrying a straw bag, and wearing scuffed white pumps. On her eyes she wore big, bright Jackie O sunglasses. All the pieces, individually, were fine. Acceptable, at least. But together on a fine autumn day they totaled a sartorial sum that I guessed only Mrs. Miller could fully comprehend.

For his part, Mr. Miller was in something close to full-blown denial about the extent of the daunting challenges he faced. He appeared to have convinced himself, at least temporarily, that a few heart-to-heart sessions of some old-fashioned talking therapy would be just the trick to help lead his wife away from the middle of the field where she'd been aimlessly wandering and ease her back onto the straight and narrow marital tracks where she belonged.

Where exactly was Mrs. Miller doing her figurative wandering?

Into another man's bed? No. Drugs? Alcohol? Nothing so pedestrian.

Mrs. Miller, it turned out, attended weddings. Usually two or three ceremonies a month, but during prime nuptial season she would do more. 'Ten one month,' Mr. Miller had reported to me over the phone when he'd called for the initial appointment. 'That's her record. This past June. The truth is she'd do ten a week if she could fit them in.'

She dressed elegantly for each one of the ceremonies. Her collection of wedding outfits numbered in the dozens, and she had an enviable assortment of spring and summer hats – Mr. Miller called them hats; Mrs. Miller referred to them as 'my bonnets.' She bought nice gifts for every one of the happy couples. Many of the outfits and all of the wedding gifts were purchased from cable TV home shopping channels. She stayed away from registries – 'Who needs to be told what to buy? My Lord,' she asked aloud during our session – and apparently her gifting tendencies leaned toward ceramic figurines of animals. Puppies and kittens mostly, but occasional angels and young children.

The wedding presents were always pricey things. 'It's her only vice,' Mr. Miller had said in admirable defense of his wife's largesse. During one particular month of nuptials every newlywed couple received – after a one-hour this-is-it closeout sale on QVC – a beautiful shiny chrome home espresso machine from Italy. The piston kind. The total tab for the machines was almost two thousand dollars.

The UPS guy and the FedEx lady who drove the routes that included the Millers' home were on a first-name basis with everyone in the household.

Other than the sheer number of weddings, and the accumulating expense, what was the problem? The problem was that Mrs. Miller had never been invited to any of the ceremonies. None. Still, she fervently believed that she was an honored guest at every one of them, and if challenged could concoct an elaborate though ultimately nonsensical explanation for her attendance.

Her typical pattern was to arrive at the church or synagogue with some breathless flair just moments before the festivities began. She'd edge herself into a prime seat for the service, usually in the second or third row right behind the family, always on the bride's side, center aisle, and she'd smile and wave at the other guests as though she knew them quite well.

She always cried during the vows.

On more than one occasion after the nuptials were complete she'd exited the church along with the bride's family and joined the wedding party for the limousine ride to the reception.

Psychotherapists are trained to ask the question, 'Why now?' Why is this man, or this woman, in my office seeking help *today*? Why didn't she come in last week, or last month, or next week, or next month? The answer to the question yields what we like to call the 'precipitating event.'

For the Millers the precipitating event for seeking psychological assistance was crystal clear. The previous weekend Mrs. Miller had, at the insistence of an irascible groom and an implacable bride, been removed from a festive wedding reception at the Hotel Boulderado by the police. The immediate precipitant for her removal was Mrs. Miller's dubious decision to break into the celebratory dance between the newlyweds and politely, but firmly, demand her turn to waltz with the groom.

'Excuse me? I think you forgot your dance with *me*,' she'd said to him with a sad smile as she tapped the groom on the shoulder. 'You'll excuse us?' she'd added for the benefit of his befuddled bride. Then Mrs. Miller held up her silk-draped arms, waiting her turn to be swept away.

The groom, it turned out, was a Boulder sheriff's deputy. Half the guests at the wedding were Boulder sheriff's deputies. Not one of them recognized the woman in the yellow silk dress. Most importantly, the bride, who knew the detailed logistics of her wedding day as intimately as a chef knows the contents of his larder, didn't recognize the woman in the yellow silk dress.

Later that day, at the police department across town, the authorities released Mrs. Miller to Mr. Miller's custody with the strong suggestion that a mental health consultation might be in order.

Enter *moi*.

My appraisal?

Based on the brief history the Millers provided, Mrs. Miller's descent into schizophrenia had been gradual. By history, I was guessing that she'd suffered her first psychotic break at around age twenty-three – she and her husband had celebrated their own wedding when she was twenty-two – and she had begun to display more intransigent symptoms of psychosis shortly after the birth of her daughter. Mrs. Miller was twenty-four at that time. The symptoms worsened once again after the birth of her son two years later. I suspected that over the intervening years her family had consistently minimized her growing list of eccentricities, and that the reclusive behavior she demonstrated – reclusive when she wasn't attending weddings, that is – had been rationalized away one way or another. Evidence of her frank psychosis had, at times, been blatantly denied by everyone in her limited orbit.

The severe mental illness was Mrs. Miller's. The conspiracy to

52

pretend it didn't exist, however, was most definitely a family affair. Her husband, Bill, was a nice guy. After five minutes in my office, I realized that he was a relentless cheerleader and a determined advocate for his wife. 'Whatever I can do to help, I'll do,' he said. 'Anything.'

It was my unpleasant task to suggest to Mr. and Mrs. Miller that before they focused on issues in their marital relationship – perhaps – Mrs. Miller should seek some individual treatment for the difficulties she was having distinguishing things that were real from things that were not.

'Is it that bad? Really?' Mr. Miller said in mutual self-defense after I'd asked how he felt about what was going on in his marriage. 'I love Rachel. In the grand scheme of things this is a small problem, right? I mean, we're talking weddings. It's not cancer. There are many, many times when she seems just fine.'

During my internship, while I was spending a rotation in an acute adult psychiatric inpatient unit, I had become extremely frustrated by one of my patients. He was a huge Samoan man, a schizophrenic whose communication abilities had devolved to the point where his speech consisted solely of multiple repetitions of a deeply baritone 'hoho,' sometimes singly, more often tendered in multiple repetitions. Despite his severe psychopathology and his immense size – the man outweighed me by at least 200 pounds – he was congenial and cooperative. We would sit for brief one-to-one 'psychotherapy' sessions a few times a week. Each meeting lasted five minutes, max. He would listen to me – I doubted at times that he comprehended the intended meaning of a single word I said – gesture in the air with his fat hands, and say, 'Hoho, hoho,' occasionally interrupting my otherwise useless intervention, sometimes waiting politely until I was done.

Infrequently he would smile or open his eyes wide in apparent wonder. More often his face would yield no expression at all.

My Samoan patient was already receiving enough Haldol to sedate an elephant, yet his mystifying psychotic process seemed immune to my best, though admittedly inexperienced and ultimately ineffective, attempts to be helpful.

I confessed to my supervisor, who knew the situation well, that I felt incompetent to treat the man. The supervising psychiatrist said two things that have stuck with me ever since. First, he told me that there are some people who are better at being crazy than I will ever be at being therapeutic. The Samoan, he said, was my case in point.

Second, he told me that from a psychopathology perspective, some of our patients have cancer. He was speaking metaphorically, of course, but I still recalled his caution on those days that my clinical skills seemed hopelessly inadequate to contain the sometimes incorrigible forces of my patients' mental illnesses.

I was tempted to share those pearls of wisdom with Bill Miller the day that he brought his wife into my office for evaluation. But I didn't. His hope was too inspiring to behold. His desire to lift his wife up was too gratifying to witness. He didn't want to believe that his wife had the mental health equivalent of cancer. I feared that indeed she might, but I wasn't ready to believe it either. That's how powerful his hope was.

Despite the fact that I thought I'd pulled just enough of my punches to allow Mr. Miller's hope to stay afloat, my ultimate assessment that day, and my verbalized prescription for further care, sucked all the oxygen out of the room.

Every last molecule.

In contrast to bipolar disease, which at its heart is a disorder of mood, schizophrenia is a disorder of thought, of perception. Schizophrenic thinking results in a myriad of cognitive symptoms. Hallucinations, delusions, and paranoia are the most common. In a schizophrenic's world, what most of us consider orderly thought begins to deteriorate, and cognition becomes subject to interferences from beyond the confines of usual perception. The process that results appears to an outsider to be bizarre, tangential, repetitive, or oddly referential.

An extreme example was my Samoan's baffling chorus of hohos. But in a schizophrenic's brain the variety of ways that faulty neurochemistry can cause thinking to deteriorate is large. In severe cases the outcomes are almost universally tragic.

The problem that was most apparent to me during my brief appraisal of Mrs. Miller was the extent of her delusional thinking – specifically her irrational belief that she had been a special invitee to all those weddings. Although the nature of the invitations remained her secret during our interview, that was where I focused my attention as I presented my suggestions to the Millers.

Mr. Miller seemed somewhat relieved by my prescription for additional help. For him, it represented an injection of helium that might provide enough lift to keep his airship of hope afloat. But Mrs. Miller resisted my recommendation and argued and bargained and then bargained some more. I couldn't follow her train of thought as she tried to explain the imperative she felt about attending the weddings. The truth was that her thinking more closely resembled a corral of bumper cars driven by preadolescents than anything like a metaphorical train.

She wept for a good five minutes before she ultimately relented to my suggestion and to her husband's gentle prodding. She only relented, I was certain, because of her husband's insistent kindness and his repeated promises that he'd be beside her no matter what, and because I'd managed to make it clear on that day that my resolve was a more than decent match for her thought disorder.

The fear in her eyes when she realized what was about to happen next was as poignant a thing as I had witnessed in my office in a long, long time. She rested her head on her husband's shoulder and with eyes full of fat tears she said, 'Okay, okay. Okay, okay. Okay, okay. Okay, okay.'

He said, 'I'm here. I'm here. I'm here.'

I'd been doing clinical work for too long to consider entertaining the clinical delusion that the fact that Mrs. Miller had relented for that moment meant that the road ahead would be smooth.

'No more weddings?' she'd asked me incredulously only a moment after her four pairs of *okay*s had trumped her husband's three-of-a-kind of *I'm here*. 'Oh Willy, does this mean no more weddings?'

Bill – Willy – looked at me for direction.

I said, 'Yes, I'm afraid it does.'

With a despair that I could feel all the way to my toes, she lamented, 'What will they do? Oh, what will they do?'

What I saw in her eyes wasn't concern, it was fear. She hadn't said, 'What will *I* do?' She had said, 'What will *they* do?' She was worried about 'them.'

I wondered, of course, who 'they' were. The brides and grooms with whom she hadn't yet celebrated? Or perhaps – and I knew this was more likely – the speakers of the voices that I suspected were whispering or shouting wicked nuptial imperatives into her ears.

I didn't know. Nor did I suspect that she would tell me. Not that day.

While the Millers were sitting in my office I'd already acknowledged to myself that I wasn't the best-equipped mental health professional in town to help Mrs. Miller with her individual treatment. I explained my rationale to the Millers, and with their consent I picked up the phone and called Mary Black – the same psychiatrist who was sharing offices with Hannah Grant before Hannah's death – and asked if she could do an urgent emergency assessment.

I'd chosen a psychiatrist to assist Mrs. Miller because I knew that the initial phases of Mrs. Miller's treatment, and likely the long-term progression of her care as well, would involve the shuffling and management of antipsychotic medications, and in Colorado the provision of those pharmaceuticals was the domain of the medical profession. I'd chosen Mary Black as a psychiatrist for Mrs. Miller not only because Mary was good, but also because she was relatively new in town and she was still hungry for fresh patients. I didn't think it was advisable for the Millers to wait weeks to see a psychiatrist and begin treatment.

Mary graciously agreed to evaluate Mrs. Miller later that afternoon. Mr. Miller had driven his wife the few blocks over to Mary's office directly from mine, and I'd never seen the Millers together again.

Months later, at a summer party at a mutual friend's house, Mary Black had suggested to me – 'You know that woman you referred to me? The wedding woman?' – that Mrs. Miller's care had quickly degenerated into a carousel of poor treatment compliance, failed trials of conventional drugs and the newer atypical antipsychotic compounds, and repeated short-term, stabilizing, acute hospitalizations.

The wedding planners and pastors and ministers and rabbis in town knew all about Mrs. Miller by then. Ushers at virtually every wedding ceremony in the county carried an eight-by-ten glossy of her in full nuptial regalia, and after six months of futile mental health treatment she was being turned away at some church or synagogue door almost every Saturday.

It was precisely the kind of outcome that I had feared.

When she was done telling me the story of what had happened to Mrs. Miller, Mary Black told me one other thing. She said, 'I don't think my husband would stand by me the way her husband has. It's inspiring. Truly inspiring. The things he's done for her . . .'

Mary's eyes told me something else: that she knew that I knew that I owed her one.

Bill Miller came back to see me a little over a year later. It was the January right after the horrid Christmas when Boulder's little blond beauty queen had been discovered dead in the basement of her home. Bill and I met for only a few minutes, maybe fifteen. He'd asked for the time so that he could thank me for my help with Rachel. I'd told him, honestly, that I didn't think I'd done much.

Although he'd suggested that his wife's treatment with Mary Black hadn't gone particularly well – and explained that he and Rachel were temporarily separated – he didn't offer any details and I didn't ask for any. We talked briefly about the Christmas-night murder of the little girl, how hard it was for his kids, and he asked me whether I'd noticed the story in the *Camera* about the young orthodontist who'd been hit by a car and killed a few days before Christmas near Chatauqua. I said I had. He told me he'd witnessed the accident, and I wondered briefly if that traumatic experience was why he had come back in to see me.

But as I waited for Bill to irrigate that wound, he moved on. He said that he and the kids were coping, and he made a particular point of explaining how well things were going for him at work – he'd just been promoted to a post he'd always coveted – as though he wanted to emphasize for me that, despite his wife's illness and his marital problems, his family life hadn't totally fallen apart.

Although I don't really remember, it wouldn't surprise me to learn that I had ended the session with some generalized offer of future help, something like, 'Let me know if there's anything I can do.'

He'd probably said, 'Thank you,' and that had been that.

11

'The girl was anxious about the holidays? And she misses her mother? That's what the session she had with Hannah was about? That's it?' I said to Diane. 'No. No, that's not all of it,' Diane said. 'Come on, I'm doing this from memory. It was no big deal at the time. I didn't take any notes. The whole consultation lasted five minutes, maybe. God, I should write things down. I just should.'

'What do you remember?'

'The girl told Hannah that her mother has a severe mental illness and had left Boulder years ago. The girl doesn't talk to her much, misses her. Hannah was speculating about the mother having bipolar disorder or schizophrenia, but she didn't really have enough information. She was worried about the girl developing symptoms.'

I wanted to tell Diane that I already knew the details. I wanted to tell her about all the weddings that Mrs. Miller attended, about the lovely bonnets and the QVC gifts, and about the delusions, and the voices. I wanted to tell her that at the time I did my eval that I thought Hannah was right about the schizophrenia, wrong about the bipolar disorder.

Instead I said, 'You can't tell anybody, Diane. You can only divulge the fact that this girl saw Hannah for psychotherapy if you have reason to suspect that there has been, or is likely to be, child abuse. Otherwise the privilege holds.'

'But she can't seek care without a parent's permission until she's fifteen.'

'You're sure about that?' I asked.

'Yes.'

Diane was often sure about things that turned out not to be true, but I suspected she was right about that one. 'Even if it's true, I don't know whether that would abrogate her privilege.'

'But it might.'

'You're not even sure it was really Mallory. You'd have to violate privilege even to be certain. God knows there would be lawyers involved, and once there are lawyers involved, anything can happen. Either way, the privilege won't evaporate today. If they started litigating this tomorrow you wouldn't have an answer before next year's aspen season. You know lawyers better than I do.'

'What do you mean? You're married to one, while I' – she paused for effect – 'am married to a Mediterranean god.'

I decided not to take that detour with her.

'What if she's dead?' Diane asked.

Shit. 'Diane, do you know that she's—'

'No, no, I don't. I don't. But if she were, if that was determined, I was wondering if I could—'

'No, you couldn't – confidentiality survives death. Well, actually you'd have to tell her parents if they asked, because they would probably have control of her estate, which includes all her medical records, but—'

'Why would they ask? If they didn't know she'd been in treatment, why would they ask?'

'Exactly.'

Diane and I had been partners longer than Lauren and I had been married. I wasn't surprised that we were finishing each other's thoughts. But the ping-pong nature of the conversation we were having felt awkward to me. Why? I suspected that each of us was in possession of some information that we weren't sure how to handle, information we didn't want to keep to ourselves, but information we weren't at all sure we were permitted to share.

'The girl also told Hannah—'

'Wait, I want to do this face-to-face. I have a patient late this afternoon at the office. I'll come downtown. You available?'

She sighed. 'I was just about to head out to the after-Christmas sales on the Mall. Things are going to get really picked over if I don't get down there soon.'

After-Christmas shopping on the Pearl Street Mall? I would have preferred to be strapped into a chair and serenaded by The Captain and Tennille.

'With Raoul?' That was wishful thinking on my part. The worse

59

the party, the more grateful I was for Raoul's company. After-Christmas shopping on the Mall sounded like a very bad party.

'Shopping? With me? Are you kidding? He won't shop with me.'

There was a caution there I knew; Raoul was a wise man. I swallowed a sigh. 'Okay, where do think you're going to be? I'll meet you someplace.'

The little office building that Diane and I owned together was an architecturally pedestrian – certainly not a painted-lady – early-1900s Victorian house on the west end of Walnut, a couple of blocks from the Pearl Street Mall. The odds of finding street parking in downtown Boulder during the closeout-sale-frenzied week between Christmas and New Year's were about the same as the odds of being eaten by a great white shark, so Diane was planning to stash her Saab behind our building and start her quest for bargains near Ninth and Pearl on the west end of downtown. Since I had a patient to see, I told her I'd park at our offices, too, and suggested we rendezvous outside Peppercorn at three.

Dirty snow from the Christmas-night snowstorm lingered in shady places along the herringbone brick pathways of the Mall, but despite what the calendar said, the day was pleasant in the sun. That's where I was sitting enjoying an afternoon interlude when Diane sauntered up to me at about ten after. She was carrying two huge shopping bags. I gave her a hug and a kiss on one cheek. She gave me one of the bags to carry. In many ways – mostly but not entirely good – Diane and I were like an old married couple.

We began walking, the sun low against our backs. From the heft of the bag in my hand, I surmised that she had been scouring the sales for either bricks or bullion.

'This doesn't happen to me, you know,' she said. 'This is the sort of thing that happens to you. This stuff with this mystery girl and Hannah. This murder and kidnapping and cops and criminals crap I seem to be mixed up with. It's your specialty, not mine.'

I was tempted to argue that it was debatable that Hannah had been murdered, and that it seemed more likely that Mallory was indeed a runaway and not a kidnap victim. But Diane's bigger point was close to the truth. Karma did seem to deliver mayhem to my door with disturbing regularity.

'If it's what you think it is, I'm mixed up in it, too, Diane.'

For a moment she was quiet. She either didn't quite hear me, she didn't quite believe me, or she was busy discounting my words as an unwelcome empathic gesture.

Finally, she replied, 'Sure, you were part of the Hannah thing. I know, I know. I know you were there. And well, now you're part of this other thing, but that's only because I've dragged you into it. Listen, if you'd rather I talk to someone else about this, I understand. But I really felt I needed a second opinion about what to do next, and I don't know anyone else who has as much experience with crazy therapy crap as you do.'

Crazy therapy crap? Once again I was tempted to argue her premise, but recognizing the futility, I said, 'The truth is that I was a little bit mixed up in the Mallory thing already, even before we talked.'

She heard me that time. Her voice grew conspiratorial. 'What?'

I shook my head and kept walking. 'I need to make this a consultation, too. My knowledge is clinical, just like yours.'

She'd grown tired of the forced-infantry-march nature of our pace and abruptly stopped walking. Once I realized she had stopped I did, too, and turned back to face her. Over the top of her head the sun was looming just above the highest peaks of the Front Range in the southwest sky. The light was sharp but gentle. It felt only faintly warm on my face.

'Tell me,' she said.

It was a shrink phrase, psychotherapy shorthand for 'go on' or 'don't stop there' or 'damn your resistance, spill the beans.'

'This is for real – a professional consultation – you can't tell anyone.'

'Holy moly,' she said.

I wished I had my sunglasses on my eyes instead of in my jacket pocket. I was squinting into the sun. *Holy moly?* 'Is that a yes?'

'I'm thinking. You get into the weirdest things, Alan. I'm not sure I want any part of whatever it is.'

She was playing with me. 'Sure you do,' I said.

'You're right, I do. I'm a glutton for punishment. Okay, go ahead and consult with me.' She raised her chin an inch and tilted it up to the side as though she were opening herself for a right cross. I opened my mouth to reply just as she changed her strategy. 'No, no, let me guess.' She made a face that a bad acting student might make to try to portray someone cogitating, contorted it a few times for dramatic effect, and finally said, 'Nope, I give up.'

'Years ago, I saw the Millers, Mallory's parents – those Millers – for an assessment. One session only. Turned out to be a long eval, over two hours. I saw them as a couple, immediately recognized that Mrs. Miller's individual problems were . . . significant, and referred her on to Mary Black for ongoing treatment and some serious pharmacological intervention. I never saw them again. Mary took over from there. Mr. Miller came back sometime later to thank me for my help. But I never laid eyes on the kids, don't even remember if I knew their names.'

Diane was a smart lady. She made all the appropriate connections instantly. 'That must be how Mallory knew about Hannah, right? Right? I bet the crazy mother parked Mallory in the waiting room while she had her psychotherapy sessions and her med consultations with Mary. Don't you think? If Hannah had seen a little girl alone in the waiting room she would have chatted her up. You know she would have. She would have made friends with her. Especially if she saw her sitting out there alone on a regular basis. That's the connection. That's it.'

'Yes,' I agreed. 'That's probably it.' Hannah's kindness was almost as legendary as her obsessiveness. I had no trouble manufacturing a vision of Hannah on her knees in the waiting room connecting with a lonely or frightened little girl who was waiting for her mother to finish an appointment with her psychiatrist.

Hi, sweetheart, what's your name?

I'm Mallory.

I'm Hannah. You waiting for your mom to finish her meeting?

'Holy moly,' Diane repeated.

Diane started walking down the Mall again. I tagged along behind. 'Holy moly' was a new phrase for Diane. I was already beginning to hope that – like most everything designed by Microsoft – it came equipped with built-in obsolescence.

I said, 'I'd bet mortgage money that her disease isn't stable. Rachel Miller sabotaged every last treatment that Mary Black tried years ago.'

Diane added an edge to her tone and said, 'Why do you say "disease"? Almost everyone else says "illness."'

62

'A lot of other people say "clients." I say "patients." Do you know why? "Patient" is from the Latin. It means "one who suffers." It fits what we do.'

She smiled, and shifted her voice into sarcasm mode. 'I bet if a new client walked into your office and had to listen to you parsing Latin all day long, she'd become one-who-suffers in no time at all. You didn't answer my question.'

'Other people say "illness"?'

'They do.'

It probably wasn't true. Diane's penchant for assuredness about this kind of thing often had scant correlation to reality. Regardless, it took me only about three steps to arrive at an answer to her question. 'Think about it. The word is *dis-ease. Dis. Ease.* It's apropos, don't you think, to what we deal with every day?'

In my peripheral vision I could tell that Diane had shaken off my explanation with the same ease with which she'd just ridiculed the tiny bit of Latin I recalled from high school. I consoled myself with the fact that she was equally dismissive as she discounted her husband Raoul's opinions about just about everything political.

Thankfully, she moved on to a fresh thought, and said, 'In case you didn't know it, she's in Las Vegas. The girl told Hannah that her mother is living in Las Vegas. She gets phone calls from her every once in a while. Her father doesn't know that they're in touch as much as they are. It's a source of conflict. The girl wasn't sure what to do.'

'Vegas?' I asked, but it was more of an 'ah-ha!' exclamation than a question. I was thinking, *Of course Rachel Miller is in Las Vegas. Where else would someone go who is addicted to weddings?*

'You don't sound that surprised, Alan. Does she gamble? Is that part of her pathology, her dis-ease?'

'No,' I said, refusing to bite. 'She goes to weddings. That's what the presenting complaint was for the couple's therapy: Rachel Miller went to lots and lots of weddings. She thought she was a special guest at all of them. It was the center of her delusional world. I suspected that she had command hallucinations but she didn't admit to hearing voices during our one interview. Her husband told me she did, that she heard voices.'

'Paranoid schizophrenia?'

'That's what I thought at the time, but a lot has changed in how we all view psychotic process, you know? I'm not sure how I'd diagnose her today.'

'Mixed thought and mood disorder? That's what you're thinking?' Diane asked.

'Something like that, yes.'

By that time Diane and I had covered all four blocks and were at the east end of the Mall. We were waiting at the light to cross Fifteenth onto the sidewalk on the still-sunny side of Pearl Street. I said, 'You want to keep going or head back?'

'I don't care. We can walk to Denver if you want, but I want to hear more about Mallory's mother and all the weddings.'

It took me a while but I explained Mrs. Miller's odd nuptial delusions to Diane, who had many questions, some psychological in nature, more having to do with wedding logistics, owning all those outfits, and buying all those gifts.

I had answers for a paltry few of the questions in any of the categories, psychological or matrimonial. After multiple prods on her part I tried to refocus her by saying, 'I only saw the Millers for that one session. That's all. Most of my energy went into trying to understand her history and then trying to prepare the two of them for a whole different kind of treatment than they'd come in the door thinking they'd get.'

'Receptions, too?' Diane asked, ignoring my pleas of ignorance.

I told her, yes, that Rachel had also attended the receptions. I shared the story about the one at the Boulderado where she'd been busted by the sheriff's deputy.

Diane had more questions. While I protested my continued ignorance about most things matrimonial, Diane chided me that it had been a very long session I'd had with the Millers, and I should know more than I was letting on.

Once Diane had – finally – exhausted her queries about Mrs. Miller and her serial wedding attendance, I had a question of my own. It was the question that I had wanted to ask Diane since the moment she told me that Hannah had done an intake with the girl who was probably Mallory. 'Do you think it's possible that Mallory went to Vegas to see her mother? Based on what Hannah told you, would she have done that? Could that be what this is all about?'

'It's possible. Hannah stressed that the girl missed her mother.

64

May even have said it a couple of times, so you have to wonder. Hannah focused on the mother/daughter relationship and the conflicts between the girl and her dad.'

'Might explain the Christmas Day stomachache,' I said. 'Her holiday anxiety, missing her mom.'

'Psychosomatic?'

'Why not? If she was worried enough to seek a therapist on her own, she could certainly be worried enough to develop symptoms.'

She paused after a couple more steps. We had walked all the way down to Eighteenth Street by then, almost a full ten blocks from our cars. I stopped and turned back to the west. The late December sun was just a slash of brilliance above the Divide and pedestrian traffic was thinning out on the Mall.

'What was the mother like, Alan? Could she have come and taken Mallory?' Diane asked.

'I suppose that's possible. Anything is, but—'

'The cops would check that first, right? They would have gone to Vegas and checked with Mallory's mother to see if her kid was there, to see if the mom had been in Boulder?'

'Yes,' I said. I was also thinking that the Boulder cops who went to Vegas would probably have found a truly disturbed woman.

Diane casually tapped me on the shoulder and handed me the second shopping bag. Like a fool, I took it.

We started walking back in the direction of the mountains. The western sky was much brighter than the eastern sky had been. She asked, 'So are you ready now?'

Segue or no segue, I knew exactly what she was talking about. We really had been friends a long, long time. 'Sure, as ready as I'll be. So what else did the girl tell Hannah?'

65

12

The moment the sun completed its descent behind the Rockies the day turned from pleasantly brisk to downright cold. What I had been considering a light breeze felt decidedly like an icy wind. Diane had seen it coming – now that I was schlepping both of her shopping bags she was able to shove her mittened hands deep into her jacket pockets for additional warmth.

My gloves were in my car and the flesh on my hands was the color of the fat on a slab of uncooked bacon.

'The kid was concerned that her dad was "up to something" or "into something." She'd left Hannah with the impression that she didn't like it, whatever it was. The girl was feeling like she had to do something about it, or else. That kind of thing.'

'"Up to something"? That's a quote?'

'Close as I can remember. It was a casual consultation – I didn't exactly memorize it. I didn't know what was about to happen.'

'"Or else"? What did that mean?'

Diane shrugged. 'I should have asked. I didn't ask. She also had some friend trouble, too, was conflicted about some guy she was seeing.'

'Boyfriend?'

'I guess.'

'It felt like typical adolescent stuff to you?'

'At the time it did.'

'And the nature of what the girl's father was up to?'

'Hannah didn't know.'

'Precipitant?'

'See, that's the thing. I asked Hannah that, too. Hannah felt there was some urgency for the girl, but couldn't get the kid to admit to anything.'

'A secret?'

'I wish I knew.'

'The holidays?'

'Hannah didn't stress that part. I suppose it's possible.'

'The police should know all this,' I said. 'Boulder's two most high-profile recent . . .'

I didn't know what to call Hannah's death and Mallory's disappearance. Diane did. 'Crimes. The word you're looking for is "crimes." "Felonies' would work fine, too.'

'Whatever. The police would want to know that there's a possible connection – a big connection – between Hannah's death and Mal-lory's disappearance. But nobody knows about it but you,' I said.

'And you,' she reminded me.

'Mostly you. It's too bad you can't tell the police.'

She skipped for one step. I think that's what she did, anyway –

just one little schoolgirl skip. Why? Who knew? 'I bet that twerp Slocum would love to know what the two of us know, wouldn't he? He'd probably cuff me again and throw me in the slammer if he knew what I was keeping from him.'

I was thinking that not only would Detective Slocum like to know, but so would Diane Sawyer, Katie Couric, Geraldo Rivera, and Oprah. Not to mention the *Enquirer* and the *Sun* and the *Star*.

And Bill Miller.

I was also thinking that Diane's continuing animosity toward Detective Jaris Slocum, though completely understandable, was one of the ways that she was postponing her grief about Hannah's death. That moment, however, wasn't the time to confront her with that particular reality. Years of experience with her had taught me that with Diane I had to pick my spots.

'Raoul wants me to sue Slocum. Did I tell you that?'

'For what?'

'He doesn't care. He calls him "that little fascist." "Let's sue that little fascist, baby,' he tells me. He hates it when I say it, but sometimes he's such an American.'

I said, 'Raoul has too much time on his hands. He needs to go start a new company or something.' Diane's husband was a legendary Boulder entrepreneur. When he wasn't nurturing somebody else's

67

start-up tech company, he was busy casting the bricks to create a new one of his own.

As we crossed back over Fifteenth to the herringbone pathways of the Mall, Diane asked the money question: 'So what do I do about all this?'

'Did Hannah leave any notes?'

'She named me in her will to handle the details of closing up her practice should anything happen to her. But I haven't found any notes about that session. Zip, *nada*.'

Few therapists show the foresight to make death stipulations in their wills. But Hannah had. I said, 'She knew Paul Weinman back when, didn't she?'

'Yes, she knew Paul.' Paul had been another friend of Diane's, a psychologist who'd skied into a tree at Breckenridge years before. His sudden death, and the subsequent uncertainty about what to do with his current cases and his practice records, had caused a lot of procrastinating Boulder therapists to make plans for what would happen to their practices in case of their own death.

'Do the police have her appointment calendar?' I asked.

'Hannah just used initials, same as us. They would have to cross-reference the calendar with her billing records or her clinical files to find out who she was seeing. Cozy is handling the cops for me, and he's not going to let them see anything confidential.'

'Anything else important in Hannah's records?'

'Not really. Closing her practice has been routine. I've done a few one-time visits with her patients to check for decompensation or acute reactive problems to her . . . death. I decided to pick up a couple of her cases. Oh, and did I tell you I'm going to see the woman who was at her office that day, the day that Hannah died?'

'The woman with the hair?' *And the Cheetos.* 'You're seeing her for treatment?'

'I am. She's having a lot of trouble. I guess it's not too surprising, considering. She's coping by becoming a little Nancy Drew, trying to solve the mystery of what happened to her therapist.'

'Isn't it kind of odd seeing her? Given what happened.'

'You don't think it's a problem, do you?'

I wasn't sure. Psychologists are prohibited from treating people with whom they have another existing relationship. It means, for instance, that I couldn't treat Grace's preschool teacher, when Grace gets around to having one. But I didn't know if the fact that both parties had been present when a possible murder victim's body was discovered really constituted a preexisting relationship. The issue had never come up before in any of the ethics discussions I'd had.

I didn't want to make Diane crazy, so I immediately resolved my ambivalence by saying, 'No, I don't think so.'

'Good. Anyway, I've referred a few of Hannah's other patients to other therapists in town. Don't be hurt. I'm not ignoring your talents – they all wanted female therapists, baby. But most of them decided not to continue for now. I'm still having her office phone lines forwarded to my number. The hardest part of the whole thing has been letting people who hadn't heard what happened to her know that she is dead. And, you know, how she died.'

'I can imagine.' We took two more steps. 'Is it possible you spoke with her?'

'With whom?'

'Mallory.'

'What do you mean?'

'Is it possible she was one of the people who called who hadn't heard about Hannah's death?'

'Oh my God.'

'Well?'

'It's possible. I had a couple of difficult calls . . . a woman asked . . . she was young – I guessed a CU student – wanted "Dr. Grant." I'm not sure I ever got a name. I told her what had happened and she . . . hung up. Oh my God.'

'When was that call?' I asked.

'Last week. Maybe Monday. Oh my God, I may have talked with her.'

'Do you remember what you said?'

'I've been upset,' Diane said, her voice suddenly hollow. 'I might not have handled it well. When Hannah's patients asked me how she died, I . . .'

'Suggested the possibility she'd been murdered?'

'It's not just me, Alan. Everybody – the papers – I'm not the only one . . .'

I touched her. 'It's okay.'

'The kid was really upset. I offered to meet with her, but she hung up.'

What did it mean that Diane might have talked with Mallory a few days before she disappeared? Maybe nothing. But it was possible that Mallory walked away from the conversation believing that her therapist had been murdered.

'What about the other call? You said there were two difficult calls.'

'The other one was from a man. Wanted to know what would happen to his therapy records. I assured him I had custody of them and that they'd stay confidential. He wouldn't give me his name, either. He asked how he could get the records. I told him. He didn't want a referral. He was almost . . . belligerent.'

I didn't reply right away. Diane wanted to move on. 'Speaking of records, Hannah's attorney – the guy who drew up her will – called me a couple of days before Christmas and asked if she had left any records that would allow final bills to be prepared.'

'For her patients?'

'Yes.'

'That's rude. Who's the attorney?'

'Guy named Jerry Crandall. I don't know him. He's a general-practice guy, doesn't do much divorce work.' Diane did do a lot of divorce and custody work; she knew all the family-law attorneys in town. 'But that's what I told him, too, that it was kind of cold. He said he had a fiduciary responsibility and that Hannah's accounts receivable are an asset of her estate.'

'Fiduciary responsibility aside, I'm not sure I'd like to get a bill from my dead therapist.'

'He's a lawyer. Can I finish?' Diane didn't wait for me to say yes. 'I told him I'd take a look and get back to him. While you guys were up skiing I checked through Hannah's practice calendar and matched things up with her recent process notes, gave him a list of unbilled sessions. When I compared all her records I realized that the session with this kid wasn't in her calendar, didn't have any notes, and had never been billed. It was the only one not in her calendar.'

'No other sessions without notes?'

'None that I found. Hannah was Hannah.' Loud exhale. 'What do I do, Alan?'

'In a word, nothing. Hell, Diane, you're not even sure it was Mallory. I think the kid is entitled to confidentiality, so you can't reveal what you know from the session.'

'It was her,' Diane said.

I ignored that. 'Any hint of abuse during the consultation?'

'No.'

'You can't tell anyone then, including the police.'

'What if the police knew Mallory had been kidnapped? If the parents got a note, or a ransom demand. Would that change things?'

I thought about it for the length of time it took to try, and fail, to pass three young mothers pushing strollers wheel hub to wheel hub on the bricks of the Mall. It was the pedestrian equivalent of trying to drive past some recalcitrant semis that were rolling side-by-side on the highway.

'Sure. Then it would be a whole different ball game. By definition a kidnapped kid is a kid who's being abused, and abuse changes all the privilege rules. If you thought you knew something that could aid the investigation into her kidnapping – once the authorities decided it was a kidnapping – you would have an ethical and legal responsibility to divulge it to the police because of the child-abuse exception.'

Diane said, 'But the police say she ran. As long as that's the current theory, I can't play the I-think-she's-been-kidnapped card.'

The holiday lights that were strung on the trees on the Mall began snapping on block by block, and within seconds snakes of twinkling dots wrapped the skeletal forms that stretched out in front of us. Diane and I both watched the spectacle develop for a moment.

'That was pretty,' I said. 'Sorry, your hands are tied.'

Hers may have been figuratively tied; mine were literally going numb from the cold and the weight of the shopping bags I was carrying.

'I suppose this means that I probably shouldn't prepare a bill for the intake and send it to Mallory's father.'

Diane's last comment was intended sardonically, but I recognized some fuzzy edges at the margins; the ramifications weren't as clear as she might have expected. 'It's an interesting point, Diane.'

'What do you mean?'

'If you were looking for a way to tell her father that you know something, sending him a bill would probably be an ethically acceptable excuse for letting him get a toe inside the consultation room door.'

'And why would I want to do that?'

'I'm not sure you would. But just for the sake of argument, let's say you believed that what you learned from Hannah's consultation might help track down Mallory.'

'And if I did believe that . . .'

'The fact that no bill has gone out yet might give you an avenue to breach confidence with her father. If you were sure the kid was Mallory. Did Hannah say anything about billing arrangements for her session with the girl?'

'Not a word. But I have to work under the assumption that the kid didn't want her parents to know about the therapy, don't I? Knowing Hannah, I bet she did the session pro bono, anyway.'

'Why? Why would you assume that the girl wouldn't want her father to know about the therapy?'

'Why? Because the kid just showed up without an appointment, and she told Hannah that he was up to something and she wasn't happy about it.'

I played devil's advocate. 'But what if he's the one who sent her to see Hannah? What if her father already knows all about whatever it was that caused her to go? Ninety-nine out of a hundred kids are in psychotherapy because somebody sends them, and the someone is usually one of the kid's parents. A kid doesn't often go on her own.'

Diane's tone grew dismissive. 'If Mallory's father sent her into treatment he'd have told the police that his daughter had seen a therapist recently, right? That would be important information to consider after her disappearance.'

'You would think.'

'And the police would have contacted that therapist, right? To try and find out what the kid was troubled about.'

I knew where she was going. 'Unless the police already knew that the therapist was dead.'

'But if they knew that Mallory was seeing Hannah and that Hannah was dead, they would have sent whoever had legal custody of her practice records – *c'est moi* – a subpoena in order to get access to the treatment notes.'

'Agreed. If the cops were thinking.'

'Well, none of that happened. None of it. Nobody from the police department has contacted me about Mallory. And I certainly haven't been subpoenaed.' As she began to connect more of the dots Diane's foot speed kept pace with her mouth speed, and I had to hustle to keep up with her. 'So I'm left thinking that Mallory sought out Hannah for treatment on her own, which would tell me that she didn't want her father to know what she was up to. Or . . . her father had sent Mallory to Hannah, which – given his subsequent silence on the matter – would tell me that for some reason he doesn't want the police to know what his daughter was up to.'

I said, 'That about covers the possibilities.'

'As a therapist, I don't especially like either theory. But I'd put my money on Mallory as the one who was trying to keep the secret.'

We arrived at the intersection with Broadway. The pedestrian signal was red and enough traffic was humming past us to rule out jaywalking. I lowered Diane's shopping bags to the bricks and lifted my hands so I could show her that my fingers were curled into hooks. I asked, 'Do you mind taking these bags back? My hands are frozen.'

She looked imposed upon.

And I realized, belatedly, why her husband refused to shop with her.

13

I had an additional tie to the Miller family, one that certainly fit any definition of tangential anyone might wish to apply, one that was marked by the requisite degree or two of separation. The link didn't come into focus for me until my solitary psychotherapy appointment late on the afternoon of the day that I played reluctant Sherpa for Diane as she trolled the Mall for Christmas bargains. The source of the connection was someone I never would have anticipated.

Bob Brandt.

Bob had been coming to me for individual psychotherapy for almost two years, and progress had been glacial. Pre–global-warming glacial. The meager speed of the treatment neither surprised nor particularly disappointed me. Diagnostically, Bob's underlying character was a caustic blend of toxic pathologies. Had he been using health insurance to pay for his treatment – he wasn't – the DSM-IV code his insurer would have required would have had as many digits as a Visa card.

The first five of those digits would have spelled out the cipher for schizoid personality disorder. In addition to having a serious schizoid character, Bob was also a chronically depressed, mildly paranoid guy. Forty-three years old, he'd been ensconced in the same dead-end clerical position in the physics department at the University of Colorado for almost two decades.

His mother and an older brother were his only living relatives. Bob had maintained contact with his mom for most of his adult life. A few years before, however, his brother had written him a letter notifying him that their mother was moving to an assisted-living facility near his house in southern Colorado. Bob had interpreted the missive as his brother's order to 'butt out,' and he hadn't spoken with either his mother or his brother since.

Where did reality lie? Sadly, I didn't know. Nor was it clear to me exactly how Bob felt about the artificial estrangement. He deflected all my inquiries about it, and resisted my occasional attempts to question his harsh appraisal of his brother's letter.

Bob had no current friends or romantic relationships and no history that I could uncover of any significant friendships since childhood, or of romantic relationships, ever. His sole social outlet was occasional attendance at local Scrabble clubs and tournaments. Mostly, though, he preferred to play his games online.

The Internet, for all its interpersonal anonymity, is a schizoid's dream.

Schizoid.

The dictionary, nonpsychological meaning of the word is the 'coexistence of disparates.' Something that is part this, part that. In mental health terms, schizoid has surprisingly little in common with either its *Webster's* definition or its similar-sounding, polysyllabic psychopathology cousin, schizophrenia. Unlike schizophrenia, schizoid personality disorder isn't a disorder of thought or perception.

Not at all. Schizoid personality disorder is a disorder of relating.

People with the malady have a history, often since early adolescence, sometimes even before that, of aloofness from relationships, emotional coldness, immunity from praise or criticism, generalized anhedonia – the inability to experience pleasure – and limited affective range.

The portrayal fit Bob like a custom-made wet suit.

Bob was, by his own description, 'a dork, a geek, a nerd, a snarf – you pick the synonym for loser, that's me.' He had a head shaped like the bow of a boat, and I surmised that his hair had been receding from his temples since the second or third grade. Exploratory surgery would be necessary to determine if he actually possessed a chin. His eyes were tiny and at times they seemed to shake in their sockets. The effect was so disconcerting to me that early in the treatment I'd actually referred him for a neurological evaluation to have those vibrating orbs assessed.

The neurologist had a name for the condition, which he assured me was benign. As was my style, I'd managed to forget the specific medical terminology by the time I was reading that night's bedtime story to my daughter.

Bob liked cars, or, more accurately, was enamored of his own car. He had a thirty-something-year-old Camaro with a big motor that he'd bought from a guy in Longmont who'd lovingly restored it to its original ebony luster. Every time Bob mentioned the old muscle car, which seemed like at least once a session, he reminded me that its condition was 'cherry,' and every month or two he assured me that it was a 'matching numbers car.'

After two years of reminders I still didn't know what that meant.

Bob lived in a couple of rooms he rented above the detached garage of a modest house near Nineteenth and Pine. He described his landlords as 'old people,' and maintained that he never spoke with them at all. Despite the fact that they lived less than fifty feet from his rented rooms, he mailed his rent check to them every month.

He could walk to work at the university from his flat and used the classic Camaro primarily to cruise around downtown or the Hill or other student haunts on weekend nights. In a rare flash of insight he'd once acknowledged that he drove his prize around town on pleasant evenings hoping that someone would find his ride cool, though the few times that he and his car had generated attention out in public he'd been pretty certain that the students had been taunting him.

After a lifetime feeling that he'd been born with the birthmark of a bull's-eye on his chest, Bob was familiar with being taunted and appeared immune to it. Frankly, the incidents with the university students hadn't seemed to trouble him. He was perplexed, however, that the kids didn't find his car cool.

To Bob, that was crazy.

Over the last year he had begun to visit Boulder's clubs and bars with some regularity, at least a couple of times a month. His pub-crawling wasn't designed to accommodate a drinking habit – a period of severe bingeing in his early twenties had actually caused him to swear off alcohol. Regardless, he was way too cheap to splurge on nightclub-priced drinks. And he didn't go out to the clubs to hang out in the glow of the pretty people. After a firm confrontation from me one day – 'Come on, Bob, why do you go?' – he admitted that he went out to nightspots to 'watch them.'

I guessed that he meant the girls, but I couldn't get him to admit it. So I reserved judgment, aware that Bob could just as well have been spying on the boys. In my presence, he'd never admitted to any feeling that I would categorize as either romantic or sexual toward people of either gender.

That's all he would say about his clubbing predilection, that he went to 'watch them.' I was left to wonder: If the watching wasn't some once-removed sexual thing, was it voyeuristic? Anthropological? Maybe part of some arcane sociological experiment? After almost two years of trying to understand such things about Bob I still wasn't sure, and on those Tuesday nights when I was driving home after I'd completed a session with him and found myself still musing about Bob's narrow life, the fact that there was so much I didn't know troubled me.

I suspected that the pretty objects of Bob's fascination were at least equally troubled when they looked up to discover Bob's shimmying eyes locked on to their own as they downed designer cocktails in Boulder's latest trendy nightspot.

I also had little doubt that Bob would avert his eyes the moment his prey noticed that he was staring. I knew it because in two years of sessions Bob had never held eye contact with me for more than a split second.

Other than the regular interaction he had with his boss in the physics department at the university – it was at her insistence that he'd sought therapy – the psychotherapy with me was, to my knowledge, Bob's primary ongoing human relationship that didn't include at least one cyber-buffer. Although I suspected that he trusted me more than he trusted his boss, I reminded myself that he didn't even trust her enough to allow her the responsibility of keeping the begonia on his desk watered during his infrequent holidays from work.

He certainly didn't trust me enough to accept my oft-repeated suggestions about the potential benefits of psychopharmacology. I raised the issue occasionally, but never pressed it. Although I held out hopes that the right antidepressant might dent his veneer of despair, the odds of medication impacting Bob's underlying character disorder were slim. But then – I had to admit – so were the odds that psychotherapy would ever make any profound difference in his functioning.

That didn't mean I wasn't going to try.

Bob did trust me just enough to come back to see me every Tuesday afternoon at 4:45. That was the foundation of our relationship. In two years of treatment, he'd missed only one session, and had canceled that appointment four weeks in advance. Forty-five minutes, once a week, that was our deal. Bob knew what time our appointment started. He knew when it ended. After a hundred tries, though, he still had only the most vague concept of what should happen in between.

I saw him on a sliding scale, discounting my usual fee by well more than half so that he could afford to come in. Bob would always pay me at the beginning of the last session of each month, just before I handed out my bills. His personal check to me was always placed in the same type of security envelope, was always folded the same way, and was always double sealed, once by licking the flap, and once by the addition of two long strips of Scotch tape.

Bob's handwriting was tiny and precise and rounded. The first time he gave me a check I had to use a magnifying glass to read the amount. I didn't know how the university credit union managed to clear his checks. But it did.

On occasional Tuesdays during our time together we did something that loosely resembled traditional psychotherapy. More often the sessions were an odd interchange that to an outsider probably would look more like social skills training than anything psychotherapeutic. Not unlike someone afflicted with Asperger's syndrome, Bob had no innate sense of how human interaction should work. He would end up being insulting when his intent was to be impersonally cordial. He would often be cruel while he was merely trying to create some protective psychological space. During the first year of treatment we'd spent a half dozen autumn Tuesdays troubleshooting how Bob might respond differently when a student walked up to his desk in the physics department and said, 'Good morning,' or 'Hi.'

His previous stock reply – 'What difference does it make?' – hadn't been working too well for him.

The most surprising thing about psychotherapy with Bob? As the months passed I'd grown fond of this man who was about as easy to get close to as a porcupine. In the lingo, I had developed a positive countertransference for him. And maybe because I'd developed affection for Bob my empathy for his plight was sometimes swollen out of proportion.

I vowed to keep an eye on it.

14

Bob's connection to the Millers didn't appear to be particularly unique or interesting. He hadn't babysat Mallory, nor had he gone to high school with Mrs. Miller. He wasn't a family friend, hadn't played Santa at any Miller family holiday gatherings. In fact, his particular connection to the girl's disappearance seemed to be a relatively common affliction that he shared with many viewers of cable news TV stations. Bob, it turned out, had quickly grown obsessed by Mallory's disappearance, which, I feared, meant that for at least forty-five minutes a week I was likely to be forced to be vicariously obsessed by Mallory's disappearance, too.

I was less than thrilled by the revelation that Bob was transfixed by Mallory's plight. As he described his fascination my silent protest was a pathetic *No, please no*. At a clinical level Bob didn't need the obsession; his pathological casserole was certainly not wanting for the addition of an obsessive crust of any description. At a more selfish level, I'd already begun hoping – like the great majority of Boulderites – that the case of the disappearing girl was going to go away gently, that Sam and his like-minded police colleagues were right and that this time the case of the disappearing girl wasn't really a case of a disappearing girl at all. Like ninety-nine percent of Boulder's residents, I was hoping that Mallory Miller – despite what I'd learned about her recent history from Diane – was just a girl who'd left home for one of the many bad reasons that young teenage girls choose to leave home.

But I wasn't to be so lucky. From the first time Bob mentioned her name – 'Do you think she ran? Or do you think she was kidnapped? Mallory?' – I became concerned that Bob and I would begin to spend some unknown number of Tuesday sessions rehashing the latest news

and gossip about her. Since Bob devoured the *Enquirer* and the *Star* –
he didn't buy them; he scoured the student union looking for discarded copies – I was even going to be force-fed tidbits about Mallory
that I wouldn't have been exposed to in the more reputable news
sources.

How did I know all this?

Because Bob had been transfixed by the Kobe thing, too. And the
Michael Jackson thing. Not to mention the Scott Peterson thing.
That's how I knew.

I was realizing, almost even begrudgingly accepting, that it was
beginning to look like I couldn't get away from Mallory Miller no
matter how hard I tried.

The Tuesday session with Bob during the week between Christmas and New Year's was like dozens before it. Bob was distracted and
distant, and we spent a chunk of the allotted time in silence. He surprised me by ending the appointment with a request he'd never made
before: He asked if we could meet again later that week.

Could I actually be witnessing nascent signs of attachment, the
therapeutic Holy Grail in the treatment of a schizoid personality?
Highly unlikely, but I gladly offered him an additional session on
Thursday, the penultimate day of the year.

15

The phone rang later that evening while I was giving Grace her bath. Lauren spoke for a few minutes before she joined me in the bathroom and handed me the portable and a towel for my hands. 'It's Diane,' she said, and I exchanged the delights of playtime in the bathtub for the dubious pleasures of the telephone.

It struck me as not a great deal.

'Hi,' I said as I moved out of the bathroom and walked across the master bedroom to the big windows facing the mountains. The still-snowy spots on the winter landscape seemed fluorescent in the moonlight.

'I've been thinking,' Diane said.

'Yeah.'

'About Hannah.'

I wasn't at all surprised. Diane and I had talked about Hannah a dozen or more times since her death. We'd do it a dozen more, and maybe a dozen more after that. My friend liked to process out loud, and Hannah's death continued to haunt her.

'These things take time, Diane. They just do. This time of year especially, you know. The holidays make it harder.'

She sighed. 'That's not what I mean.'

I stuffed my repertoire of grief platitudes back into storage and said, 'Okay.'

'What if this is why she died? Because she met with Mallory Miller. What if somebody killed Hannah because she met with the kid that one time?'

'I'm . . . listening.'

'Don't use that voice. I hate that voice. You think I'm crazy? Tell me this didn't cross your mind.'

'I can honestly say it didn't cross my mind.' It had – briefly – but I wasn't about to admit it and inadvertently provide monster chow for the dragons inhabiting Diane's cave of paranoia.

'Hannah might have been murdered, right? That's a possibility?' Diane's tone was hoarse, slightly conspiratorial. I couldn't figure out why.

'Are you at home?'

'Yes.'

'Why are you whispering?'

'I don't know. This is the sort of thing people whisper about, isn't it?'

'Okay, just wondering.'

'Now answer me.' She was still almost whispering. 'It's a possibility that Hannah was murdered, right?'

'Yeah.' The coroner's finding on manner of death was 'undetermined.' That conclusion didn't mean Hannah had been murdered, nor did it mean that she hadn't been murdered. We both knew Diane had her own hypothesis on the matter.

She spelled out her theory for me anyway. 'Slocum hasn't been able to identify a motive to support a conclusion of homicide, right?'

'Yeah.' I could graciously grant Diane the motive argument, fully cognizant that Slocum hadn't been able to identify means or opportunity, either. He was 0-for-3.

'Well, what if this was the motive? Something Mallory told Hannah. Something that needed to stay secret.'

I tried to imagine some possibilities. Couldn't. The time frame seemed wrong. Hannah had died over a week before Mallory disappeared.

'Like?' I asked.

'I don't know. I thought you would have . . . an idea. This is your bailiwick, not mine.'

Bailiwick? I was hoping it wasn't a new companion word to *holy moly*. Regardless, Diane was doomed to be disappointed by the sparse contents of my bailiwick. I didn't have any theory about the secret that Mallory might have shared with Hannah.

From the bathroom Lauren called out, 'Check the stove for me, sweetie. I have something cooking.'

I inhaled, and followed the tantalizing aroma of spicy hot cider all the way to the kitchen. A cinnamon stick and some cloves were floating in a steaming apple brew. Lauren had been preparing a treat for us when the phone rang. I shut off the gas to the burner but stayed close by so the steam would rise toward my face.

Diane wasn't patient about the delay. 'You still there?' she asked.

'I'm thinking.' What I was thinking about was whether I should add some good whiskey or a dollop of rum to my cup of hot cider.

'You done yet?'

I said, 'Maybe if Hannah had died after Mallory disappeared, it might make some sense to wander down this road. But Hannah died first. And that was over a week before Mallory disappeared.'

'You think I'm crazy.'

It wasn't a question. 'No crazier than I thought you were before you called.'

'Funny.'

'Based on what you told me there was nothing incendiary about the session. Nothing worth killing Hannah over.'

'She said her father was "up to something." Remember?'

'But the question is what? She may have meant that he wanted her to take up the viola, or change schools, or get braces. Who knows? Hannah didn't spell it out.'

'I expected you to be more helpful, Alan.'

No doubt because this is my bailiwick. I said, 'Sorry.'

'You don't want to do this, do you?' she asked.

Her question wasn't an accusation. Diane was belatedly recognizing my resistance to be involved with anything that had to do with Boulder's latest missing girl.

'No, I don't. But I will.'

'Is it because of Grace?'

'I'm sure that's part of it.'

'What then?'

'I'm working on that. I don't like the parallels to eight years ago. The whole thing is creepy. I'm a father now, it's . . .' I could have just admitted that I wasn't working on it very hard, but Diane wouldn't have let me off the hook. The truth was that I wanted the whole Mallory Miller thing to go away.

She softened. 'Think about it, please. See if anything jumps out at you. Can you at least do that?'

'Sure,' I said. 'I can do that.'

Grace was in fresh jammies, Lauren was swathed in soft flannel, her slender feet cushioned in sheepskin Uggs, and the mug of hot cider, with a little bourbon, was warming my hands. The three of us sat together on the couch in the living room and read bedtime stories about little girls and flowers, and dogs and friends.

Grace cackled and giggled and was delighted at the pages.

I held my daughter a little tighter than usual as Lauren's late-day gravelly voice soothed us all.

I waited until Grace was in bed and Lauren was settled into the soothing rhythms of a game of pool in what – had we possessed a table and chairs instead of a tournament-quality pool table – should have been the dining room, before I went downstairs and climbed on the road bike that I'd set up for indoor workouts in the basement. I warmed up quickly, maybe too quickly, and soon had my spin up where I wanted.

If a girl, I wondered, a fourteen-year-old girl, had shown up in my waiting room wanting an emergency appointment, what would I have done?

Mallory had probably told Hannah it was 'important,' or something similar. I didn't know a therapist, myself included, who wouldn't have listened to what she had to say. Why? 'Important' could have meant she wanted to report abuse. And if a kid wants to report abuse, it's the responsibility of adults, especially mental health professionals, to bend over backward to listen.

I also wondered whether Hannah had made the connection between the teenager in her office and the little girl she might have seen in her waiting room ten years or so before. Had Mallory said anything to remind her?

Remember me? I'm Mallory.

I tried to put myself in the same circumstances. Would I remember a kid so many years later? Would I even recognize that it was the same kid?

I didn't think I would. Miller is a common name. Sometimes my friends' kids changed so much in only a couple of years that I hardly recognized them. Adrienne's son Jonas had grown so much in the past year that he looked like a completely different child. Sam's son Simon had gone from little boy to man-child, it seemed, in weeks.

Even if Hannah had remembered the small child she had befriended in the waiting room, the memory wouldn't have given her many clues. Hannah would have no reason to know anything about the details of Mary Black's care of Rachel Miller.

But why was Mallory so vague about her concerns about her father?

That was my most troubling question: Why would a girl insist on a session with a therapist and then be vague about what was happening at home?

I made some assumptions about the session that I thought were safe.

Hannah would have asked Mallory directly about drug use, specifically about alcohol. Hannah hadn't told Diane about any concerns with substance abuse, so apparently she felt satisfied with whatever answer she'd received from Mallory.

Given that Mallory had revealed her mother's history of mental illness, I suspected that Hannah had directly or indirectly done some version of a mental status exam during the interview to see if what afflicted mother might also be afflicting her progeny. Had Mallory passed?

I didn't know that. Probably. But there were plenty of unknowns.

I listened for a moment to the sharp cracks and gentle taps that punctuated Lauren's pool playing. Returning my attention to the bike, I reminded myself that I was doing a lot of speculating.

Mallory had said her father was 'up to something.'

But what had he been up to?

Was it related to Mallory's anxiety about the holidays?

And why had Mallory chosen that day to sit in the waiting room to see Hannah? A great question. I didn't have a great answer, or even a good one.

16

Coloradans don't tolerate gray skies with any equanimity.

Other weather we endure. Gray skies, no.

On the high desert landscape where the Great

Plains rise into the Front Range of the Rockies, we live through the often relentless heat of June and July with little complaint, reassuring each other that even though it's 103 degrees outside, at least it's a dry heat.

Our once-a-decade oh-my-God blizzards, or our annual winter cold snaps of day-after-day temperatures below zero and wind chills that feel arctic? Most of us write them off as the price of living in close proximity to the best skiing on the planet.

The hundred-mile-an-hour winter Chinooks blowing out of the mountains in January and February? *Hey, lean into it, it's only a little wind.*

Golf-ball-size hail? Fierce summer thunderstorms? *We live in a desert. We need the moisture.*

But the absence of sunshine?

After two consecutive overcast days the grumbling begins, everyone's temper shortens, traffic cops stop giving warnings, and people aren't quite as nice to their dogs. Add a third or, God forbid, a fourth day of concrete-colored skies, and most of the state's residents, especially the natives, begin to wonder for what it is they're being punished. A few furtively check their IDs to see if they've been magically relocated to Seattle or Cleveland or Buffalo or some other sunshine-deprived location as penance for an obviously serious transgression against humanity.

It's not that it's always sunny here. But I have to admit that it feels like it's always sunny here. The tourist board throws around statistics:

We have 300-plus days of sunshine each year, we're sunnier than San Diego, much sunnier than Miami. I don't know if any of it's true. But I do know that the reality is that in Colorado I awaken every morning expecting to see the sun for a healthy chunk of the day.

One day of gray is disappointing. Two days in a row becomes a mini-crisis.

Anything more is cause for alarm.

Once the sun had set on Diane and me as we walked the Mall sharing our secrets about the Miller family, the rest of that week between Christmas and New Year's – the week after Mallory disappeared – was meteorologically bleak. Thursday brought constant flurries under steely skies. Friday taunted – the sun's silhouette was occasionally visible behind quickly passing clouds, but warming rays never reached the ground in a way that left behind even a hint of a shadow. Saturday, snow flurries fell intermittently all day long, icy winds howled from Wyoming, and by nightfall downy drifts began to cushion the bases of fences and the low sections of walls that dared to face north.

The sun had disappeared from our state – probably forever – it seemed.

A googol of reporters was camped out in Boulder, still expecting – or, God forbid, hoping for – a garroted body to emerge from a Boulder basement.

But Mallory Miller stayed stubbornly missing.

I was getting dragged into the riddle of her absence further and further.

Everybody was cranky.

Everybody, that is, except Sam Purdy.

And Sam probably should have been cranky. He had been for all of the many years we'd been friends. A lot was going on in his life. He was on the cusp of completing his first holiday season as an unmarried man. He had just celebrated the anniversary of surviving for a year after a heart attack – he'd reminded me that it beat the alternative, hands-down – and he had just managed to complete twelve-plus months without developing a fresh gallstone.

He was still learning the ropes of single-parenting his son, Simon.

And because of Mallory Miller, he was being forced to work overtime on a high-profile holiday crime, not exactly his thing, as part of a team of many detectives, most definitely not his thing.

But Sam's mood was good. Boulder's streak of gray days was nothing compared to the winter stretches he'd endured in his family home on Minnesota's Iron Range. His health problems? He had grown philosophical about them, felt he was doing all he could – with diet and exercise – to manage them. His divorce? Despite some stumbles he thought that he and Sherry had handled it all like grown-ups. Was there enough money to go around? Of course not – as Sam had indelicately put it, 'I live in fucking Boulder. How could there be enough money?' Sam's son Simon? He was a good kid. He had some emotional bruises from what his parents' marital disruption had forced him to endure, but Sam was confident that his son would do okay.

I didn't disagree.

The Mallory Miller case? Right from the start, Sam had pitched his tent in the don't-get-too-worked-up-about-this, she's-a-runaway camp. But he was a professional cop, and until his captain told him otherwise he planned to continue to investigate the details of her disappearance as though she might have been kidnapped by some mysterious intruder.

I knew the truth about Sam's personal life. I knew that Sam's pleasant demeanor wasn't due to his positive outlook, but rather that his positive outlook was due to a girl.

Okay, a woman. Her name was Carmen Reynoso. She was a cop, another detective, a class act who lived somewhere within commuting distance of the police department in Laguna Beach, California, and she and Sam were in love. They had met a little more than a year before while on the track of a serial killer.

It was a long story in which I'd had a part, and I liked to think I'd introduced them.

Sam and Simon had tickets, or some airline's digital equivalent, to fly to John Wayne International Airport to spend the New Year's holiday with Carmen and her daughter, Jessie. Jessie, a student at UC Santa Cruz, had promised Simon a trip to Disneyland during the visit.

In Sam's world, gray skies or blue skies, all was cool.

I met Sam at the new ice rink off the Boulder Turnpike in Superior, where Simon's peewee team was playing on the Wednesday night that fell within our streak of end-of-the-year bleak weather. Simon – who, unlike his father, played offense – was doing a sleepover at a teammate's house after the game and Sam and I were going to go someplace for a beer. It had been a while since we'd had time to get together socially.

Perhaps the flyers that were posted all over the ice rink doors should have been a caution for me about how the evening might progress, but, like most people in Boulder County, I was already growing somewhat immune to them. Two types predominated. Each version was on a standard eight-and-a-half-by-eleven sheet of paper. One was on brilliant yellow stock, screamed 'MISSING!' and had a black-and-white photograph of Mallory – she was airborne, just launched from a trampoline – above a brief physical description. The other flyer was on white copy paper and was adorned with a color photograph that had been taken by a school photographer who had already taken too many pictures that particular day. Large block letters asked, 'HAVE YOU SEEN HER?'

No, was the short answer.

I hadn't seen her. But in the few days since Mallory's disappearance I'd seen, literally, thousands of the flyers. Volunteers had papered almost every vertical surface Boulder had to offer, and some horizontal ones as well, with a yellow flyer or a white one, or more often, with multiple copies of each.

Towers of Mallory.

White and yellow checkerboards of Mallory.

Although I was growing inured to the posters themselves, the messages weren't lost on me. MISSING! and HAVE YOU SEEN HER? ran through my mind like an ever-repeating crawl at the bottom of some cosmic TV, the messages as insistent as the lyrics of an annoying jingle.

The two photographs of Mallory – one smiling and content, the other mischievous and teasing – had a much more subtle effect on me than did the banner headlines. The photos of the young girl lingered in my preconscious and provided fodder for unsettling dreams of the things that fathers dread. More than once I woke with a startling sense of vulnerability, a visceral awareness that I had a daughter and that it could have been she.

Sam had lost a lot of weight – I was guessing thirty-odd pounds – in the last year, but none of it in his face. He still had the face of a big, round guy. Much of the motivation for the weight loss had been medical. The past few years had confronted my friend with a minor heart attack, kidney stones, and gallstones. A new, healthy diet was one of his ways of fighting back.

He'd sworn off doughnuts and bacon and brats, and hadn't had a burger and fries in most of a year. He was learning to cook and he'd already warned me that he was going to count on me to be his running buddy while he trained to run his first 10K, the late-spring Bolder Boulder.

Health aside, most of the motivation for his self-improvement program, though he'd never admit it to me, was his recent separation and divorce, and that new girlfriend in California. Sam was a mature guy, a serious cop, and a devoted father. Still, he wanted to be buff so he could get the girls.

Prior to that night, I'd never observed Sam watching his son play in a competitive game in any sport, and anticipated that it wasn't going to be an inspiring sight, especially given the fact that the sport was hockey. Sam had a little bully in him – ask me, all effective cops do, they have to. In addition, Sam had the natural-born arrogance of Minnesotans who believe that they know more about hockey than any native – read: citizen of the United States of America – referee who might tie on skates and pull on a striped blouse in some Colorado barn. Sam granted Canadians special hockey dispensation.

I feared that it was a combustible combination of traits, and that I was about to discover that Sam was going to be one of those parents who give youth sports a rotten name. If, or when, he got too embarrassing to be with, I was more than prepared to move to a seat in the arena as far from him as possible.

Sam, as he often did, proved me wrong. Every word he screamed at the game was a word of encouragement. He knew the names of every one of Simon's teammates and lavished praise on the kids for their shots and their passing, but especially for their positioning and their defense. He even screamed out some kind words for the opposing players.

The two times he yelled out to the referees it was with a hearty, 'Hey, good call, guy. Let's keep 'em safe out there.'

Between periods I asked, 'Case driving you nuts?'

'Nah,' he said. But he knew what case I was talking about. 'If cases like that drove me nuts, I'd have been hanging out in your office a long time ago.' That thought caused him to chuckle to himself; Sam's opinion of psychotherapy wasn't particularly benevolent. Then he lowered his voice and tilted his big head toward me. 'There're still some guys who think somebody took her, a few. But it didn't come down that way. She was a kid with issues, Alan. The girl ran, plain and simple. Because of all the media and, you know – that other girl, back when, and what happened to her – the bosses have to go overboard on this, look for intruders under rugs, dot all the *t*'s and cross all the *i*'s, but everything or damn near everything says that she ran.

'Hey, a fourteen-year-old girl gone from home? It's a sad thing. Worse around Christmastime. But it happens. This time it happened at the wrong time in the wrong town in the wrong neighborhood under the wrong circumstances, so now the whole world is watching one family's tragedy unfold. But that's all it is: one family's tragedy. I'm afraid that the real tragedy is what happened to her after she ran; that's what keeps me awake at night. Is she in a ditch somewhere? Discarded by the side of some highway? In some asshole pimp's hands? When I hear what happened to her I think it's going to break my heart. My advice? Leave it alone.'

He was probably right. But Diane's story about Hannah Grant's intake interview with Mallory was still haunting me. I wasn't able to leave it alone.

'What about the guy that the Crandalls saw, the neighbors? The one they thought was loitering on the block before the snow started?'

Sam grimaced. 'If those people were really so concerned, why didn't they call us when they saw him? He was probably just some guy out for a stroll, trying to walk off his Christmas dinner. Maybe his kids were out caroling and he was keeping an eye on them. You know what it's like after something like this. People think they've seen all kinds of things.'

'What about the blood?' I asked.

Sam looked at me sideways, as though that question had surprised him. 'Simon cut his heel on the back door last summer, on the screen. My God, did it bleed. He hopped all over the house looking for me to get him a bandage and by the time he found me, there was blood everywhere. I still don't think I got it all cleaned up. I'm not the world's best housekeeper, and I promise you that I wouldn't want the crime-scene guys checking my house for splatter. The fact that there's some blood in the Millers' house doesn't mean any felonies came down. Hey, I bet if I walked in with some Luminol I could get your house to light up, too.'

'Well, then what about the snow thing?'

17

The snow thing.

Christmas had been on the previous Saturday. The day had been clear and cold with a high temperature in the mid-twenties. An up-slope developed and snow started falling in earnest in Boulder some time around seven o'clock in the evening. At first, it had been a steady snow; three quick inches fell before the wind shifted directions around 9:30 and the snow paused for an hour. When the upslope resumed so did the snow, which fell insistently until early morning.

'All these questions? It isn't like you,' Sam said. 'You working as a stringer for the *Enquirer* in your spare time?'

'Actually, I've been trying my hardest to keep my head in the sand about this whole thing.'

'You're failing miserably.'

'I don't get the snow thing. Humor me.'

'I don't either,' Sam admitted.

Bill and Reese Miller left Mallory at home alone with her stomach-ache around 6:30, just before the snow started. Her cell-phone records show that Mallory made a few phone calls – all to girl-friends – in the next couple of hours, and received a few others. The first call out was at 6:39. The last call in came at 8:47. It was from her father, checking in on her from the Christmas gathering, and letting her know they'd be home soon.

Bill Miller said that his daughter answered the phone, and reported to the police that Mallory told him she was doing okay. She was all packed up for the next day's ski trip, had a heating pad on her belly, and was watching a DVD she got that morning for Christmas.

'The snow thing isn't important?' I asked Sam.

93

'I didn't say that. I said I don't get it. There's always something in every case that I don't get. Always.'

'Where are her footprints?'

'I said I don't know. I wasn't kidding – I really don't know.' He popped a peanut into his mouth and pointed toward the ice. 'So where do you think a place like this gets money for a Zamboni like that?'

The Zamboni that was scooting around the rink between periods grooming the ice surface looked brand-new. All shiny and painted a shade of green that was much too close to chartreuse for my comfort. It was covered with more commercial messages than the NASCAR champion stock car.

'I don't know,' I admitted.

'When I retire, I think I'd like to drive a Zamboni in a place just like this. I'd do it for free, just for the fun of it. For the kids. You know about Zambonis? How they got started?'

I admitted I didn't.

Sam did. He explained the whole history of the Zamboni as though he'd grown up with Mr. Zamboni's daughter and lived through the experience himself. I listened with some wonder, not because of any particular fascination with Zambonis but because of the extent of Sam's knowledge base. The truth was that Sam knew a lot of crap. He was the kind of guy with whom you did not want to play Trivial Pursuit.

'How come you know so much trivia?' I asked him when he'd exhausted the Zamboni tale.

'I just remember stuff. It's one of the things that makes me a good cop. And I don't consider it trivia.'

'No?'

'No. I like to think of it as information of infrequent utility.'

'It's occasionally important to know that the first Zamboni was made from an old army Jeep?'

'That's the thing. You never know what might be important. It's all just information and then, out of nowhere, something becomes useful. I just store it so it's there when I need it.'

Like the snow thing, I thought.

The Millers' home was on the eastern side of Twelfth Street, facing the mountains that rise dramatically only a dozen blocks away. How dramatically do the Rockies jut out of west Boulder? On one side of a street you're on a gentle hill. On the other side, you're on the slope of a mountain.

But that's to the west. A block to the east – in that part of the Boulder Valley 'east' means downhill – and a few doors north of their home, the Millers had a new neighbor. A neighbor they had probably never met. The new family, the Harts, had moved into their brick Tudor the previous spring and within two months of unpacking their moving vans had begun diligent work on the family passion – which involved turning the facade and entire front yard of their house into a garish, illuminated, motorized tribute to the Christmas holiday.

The number of lights involved – all of the family members seemed to prefer to call them 'points' when they spoke to the media, which they did frequently – ran well into five figures. Six major illuminated displays – exactly half were loosely biblical in theme – ranged from three feet to nine feet in height, and eleven different motorized extravaganzas kept elves bowing, stars shooting, donkeys walking, and reindeer flying all over the front of the house and far up into the trees. An enterprising reporter with an incipient personality disorder found 116 distinct representations of Santa Claus secreted in various locations. On the wide expanse of roof beside the center gable of the house a huge arched sign of shimmering red neon announced to all that this home was indeed 'The Very HART of Christmas.'

It was something.

Families who like to make an annual trek through other people's neighborhoods in search of the best and brightest Christmas decorations seemed to adore what the Harts had done to their home. The Harts' neighbors, and the neighbors of the Harts' neighbors, all of whom had to endure the endless crawl of traffic down Thirteenth Street, were probably not quite so enamored of the family's efforts.

Boulder being Boulder, the controversy became sport, and arguments flourished about light pollution and the environmental consequences of all that electricity being used on something so, well, garish and transient. The local paper, the *Camera,* actually published a series of letters about the brouhaha, the first of which compared the Harts' extravaganza to one of Christo's installations. Follow-up missives predictably belittled the aesthetic sensibilities of anyone who could possibly think that way.

'But,' I asked Sam, 'do you think the news footage shows what everybody thinks it shows?'

'Pretty much,' Sam said. 'It shows what it shows, I guess. I don't have much argument with Fox News. Well, that's not exactly true. Let's just say I don't have much argument with what Fox News has to say about those few minutes in the Millers' neighborhood on Christmas night.'

'So?' I said. 'Explain it to me.'

'What?'

'The snow thing.'

'I can't.'

'You can't?'

He smiled. Not at me, exactly. He smiled as though he were enjoying my consternation. 'So that's it? You can't explain it?'

What he couldn't explain was the footage that had been shot by the Fox News helicopter on Christmas night. The shot was live for their 9 P.M. newscast – which had included an announcement of the three winners of Fox's best-holiday-decorated-house-in-the-metro-area contest. The Harts' home had been awarded a disappointing, to them, third place, which earned the earliest appearance of any of the winners on that night's evening news. Records revealed that the live chopper footage from Boulder was aired beginning precisely at 9:16. Viewers eager to see the ultimate champion would have to stick with the newscast until the bitter end because the helicopter would have to make a trek across the entire metro area to Aurora for a shot of the grand-prize winner.

'Snow started sticking right away, yes? Around seven?' I asked.

'At my house it did.'

'And phone records show that Mallory was still home at eight forty-seven?' That tidbit of information had been leaked to the media earlier in the week. Locally, it had been played up by one of the TV affiliates as though the scoop was as important as a cure for cancer.

Before Sam had a chance to reply the kids skated back onto the ice to warm up for the next period. 'For the sake of argument, yes, let's say there was phone activity at eight forty-seven,' Sam said. 'I don't want to talk about this during the game, so make it quick. I'm getting bored.'

After the news helicopter completed its shot of the Harts' home, it had banked away for a wide shot of the neighborhood, which included, for about three seconds – Fox timed it at 2.8614, and who was I to argue with that – the Millers' totally undecorated house on Twelfth Street. Two days after Mallory's disappearance, an astute Fox producer realized what the station might possess in the additional neighborhood footage that had been shot on Christmas night, and Fox launched a huge advertising blitz to promote its 'crucial new information in the Mallory Miller case. Tune in Tuesday. Exclusively on Fox News at Nine.'

'Mr. Miller and Reese got home around nine-twenty, right?'

'Give or take.'

'But close.'

'Close.'

'Mallory was gone by then.'

'Correct-o. We think. Nobody actually looked for her until the next morning. People forget that little detail. She had a big head start.'

'You think she was home at nine-twenty, Sam?'

'No, I think she'd already split. But I do like arguing with you. That part's kind of fun.'

Fox had done digital magic to the Christmas night footage. The resulting images of the Miller home were grainy, and the shadows were darker in a few places than was ideal, but the video was clear enough that the conclusions Fox reached really weren't controversial.

'The helicopter footage from Fox shows no footprints in the snow around the Millers' house. Not on the walk, not on the driveway, not through the yard. And no tire tracks up the driveway into the garage.' I waited for him to disagree, but he seemed to be ignoring me. Finally, I added, 'And lights were on in the house, right? Both floors.'

'So what? You know any kid who remembers to turn off lights?'

'All that's at nine-sixteen?'

The buzzer sounded. Sam said, 'It was actually nine-eighteen by then. But why quibble? We're friends.' He pointed at the fresh sheet of ice down below. 'Game's starting.'

'So are you saying you think that Mallory just happened to hustle out the door between like nine-eighteen and nine-twenty?'

Sam smiled at me pleasantly and said, 'Maybe she was watching the Christmas thing on Fox News and timed her exit perfectly to confound the helicopter. We hear she's a bright kid.'

I made a face that expressed my displeasure at his condescension.

He kneed me gently. 'Hey, Alan, so far I've just been agreeing with you about stuff you learned from somebody else. Maybe some of it's right. Maybe it isn't. But I can't tell you what I think, you know that, not if it involves what I know as a cop. But you know what else? Intruder theory, runaway theory – it doesn't make any difference. None. The lack of footprints in the snow on Christmas night is an anomaly no matter what theory you like. The kid got out of the house without leaving a trace. How? Microclimate? I don't know. Come on, it looks like Simon's on the ice for the start of the second period. Let's give the kids some support.'

Simon was indeed on the ice, at left wing. Both teams were sloppier with the puck at the start of the second period than they had been in the first. I was about to ask Sam whether the kids might be having trouble with the fresh ice laid down by the Zamboni when he spoke first.

'Reese Miller's a hockey player. Did you know that? I've seen him play a few times. He's good.'

I hadn't seen any mention of Mallory's little brother's hobbies in the paper. But then I'd been making a concerted effort not to read about the more gossipy aspects of the case. 'No, I didn't know that.'

'He's had some trouble.'

I leaned forward so that Sam would know that I was looking at him. 'And you know this as a cop or as a parent?'

'The latter.'

'What kind of trouble?'

'God, you're nosy tonight. You heard that his dad sent him out of town for a while until the commotion dies down?'

'To visit family?' I asked. I hadn't heard.

'I shouldn't say, but yeah,' Sam said. 'I'm not sure I would have done that. Seems like a time when you'd want your kid close by.' I opened my mouth to agree, but Sam was done with the conversation. 'Let's watch the game.'

18

Bob entered my office for his additional, day before New Year's Eve appointment carrying a boom box.

Mallory Miller had been missing for five days.

He and I had met almost a hundred times by then and he had never walked in the door with a boom box, or any other prop, for that matter. Without preamble, but with an almost sinister smile that underscored the fact that he seemed to lack a chin, Bob set the stereo on the table between us and pressed the 'play' button. I didn't recognize the tune at first – maybe because I'd managed to make it through the years on both sides of the recent cusp of centuries deprived of any familiarity at all with boy bands – but I realized soon enough that I was listening to a disappointing cover of Del Shannon's glorious 'Runaway.'

A run run run run runaway.

Bob's preferred, but dubious, choice of versions was a seriously overproduced adaptation of the classic featuring a harmony of voices obviously lacking in testosterone. I patiently adopted the role of audience, unsure why that day's psychotherapy required musical accompaniment, and unsure why – if we required music at all, and that song in particular – we couldn't be listening to the almost flawless original. At what appeared to be a predetermined moment Bob decided to turn the session from surreal soundtrack to painful karaoke. His voice, a strange mix of soprano and something else, added a decidedly creepy new layer to the sugary harmonies that were filling my office.

Bob had chimed into the song at the precise point that the lyrical progression had reached *And I wonder / I wa wa wa wa wonder.* But he didn't stop there. He sang, '*Why / why why why why she ran away / And I wonder where she will stay.*'

He reached forward and hit the 'stop' button.

I wondered if I was supposed to clap.

Bob could carry a tune. I had to give him that.

Once I was certain he was finished, at least for the moment, I tried to think of something intelligent to say. I failed.

Sitting back, Bob was quiet for most of a minute before he said, 'I'm writing about it.'

'You are?' I asked, trying not to reveal the true level of stupefaction I was feeling at what was happening in my office. Was Bob writing songs?

'Yes.'

Bob played board games. His favorite was Scrabble, but he'd always maintained that he was a pretty decent chess player, too, and I had no reason to doubt him. And I knew that he'd once driven all the way to Laughlin, Nevada, in his Camaro for a big Monopoly tournament at one of the casinos. Ideally, Bob's vision of ideal human interaction was that everyone should follow game protocols, that people should take turns, that everyone should know the rules, and that any and all disputes should be handled via consultation with a reference manual.

Needless to say, since most people acted as though life had no rules and as though there were no manual to consult, in real life Bob was frustrated more often than not by the manner that people behaved.

In Bob's game-centered worldview – a perspective that he definitely applied to conversations – it was my turn to speak. His hollow yes had constituted the totality of his turn and started the clock on mine. Given the presence of the boom box on the table between us, and the revelation about the writing he was doing, that probably wasn't a good time to reiterate a salient point I'd been trying to make for most of a year about the actual parameters of human communication. I took what I hoped was a safer road. I asked, 'What kind of writing are you doing?'

'A story. I think it'll be a novel. I don't know.'

My turn again. 'What . . . are you writing about?'

I knew, of course. I was hoping that I was wrong, but I knew.

'I know some things about what happened to the girl. That's what started it but it's mostly stuff I'm making up.'

'You know some things?' I said, trying to smother the skepticism that had crept into my question.

'Things that aren't in the news. I'm thinking I might call it *My Little Runaway*.'

And thus the song.

'The girl' had to be Mallory, right? She was Bob's current obsession, wasn't she? Had to be her.

Maybe, maybe not. In psychotherapy, assumptions are termites. Let them survive unchallenged and they'll eat away at the foundation. In an effort to exterminate at least one termite, I said, 'Mallory Miller? You know some things about what happened to her?'

'Yes.' He leaned forward, his elbows on his knees, his hands clasped in front of him.

Bob leaning forward startled me. Why? Simply because it brought him closer to me, and 'closer' wasn't one of Bob's things. 'Closer' is what schizoid personalities try to avoid the way arachnophobes try to steer clear of spiders. For a moment I considered the possibility that Bob had only leaned forward to once again turn on the boom box so that he could sing along to another song.

But he didn't touch the stereo. He had leaned closer for some other reason.

Belatedly, I realized that it was again my turn. All I could think of to say was 'Wow.'

Bob nodded an acknowledgment that I'd caught up with the conversational progression. 'What she was thinking. You know, like that. Nobody else knows it.'

With those words I decided that Bob had indeed leaned forward to share a secret with me. From a therapeutic perspective, it was a sign of true progress. I began entertaining the possibility that he might, against all odds, be getting better, but that fantasy was short-circuited by my wish that Bob had shared a different kind of secret with me – something about sex, or petty theft, or self-medication, or violent dreams. Just about anything else.

Anything other than something about Mallory.

Bob had many personal faults. Some were born of his underlying pathology; some were more difficult to explain. He was cold. He was irritable. He was intolerant. I suspected he was a bigot. He was mistrustful. Organic vegetables were more compassionate than he was.

The list could go on. And on. But as far as I knew – and after two years of Tuesdays I knew as much about him as anyone – Bob wasn't a liar.

Which meant one of two things. The first possibility was that Bob somehow did know some details about Mallory's disappearance, or at least about her state of mind prior to her disappearance.

The other option that I was considering? That Bob just thought he knew those things.

But was it likely that he could be so wrong? The natural history of schizoid personality is not that it's a precursor to schizophrenia. Although schizoids may display idiosyncratic thinking, failure in relating typically doesn't lead to psychotic failures in thinking. But, I reminded myself, the natural history of schizoid personality doesn't rule out progression to serious thought disorder either.

I forced myself to entertain the possibility that I was witnessing initial signs that Bob might be showing signs of decompensation. Usually the resolution to such therapeutic quandaries mattered little, if at all, outside the confines of the consultation room. That time? That time it might make a hell of a lot of difference. The girl in question, Mallory, was still missing, and . . . I realized that I didn't know how to finish that sentence, but also realized, belatedly, that it was my turn to finish some sentence. I said, 'You know things that the police don't know?'

He replied to my question with an apparent non sequitur. 'I rent a garage for my Camaro. I've told you that. It's why it's still so cherry.'

'Yes, we've talked about the garage.' I had to try not to sound exasperated.

'Well, the garage is right next door to Mallory Miller's house.'

He paused a long time, long enough so that I considered that it might, again, be my turn to speak. Although his news was interesting, I was getting ready to squander my move intentionally by saying something innocuous, like, 'It is? Right next door?' But Bob wasn't really done with his turn – he was the hesitant chess player who hadn't quite lifted his fingertips from the piece he'd just slid across the board.

He said, 'See, I know things. They say "write what you know." Well, I know about . . . this. At least a little.' He grimaced. Before I had a chance to respond and ask him about the reason for the grimace, he explained on his own by saying, 'But I don't want to be on TV.'

Although I'd not heard a direct answer to my earlier question – 'You know things that the police don't know?' – I was left with the impression that the answer was yes. Still, despite some concerted effort, I couldn't get Bob to say another word about Mallory that day. My intuition told me that his provocative tease about the missing girl would lose its energy if a long weekend intervened. I said, 'Let's continue this tomorrow.'

'What?'

'This seems important. Can you come back tomorrow for another session?'

'Because of her?'

'Because it seems like a good idea. To me.' What I didn't say was that scheduling three appointments with a schizoid personality in the same week was a clinical strategy that bordered on the absurd.

'I can't afford it.'

'I'll work with you on that.'

He didn't agree; he acquiesced.

His departure at the end of his session was much less dramatic than his boom box entry had been. As he did sometimes, he asked for permission to leave using the French door that led directly outside from the back of my office. The alternative route – returning down the hallway that my office shared with Diane's and then out through the waiting room – brought with it the risk for Bob of confronting another human being, an option that, on most days, he was unlikely to choose. I assented to his request, of course, and he grabbed his things and walked into the cold without a thank-you or a good-bye or a see-you-tomorrow.

I kept my eyes on him until he'd traversed the small backyard of the old house, scissored his way over the poor excuse for a fence on the south side of the property, and begun to close in on the distant sidewalk along Canyon Boulevard.

As I watched him trail away, I belatedly wondered whether I should have pressed him harder about Mallory and what he knew. But the truth was that at that moment, were I a betting man, I would have wagered that Bob's knowledge of Mallory was something that approached delusion.

The conclusion saddened me. Regardless, I'd know more soon enough.

My last clinical appointment of the year was going to be the next day, with Bob Brandt.

19

Diane didn't miss much.

'Did your schizoid man bring that boom box with him into therapy?' she asked me as we both rushed toward our office suite's only bathroom in the few moments that we were stealing between sessions.

I'd never told Diane that Bob suffered from schizoid disorder. But she was an astute diagnostician and had probably come to her own DSM conclusion about him after one or two awkward encounters while she was retrieving a patient in the waiting room.

For appearance' sake, I played coy. 'My last appointment brought a boom box with him, yeah. Actually played me a song on it. Could you hear it through the wall?'

I slowed so that Diane could make it through the door into our tiny kitchen before I did. As she crossed the space and spun into the adjacent bathroom she didn't pause to thank me for my gesture.

'What song?' she called through the closed door.

Diane was just making conversation. She didn't really care what song. I was pleased that her mood seemed improved. She hadn't enjoyed too many good days since Hannah's death.

'"Runaway."'

'Del Shannon?'

'No, some boy band.'

'Holy moly. Which one?'

To my dismay, 'Holy moly' had apparently survived the cut. 'How the hell would I know? All I listen to anymore is Raffi and The Wiggles.'

'Your boy-band days will come sooner than you'd like and you'll look back wistfully on the Raffi period. Was it about Mallory? Is that why he played the song?'

The toilet flushed loudly as I pondered the eerie accuracy of Diane's associative intuitiveness. 'Why would you guess that?'

Efficient sink sounds. The door opened. Finally.

'Because I am the psycholog-ess,' she offered, as though it somehow explained her rare perceptive skills.

'What?'

'Never mind. Could he be an Asperger? Your guy? Mr. Boom Box.'

Diane's question knocked me off balance just a little. Fortunately, I'd already given the issue some thought. I said, 'From a pure social-skills point of view, maybe. But the criteria for schizoid fit him like a glove.'

'It's trendy, you know. Diagnosing Aspies. Schizoid is so . . . sixties.'

'Yeah.' I squeezed past her into the bathroom. I didn't feel comfortable discussing Bob's diagnosis and, anyway, my bladder was screaming.

'You want coffee?' she asked.

'No thanks,' I called through the door as I fumbled with my zipper. At that moment, the thought of adding another liquid, especially a diuretic, to my system seemed masochistic.

Diane said, 'I still haven't heard from the cops about Hannah's session with Mallory. I kind of thought I would.'

'After this much time I don't think you're going to.' The relief I'd begun to experience in the privacy of the bathroom was exquisite. Talking out loud felt like a particularly intrusive chore.

'Do you think she ran?' Diane asked.

'I do.'

'Someone should know what I learned from Hannah.'

I moved to wash my hands, but didn't reply. Wasn't sure how to reply. Eventually I said, 'It'd be great if you could say something, but you can't.'

'Too many people think they know what was going on in that family. The media does, the cops do, Mallory's father probably does, too. Truth is that it seems like a lot of people all know a little bit but nobody is talking to each other. Nobody has the whole picture.'

I dried my hands while I considered her point. I had to admit she had one. Although I could have argued that the same thing was true about almost any family anywhere, the Miller family was a special case. It seemed likely that despite the intense law enforcement and media assault on their privacy, no one had developed a complete picture of what had been going on in the Miller household prior to Christmas night.

'I've been wondering,' Diane said. 'Do you think Mary Black would talk to me?'

I opened the door. 'About what?'

Diane had one hip against the kitchen counter. She was sipping from a big pink mug of coffee. 'Mrs. Miller, Mallory's mom.'

'No, of course not. Why would she?'

She ignored my question. 'Would she talk to you, then? You referred Mrs. Miller to her.'

'Last time I checked it didn't give me lifetime access to the woman's mental health records.' I squeezed past Diane, and began to snoop around in our little refrigerator for something with caffeine. 'What do you hope to find by talking to Mary, anyway?'

'I can't talk to her father. There has to be some way to pull all this together.'

'"All this" being the Millers' family situation?'

'Yes . . .'

She'd spoken the simple affirmation as though it constituted an incomplete sentence. I suspected that the other part of the sentence – the part she'd kept to herself – would be something about Hannah's death and Diane's ongoing lament that the cops – specifically the evil asshole, Jaris Slocum – weren't doing much to find Hannah's killer.

Diane remained certain that out there – somewhere – was Hannah's killer.

For whatever reason, she decided that it wasn't judicious to go there with me right then. I couldn't see a reason to quibble with that judgment so I spent a silent moment reflecting on some of the crazy cases I'd been involved with over the past few years, looking for lessons on how to 'pull all this together.'

All I saw were ways to repeat mistakes I'd already made; I couldn't see a single advisable choice. I said, 'Sometimes there isn't, Diane. Sometimes we end up knowing things that other people should probably know. But that's just the way it is.'

Her reply? 'This coffee's old. When did you make it?'

'Before lunch.'

She poured the contents of her mug into the sink. 'I know somebody who might talk to me. Fill in some pieces.'

'Yeah, who?' I expected a punch line.

She fumbled around in a cupboard and came out with a mint Milano. 'I never got my trip to Vegas.'

I wondered where the cookie stash was hidden; I hadn't spotted them earlier in the day. A millisecond after I absorbed her taunt I realized that she might not be joking. 'Diane, you wouldn't.'

'I wouldn't? Watch me. It's winter and it's cold here, if you haven't noticed. It's warm there. The craps tables are open twenty-four seven. Want to come?'

She'd stepped out of the kitchen and started back down the hallway to her office.

I stuck my head out the door. 'You're kidding, right? Tell me you're kidding.'

As she turned the corner toward the waiting room to retrieve her next patient she wiggled her ass in reply. Over her shoulder she called out, 'For the record, I think he's schizoid, too. Asperger, my . . .' She gave her ass one final shake to finish the sentence.

20

No boom box on New Year's Eve afternoon during Bob's additional, additional therapy time. I wasn't surprised; I actually half expected that he would behave as though our conversation about Mallory had never taken place.

Bob slipped his ancient leather-bottomed North Face backpack from his shoulder onto the floor and sat heavily across from me. He didn't bother to remove the well-worn fleece-lined denim jacket that covered one of the button-down blue oxford dress shirts he wore year round. Bob had two denim jackets. This one, with the fleece, was the winter version. The other one, unlined, was reserved for spring and fall.

He didn't say hello to me. He hadn't looked in my direction since I'd retrieved him from the waiting room and led him to my office. I thought he looked particularly tired and distant, which left me again questioning the wisdom of scheduling a third session with a man who used so much of his energy to maintain interpersonal distance.

I said, 'Hello, Bob.'

His gaze was locked on a particular spot on the wall behind me, over my left shoulder. I was tempted to turn and see what was so interesting to him, but I didn't. I knew I'd discover nothing there but paint.

If you were to examine the family histories of the last hundred patients who had sought my help, you would find quite a few who had, arguably, suffered worse childhood trauma than Bob. I don't say that to minimize what he endured when he was young, but rather to create some perspective.

As adults, none of those other patients was as psychologically damaged as Bob. To me, that meant that Bob's unfortunate childhood wasn't sufficient to explain his psychopathology.

Bob's father – the man had been emotionally abusive, and I wouldn't have been at all surprised to learn someday that he had been physically abusive as well – had abandoned the family when Bob was only four. Bob's older brother – the one who lived near his mother – was a high school football star who'd become a college football star who'd become a successful tax attorney. Bob had more than enough insight to know that despite the fact that they had shared a house growing up, he and his brother had never really lived on the same planet.

His sister, five years older – Bob's memory of her is innocent, and his worship of her saintlike – died of leukemia a year after their father deserted them, on the very day that Bob entered kindergarten.

She'd died at home before breakfast and Bob's mother didn't permit him to miss his first day of school.

His mother was, by Bob's description, a hot-and-cold, smother-and-reject kind of caretaker whom I surmised, had she made her way into a clinician's office for a diagnostic sit-down, would probably have walked out with the dreaded 301.83 label of borderline personality disorder.

As a childhood tableau, it was an awful set piece. But sadly, I saw worse all the time.

All the time.

If a traumatic upbringing wasn't responsible for Bob's seemingly intractable character pathology, was nature to blame? Did the shuffle and deal of genetic bounty leave Bob with a particularly bad hand? Possibly.

Most likely, though, it was some combination of two powerful forces, some unpredictable interaction between Bob's genetic fabric and the bedeviled caprice of his human family.

But I didn't know for sure. The only solace I could find was that a lot of work was being done on the spectrum of disorders that covers the broad territory from autism to schizoid personality. Someday soon, maybe, we'd learn something that would allow me to be a more effective therapist for people like Bob.

Bob said, 'When Doyle sells it, I'm going to have to find a new place to garage the Camaro.'

Something I'd learned about Bob over our years of Tuesdays together was that he often started our conversations midstream, as though an important dialogue had been going on in his head and at some point in my presence – a random point possibly, but more likely not – he decided to put voice to one of the thoughts. I was left to wonder why segue, context, and transition were absent from those rhetorical equations. For the time being, until the long list of goals that comprised my treatment plan for Bob was completed, keeping up with the nature of the progression of his thinking was part of my responsibility.

That day, though, what I was most aware of was that Bob hadn't started the session talking about Mallory.

'Doyle is . . . ?' I asked.

'The guy I rent the garage from. For my Camaro.'

Bob explained the simple fact as though he was annoyed that he was being forced to repeat it for my benefit. Although Bob had mentioned the garage arrangement already that week, the truth was that I'd never heard him mention anyone named Doyle before. I was certain.

'And he's selling . . . ?' I guessed that Doyle was selling the garage.

'The house. It's been on the market for a while, since fall. When he sells it, I'm going to have to move my car, obviously.'

Bob garages his car next door to the home where Mallory Miller lives with her father and brother. And a guy named Doyle owns the house.

Interesting. Lauren hadn't mentioned that last fact to me. Nor did I think I had seen that tidbit in the paper. Not in the Boulder *Daily Camera*. Not in the Denver papers.

The house had been on the market for a while before Mallory disappeared. Had I seen that detail in the paper? I wasn't sure about that either. Maybe. I reminded myself that I wasn't exactly a student of the case.

Bob is concerned about losing the garage for his Camaro.
Check.

'Have you spoken with this guy Doyle, Bob? Do you know his plans for the . . . garage?'

With Bob, where interpersonal relationships were involved, the obvious step often wasn't obvious at all.

'He's selling the house. There's a sign up outside. What's to ask? He moved out a couple of months ago. It's a nice place. I can't afford to buy anything like that.'

Bob's reply was edgier than usual. I noticed that I was tiptoeing with him. I wasn't sure why I was doing it, but I could feel the care I was forcing into my words as I said, 'When he sells the house you'll have to look for a new place for your car?'

Bob was pulling his lower lip across the sharp surface of his front teeth. He did it three or four times before he said, 'I don't actually pay him.'

It was my turn. 'You don't pay Doyle? For the garage?'

'He, um . . . builds fountains and ponds and streams and water-falls, you know, crap like that for rich people. That's his . . . his business. He does pretty well. I mean, to buy that house, right? It has a theater – a real theater – in the basement. It's like . . . a great place to watch movies. So cool. He has to be doing okay. I help him some-times, on weekends mostly. He lets me use the garage for the Camaro, and lets me watch movies sometimes. The Trilogy down there? Oh, that's the deal. That is the deal. It may turn out I've been getting screwed. I don't know. I really should have done the math.'

For two years I'd known Bob and I didn't know anything about Doyle, nor did I know anything about his weekends spent building fancy water features for people self-indulgent enough to expect to have large quantities of scarce water decorating their high desert properties. What else didn't I know about this man across from me?

Experience had taught me that with someone like Bob, the scope of my ignorance could be breathtaking.

'The Trilogy?' I asked, trying to fill in at least one blank.

'*The Lord of the Rings?*' he explained as though I were a dunce.

'Of course,' I said, feeling appropriately chastised. *Of course.* For Bob, what other trilogy could there have been? 'I didn't know you worked for anyone else, Bob.'

'It's just moving dirt.'

'And that means it's not important?'

'What's the big deal? We put down liners. Move rocks. Lay down some pipes, attach pumps. It's pretty easy. But people pay him a mint for this stuff. You should see his yard. Surrounded by berms and rocks. A big pond, a stream, a bridge, two waterfalls. Those fish –

koi. It's pretty cool. We moved a lot of dirt for all that. I like driving the little tractor, the Bobcat? That's a trip.'

'But no more?'

'I told you, he moved. I'm watching his house now until it sells. Keeping the walks shoveled, sweeping up, checking on stuff. Timers, lights. Like that. I think I will go back and do the math. I probably got screwed in the deal.'

If he had been screwed, he didn't sound too upset about it.

Assuming that he had one, I wasn't certain precisely what emotional point Bob was trying to make. Was he aggravated at losing his garage space? Was he sad that he would no longer have a part-time job building water features? Was he going to miss whatever relationship he had with Doyle?

All of the above? I had no idea.

'Will you miss it?' I asked. The 'it' was deliberate on my part. Bob could select an object himself. Garage, job, friend. His choice.

'Miss what?' he asked, instantly abrogating the intent of my clever quiz.

Forcing myself to remain placid, I asked an obvious shrink question. I said, 'I don't know. What do you think you will miss?'

Bob sometimes did this thing with his head that was exactly half of a shake. He'd turn his head to one side – I thought exclusively toward the right, but I wasn't done testing that hypothesis – and begin a head-shaking motion, but he would interrupt the arc of the shake precisely at the moment his nose was back at the neutral position. The movement wasn't graceful; it was abrupt. His face would jerk to a stop as though it had smacked into an invisible obstacle. Typically he accompanied the motion with a verbalized, 'Sheeesh.'

Years before, I'd had another patient who possessed the same bizarre affectation. I found that curious; it was like knowing two people who each had a sixth finger growing out of his elbow.

Bob chose that moment – after I pressed him a second time on what he would miss were Doyle to sell the house – to do the half head-shake thing, and he included the exasperated 'sheeesh' for emphasis.

As I always did, I interpreted the little choreography as a sign of his impatience. With many patients I would probably have kept my interpretation to myself, but with Bob I tried to do as much as possible out in front of the curtain. Human behavior was already enough of a mystery to him.

'You didn't like my question?' I said to reveal the progression of my thoughts.

'I don't like anybody's inane questions.'

The 'anybody's' was Bob's way of cushioning the blow, of telling me not to take his 'inane' rebuke personally. I considered the fact that he was depersonalizing the insult as another sign of clinical progress. On another day I would have been patting myself on the back at the emergence of even that paltry evidence of Bob's growth in compassion.

Not that day, though. I knew it was my turn to speak, but I decided to pass. Where Bob chose to go next would tell me something.

I figured that Bob was waiting for me to take my turn in this real-life board game of ours. After a long pause, he shifted his gaze from the fascinating blankness on the wall behind me, chanced the briefest of glances at me, and then began looking at his hands. His eyeballs began to shimmy.

As always, it gave me the creeps.

Finally, resigned that I was upsetting the world order by skipping my turn, he said, 'It's not safe yet. I'm not sure what I've gotten into. It's just too soon.'

Huh? 'What's too soon? I don't think I understand.'

'There's a lot I don't get,' Bob said.

What the hell are we talking about? 'For Doyle to sell his house?'

'I'm not sure everything is turning out, you know, the way . . . It might have been a mistake. I stumble into stuff, I do. Not very often, but, boy, when I do . . .'

'Are you talking about Mallory again, Bob?'

He did the half head-shake thing one more time and exclaimed, 'Sheeesh.'

21

I am – almost without fail – thoughtful during psychotherapy sessions. My words are measured. My mannerisms are controlled. It is unusual that I say or do anything while in a treatment session that is not considered and deliberate. That is not to say that I don't often say things that are, in retrospect, ill advised or outright stupid. Rather it is an acknowledgment that when I do, it turns out that I have made the ultimately questionable move with conscious intent.

But the next question that I asked was actually no more deliberate than had been my decision to reach across the hall and try the knob on Mary Black's office door on the day that Hannah Grant died. What I said was, 'Why don't you tell me about Doyle?'

Doyle *had* to be important. Bob, who lived his life devoid of relationships, apparently had one – however loosely defined – with this guy Doyle. In this psychotherapy, with this patient, with his problems, that was monumental news.

Was the presence of Doyle in Bob's life a sign of some drift in the continental plates of Bob's pathology? I had to suppose that it was. Could Bob really have a friend? But if Doyle was important, why hadn't Bob mentioned him to me before that day?

Did Doyle's sudden appearance say something I couldn't afford to miss about my relationship with Bob? Or perhaps, more importantly, about Bob's perception of his relationship with me?

The context of Doyle's emergence in Bob's psychotherapy was significant, too. Bob had decided to talk about Doyle while he was discussing loss. The 'loss' in question was, at the surface, the loss of a garage for his cherished Camaro, but the fact that he raised the issue of Doyle in the context of any attachment had to be significant. Right?

Maybe. I admit that I wasn't totally certain. Part of me thought I might be making a classic psychotherapy reach.

This work I did was much more art than science.

'Doyle's just a guy,' Bob said in reply to my question.

With as much nonchalance as I could muster I said, 'But you've known him a while? I don't think you've mentioned him before.'

'I don't *know* him. I park my car at his house. And I'm *sure* I mentioned him.'

'And you work for him sometimes.'

He pondered my words for five seconds before he said, 'I work for the state of Colorado, too, but I don't know the governor.'

It was a good retort; I reminded myself that Bob was a smart guy. As an employee of a university that was suffering through an era of eroding state support, Bob wasn't terribly fond of Colorado governor Bill Owens's style of leadership. When Bob mentioned the gov during one of his not-infrequent political rants, he typically called him 'Invisi-Bill,' not 'Governor Owens.'

I chose to avoid the partisan detour. 'Before last week you hadn't mentioned Doyle.'

He backed off his earlier position. 'So you say. Unless I've been misunderstanding something, I'm here to talk about problems. Doyle hasn't been a problem. He's a guy. I do some work for him; he lets me use his garage. That's all, folks.'

The Looney Tunes allusion was an interesting addition to Bob's repertoire. I hadn't heard it before; with him, comical touches were as rare as zits on starlets. But I convinced myself to ignore it, confident it would come back around if it was important. I could've let the Doyle thing drop, too, maybe should have. But instead I chose to push a little harder. 'I find it interesting that you've never mentioned him before.'

His frustration blossomed. 'Really? You find that interesting? I haven't talked about the teller I use at the bank either. But I see her every week, too.'

Did he say 'use'? He 'uses' a teller? And who, in the age of ATMs, lays eyes on a bank teller every week? Wouldn't a schizoid guy love the age of ATMs?

I had a few choices as to where to go next, one of which was the tempting bank teller/ATM question, but I suspected that it – like Invisi-Bill and Looney Tunes – was a blind alley. I went with what looked like the no-brainer: 'By talking about him now are you suggesting that Doyle has become a problem?'

'Only if I need to find a new place to park the Camaro. When that happens, then, well . . . then I have a problem, don't I?'

'If Doyle sells the house?'

'When. Yes.'

'And your current landlord doesn't have any garage space you can rent?' I wouldn't have asked most patients that question. But Bob often missed the forest for the trees, or vice versa, and part of my job was to help him understand how the world works, especially those parts of the world that are inhabited by other people.

'He owns some big stupid supercab macho truck. There's no room in the garage.'

I leaned forward slowly, resting my elbows on my knees, slightly closing the space between us. I was almost certain that Bob felt my postural readjustment as an unwelcome intrusion. That was okay; it was my intent. 'You said it wasn't safe yet. What did you mean? Was that about Doyle?'

I was challenging Bob much more than I usually did. For many patients, perhaps most, my insistence on talking more about Doyle and the garage would not have been perceived as much of a confrontation. But Bob was feeling pressured by my persistence and he was figuratively reaching out behind him, searching for the perimeter of the corner I was edging him toward. His breathing grew more rapid and his normally pale cheeks drained even further of color.

'Yes,' he said, but it was tentative. His defenses were much more nimble than I would have predicted.

As I swallowed a silent question to myself about whether my persistence was really therapeutically indicated, I made the point I'd been leading up to for minutes, 'And I thought you were implying that you're concerned about Mallory.'

He snapped back, 'Isn't everyone?'

Another good reply. I was impressed, but perhaps I shouldn't have been. The one thing that schizoid personalities usually have mastered is distancing behavior.

Two years and counting and I was still learning things about Bob.

The banter was therapeutically enlightening, but I wasn't about to be deterred from my quest to understand more about his surprising revelations about Doyle, and his intimations about Mallory. 'Earlier in the week – when you played the song? – shortly after you mentioned the guy you rent the garage from, you specifically expressed concern about Mallory, and talked about the writing you're doing. And today you said, "It's not safe yet."'

'So?'

'What connects Doyle's garage, your writing, and Mallory?'

Bob's mouth was open about half an inch and he'd thrust his jaw so far forward that it momentarily appeared as though he had a chin. He said, 'She's been gone a . . . while. Everyone's concerned. I bet even you are. Aren't you?'

Even me? 'Bob, this is important. Do you know if Doyle has anything to do with Mallory's disappearance?'

He shook his head. 'You never really know about people, do you? You think you know . . . but then,' he said, his voice unsteady. 'I think . . . things always turn out to be different.'

Bob's platitude was true, of course. And Bob's psychopathology probably left him more vulnerable to doubt about other people's motives than most of us. But I also knew that Bob's statement hadn't been an invitation to parse psychological principles. I asked, 'What are you thinking specifically?'

'Nothing,' he said. Then he added, with a side of sarcasm, 'My mother.'

I went back to the beginning. 'Why don't you tell me about Doyle?'

Bob stuck his tongue between his teeth. When he released it, he said, 'I know her. Mallory. I didn't think you'd . . .'

What? You didn't think I'd what?

22

I know her. Mallory.

Interesting non sequitur. Or apparent non sequitur. He hadn't answered my question about Doyle. Instead, he'd turned my attention back to Mallory. Or . . . perhaps talking about Mallory was his way of talking about Doyle.

Patience, Alan.

'You do?' I asked. 'You know her?' Despite what I'd learned about the location of the garage, and about Doyle, I wouldn't have guessed that Bob knew Mallory. Why?

Because Bob was Bob.

'We talked. While I was working at Doyle's. She'd come by sometimes. She was curious what we were doing. She liked the fish. And the waterfall. She said she could hear the water running from her bedroom window. I saw her up there sometimes. At her window. When Doyle wasn't home she'd go down and sit by the pond and watch the fish.'

Bob was having trouble stringing the short sentences together. Something was aggravating his natural wariness. Was it thoughts of Mallory?

Had to be. Or maybe Bob's admission about Mallory was diversion? Was he uncomfortable talking about Doyle and was he taking me someplace he figured I'd willingly go instead? Was Bob that cunning? I didn't think so, but I couldn't rule it out.

'We talked through the fence,' he added, not waiting his turn. 'A few different times.'

Not waiting his turn was another sign of his discomfort. The fact that he and Mallory talked through the fence? I suspected that the physical separation of the barrier made the conversation more

119

palatable for Bob, maybe even made the conversation *possible* for Bob. Metaphorically, it was elegant.

But still . . . 'Go on,' I said.

'She's a nice girl.'

'And you spoke with her?'

'I have, yeah. A lot of times.'

Well, Bob, was it a 'few times' or 'a lot of times'?

He squinted his eyes and tightened his jaw. The grimace caused his chin to retreat. It looked for a moment as though his face just melted away half an inch below his lower lip. 'She's my . . . friend.'

As surprising as it might sound, the fact that Bob had personally met Mallory was merely a curiosity to me, another one of those 'I know someone who' anecdotes that were still swirling around Boulder about the Millers. But the fact that he'd conversed with Mallory on a personal level? And multiple times? And that he considered her a friend? That was epiphany-quality news where Bob was concerned.

From what I knew about him socially – and before that day's session had started, I thought I knew most of what there was to know – Bob didn't have repeated personal conversations with people with whom he wasn't somehow compelled to relate.

He just didn't.

'She's your friend? You talked about . . . ?'

'I told you. The waterfall, the pond. The fish. She loved the waterfall. Other things. She likes my car.'

'Other things?' I was reaching. I knew I was reaching.

'Yeah.'

'Such as . . . ?'

Another grimace. Then, again, 'My mother.'

I went to safer ground. I didn't want to. But I felt I would push him farther away if I came any closer. 'And you thought she was nice?'

Shortly after the words exited my mouth, I realized that my caution had come too late and that our rat-a-tat conversation was over. Silence descended on the room the way darkness follows a closing curtain. I waited. Bob had started breathing through his mouth. Each exhale was accompanied by a faint whistle.

Finally he spoke. He said, 'She doesn't look fourteen.'

My spleen spasmed. At least I think it was my spleen – something in there suddenly got twisted into a big, fat knot. I hadn't been aware that I didn't want to hear those specific words from Bob, but now that he'd said them I knew that I hadn't wanted to hear them.

'Time's up,' he said.

I looked at the clock.

He was right. Time was up.

Didn't matter to me. I needed some magic that would encourage Bob to stay and tell me what was haunting him. Because something was haunting him. I couldn't find any magic, so I focused on what I feared: 'You don't think she looks fourteen?'

'Do you?' he asked.

Frankly, no. In Boulder, most eleven- and twelve-year-old girls look fourteen. Fourteen-year-old girls look, well, older – sometimes a lot older. Sometimes way too much older. But I wasn't about to tell Bob that. I suspected his comment about Mallory's age had little to do with musings about the sociological implications of the increasingly early psychosexual maturity of adolescent girls.

I said, 'Bob, look at me. Please.'

He did, holding the connection for almost two entire seconds. I asked, 'Do you know something about Mallory? Where she is? How she's doing? Had she said something to you? Has Doyle?'

Way too many questions on my part. Way too many. A rational observer would have had a hard time determining who was more flustered at that moment, doctor or patient.

'Maybe you know something you should tell the police,' I added – my way of adjusting the seasoning on a therapeutic dish I was already responsible for overcooking.

Bob did the half head-shake thing again, this time minus the 'sheeesh,' before he said, 'I have to go.'

I barely heard his words. The echoes of his earlier pronounce-ment – *'She doesn't look fourteen'* – were gaining volume in my head. Silently quoting Diane, I thought, *Holy moly.*

'Did you talk to Mallory just before Christmas, Bob? Did you know what was going to happen?'

'I have to go.'

'I have a few extra minutes. We can go on.'

Bob didn't acknowledge my offer. He stood, grabbed his daypack,

121

and stepped toward the French door that led outside toward the backyard, but he didn't ask me for permission to use it as he had on previous occasions. As he pulled the door open, air that was much colder than I expected flooded into the room, chilling my feet. He paused in the open doorway and turned his head back in my direction.

Our gazes failed to connect by about ten degrees. It was as though he were blind, wanted to find my gaze, but couldn't quite manage to make eye contact.

He said, 'Is something a secret if nobody knows you know it?'

My gut was still in knots. 'I don't know what you mean.'

'For something to be a secret, somebody else has to know it, right? Or . . . do they? I tell you things and you have to keep them secret. But I've never been . . .'

Been what?

I suspected that Bob's naiveté was talking, or that he was posing a trick question – a-tree-falling-in-the-forest clone – but I couldn't find the trap. Reluctantly I said, 'A secret is a secret, I guess.'

He suddenly shifted his gaze and we locked eyes for a period of time that was about the duration of a solitary flap of a hummingbird's wings. There, and then gone. He persisted. 'If nobody knows something but the person who knows it, is it really a secret? Or is it something else? What would that be?'

'What are we talking about, Bob? Is this . . . something about Mallory? Is she okay? Do you know something about where she is?'

'Other people have secrets. I didn't really know that. I mean I knew it, but I didn't . . . I don't know everything yet, but it's not as simple as I thought at first. I'm not even sure about what I know. Does that make sense?'

No, it doesn't.

I could feel him pulling away. He hadn't moved an inch farther away from me, but this prolonged connection between him and me had existed at a level of intimacy that I knew Bob couldn't tolerate for long. Now he was floating away like a helium balloon in a stiff breeze.

I tried to grab for the string that would bring him back. I said, 'But you know something? You know a secret?'

I kept thinking, *You know that she doesn't look fourteen.*

'You know secrets, too,' he replied. 'People tell you things. I do. Therapists.'

What did that mean? Was he speaking generally or was he referring to something specific that he thought I knew?

I didn't know.

He pursed his thin lips and shook his head, just a little, as though he was mildly disappointed with me. 'The story's not over. I have to figure stuff out, who to trust. I think I've already been wrong once. Doyle's not . . . the guy I thought he was.'

Trust me. Please.

'Doyle's not what? What do you mean?'

'Maybe you should read it. What I wrote.'

I opened my mouth to reply, but Bob closed the door behind him.

I was about to say, 'I'd love to.' The cold air that had rushed in wasn't the only cause of chill in the room.

I stepped outside into the frigid air. 'Bob,' I called. After two more steps across the yard he stopped and turned to face me. He didn't bother to look at me, but he faced me. I said, 'Tuesday, our regular time, okay?'

'Yeah.'

'If you'd like to meet before then I can do that. Don't worry about the money.'

He said, 'Okay,' hunched his shoulders forward, dropped his poor excuse for a chin, and paced off into the night.

23

Sam had blown some serious bucks at Runners Roost.

A year before if you had asked me what was more likely, a giant meteor destroying our planet, or Sam Purdy adorned in head-to-toe burgundy running Lycra, I would have been warning everyone to duck. But there Sam stood, right at my front door, jogging in place, his breath puffing out in little frosty clouds that stood out like flares against a sky the color of deep water.

It was 5:10 in the frigging morning on the first Monday of the year. My initial thoughts upon waking had been about my disconcerting session with Bob a few days before.

'You ready?' Sam asked. 'I say we do a couple of slow miles, then we try to bring one in around nine. What do you think? We'll work up from there.'

I tied both of my shoes before I replied. 'I think it's January, Sam, and this could really wait until March or April. The race isn't until May, for God's sake.'

The race on Sam's radar was the Bolder Boulder, the Memorial Day Weekend 10K classic, and for some reason Sam had decided that his training regimen couldn't be put off until spring. I'd volunteered to be his workout partner, and unfortunately for me his ardor for physical fitness was that of the newly converted.

'Emily coming with?'

Sam was asking about our Bouvier des Flandres. Emily was a big bear of a dog and her natural instincts spurred her more toward herding livestock than jogging on a lead alongside human beings. 'Maybe next time. Running in straight lines isn't one of her best things. She likes to roam. Let's see how it goes without her this time.'

'What about the little one? Anvil?'

'Hardly. Three miles is a marathon for a miniature poodle. At least it is for him. I'm afraid it's just you and me.' I stared out into the darkness. 'I don't even think we'll see the milkman or the paperboy at this hour.'

'Cool, let's go.'

Although it was contrary to his character to yield control, Sam wanted me to set the pace. Two reasons: From a thousand dog walks I knew the trails in the nearby hills, and since I'd run a couple of Bolder Boulders when I was younger he was granting me the status of running guru.

I knew the status assignment wouldn't endure for long. Near the end of mile one, I asked, 'What kind of trouble has Reese Miller been in?'

Sam didn't move lightly. I don't know whether it was inexperience, poor technique, just the fact that he was a big guy, or what, but the pounding beside me on the dirt trails of Spanish Hills sounded more like the *clop, clop* of a Clydesdale than the heel-toe patter of a jogger. I'm not much of a runner. Bicycling is my thing. But running beside Sam and his plodding strides I felt like I was floating.

'Fights.'

I didn't expect that he'd answer me at all, but his reply was too parsimonious for my taste. I considered the possibility that Sam was too winded to be more expansive, but he was in better shape than at any time since we'd met and I decided that the brevity was an indication of caution while he figured out where the hell I was coming from.

'Hockey fights?' I asked.

'Some.'

'But some not?'

'I think you're watching too much cable. It's bad for your health.'

I probably had been watching too much cable news, but I wasn't about to admit it to Sam. Blame it on Bob, and Diane. 'I don't know. I'm curious, I guess.'

'Ask me, there's already way too much curiosity about that case.'

'You brought up Reese, Sam. Not me.'

'First time, I did. And I regret it. This time you did. You still pissed at Jaris Slocum?'

I wasn't surprised that he'd changed the subject; I was surprised where he'd gone. 'What he did to Diane? Of course. He was an asshole.'

'There're reasons. Not excuses. Reasons. Cops feel pressure, too. Just like everybody else.'

'Reasons to rough up a witness who's grieving about finding her friend dead? Yeah? Like what?'

'Maybe you could cut him some slack, get over your hurt feelings. In the end it's not about what he did, it's about whatever happened to that woman.'

'That woman' was Hannah. 'I'll think about it,' I said, curious as to why Sam was suddenly so concerned about Jaris Slocum's welfare.

'You have other reasons, don't you?' he said.

'What?'

'For asking about Reese.'

The boomerang of subjects threw me. All I managed was a solitary, 'What?'

'Thought so.'

I had been trying not to sound defensive; apparently I wasn't succeeding. The truth was I wasn't that interested in Reese. Reese was a foot in the door. I wanted to hear Sam's thoughts on anything to do with the Millers, hoping to hear something that would ease my mind about my last meeting with Bob.

I said, 'No, no. What you said at Simon's hockey game got me thinking, and I've been wanting to hear what you know about Reese. Not as a cop, just as a parent.'

'Yeah? That's all you're wanting to know, what I know as a parent?'

'Exactly.'

'Pardon me if I don't believe you.' Sam's thunderous strides punctuated the silence that followed. *Boom, boom. Boom, boom.* He broke the tension by asking, 'What do you know about the Pearl Street Mile? I'm thinking it's more my distance than 10K.'

The Pearl Street Mile is a summer evening race run around the Downtown Boulder Mall. Compared to the carnival spectacle of the massive holiday weekend Bolder Boulder, the Pearl Street Mile is a relatively sedate event.

'Not much.' I told him what I knew, adding, 'You're going to pass on the Bolder Boulder?'

'No. Just trying to find the right distance for my running style.'

'And you're thinking you're built for speed, not endurance?'

My sarcasm was rarely wasted on Sam.

'You take what God gives you, you know.'

Nor his on me.

'I know.'

Sam pulled up short and put his hands on his ample hips. I stopped a couple of strides later and turned back to face him. He wasn't breathing hard but each exhale temporarily hid his round face behind a miasma of fog.

My neighborhood, Spanish Hills, is a rural enclave of mostly elegant homes – ours was one of the few exceptions – on the hillsides that comprise the eastern rise of the Boulder Valley, not far from the scenic overlook on the Boulder Turnpike. The western rim of the valley is formed by the Front Range of the Rocky Mountains, and by comparison the vanilla hills of the eastern rim are, well, wimpy.

The spot where Sam paused on our run was on the top of a rounded ridge just north and east of my house. From where I stood, Sam's right ear was totally obscuring the rock formation known as Devil's Thumb. I'd always thought that the huge natural sculpture more closely resembled an altogether different part of the devil's anatomy, but maybe that was just me.

'What?' I asked for about the tenth time that morning.

'You got something. So tell me what it is, get it off your chest. No secrets, just get it off your chest.'

Sam wasn't being a bully. He was perfectly capable of it, but at that moment he was merely making me an offer. The features on his face suddenly lit up just a little. The phenomenon was illumination, not insight. Far behind me the morning sun was breasting the almost imperceptible arc of the wide horizon of the Great Plains.

Sam and I had been here before. I knew something I'd learned in therapy that I thought he should know, but I couldn't tell him about it. With a few exceptions, the rules said I couldn't tell Sam anything a patient had told me. Life had taught me over the past few years that assiduously adhering to those rules was sometimes as dangerous as breaking them. I was confident that I would ultimately decide what to reveal based on that reality, and that with enough creativity I could find a way to tell Sam what I wanted to tell him without the rules ever knowing they'd been sullied.

Below us, the headlights of a car snaked down the dirt and gravel lane that led to my house. In the predawn shadows I couldn't identify any features of the car. The guy who delivered the morning paper? No, it wasn't him; he had a rusty, old post–World War II Dodge Power Wagon that sent its bass rumble bouncing through the hills. In its own way, the sound was as distinctive an announcement siren as the syrupy melody of the ice cream man.

I watched the car's progress until it disappeared behind the contour of an intervening hill. It was probably the nanny that Adrienne, our urologist neighbor, sometimes brought in to watch Jonas at an ungodly hour so she could keep her morning surgical schedule.

To Sam, I said, 'Do you guys know much about the house next door to the Millers? The one that's for sale?'

'Us guys?'

'The cops.'

Sam started jogging in place. The sight of the ruby fabric stretching across his thick thighs made me think of a matched pair of prosciutto di Parma.

He took off down the trail. I did, too. Over his shoulder, he said, 'There something you think we – us cops – should know about the guy next door?'

After a few strides I replied, 'Not really.'

'Not really? Or not at all?'

I didn't know enough about the Millers' neighbor to answer Sam's question, and I wasn't totally comfortable with the territory I was taking him, so I asked, 'What kind of fighting did Reese have trouble with?'

'If you've been watching all that cable then you know what those kids have been through. He's a good kid.'

He hadn't answered my question. I was forced to hustle to keep up with him; the pace he was setting for the second mile was way too fast. 'You mean been through with his mom?'

Without any hesitation, Sam said, 'What do you know about the trouble with the kids' mom?'

Startled, I realized three things. The first two? The eastern sky was brightening, and the day had begun. Number three? Maybe there hadn't been anything in the news about the difficulty that the Miller children might have had with their mom, and I'd just told Sam Purdy that I knew something he didn't think I should know.

Oops. The information wasn't particularly important. The fact that I had an avenue to know it? Sam would find that important.

24

The pace that Sam set for the last mile and a half of our run precluded chatting. Despite my usually rigorous bicycling regimen I was seriously winded by the conclusion of our morning jaunt. To my relief Sam was, too.

As soon as we'd come within sight of my house I'd started looking around for the car that had come down the lane a little earlier. It wasn't there. It wasn't in front of our house. It wasn't in front of Adrienne's either.

The hue of the sky told me that we'd arrived back where we'd started shortly before six. I invited Sam in for coffee. He declined. 'Sherry has Simon. She's bringing him back over early so she can get to class. I need to be home to feed him and get him off to school.'

Sherry was Sam's ex. She was living in Northglenn, a suburb north of Denver, and attending school at Auraria. She'd sold her flower business and was studying to be an EMT. The custody arrangement that she and Sam had negotiated was so complicated that I thought it would require single-variable calculus equations to put it on paper. But the plan worked; I'd not once heard Sam complain about the convoluted logistics.

He opened the door to his old navy Cherokee. In the thin light the dried muck on the lower third of the squat body made the car appear to have a custom paint job. Almost. 'How many miles you have on this thing?' I asked.

'Odometer broke at one-forty-seven-something. That was on the day that the Supreme Court decided who our president was going to be. So more than one-forty-seven. Plenty more than one-forty-seven.'

'How old is it?'

'It's a '90.' He climbed in. The concave driver's seat accepted his rear end the way Lauren's out-thrust hip supported our daughter's cute butt. Naturally. With just the slightest trace of a smile in his eyes – it was impish, almost ironic – he said, 'You know what? That makes this car the same exact age as Mallory Miller.'

I didn't know what to say to that.

He wasn't done. 'And the other girl, too. I'm sure you remember her. She was a 1990, too.'

The one who had been murdered in the dark hours overnight on another Christmas Day. The pretty little blonde whose one-time beauty-queen momma wanted her daughter to be a beauty queen, too. The one whose pathetic father had carried her lifeless body up the stairs from the basement like a spray of damaged flowers. Yes, I remembered that other girl. Too well.

'See you,' Sam said. 'Thanks for the run.'

The Cherokee chugged north down the lane. Before it was out of sight the rumble of the old Dodge Power Wagon signaled that the newspaper delivery guy was heading in our direction. I watched his headlights dance in the grasses before I stepped inside and started a pot of coffee. A few minutes later I was still wet from the shower when Grace announced the beginning of her day. My sleepy wife crashed into me in the doorway as we rushed toward our daugh-ter's room.

I cherish morning in our home. I love the soft carelessness of my wife after she's slept, her flesh exposed near the unbuttoned top but-ton or two of her pajamas. I love the fragrance at the nape of my daughter's neck after a night of sweet dreams. I love the frantic energy that the dogs bring to each and every dawn.

I adore the tang of fresh juice and the texture of bananas and the yeasty smell of toasted Great Harvest bread. I adore the first sip of hot coffee almost as much as I adore the aroma, and I relish the light that pours over the infinite plains and fills our little kitchen seconds before it jumps up and causes the crystalline formations on the Flatirons to sparkle like the facets of diamonds.

No, that day I wasn't necessarily thrilled about running around like a madman in order to make it to my office for my 7:15 appoint-ment downtown, but it was, I figured, all part of the package.

And all in all, it was a damn good package. I felt that way almost every morning and felt great fortune that almost every day in my home started with the unspoiled promise of fresh bliss.

131

A year and a half earlier, Lauren had bought me a new BMW Mini as a gift. The generous gesture was intended to snap me out of a professional funk that I'd been sliding into, and her choice of cars paid homage to an old love of mine, a classic Mini Cooper named Sadie that I'd adopted in my youth. I drove the gift Mini on nice days for over a year before I sold it. I didn't sell it because I didn't like it. I sold it because every time I drove it I felt as though I was taking a holiday from responsible parenting. All the data said it was a safe car for its size. The problem, though, was its size. Compared to an elephantine Ford Expedition – and way too often on Boulder's roads that was exactly the comparison I was forced to consider – my little Mini felt like a dainty ladybug.

I'd put an ad in the paper after the previous autumn's aspen season had peaked and ended up selling the Mini to a sophomore volleyball player from CU who had apparently convinced her parents that the little car was safe enough for her.

When I pressed the button that opened the garage door the car that was waiting to take me downtown to my office was a three-year-old, four-wheel-drive Audi wagon with 27,000 miles on it. I'd bought it from Diane's next-door neighbor when she moved to Phoenix to trade the cold of Colorado's winters for the heat of Arizona's summers. The Audi was a fun car. Not as much fun as the Mini. But fun enough. It could handle all but the deepest snow, there was room in the back for both dogs, and – most important – it had more airbags than cylinders, much more sheet metal than the Mini, and, rational or not, I didn't feel like a lunatic when I strapped Grace into the backseat.

I was only two steps away from the open garage door when I spotted a fresh set of headlights snaking down our lane.

I stopped. Four cars at my house before 7 A.M.? For us, that constituted a parade.

The approaching car had a throaty rumble, not as *thumpy-thumpy* as the newspaper guy's Power Wagon, but certainly not that of a lightweight, well-muffled, catalytic-converted Honda or Subaru either.

Despite the incipient dawn the headlights were aimed right at my eyes and they blinded me until the car was about twenty feet away. I stood still, waiting for the reveal. Finally, the driver turned the car abruptly to the left and pulled it to a stop that was short enough to cause the vehicle to slide a foot or so on the dirt and gravel.

The car was a shiny black Camaro that was much, much older than Sam's Cherokee, but still a modern automotive wonder compared to the paper guy's ancient Dodge truck.

Bob Brandt climbed out from behind the wheel. He didn't kill the engine, however, and the growl of the big motor in the Camaro continued to thunder off the hillsides. Bob didn't say 'Hi,' or 'Good morning,' or 'Sorry to intrude,' or anything else that most people might say in similar circumstances.

I didn't say some things, too. I didn't say, 'What are you doing here at this hour?' or, 'How the hell do you know where I live?'

My home phone number wasn't listed. My home address was a carefully guarded secret. I didn't encourage patients to call me after hours. I certainly didn't encourage them to drop by whenever the hell they felt like it. Whatever early-morning calm the serenity of my family in my home had afforded me evaporated like the steam from pancakes on a hot griddle.

I was feeling violated by Bob's presence in front of my garage. But at some level I also felt grateful for another opportunity to connect with Bob about Mallory Miller.

Bob spoke first. That was fine; it was definitely his turn. 'What do you think about my car?' he asked. The Camaro's motor – had he told me once, or twice, or ten times that it was a 396? – provided a percussive accompaniment that sounded like a big sub-woofer with an electrical short.

I had no intention of chatting about cars with Bob at seven o'clock in the morning only steps from my front door and my darling daughter. 'Good morning,' I said, while I told myself that Bob must have a reason – a good reason – for mounting this kind of intrusion.

Bob was dressed in his ubiquitous outfit. Chinos, long-sleeve blue dress shirt, denim jacket – the fleece-lined one. Trail runners. He appeared nervous. I'd never before seen him outside the confines of my office, though, and was more than prepared to believe that he spent much of his life appearing nervous.

'I have something . . .' He was looking at my Audi. 'That yours?'

He sounded surprised, as though he expected someone else's car to be in my garage. 'Why did you get rid of the Mini?'

He asked as though he been wondering about it for a while and thought that he deserved an explanation. I wasn't going to go there with him, either.

'You like this better?' he asked, perseverating on the car.

I counted to three. 'Bob, you said you have something . . . What? Something you wanted to tell me—'

'Something to give you. Is it the turbo? That's the turbo, isn't it?' He was still focused on the wagon. 'Fixated' might be a better word.

'I assume you came to my house because something feels urgent, Bob.' I could have just said, *'Why are you here?'*

Bob didn't get my drift. He thought about my question for a few seconds before he said, 'Should it?'

Seriously schizoid people relate the way people with sleep apnea breathe at night: in fits and starts. No organic rhythm. Just enough to maintain life. Sometimes not even that much. Nothing that should be natural and predictable about interacting with another human being is natural and predictable for them.

Allowing the realization to settle that Bob's appearance at my home at dawn was undoubtedly meaningful, I forced my discomfort that he knew where I lived away from center stage and stuffed some composure into my voice. I asked, 'What brings you to my home so early in the morning, Bob?'

What was I thinking? I was thinking *'Mallory.'*

'I have to . . .' he said. I thought he'd stopped himself before he completed the sentence. 'I wanted to give you . . . what I've been writing. We talked about it. Remember?'

You bet I remember.

He leaned into the Camaro and came back out with an old, beat-up, dark-blue box imprinted with the logo of Kinko's, the copy palace.

'Here it is. It's not done,' he said.

He held it out for me. I took it. The ream-sized carton was far from full. I guessed it held fewer than a hundred pages. I was already wondering: *Is this it? Is this really the reason he's come to my home shortly after dawn? To give me part of a novel?*

'Don't read it, yet. I'll tell you when.'

'You want me to have it, but not to read it?'

'Yes.'

I thought my question warranted a better explanation. Bob, apparently, didn't agree. 'That's it?' I said.

'I have a long way to go. I'm still trying to get it . . . I want it to be right before you read it.'

'Couldn't you have just held on to it until you decide that you would like me to read it?' *Or until you see me tomorrow?*

He chanced a glance at me. The tenor of his look was questioning whether I had suddenly become mentally challenged. As though it would explain everything, he said, 'This is a copy. It's not the original. I have one, too.'

He'd totally missed the point of my question. With Bob, that happened with some frequency.

'Okay,' I said. I was already putting together a list of things we'd have to discuss during the next day's session.

'You'll understand,' he assured me. 'When I tell you it's okay to read it, you'll understand.'

'You'll explain?'

'Yes. You like it?'

I raised the box up a couple of inches. 'I'll let you know. After you tell me when I should read it.'

'I meant the Camaro. It's cherry, don't you think?'

I gazed at the glossy black car, its pristine paint marred only by the faintest hint of Spanish Hills dust. 'Sure is,' I said. 'It sure is.'

'Yep,' he agreed.

I took a deep breath and asked, 'Bob, have you thought more about the question I asked you last week? Whether you know something about Mallory Miller that you should share with the police?'

He kicked at the dirt. 'You know the . . . that woman who was killed? Who died? On Broadway? The therapist, like you?'

Like me? I felt gooseflesh on my back. 'Hannah Grant? A few weeks ago?'

'Her. She was Mallory's . . . therapist. Mallory was afraid after she died. Really afraid. She thought . . . Mallory has this thing about Christmas. The guy that the neighbors saw? You know about that?'

Oh shit. 'Which guy? On Christmas night? Outside? That guy?'

135

If Bob knew anything new about Mallory and the Christmas guy it meant that he'd seen Mallory since she disappeared.

'I was watching a movie.'

'At Doyle's house? You were there?'

'Before Christmas she thought someone may have found out about . . . oh boy. And because of . . . that's why . . . she wasn't comfortable. No, not at all.'

'That's why what?' There was enough pressure in my questions to launch a rocket.

Smooth, Alan. Real smooth.

'She doesn't really like Christmas. I don't either. She was scared that she might be – Sheesh. I can't, I shouldn't . . . It happened once, it could happen . . . I have to go. I don't want you to . . . ,' he said. 'Anyway, I don't like to be late.'

You don't want me to what? 'I'm very interested in hearing more, Bob. It will just take another moment. You came all the way out here.'

I'm sure I sounded pathetic.

'I have to go.' He opened the door and climbed into his car. The vinyl seats were so cold that they squeaked with his weight.

'Are you scared about something, too, Bob?' I asked through the glass.

He shook his head.

'Do you know anything about where Mallory is? Anything? Please tell me.'

'I'm late.'

'I'll see you tomorrow then,' I said.

'Sure,' he said, barely loudly enough so that I could hear.

He fishtailed a little as he spun around to head out the lane. The rumble of his motor was almost enough to stifle the pounding in my ears.

She was scared. He'd said she was scared.

Was I tempted to read what Bob had written? Of course I was, right that minute. I was also certain that my temptation was part of the challenge that Bob was positing.

Why was he setting things up to tantalize me that he might know something about Mallory Miller's fate and then keep the evidence of

136

what he might know just out of my reach? He had taunted me already with the proposition that he knew her, was friends with her. He had just added the proposition that he knew that Mallory had seen Hannah for psychotherapy. And he'd added the tantalizing possibility that he'd been right next door in Doyle's house on Christmas night. He'd said that Mallory was scared.

I didn't know what Bob was up to with Mallory. Far from it. But trust – therapeutic trust between Bob and me – was on the table in the form of the manuscript in the Kinko's box. That much was perfectly clear.

What were the odds that Bob actually knew something crucial about Mallory?

Low, really low.

Bob's life was smoke, not fire. Heat, not light. Bob hadn't told me anything that was really new to me. I was already aware that Mallory had seen Hannah for psychotherapy. I already knew about the man who had been loitering outside, everybody did. All Bob had really added to the equation was that Mallory was scared.

And that he'd been next door watching a movie.

Hopefully, the next day I'd learn what Bob thought Mallory was frightened about. I could wait until then.

Long before the dust had settled on the lane from the Camaro's too-rapid departure, I'd flicked off the lid of the Kinko's box and looked inside. The flimsy cardboard box was less than a quarter full of $8\frac{1}{2} \times 11$ sheets. The title page was simple, the typeface minuscule.

My Little Runaway
By R.C. Brandt

In the lower right-hand corner Bob had carefully sketched the encircled *c* of the copyright symbol and beside it had typed out the word 'copyright' and beside that, the year.

I closed the box.

25

I didn't see patients most Fridays. Diane skipped most Mondays. So I wasn't at all surprised that her Saab wasn't in its usual spot in front of our wreck of a garage all day Monday while I was at the office. Anyway, she'd asked me if I would cover her practice in case she and Raoul went away for the weekend, and weekends for Diane almost always included Mondays.

But the phone call she made to me that evening caught me off guard. Dinner was done, the kitchen was clean, Lauren had Grace in the tub for a mother-daughter bubble soak. Their giggles and laughter filled the house and buoyed my spirits like a healthy dose of rock and roll.

I had the dogs at my feet. Life was good.

'Can you hear that?' Diane asked.

I heard noise but it sounded like nothing more than routine mobile-phone clutter crap. I figured Diane was in her Saab, driving behind the spine of a hogback someplace, or in the deep recesses of one of the many canyons that snake west out of Boulder into the heart of the Rockies.

'No, I don't think so. You're breaking up.'

Then I heard it – the frenetic calliope melody of a slot-machine jackpot followed by an orgasmic scream of 'I won! I won! Yes! Yes! I told you about this machine. Didn't I?' I could almost hear the cascade of dollar coins tumbling into the stainless-steel tray.

'You up in Blackhawk?'

'Nope.'

'Central City?'

'One more try.'

I could have wasted my third guess on Cripple Creek, the final member of the triad of Colorado pioneer mountain towns that the electorate had burdened with legalized gambling. Instead I went for the jackpot.

'You're in Vegas. You really went.'

'Told you.'

'How much of Raoul's money have you lost?'

'I make plenty of my own money.'

'Yeah, but you told me once that you only gamble with his.'

'I forgot I told you that. I can't believe I told you that. I'm down a grand or so.'

'Or so?'

'Maybe a little more. Single digits.'

'Single digits plus, what, three zeros?'

'My luck will change. I rescheduled my patients until Thursday. That's a lifetime in craps. Can we talk about something else? How about matrimony? You want to talk about matrimony?'

Part of me didn't want to know. But I said, 'Sure.'

'I found her. Mrs. Miller. She was hanging out at a place called the Love In Las Vegas Wedding Chapel.' Diane made sure that her pronunciation of 'love' had two syllables. 'Everybody knows her in the Vegas wedding racket; she's kind of a local legend. I only had to go to three chapels and ask a few questions.'

I had a picture in my mind.

A woman who had once been pretty dressed in an outfit that had once been fashionable topped by a hat that had once been fresh was sitting by herself on the bride's side of a chapel that had never, ever really been pretty or lovely or fresh, and she was celebrating the nuptials of two people who had known each other for hours or days or months or years.

Elvis was there, too, or he wasn't.

The woman heard voices in her ears saying cruel, frightening things and one glance at her made clear that she spent many more of her waking hours tormented than she did at peace. Her face was sometimes molded into odd grimaces with tight, scared eyes, a cockeyed mouth, pursed lips, and a protruding tongue. She mumbled replies to the voices at inopportune moments and strangers in all walks of life kept their distance.

Her hygiene was lacking, her makeup was abundant and applied with idiosyncratic whimsy, and she'd resorted to wearing bad wigs to cover a tangle of hair that, during moments that approached sanity, she realized she could no longer manage.

Her teeth had begun to rot and her breath smelled like roadkill.

She lived in a homeless shelter, or worse.

She had a paper bag full of medicines but most days she hated the side effects more than she hated the voices. Although she would occasionally take a pill or two or three to quiet the rageful ranting, or to still the incipient panic, or to dull the despair that urged her closer and closer to the futility of suicide, she lugged the stained brown bag of pharmaceuticals around more as a totem than anything else.

She was a lost life who was ordered by unseen powers to celebrate the marriages of pairs of strange people eager to believe that their own lives were full of nothing but promise. As each newlywed couple walked out the door of some tacky wedding chapel, whatever future the woman saw in them would disappear like a convention-eer's promise to his wife to behave himself in Vegas.

That was the picture I had in my mind.

'Is this going to make me sad?' I asked Diane. 'Is it going to do me any good to know?'

Lauren sometimes asked that exact question of me late in the evening when we were in bed and the late news was on TV. A story would start to air – something about murder or rape or previously unimaginable despair or desperation in a part of the world that seemed always to bring unimaginable despair and desperation. The anchorperson's eyes would be stern, his voice would be grave, and Lauren would hit the mute button and ask, 'Is it going to do me any good to know this?'

The carnival midway refrain of another jackpot, this one at a more distant location in the casino, filled my ear. Almost as if prompted by the loud celebration that followed the slot machine victory, Diane said, 'This is Vegas. You can't stay sad here long.'

She said it, I was sure, for her own benefit as much as for mine.

'Something tells me that she's managed to stay sad.'

'Mallory's mom? Yeah,' Diane admitted. 'I think she has.'

I was thinking *Reese's mom, too*, but I didn't throw his name into the mix. The refrain from the previous week's morning run with Sam was still part of the soundtrack spinning in my head.

'She's still crazy?' I asked. My question was irreverent and my choice of descriptors pejorative, but Diane knew that I was asking with a heart laden with pathos.

'You know,' she said.

I did know. It was because I knew that I was so certain that it was going to make me sad. 'Did you learn anything?' I said, but I was thinking: What could she have learned? What could Mrs. Miller know? I didn't think that Mallory had gone to Vegas to see her mom. I didn't think that Mrs. Miller would know anything that would help Diane understand the connection between Mallory and Hannah.

'It's not what you think, not what I thought. Coming here to see her? It's like poking at a hornet's nest, for some reason it gets a lot of people stirred up. It's . . . just a sec. I can't talk here – I'm going to go outside, or at least to a quieter part of the . . . It's such a trek to get out of the casino from here; if the call gets dropped I'll phone you right back. You really need to hear this.' Her next words were a simple, pleasant version of 'Yes, I'm out.' I suspected the message was intended for the croupier or whatever you call the person who handles the dice and the chips at a craps table.

Diane dropped the phone on the floor – at least that's the way it sounded – cursed, kicked it, picked it up again, and asked, 'You still there?' She laughed. 'The phone slipped out of my hand while I was trying to pick up all my chips.'

'I'm still here.'

'Good. I won five hundred or so. That's pretty good. This place is so huge.' A moment of silence. Then, 'Hi. Do you know which way's the door?'

Hi? Was she talking to me?

'Which means you're only down . . . what?' I asked.

Thud. I thought the phone must have fallen out of her hand again. 'Diane? You there?'

That's when the call died.

Diane didn't call right back.

I gave her five minutes before I tried to reach her. Her cell phone rang and rang and rang before it clicked into voice mail.

I waited half an hour, hitting redial again every ten minutes or so with the same result. I was chewing on the possibility that technology had failed somewhere, that her phone had died or that the network had burped.

Soon I started thinking that she'd simply changed her mind about talking to me right then. Maybe she'd passed an open seat at a twenty-dollar blackjack table that she was sure had her name on it in raised gilded letters, or she'd eyed a spot at a new table and thought she'd seen steam rising from those dice.

I also considered the possibility that she'd run into someone she knew – Diane knew more people than anyone I'd ever met – while making her way out of the cavernous casino, and that they had headed somewhere for a drink or a meal or . . . what?

Diane, I guessed, was staying at the Venetian, the mid-Strip gambling palace that was decked out to look like Venice, Italy; that's the hotel where she'd booked us to stay the weekend after Hannah's death. I'd never been, but she'd told me that the canals in the hotel were lined with shops and I knew from long experience with Diane that a garish SALE sign in a store window could have distracted her. Easily.

All were reasonable explanations. But none, I thought, were likely.

Had her plans changed, Diane would have called me back and told me she'd talk to me later. She certainly would have picked up my call to her cell. Were her cell not working properly she would have gone to a pay phone and called me the old-fashioned way. After tracking down the mother of a missing girl – a girl who was the patient of Diane's dead friend – and after telling me she had news I needed to hear, Diane would have done something to reach me. She wouldn't have left me hanging, waiting, wondering.

She wouldn't.

I called Raoul at home to see if he'd heard from her. He wasn't there.

I followed happy voices down the hall and found Lauren and Grace on the bed in the master bedroom, where I interrupted Lauren's dramatic rendition of *Alice in Wonderland*. She told me she thought she had Raoul's mobile number in her Palm. With monumental inefficiency, and only after pecking enough tiny faux buttons to book an entire round-trip flight to Kathmandu – including arranging for Sherpas – I tracked down Raoul's mobile number and dialed the ten digits.

'Raoul,' he answered almost immediately.

He sounded tired. The usual gorgeous timbre of his voice was disguised by the wireless ether.

'Hey, Raoul. It's Alan. Where are you?'

'San Francisco, consulting at a clueless incubator. How these people expect to make any money is beyond me. What's wrong?'

His question made perfect sense. I don't think I'd ever before called Raoul on his mobile phone. Instinctively, he knew I wasn't calling him in San Francisco to recommend a restaurant.

'It's probably nothing,' I said.

He replied, *'Mierda.'*

26

Raoul's voice, when he wanted it to, carried no echoes of his childhood in Catalonia. I'd never given much thought to whether or not the tonal charade required much of his energy or attention. I'd always assumed that he could move back and forth between the American and Catalonian accents effortlessly, the way that a skilled actor does Kerry one minute and New Jersey the next. Raoul said, 'Back up. When did all this start? When did she call you?'

I heard echoes of Barcelona, and of worry, in his perfect English. I supposed that I was hearing the Barcelona only because I was hearing the worry. The caller ID unit by the phone told me that Diane's call to me from the craps table had come in exactly forty-seven minutes earlier.

'Forty-five minutes ago,' I told Raoul.

'So she's been out of touch less than an hour?'

'Right.'

'That's not a big deal.'

I'd been doing the same comfort calisthenics. But I clearly remembered the intensity of Raoul's barely contained outrage while Jaris Slocum was holding Diane hostage in the backseat of the patrol car after Hannah Grant's death, and I remembered how resistant he'd been to any reassurance at that time. I knew that all the fret-yoga he was doing to convince himself that the current circumstances were some version of ordinary wouldn't, ultimately, do him a bit of good. Diane being out of touch for forty-seven minutes in the current circumstances required explanation.

And when I told him what I knew, I knew he'd agree with me.

'Raoul? Do you know why Diane went to Las Vegas?'

He spent a couple of heartbeats mining the apparent innocuousness of my question for innuendo before he replied, 'She likes it there. She missed her chance last month when . . . you know.'

'Do you know why she went now?'

There it was again. The shrink's 'precipitating event' question. *Why now?*

Raoul was one of the brightest people I'd ever met. I could almost hear the gears turning in his head as he tried to make sense of the bare glimpse he was getting as he strained to see where it was that I was leading him.

'She told me that a patient's mother was there. In Vegas. Somebody she wanted to talk to about a case. That was her excuse, but she really wanted to play craps and the mountain casinos have a five-buck limit. Small bets bore her.'

'It wasn't one of *her* patients' mother she was planning to talk to, Raoul.'

'I don't follow.'

'The patient whose mother is living in Las Vegas? That patient wasn't Diane's; it was Hannah Grant's.'

I could hear his breath blow hard against the microphone. 'And you knew this? You knew that was why she was going?'

It was an accusation. His unspoken words were *'And you let her?'* I felt his finger pointing at me physically, felt it mostly in my gut. I could no more have stopped Diane from going to Las Vegas than I could prevent January from being colder than July. But that didn't matter to Raoul, not then.

'She told me she was thinking about it, about going to Vegas to talk with this woman. But I thought she was just being provocative with me. You know how she is. I didn't think she'd really go.'

'Diane always does things that other people don't think she'll do. It's who she is.'

It was another accusation. And it was right on target. 'I wish I'd listened to her. I'm sorry.'

Raoul had no time for my *mea culpas*. 'Had she talked to this person, yet? This mother?' he asked.

Before I replied I used a moment to recall the specifics of my last conversation with Diane. 'When we talked, she told me that she'd found her, tracked her down. I don't know whether or not she

145

actually spoke with her. I think that's what she was going to tell me when she got outside. She said it was important.'

'You know what patient it is, don't you, Alan?'

My impulse was to hesitate, to cover my ass. To my credit, I didn't. I mouthed a simple 'Yes.'

'You know who the mother is, too?'

'Yes.'

'You're going to tell me.'

'You know how this works.'

Raoul was the husband of a psychotherapist. Spouses of mental health professionals know the rules. He said, 'This is Diane we're talking about. You are the one who had better know how this works.'

I tried to deflect him, to steer him back to the current crisis. I said, 'I don't even know where's she staying. Where do you stay when you're there?'

He took a deep breath. 'I try not to go at all if I can help it, but where faux Italian is concerned I prefer the Bellagio. The fountains are . . . something. She's at the Venetian,' he said, confirming my suspicion. 'She likes the canals. I take her to Venice, I take her to St. Petersburg, I take her to Amsterdam; it turns out the canals she likes best are inside some vapid casino in Las Vegas.'

'I'll try her room and call you back.'

'You've tried her mobile?' he asked.

'A few times.'

'*Merde.*' I recognized the move from Catalonian to French. The man could curse in more languages than anyone I knew. He never cursed in English, however. Not in my presence.

'It's probably nothing.' I didn't believe my own words. I said it because it was just one of those things that people say in circumstances like those.

While Raoul was still on the line, I pulled Lauren's cell from her purse and punched in Diane's mobile number. After three rings someone answered.

A female voice, not Diane's, said, 'Yeah? Who is this?'

Speaking into both phones simultaneously, I said, 'Hold on a second, Raoul. Someone's on her cell.'

'Go on,' he said. '*Allez!*'

The voice on Diane's phone demanded, 'Who's Rule?'

The lilt of the woman's voice triggered some clinical trigger in my brain. Instinctively I went into therapist mode, specifically I went into psychiatric-emergency-room therapist mode. My voice calmed, my hearing sensitized for the unexpected. Psychologically speaking, my weight was on my toes; I was prepared to change directions in a heartbeat.

'This is Dr. Gregory, may I speak to Dr. Diane Estevez, please? You answered her phone.'

'Well, she's not home.' The woman laughed. 'No one's home. That's the whole point, isn't it? Not being home? This is about as far from home as I get. So there.'

I considered the possibility that I'd dialed Diane's number incorrectly and that I was simply being confused by the lottery of errant connection. Then I heard the familiar frantic calliope riff of a slot machine jackpot and I knew that what had happened wasn't a simple wrong number. This woman was in a Las Vegas casino and she was holding Diane's phone in her hand. Why?

'The phone you're holding belongs to a friend of mine. Do you mind if I ask how you got it? Did you find it?'

'The doctor? It belongs to the doctor? Rule? Dr. Rule?'

'Yes.' I let it go. I didn't want to try to explain to this woman who Rule, or Raoul, was, or wasn't.

'Well,' she said. 'I would guess he's out playing golf.' She laughed again. Her cackle was sharp and high-pitched – the yelp of a distressed tropical bird. You wouldn't want to be sitting in the vicinity of this woman in a movie theater during the screening of a half-decent comedy.

'That's pretty funny,' I said in a voice intended to convey that, against all odds, I found her act cute. 'But I'm actually being serious. Where exactly did you find my friend's cell phone? It's important. She'll want to know when she . . . thanks you.'

'I'm playing slots. Two machines – I always play two machines. It was in the tray on the left when I sat down. Or is that the right? I get my lefts and my rights mixed up, especially when I've been drinking, and I've been drinking. Who the heck are you?'

I played the doctor card. 'I'm Dr. Gregory.'

'You out playing golf, too?' She laughed again. I had to hold the phone six inches from my ear to provide a cushion from the intensity of the din.

Diane had dropped her phone on the way out of the casino. That

147

was the explanation for everything. That was why she hadn't kept her promise to call me back as soon as she was outside the casino. That was why she hadn't been answering my repeated calls to her cell phone.

Simple. 'You're in the casino at the Venetian?'

'You wanna bet?' She laughed. 'Or, I . . . wanna bet. I guess I'm the one who's betting.'

'What's your name?'

'Michelle. You know about Harvey Wallbangers?'

'A cocktail, right?' I reminded myself to be patient. *Corral her*, I thought, *don't lasso her.*

'Ver-y good. Nobody here knows how to make 'em. Nobody. I order one and I keep getting Tequila Sunrises. Can you imagine? I don't like the red stuff, I like the yellow stuff. In the tall bottle? You know what I'm talking about?'

'How many have you had?'

'Three, or . . . not – no, four.' She paused. 'Four. Not counting this one. Oops, this one's almost gone, too. Do you know how hard it is to make any money playing nickel slots? Well, it is. Even if you max your bets, and I do sometimes, I really, really do, it's like . . . when you win you still just get . . . well, nickels. Is that fair?'

'So you're playing nickel slots at the Venetian?'

'I am.'

'Are there any casino employees around, Michelle? Maybe right behind you? Somebody in a uniform, someone making change or . . . serving cocktails, or something? An attendant?'

'Yep, there's one right there – how'd you know? Is there a camera on me? Am I like on one of those TV shows or something?'

'Could you please give my friend's phone to the person who works for the casino? Tell him I would like to speak with him?'

'Her.'

'Her. Fine.'

'Here,' she said to somebody, possibly the casino employee, but certainly not to me. 'Some doctor named Rule or . . . Gregory or something lost his phone while he was playing golf. Here, you take it, go on. I don't want it anymore. I need more nickels.'

A heavily accented voice – Caribbean? Jamaican? – said, 'What you need, ma'am? Change?'

And that was the end of that call.

* * *

'Raoul, you still there?'

'Of course.'

'Diane doesn't have her phone with her. Some drunk woman in the casino found it, just turned it over to a casino employee. The call died. I'll try calling back again in a minute. Diane must have lost her phone.'

'At the Venetian?'

'That's what the woman said.'

Raoul said, 'I'll call her room. Keep your line open in case she calls you.'

'Of course. Raoul, I'm sure it's okay. There will be a simple explanation for this.'

He'd already hung up.

Diane had lost her phone. Raoul would call her hotel room and find her sitting on her king-sized bed lambasting somebody from hotel security about the casino's inefficient lost-and-found procedures. That's what I was telling myself. No big thing.

In my heart that's what I didn't believe. As innocuous as the events sounded – a friend failed to keep a promise to call another friend for less than an hour – my heart told me that something sinister had occurred.

You really need to hear this, she'd said. Diane would have found a way to call.

I tried Diane's cell one more time. Without even a single ring, my call was routed to voice mail. I left a simple message, 'Hey Diane, it's Alan. Still trying to reach you in Vegas. Give me a call. I'm getting a little worried. Raoul is concerned, too. Call him.'

I surmised that the casino employee who possessed Diane's phone had killed the power and that Diane's phone was programmed to send power-off calls to voice mail.

I walked down the hall to find Grace and Lauren asleep together on our big bed. One big spoon nestled protectively around one little spoon. I adjusted the comforter so that it covered both of them, flicked off the lights, took the bedtime volumes away from the pillows, and kissed them each on the head before I retraced my steps back to the kitchen counter. I'd carry Grace from our bed into her room later on.

The phone chirped in my hand. I caught it after half a ring. Raoul. He said, 'She's not answering. *Quin merder.*'

It was my turn to curse. I'm not multilingual; I said simply, 'Shit.'

27

'I tried her cell again,' I said. 'I think someone turned it off. The call went straight to voice mail.'

'That's enough for me. I'm going to call hotel security,' Raoul said. 'Get them on this.'

'Get them on what?' I asked, gently. 'You'll tell them you've been unable to reach your wife for an hour? So what? In Vegas terms that's an eye-blink. You know what the security people will say: She met somebody she knew, got distracted. She met somebody she didn't know, got distracted. She went to a show, went to a club, went for a walk, found a hot slot machine or a hotter craps table, went out for a meal, went out for a drink. So she's been gone for an hour? Nobody's going to care. Not for an hour, not for a day. Maybe not even for a week. Not in Las Vegas.'

'They don't know Diane. I do. You do, too. This isn't like her. If she said she was going to call, she would've found a phone. She would've called.'

'But that's the point. They don't know Diane. To them, she's just a tourist who lost her cell phone. Big deal.'

Stubbornly, Raoul said, 'I'm going to call hotel security.'

'Okay,' I said. I knew that were I in his shoes I would want to do something, too, no matter how futile.

'Write down my hotel number here.' He dictated it. 'Call it if you hear from her. I'll be on my mobile.'

I curled my tongue against the roof of my mouth and forced just enough air through the gap to cause a high-pitched, low-volume whistle to emerge. Emily, the big Bouvier, responded immediately. I could hear her lumbering in my direction from the other side of the house.

The sharp tips of her nails *click-clacked* as she made the transition from carpet to hardwood. I knew that Anvil, the miniature poodle, would follow her. He'd follow not because he found my whistle alluring. He'd follow because whatever Emily found alluring, he found alluring.

In our tiny neutered dog pack, Emily was the alpha-Amazon and Anvil was the eunuch slave.

The dogs waited impatiently while I pulled on a jacket and stuffed the cordless phone from the kitchen into one pocket and Lauren's cell into the other. We all crashed together heading out the front door.

Emily ran immediately across the lane toward Adrienne's house. For her it was like visiting extended family. I stage-whispered to her that everybody was in bed; she apparently didn't care. Anvil peed copiously in the dust before he loped off in the same general direction.

Raoul's version of my predicament was simple. In his view I possessed information that might help him find his wife. Sure, he'd been married to a psychologist long enough to know that the information he wanted was privileged. Realistically, of course, he didn't care. Who in his position would?

The fact that I'd already revealed that the information had at least a tangential tie to Hannah Grant's unfortunate demise would only aggravate his insistence that I breach confidence and tell him what he wanted to know. But what he also didn't know was that the patient of Hannah Grant's whose mother was in Las Vegas was Mallory Miller and that the reason for my anxiety over Diane's sudden vanishing wasn't only because I was concerned that it might have something to do with Hannah's death, but also because I feared it might have something to do with Mallory's disappearance.

I'd already decided that, ethical or not, as soon as I felt that Diane had been sucked into that vortex I'd tell Raoul whatever I knew. It wasn't the way the rules were written. But so be it.

Ten minutes outside with the dogs and I was getting cold. It was apparent that Emily – she didn't get cold until wind-chill numbers were in double-digit negatives – was eager to head down the lane on her usual evening jaunt, but I feared that kind of walk would yank us out of range of the cordless phone so I forced both dogs to roam the area between our house and Adrienne's. Emily found some smells that were compelling and she adapted. Anvil hung around close by. Raoul called back just as I was coaxing the reluctant dogs back inside the front door.

'Hi, Raoul?' I answered. 'You hear anything?'

'Not from Diane. Security's not going to help. I'm in a cab on the way to the airport. I'll be in Vegas in a couple of hours.'

'You're sure that's a—'

'Yes, I am. You didn't hear from her?'

Raoul's interruption shouted at me that his usual unflappable civility was developing fissures. 'No,' I said.

'Sometime tomorrow morning, if I'm not waking up next to my wife, I'm going to want to talk to this patient's mother, Alan. Be prepared to help me find her.'

'Raoul, I—'

He hung up.

'—will do whatever's necessary.'

28

Diane's husband was wealthy. She didn't work the long hours I did. She didn't have to.

On a typical weekday before eight in the morning my car would've been the first to slide into the parking spaces beside our office building. That Tuesday should have been no different. On a typical Tuesday morning, Diane would show up at around 9:00, or 9:30. That Tuesday should have been no different.

She'd told me on the phone the evening before that she'd already canceled her appointments until Thursday. Still, given the events at the Venetian, the driveway felt empty without her Saab, the waiting room felt empty without her patients, and the offices felt empty without her laugh.

Raoul had called me near midnight the night before from the room he'd checked into at the Venetian after flying to Vegas from San Francisco. He had a suite fit for the doges overlooking the Rialto Bridge, but he didn't have any good news to report. Diane hadn't phoned him. The fact that she hadn't at least left a message on Raoul's cell was unprecedented between them. When one of them was traveling they always talked at the end of the day – always. When they were traveling separately they always talked at the end of the day.

After a lot of cajoling, and a five-hundred-dollar incentive, Raoul had finally persuaded a housekeeping manager to agree to check Diane's room for him. The manager wouldn't give Raoul the location of her room, but reported back that there was no sign of anything out of the ordinary, nor was there any indication that she'd been there since late that afternoon. No phone calls had been placed on the hotel room phone since midafternoon. The minibar was untouched after it had been replenished midday. The housekeeper who cleaned the room reported that she'd finished the evening turndown service around 6:30. From all appearances, no one had disturbed the bed or bath linens since that time.

The casino attendant who'd been given Diane's cell phone by the drunk woman who played nickel slots and inhaled Harvey Wallbangers had promptly turned it in to the casino's lost-and-found department.

Diane had not inquired about it.

Raoul had also begun what he anticipated would be a long, difficult process of badgering the hotel security officers to review the casino security videotapes for the time that Diane was walking across the gaming floor talking with me on her cell phone. He assumed that hotel security cameras videotaped every square inch of the casino twenty-four hours a day. Security was resisting his pleas to review that section of the tapes.

Their argument? What his wife did when she was in Las Vegas was her business, right? Not her husband's, right?

He was European, he understood. Right? They can't very well start showing videotapes of what one spouse does in their casino to another spouse, can they? Would that be fair? What happens in Vegas stays in Vegas, right?

Raoul knew that it was hard to disagree, unless you knew her.

Raoul knew her. I knew her.

Venetian security didn't know her. The identity of the person she'd run into as she walked across the casino floor? Venetian security thought that was her business.

How had she lost her cell phone? Venetian security thought that was her business.

Had she left the casino at all? Her business.

What else had Raoul accomplished by midnight Colorado time?

He'd called all the hospitals in a ten-mile radius of the Strip, searching for even the barest hint that his wife might have been treated or admitted that evening. He'd learned nothing that helped.

He'd called the Las Vegas police, seeking any indication that the local authorities had crossed paths with someone who even vaguely resembled his description of Diane. He'd learned nothing. He'd called American Express to see if he could get a list of charges she'd put on her card in the previous twenty-four hours. A supervisor would speak with him in the morning.

He'd tipped the concierge at the Venetian a hundred bucks to find a twenty-four-hour copy shop that could blow up and print a hundred copies of the photograph of Diane that he kept in his wallet.

She promised him that the prints would be waiting for him before breakfast.

'I eat early,' he'd told her, suspicious of her promise.

'I stay up late,' she'd replied with a smile.

'It's the suite,' he explained to me. 'They must have run my credit report. I think she's hoping I'm a newly calved whale.'

The midnight call from Raoul had awakened Lauren. I didn't see any advantage to be gained by alarming her into having a fitful night's sleep, so I'd explained, benignly, that Diane was in Vegas and that Raoul hadn't heard from her, that he was worried, and he'd called to see if I'd talked to her since early that evening.

Had I? My wife wanted to know. I had not, I told her, not since early evening. I kissed her, and murmured that she should go back to sleep.

Over coffee in the morning, I explained the rest of the mess to Lauren, obliquely highlighting the slippery ice of the confidentiality hazards that were out in front of me, and specifically including the fact that before we'd hung up the night before, Raoul had reminded me that he wanted to know which patient's mother Diane had spoken with the previous day. Lauren, of course, knew nothing about my patient Bob and his odd connection to the Millers' neighbor, Doyle. And she certainly didn't know that the patient's mother that Diane wanted to see in Vegas was Mallory's mother, Rachel.

'What do you think about Diane not calling?' Lauren asked me as I was kissing her and Grace good-bye before leaving for my office.

'I'm worried. It's not like her.'

'There's probably an explanation,' she offered.

'I hope you're right. But I can't think of what it might be. Diane's a stay-in-touch kind of person.'

'She's always been unpredictable.'

'About some things, yeah. Not about staying in touch. About that she's as reliable as sunrise.'

She kissed me again. 'If Raoul doesn't hear from her by midday, let me know, and I'll see if there's anything I can do. Maybe some-body knows somebody in the DA's office in Las Vegas. Okay?'

'Thanks.'

'Sam might be able to reach out, too,' she added. 'He might have cop contacts out there.'

And what, I thought, was I going to tell Sam about the Millers and Bob and Doyle and Hannah Grant that might entice him to reach out to cop colleagues in Las Vegas? 'Maybe she'll call,' I said, not quite believing that she would.

I unlocked the front door of the building, flicked on the lights in the waiting room, and started a small pot of coffee in the tiny kitchen. At 7:43 the red light that indicated that my first patient had arrived for her 7:45 appointment flashed on in my office.

It was time to go to work.

29

Raoul had my pager number. I'd told him to use it as soon as he knew anything about Diane and that I'd call him back as soon as I could.

Lunchtime came and I didn't hear from him. I tried his cell phone. My call was routed to voice mail; I left a message asking him to phone me with news immediately.

Nothing.

Midafternoon I went through the same routine with the same result. Just to be certain that my bases were covered, I left an additional message on Raoul's hotel room voice mail at the Venetian.

Nothing.

When 4:45 came around and the red light on the wall in my office flared on, I found myself becoming alarmed that almost an entire workday had passed with no news about Diane. My level of concern for her was approaching ten on a ten-scale.

I walked down the hall to get Bob. My apprehension about the session was high. I had almost convinced myself that Bob really did know something important about Mallory.

Bob wasn't sitting in the waiting room. No one was.

My first reaction? *Who flicked the switch that had turned on the red light?*

I checked my watch. Four forty-four.

I waited a minute. Four forty-five. Had Bob ever before been late for therapy? Maybe once or twice, but his absence from the waiting room was certainly an anomaly. Had he forgotten that we'd made this appointment the day before? How could he have? Given the drama in front of my house at dawn, I was sure Bob would have remembered his usual appointment time.

I flicked off the switch that illuminated the red light and returned down the hall to check my calendar and my voice mail. I was still thinking that Bob would show up any minute.

I was wrong.

Five o'clock came and went, then five fifteen, and finally five thirty, the time that Bob and I would usually be finished with his session.

The reality was that patients missed scheduled appointments all the time. If I had a busy week I could usually count on at least one no-show among my patients. Sometimes patients forgot their appointments and that was that; other times patients spaced out their appointments and the fact that they'd forgotten was ripe with therapeutic meaning. Sometimes life intervened. An injured child, a traffic accident, a late flight.

But Bob? He'd never missed a scheduled appointment. Never.

I thought about the midnight-blue box with the Kinko's logo that was sitting in the file cabinet near my desk. Bob had said, 'Don't read it yet. I'll tell you when.'

After he'd handed it to me I thought I'd said, 'I'll see you tomorrow then.'

I thought Bob had replied, 'Sure.' Was it possible that Bob had known he wouldn't be showing up for this appointment? With most patients, I would have simply packed up my things, gone home, and not given the missed session another thought. But Bob wasn't most patients: Bob was Doyle's friend, and Bob knew Mallory.

Bob thought he knew what Mallory had been thinking. Bob had been next door the night that Mallory had disappeared. Bob had written a story about Mallory's disappearance. Bob thought Mallory was scared.

I had a copy of what he had written.

But he'd told me not to read it.

Powered by the pair of fresh batteries that I'd installed that morning, the pager on my hip vibrated with irritating insistence. The number that flashed on the screen was for Raoul's cell.

I dialed immediately. 'Raoul, it's me: Alan.'

'I'm ready to kill these people. Tell me something: Does Nevada have the death penalty? I think I'm becoming a proponent.'

'Which people?'

'Take your pick. The Las Vegas police. The fascists in Venetian

159

security. Even the damn minister at the Love In Las Vegas Wedding Chapel. He might be first.'

'What?'

'I gave the housekeeping manager two hundred more bucks to look for Diane's calendar in her room. It wasn't there, but she let me see the notepad by the telephone. Diane was visiting wedding chapels. She wanted to talk with somebody named Rachel at a wedding chapel. She had a list of them on the notepad. I visited all three. Love In Las Vegas was the most promising.'

Without much thought, I said, 'I'm glad you found that . . .' I didn't know how to end the sentence.

Raoul did. 'On my own, you mean,' he said.

'Yes. Did you talk to this . . . Rachel?'

'Nobody at the chapel will tell me anything. But they know her, that's clear enough. The minister is a guy with a fake British accent who prances around like he's on holiday from his day job in the House of Lords. He acted really cagey when I mentioned Rachel's name. I'll find her tomorrow.'

'Diane?' I said, hopefully.

'I pray. But I'll find Rachel, and she'll help me find Diane. Despite the neon carnival and depraved World's Fair ambiance of the place, Las Vegas feels like a small town. Money is ammunition here. That works in my favor. I'm well armed.'

'The police are uninterested?'

'"Uninterested" is a generous word.'

'And Venetian security?'

'I think they went ahead and looked at the videotapes of whatever happened while Diane was walking out of the casino. When she lost her phone.'

'Did you get the impression it seemed significant to them?'

'It raised an eyebrow or two. But they won't tell me why.'

'What happens in Vegas stays in Vegas?'

'Like that. There's one woman on the security team who wants to talk with me. I flirted with her a little, and I'm going to see if I can catch up with her later on when she gets off work. Her shift ends at eight.'

I tried to imagine Raoul's frustration. His determination was apparent, but whatever he was doing to mask his frustration was admirable. I asked him, 'Why aren't you bugging me for more information about Rachel?'

'Diane wouldn't want me to. She didn't talk to me about her clients. One of the things she respects about you is how you've kept your mouth shut through all the . . . difficult situations you've been in over the years. I'm trying to respect what she respects.'

'I appreciate that. I'm in another difficult position right now. I'd really like to be more helpful, but Diane's not the only one who's . . .'

'Who's what?'

'Mixed up with Rachel's . . . problems. I've already told you more than I should.' I knew I sounded lame. If I were in Raoul's shoes, I think I'd want to string me up by my thumbs.

In a tone that was intended not only to sound calm but also to communicate his increasing desperation, he said, 'It's a reprieve, not a pardon, my friend. As soon as I run into a dead end with this Rachel person I'll be back in your face, insisting. Or worse.' At the end he managed a little laugh.

'I can't wait,' I said.

'I have to go. Before my date with this security lady later I'm going to try to see if I can find any gamblers who remember seeing Diane at the craps tables last night. I hope that some of the same people will be playing again. I'll be in touch. *Adeu.*'

'*Adeu*' is Catalonian for good-bye. Other than profanity, the only other Catalonian Raoul had taught me during the many years of our friendship was how to ask if there was a good bar nearby. At that moment, had I been on a beachfront up the coast from Barcelona, I would have been sorely tempted to try out the phrase.

I said, '*Adeu*, Raoul.' But he'd already hung up.

After only a moment's hesitation I opened the drawer to the file cabinet and withdrew the Kinko's box that Bob had given me. Almost reverentially, I lifted the lid off the box, and raised the title page in my hands.

My Little Runaway
By R.C. Brandt

A quick, surreptitious glance at the open box revealed that the top sheet in the pile of paper that remained in the box wasn't the beginning of Bob's story. The second page was handwritten. In his

161

familiar, neat, incredibly cramped script, Bob had written me a note.

> *Dr. Gregory,*
>
> *If I've told you to go ahead and read this, this is the page that I want you to throw away. You can go ahead. If I haven't given you permission, this is where you should stop. Remember, I'm trusting you. I'll tell you when.*
>
> *Bob*

His tiny scrawl seemed indecipherable, a missive intended for selected residents of Lilliput. I guessed that the first line was my name and the last line was Bob's, but I couldn't read the two lines in between all the way through, not at first. Only by holding the paper farther and farther from my eyes until I got it all the way out to arm's length did the script come sufficiently into focus. 'Dr. Gregory,' it read. 'If I've told you to go ahead and read this, this is the page that I want you to throw away. You can go ahead. If I haven't given you permission, this is where you should stop. Remember, I'm trusting you. I'll tell you when. Bob.'

Reluctantly, I replaced both pages – the title page and the warning page – and fit the lid back onto the box.

What could be the harm of reading the damn thing?

Bob's handwritten note had spooked me. How had he anticipated that a second caution to me about not reading his manuscript would be necessary? I decided to ask him. After checking my address book for the number, I called his home.

The phone rang and rang. No answering machine ever kicked in. As I hung up, I admitted to myself that I'd just done something that I rarely, if ever, did. I'd just tried to check in with a patient because they'd missed a session. What was my typical practice? I usually just let the issue simmer until the next scheduled appointment.

This time, that didn't sound like a judicious plan.

30

I thought she was maybe fifteen years old, but she swore she was seventeen. I didn't have to ask her age; she was apparently accustomed to protesting that she was older than she looked, and before I'd known her for a full minute she'd insisted she was seventeen, really. Her name was Jenifer Donald. The Jenifer was leavened with only one *n*, she'd pointed out – the result not of a spelling failure, but rather, I was guessing, of a momentary lapse in judgment by young parents who were intent on making sure their daughter went through life with a distinctive name.

Jenifer was from Clemson, South Carolina, and was in Boulder visiting her grandparents, who lived on the northern edge of Boulder's original downtown near the intersection of Eighteenth and Pine. 'They're so cute. They really are,' she said, referring to her grandparents. 'Some of my friends' parents are as old as my grandparents. But my grandparents are just so cute.'

'Clemson? That's where the college is?' I asked.

'The university,' she corrected. It was clear that the distinction was important to her. 'It's where I want to go. I'm hoping for a scholarship, for band. I'm a drummer. I have a good chance, I think. My PSATs were better than I expected. Much better. I take the SATs next month – I hope, I hope, I hope I do well. My parents and my grandparents want me to look at CU, too. I told them I would. That's why I'm here.' She rolled her eyes. As if *anyone* would choose the University of Colorado over Clemson.

I found myself warmed by the unfamiliar melody of her lilting voice and loving the openness with which she'd greeted me at the front door of the brick two-story home. Jenifer's pretty face was as

163

welcoming as her manner. Her blond hair fell in a straight shot well past her shoulders. 'What kind of doctor are y'all?' she asked. Her question wasn't at all suspicious, merely friendly.

When she'd opened the front door, I'd introduced myself as 'Dr. Gregory,' hoping the appellation would grant me some advantage with the kid who'd responded to the doorbell. I was already regretting having done it; I couldn't very well tell her I was a clinical psychologist without leaving her with the implication that Bob had a reason to be seeing one.

'So Bob's not here?' I asked, changing the subject.

'The guy upstairs in back? That's Bob? Grandpa calls him "the tenant." Don't think so.' Jenifer said 'the tenant' in a deep, gravelly voice, mimicking, I guessed, her grandfather's delivery. 'I haven't actually seen him this visit. I just got in to Boulder today – it's so cold here, how do you stand it? My grandparents have an appointment somewhere. Pill-ottos, pill-ah-tees. Those machines? We don't do that much of it in South Carolina.'

She laughed; and her laugh made me smile. She really thought her grandparents were cute and that Boulder was exotic. 'Yes, those machines,' I said.

She smiled back and shook her head. 'Would you like to come in and wait for him? I'll fix you something.'

'Thank you,' I said, stepping past her into the house. 'You're a drummer? Marching band?'

'And orchestra,' she said.

A short hallway led to the back of the house. Through a kitchen window I could see the curtained rooms above the garage. 'That's Bob's?' I asked.

Jenifer said, 'You bet.'

'Where are the stairs?'

'Other side, on the alley.'

A pile of mail was visible in a basket on the back porch.

Jenifer saw me looking. 'See that? I'm sure your friend Bob would have picked up his mail if he was home.' She lowered her voice to a whisper before she added, 'He sure gets a lot of catalogs.'

'I'm sure you're right. He must not be home.'

'Hey, I'm a pretty good cook. Y'all like grilled cheese? I make a mean Swiss on rye.'

Jenifer managed to make 'Swiss on rye' sound almost as alien as blowfish.

I said, 'I'm actually kind of worried about him. He and I were going to get together earlier today but he didn't show up, which isn't like him.'

'Are you thinking maybe he's sick?' Her voice blossomed with concern.

I shrugged my shoulders. Bob could indeed be ill; it would explain a lot. I asked, 'Is it okay for me to go knock, you think?'

She hopped past me and bounded out the door and across the back porch. 'I don't see why not. Knocking never hurt anybody, did it?'

She lifted the rubber-banded stack of mail from the basket, led me around to the alley, ran up the stairs, and knocked on Bob's door. Two sharp raps. She cooed, 'Knock, knock,' for good measure.

While we were giving Bob much too much time to make his way to the door, Jenifer seemed to be examining my face. She finally scrunched up her nose a little bit and asked, 'You really are worried, aren't you?'

I said, 'Yes, I am.'

'That's so sweet. Wait here.' In one fluid motion she jumped down the stairs, and disappeared around the corner. She returned seconds later with a fistful of keys, popped back up the stairs, unlocked the lock, turned the knob, and threw open the door.

'Go have a quick look,' she said. 'I'm sure he wouldn't mind. I'll just toss this mail in here so nobody—'

Jenifer took a half step into Bob's apartment and immediately screamed, hitting a note that – despite a volume that would have made a siren engineer envious – was so high in pitch that it almost disappeared into the range undetectable by human ears.

I hurdled up the steps three at a time, 'What—'

31

'Detective Sam Purdy, this is Jenifer Donald. She's visiting her grand-parents from South Carolina.'

'Pleased to meet you,' Sam said.

I was tempted to tell Sam that Jenifer was as sweet as an August melon, and warn him that she was older than she looked, but I didn't. He'd figure it all out himself before too long.

He flipped open his badge wallet for her benefit. Jenifer hopped back from it as though it were cocked and loaded.

'So you don't actually live here, Jenifer? This isn't your house?'

'No, sir. Should I call you "officer"?'

'Detective. Dr. Gregory told me that you're here visiting your grandparents. They are due home when?'

Sam was dressed in new clothes, or at least clothes I'd never seen him wear before. Two factors were at play: One, he'd lost a lot of weight over the last year and his old stuff didn't fit. Two, he actually seemed to have started caring how he looked. The ensemble he was wearing was composed of a pair of jeans from the Gap and a striped wool v-neck sweater over a white T-shirt that hadn't even considered turning yellow. For Sam, the outfit constituted styling.

Jenifer's acute anxiety that she had done something to lure a po-lice detective to her grandparents' door was making me nervous. She said, 'Soon. They're due back soon. Any minute I bet. But I'm not sure. They're out doing that pill . . . thing. Exercise, you know? With those machines?'

Sam sighed. He knew. Eating a healthy diet was something Sam had embraced. Exercise? That had become cool with him, too. But Pilates and yoga? For Sam, they were still on an astral plane with tats and piercings. He wasn't quite there yet. At his partner Lucy's insis-

166

tence, he'd accompanied her to a solitary session of Bikram yoga – the kind that's basically done in a sauna – and was astonished, and dismayed, to learn that people were physiologically capable of sweating out of their noses.

Profusely.

And that they would pay dearly for the privilege.

I thought it would take him a while to come around to being open-minded about yoga and Pilates.

'And this guy, Bob, is your grandparents' tenant?' he asked Jenifer. 'He rents a room?'

'Two rooms. Yes, sir. And he has his own bathroom, of course. Hot plate, microwave. You know. I used to stay up there when I was visiting. It's nice. You can see the mountains real well when the leaves are off the trees. Or is it "real good"? No, no – it's real well.'

We were all standing out near the alley at the foot of the stairs that led up to Bob's rented rooms. Sam looked at me before he asked Jenifer the next question. 'And which one of you actually entered Bob's rooms?'

Jenifer swallowed and her eyes got as big and bright as table grapes. 'I did. That's when I saw – I shouldn't have done that, should I? Oh my Lord. Am I in trouble? The doctor was worried and I thought that he . . . oh my Lord! Oh my Lord. I'm so sorry. Back home, we'd – but, oh, I really am sorry. I'll never do it again. I promise. Please don't . . .'

She couldn't even bring herself to say 'arrest me.'

'"The doctor"' – Sam glared at me – 'said you saw some blood when you were inside? And a mess?'

'I did. I'm so sorry. I don't know what I was thinking. I really don't know what I was thinking. Going into a stranger's place like that? We might do it back home, but I'm not – Y'all—' She sighed. 'I screamed. The blood, the mess. I'm so, so sorry.'

'It's nothing,' Sam said, in his best fatherly voice. 'Don't you worry; you did what you thought was best.' Sam climbed the staircase toward Bob's rooms. He stopped near the top, turned to Jenifer and me, and said, 'What I'm going to do is something that law enforcement calls a "welfare check." All that means is that I'm going to make a quick walk through his place, make certain that there isn't someone inside needing assistance, then I'm going to come right back

167

out.' He focused his eyes on me before he continued. 'Just in case anyone's ever curious about exactly what I did in there. Understand?'

'Yes,' Jenifer replied, although it hadn't been her understanding Sam had been seeking.

He edged into the flat without touching a single surface and was back out of Bob's rented rooms in a little over a minute. Because of the way the door was situated I wasn't able to follow his progress. Once he was back on the landing at the top of the stairs, he looked at me and shook his head, 'Nobody in there. Some blood, not too much. Just what you saw near the door. And it's a mess in there, too, Jenifer, just like you said.'

'There they are. *Finally*,' Jenifer said, pointing down the driveway that led out to Pine Street.

A huge dark GMC pickup with a camper shell was pulling into the driveway. We all waited.

The second her grandparents made it out of the truck, Jenifer announced, 'The police are here about the tenant. There's blood. I looked inside. I'm so sorry. I am.'

32

'Get in,' Sam said. He pointed at his Cherokee.

I got in. The consequences of being obstreperous at that moment were too much for me to contemplate.

'There's not that much blood,' he said.

'It's relative,' I argued. 'If it was yours, I think you might consider it a reasonable quantity. Anyway, isn't that exactly what you said about Mallory's blood on the day after Christmas?'

'And it turns out I was right about Mallory's blood on the day after Christmas. Kid got nosebleeds. The splatter in the house was consistent with a sudden nosebleed.'

I could have argued the point, but it was clear that Sam was holding trump cards. 'What about the mess?'

'You really didn't go in?'

'I peeked, Sam. I was worried.'

'Being messy isn't a crime. I see teenagers' rooms that are worse all the time. There's no visible evidence that a crime was committed in the guy's flat. The kid's grandparents heard nothing. There're a few drops of blood on a wall and some bad housekeeping. Hell, he could be over at Community right now getting his finger stitched up. ER doc told me once they see people all the time who slice their hands up while they're cutting bagels. I hadn't known that. Bagels.'

'There was blood on the carpet, too,' I argued.

'You said you didn't go in.'

'You can see it from the door.'

'There wasn't that much blood on the carpet.'

'Was it fresh?'

'I didn't stop to test it.'

I opened my mouth to ask another question, but Sam stopped me.

169

'We have rules, Alan. Bill of Rights ring a bell? I did a welfare check. I didn't find anyone in need of assistance or see any other reason to stay in the man's home uninvited, so I left. Done.'

'You're not going to investigate, are you?'

'Investigate what?'

It was exactly the response I'd dreaded. 'He's missing. His place was tossed.'

'Tossed? So you say. You know any of this for sure?' He waited long enough to see if I was done arguing with him. 'Didn't think so.' He went on, making his case, 'Jenifer's grandparents say that they're sure Bob was home alone when? Last night?'

'Night before, actually. And they said they thought he was alone because he always is. They don't actually know he was alone.'

'Okay, they weren't sure about last night. And now it's early evening and he's not home. Big frigging deal. Where's the crime? The only crime I see is that Jenifer's grandparents are in violation of zoning codes for having a tenant and a crappy makeshift second kitchen in those rooms. But I'm going to let that one slide.'

'Big of you,' I said, trying not to sound too sarcastic. The truth was that I didn't know how to answer any of Sam's questions without telling him things I wasn't allowed to tell him.

Sam probed the contours of my silence and came to the conclusion I figured he would get around to. 'He's one of yours, isn't he? Your . . . clients?' Sam asked, not expecting me to answer. 'And . . . let me guess, he didn't show up for his appointment with you. He's usually as reliable as milk of magnesia about showing up on time, so you're worried.' Sam didn't even bother to make these statements sound like questions.

I didn't deny anything. Didn't confirm anything.

'You want me to be worried, too,' he added.

I was relieved to be given a prompt I could actually respond to. 'That would be nice,' I said.

'Why didn't you just call nine-one-one? Why'd you call me?'

I stared at Sam for a moment. I could've told him that I called him because I trusted him and didn't call 911 because for all I knew I would end up having to introduce Jenifer, with one *n*, to Jaris Slocum. It would have suggested to Sam that I still wasn't prepared to cut Jaris Slocum any slack, and that was one argument I didn't need rewound.

I played another card instead. I suspected the card I played broke a rule, but I convinced myself that the rules were gray about whether or not I could play that particular card. 'I wonder if he has a car. That might help us find him. His car.'

Sam gave me about an eighth of a smile. 'You wonder if he has a car?' He lifted his chin half an inch and groomed the grain of his mustache off to the sides with the index finger and thumb of his right hand. 'Stay here while I go back inside and ask Bob's landlords a few more questions that I'm sure you could tell me all the answers to if you didn't suffer from such serious constipation.'

He added a comment about Jesus before he was out of earshot.

While Sam was gone, I phoned Lauren and told her I was going to be even later than I had told her I was going to be the last time I called. She wanted to know if she should hold dinner, and she wanted to tell me about the new ways that Grace was being cute, and chat about why I was tied up so late, and she wanted to know what was new with Diane and Raoul. I explained I'd fill her in on everything when I got home and told her to give Grace a kiss for me. Dinner? I'd fix something for myself.

Sam returned after about five minutes. He settled onto the driver's seat and crossed his arms. The front of the Cherokee was pointed toward the southwest, and from the shotgun position there was a break in the trees that allowed me to see the vault of the second Flatiron outlined against the night sky. The light of the fractional moon was reflecting just right.

Sam said, 'He has an old muscle car. A Camaro. Keeps it garaged at a house over on Twelfth Street.'

I caught myself holding my breath and forced myself to inhale, exhale, act natural. 'Where exactly on Twelfth?'

'You're really going to pretend you don't already know all this? Okay, I'll play along. Mr. Donald doesn't know exactly where. But I have a suspicion you might be able to find it for me, you know, like those good ol' boys can find the exact spot you should drill your new well. What are those boys called? The ones with the forked sticks? Are they called dowsers? Ah, who cares? We're going for a little drive.'

Sam started the Jeep and made his way across downtown until he

171

got to the Hill and turned on Twelfth Street. We were heading south, paralleling the mountains that loomed a dozen blocks away. He pulled to a gentle stop at the curb halfway between the instantly recognizable home where Mallory Miller had disappeared and the smaller place that was next door on the north side.

Doyle's house.

'I'm guessing that's where this guy Bob keeps his muscle car,' Sam said. 'Just a suspicion. Call it cop's intuition.'

I didn't bite. Sam picked Doyle's house either because the Donalds had actually told him exactly where he could find Bob's car, or he picked it because during our morning jog I'd already mentioned the Millers' neighbor's house to him. Sam didn't misplace much information.

I was busy eyeing the real estate sign in front of the house, trying to cram the listing agent's name – *Virginia Danna, Virginia Danna* – into my memory. I asked, 'So are you going to check for a car in the garage?'

'Sure we are. Come on.'

The front yard of Doyle's house was terraced. Undulating, mortarless flagstone walls of varying heights supported a series of planting beds that radiated away from the curving center walk like the lines on a topographic map. Dried ornamental grasses were interspersed with globe evergreens and other Xeriscape-y things I didn't recognize.

I stuffed my hands into my pockets to try to ward off the January cold and followed Sam down the front walk until he moved onto a path that intersected with it and led around to the back of the house. After a few more steps, I could see the gable of a single-car garage roof toward the rear property line.

'You're not going to introduce yourself to whoever lives here?' I asked innocently.

'Place is empty. Owner moved away a couple of months ago. Guy's asking way too much is what I hear. You know, given the market and interest rates and all. But who the hell knows what's up with Boulder real estate these days? Did I tell you some agent's been dropping by begging me to sell my place? Says he already has a buyer and can get me a fortune for it. I think he's a developer and wants to scrape my shack and put up a spec. I could take the money but I'd have to move halfway to Wyoming to find someplace new to live. What's the point of that? It would mean commuting for me, and new schools for Simon.'

A casual observer might have mistaken Sam's ramblings for whining, or for the opening gambit in a friendly discussion of Boulder County property values and the moral and economic consequences of chasing the appreciated dollar. I knew better. Sam's moves were misdirection. From experience, I knew that he used misdirection the same way magicians used it.

So what was it that I was not supposed to notice?

Sam has been in Doyle's yard before.

I was sure of it. Despite the darkness he was leading me across the property as though he'd sat in on the design meetings with the landscape architect. Once we made it to the backyard, he followed a flagstone path over a little wooden bridge that spanned a curving faux streambed. When the path split, Sam chose the fork that ran toward the rear of the lot.

Only the top half of the garage was visible behind a stunning series of man-made granite – for want of a better word – cliffs. At the bottom of the natural-looking walls was a good-sized, but drained, pond that would flow into the streambed we'd crossed earlier. I had no trouble imagining the waterfall that would cascade down those rocks into that pool come spring.

'This way,' Sam said. He stopped at a garage window and shined the beam of a flashlight through the glass. The garage was clearly empty.

No cars. No cherry Camaro.

'There you go,' Sam said. 'Your guy took his car and went somewhere. Free country. Mystery solved. Nothing that requires the services of Boulder's finest.'

'You?'

'Me. This is the right house?' Sam asked. He was holding the flashlight between us down near his waist, aiming the beam straight up toward the night sky. With the up light his forest of nose hairs was illuminated with way too much clarity for my taste. His face and head took on eerie contours inside the fog of his steamy breath.

I felt like saying something in reply to his question but couldn't figure out anything that confidentiality permitted me to say.

173

He smiled, recognizing my conundrum. 'Thought so.'

Over his shoulder I saw movement in the Millers' home. A silhouette in the upstairs window. I tried to watch it without watching it. I said, 'I'm worried about Diane.'

'What?'

I had his attention. I repeated my concern.

'Your partner? That Diane?'

'She went to Las Vegas a couple of days ago. I was talking with her on the phone last night from one of the casinos and the call suddenly went dead. She's disappeared. Her husband flew out there a couple of hours later and he can't find a trace of her. The Vegas cops aren't interested.'

Sam moved the flashlight beam away from our faces. A second glance next door revealed the silhouette moving from the Millers' window. In an instant, it was gone.

'Your friend Diane went to Las Vegas?'

Sam knew precisely what I had told him by telling him that fact. With Sam I rarely had to say things twice. 'To talk to someone,' I said, as a way of underlining my point, just in case.

He nodded, wetting his lower lip with his tongue. 'You're looking at something behind me. Don't do it again. Look at me. Eye contact. Good, good. What is it?'

'Somebody watching us in an upstairs window.'

'Still there?'

I shook my head.

'Dad?'

'Couldn't say. Just a silhouette.'

'Which window?'

'Closest to the street.'

He nodded and ran his fingers through his hair before he stuffed his free hand into the back pocket of his jeans. 'Diane went to Las Vegas to talk with someone and then yesterday she vanished? Now you have a client you're worried about that you think may have just vanished, too? You and I are standing in the backyard of a house on Twelfth Street where said client garages his old car. Right next door a young girl happened to disappear on Christmas Day. I got it all right, so far?'

'You're doing pretty well.' *The car part is a little off*, I was thinking. *The Camaro may be old, but it's cherry.*

'Great, glad to hear it. Let me add a couple of things to the list, things I've already been a little concerned about. You know something about Mallory Miller's mother that in my book you don't have any reason to know. You probably even know she lives in Vegas. You're way too curious about Reese's aggressive tendencies for my taste. And it was not too long ago that you kind of predicted that you and I were going to knock heads about this house next door to the Millers.'

'That's three things, Sam, at least.'

'Do me a favor, ignore the arithmetic.'

'I can't confirm some of what you're saying. But I can't argue with what you're saying, either.'

'From you that's a ringing endorsement.'

I shrugged.

With gorgeous understatement, Sam said, 'Well, too many missing pieces. It all sounds too goofy for words to me.' He began walking. 'Come on. I want to hear more about Diane and what's going on with her in Las Vegas.'

He led me back out through the dormant water features of Doyle's yard. Just before we got to Sam's car at the curb I said, employing a voice that was much more measured than I was feeling at that moment, 'Diane and I were both there the day that Hannah Grant died.'

Without even a glance in my direction, he said, 'I know that. Don't you think I fucking know that?'

33

My car was across downtown outside the house where Bob rented rooms from the Donalds. After pressing me for some more details about Diane's disappearance in Las Vegas, Sam headed toward Pine Street to drop me off.

'So what do you know about the owner of the house with the water park?' I asked.

He killed the volume on the radio, squelching some country lament that I didn't really want to hear. While I waited – rating the odds at three out of ten that he'd actually answer my question about Doyle – I was thinking, and not for the first time, that most of Sam's favorite country artists could use a few sessions of psychotherapy.

'Owner's been out of the house for a while; it's vacant now, was vacant over Christmas, too, if that's what you're wondering. And yes, we've talked to him – the owner – got in touch with him right away through the real estate lady who's listing the house.'

Sam paused poignantly. Okay, provocatively. I thought he was waiting to see if my sense of self-preservation was so impaired that I would choose that moment to remind him of something he had once confessed to me about the last time – the Christmas when the little blond beauty queen was murdered three blocks away. That time, Sam admitted one night over beers, eleven long months passed before any cop, any DA's investigator, any FBI agent – anyone in law enforcement – got around to interviewing one of the dead girl's family's nearest neighbors.

For eleven months after a child was viciously murdered, the cops had failed to interview the residents of a house with a perfect view of the crime scene.

To me, unbelievable.

But I didn't remind him. He didn't need reminding.

He went on. 'The owner gave us permission to search. No hesitation, no bullshit, totally cooperative. Agent unlocked the place and we searched it. Nothing. And all this happened in the first few hours after Mallory's father reported her missing.'

'Is the owner in town?'

Doyle. I wanted to use his name out loud, but I couldn't. I wanted to know if Doyle was in town.

'No.'

'You guys thought Mallory might have been in there after she disappeared?'

'Vacant house right next door? It's one of the first places we look.'

'But nothing?'

'Just a vacant house. Kitchen's hardly bigger than mine. Terrific yard, sure, but no place to toss a football. Definitely overpriced. Hey, what isn't in this town?'

Sam pondered the inflation of Boulder's housing stock more than I did, but taking that detour didn't seem productive to me. I asked, 'Was the Camaro in the garage when you searched the house at Christmas?'

'Now there's a good question. I don't recall that it was. If it had been, somebody would've run the tags and talked to your guy. I'm sure of that. And I don't think we've ever talked to your guy.'

I could tell that I had only about half of Sam's attention. He was considering some angle I couldn't see. His answer to my last question was probably in the vicinity of honest but he wasn't telling me all that he could. But then I wasn't telling him all that I could, either. 'Something else is spinning in that big head of yours. What is it?'

He startled a bit at my question as he pulled from Ninth onto Pine. 'I'm connecting dots, looking for a damn crime. I need a rationalization I can use.'

'What do you mean?'

He didn't answer right away, not until we were almost on the Donalds' block. My car was just ahead. The lights were still off in Bob's rooms; I would have been truly surprised if they weren't.

Sam flashed the Cherokee's headlights at a van coming at us from the other direction. The driver of the van responded by flashing to his low beams for half a second before he went right back to his brights.

He beeped his horn to underline his aggravation that another motorist would deign to question his choice of headlamp settings. I couldn't see the van driver through the high-intensity glare but I would have bet he was flipping Sam off, too.

I said, 'Asshole's tugging on Superman's cape.'

'He's lucky I'm in a good mood.'

I smiled out loud.

'There's nothing here for me, Alan. Your guy's been gone, what? A day or two maybe? There's half a thimble's worth of blood near his door – and some clothes on the floor. No sign of forced entry. No witnesses. Guy's gone. His car's gone. Ergo: He split. People do it all the time without warning anybody, without telling anybody. Even their therapists. I have nothing I can give my bosses that they'll find the least bit interesting. I take this in, I know what I'm going to hear: So far this isn't a police matter. So that's what I tell you: So far this isn't a police matter.'

'Okay,' I said.

'And your friend, Diane? She's so far out of my jurisdiction it isn't funny. I put myself in the Vegas casino's shoes and I'm not going to give a crap about her welfare until another few days pass and the hotel needs her room for the next convention. I put myself in a Vegas cop's shoes, I feel basically the same way. Grown-ups do what grown-ups do. But say she's really missing? By the time people get worried enough to look for her, it will probably be way too late to do anything to help her. I pray she's okay, but just disappearing off a casino floor like that? I don't like what you're telling me. That's just the truth. I wish it were different.'

Sam pulled the Cherokee to a stop nose-to-nose with my wagon and doused the headlights. The glow from a streetlight washed into the car from the driver's side, silhouetting Sam against the glass.

'The dots I'm connecting are actually way more interesting to me,' he said. 'See, if I put on my decoder glasses I see your footprints just about everywhere I look, which shouldn't be too surprising considering your history with this kind of thing.'

I opened my mouth to disagree. Closed it. What was the point?

Sam went on. 'First? I think maybe you and your partner, Diane, have some connection to the Millers – I'm guessing Mrs. Miller, Rachel – that I don't know about. Want me to guess? Okay, I suspect it goes back a few years, maybe more. Could I guess what it is? Yes, I could.' He paused, allowing me to digest his conclusion.

'Next? I think that the Camaro man has some connection to the guy who owns the water-park house and for some reason that connection makes you much more nervous than a simple rented garage should make you. So it's something else entirely. I'd like to know exactly what that connection is, but experience tells me I'm not going to get shit from you tonight, so I'm trying not to give myself a headache about it. My assumption at the moment is that you think it has something to do with Mallory Miller. Frankly, that worries me. It worries me that you're playing detective again, and it worries me just the slightest little bit that you might be on to something that we don't know.'

The sound of Sam's stomach complaining that it hadn't seen a meal in a while filled the car. The growl made me realize that I was hungry, too. I wondered if Lauren had saved me some dinner.

'More? We already know that you and Diane were the ones who found that vic on Broadway. And—'

'Sam, you just called Hannah Grant a "vic."'

'I shouldn't have said that. She was your friend. My apologies. Habit, I'm sorry.'

'That's not what I meant. You think Hannah's a victim? You think her death was a homicide? The coroner called it "undetermined." Has that changed?'

'It's Slocum's and Olson's, not mine. I'm not the authority on that case. Manner was undetermined yesterday. Manner is undetermined today. End of story, sorry.'

In almost any other circumstance I would have pushed him. But I needed Sam to stay interested in Diane and Bob. We could get back to Hannah later. I couldn't help but wonder, though: *What do the cops have?*

'What else?' I asked. 'You were going to say something else.'

'Reese Miller,' Sam said. He'd forgotten which finger he'd used to keep track of his last point. By default, he chose his thick thumb to represent Reese Miller. 'Why are you so interested in him? Where the heck does he fit into this puzzle?' He turned his head toward me and looked right at me. 'Do you even know?'

I opened my mouth, closed it, and emitted some sound that was closer to a sigh than anything else. Reese was an unknown to me. I said, 'No, I don't really know anything about him.'

'Good,' he said. 'Listen, I have to get the babysitter home and I promised to help Simon with a poem he's writing. Did you have to write poems at his age? It's a good thing. Getting kids to write a lot. Keep me up to speed on Diane.'

I opened the Jeep's door and was freshly surprised by the bitter chill of the January night. 'Thanks, Sam.'

'Yeah,' he said. Then: 'Wait.'

I leaned back into the car. Sam looked away from me for a couple of seconds before he turned back. 'I know you expect me to find a way to help you. But I can't. There's no hook for me. There has to be something I can grab on to.'

'I don't especially want anything to do with this either, Sam. Since the day that Mallory fell off the face of the earth I've tried like hell to make this leave me alone. But it keeps tracking me down. From my point of view, you get close enough to this thing and you'll find it has as many hooks as a square foot of Velcro.'

I slammed the door shut and he drove off.

34

The clock read just shy of 8:30 when I walked in the front door of my house. Emily greeted me exuberantly, but I found my other two girls sound asleep in the master bedroom curled into the familiar big spoon/ little spoon configuration. They were surrounded by that night's bedtime books and Grace's favorite stuffed animals. Our not-so-stuffed poodle, Anvil, was curled into a tight ball at Grace's knees.

I was feeling remorse that I'd been missing out on the bedtime ritual so often.

Sound asleep at Grace's bedtime was a little early, even for Lauren, but the energy depletion that she suffered as a result of multiple sclerosis wasn't always easy to predict. If you asked her on a day when she wasn't suffering any of the acute effects of one of the disease's myriad symptoms, she'd tell you that what she hated most about the illness was that it made her days so much shorter. As each successive year took its toll, Lauren had fewer good hours, fewer strong hours, fewer waking hours, fewer hours when pain or weakness didn't drive her to bed. Ask her what she'd most like to change about having MS, and she'd tell you she wished her days were longer. She'd tell you that on most days her energy lasts about as long as daylight endures on a December day in Anchorage.

This had apparently been one of those Yukon days. That's what she called them. I'd call her from work and find her at her desk at the DA's office. I'd ask how she was doing. Too often she'd say, 'You know, babe. It's a Yukon day.'

I rearranged the comforter so that it provided some cover for both mother and daughter, kissed the tops of their heads, lifted Anvil from the sheets, and led the dogs outside to pee. Once the odd canine couple had done their thing and our little parade was safely inside the house, I checked for a message from Raoul or, even better, Diane.

Nothing.

I scrambled a couple of eggs, folded them into some honey wheat toast, and carried my plate into the living room. I ate standing up at the big windows that faced down into Boulder, trying to spot the house where Jenifer Donald was visiting her grandparents, trying to spot the overpriced house with the water park up near the foothills on Twelfth, trying to spot the small house on Broadway where Hannah Grant had died.

Far to the west, on the other side of the vast mountains, I wondered if Raoul was on his date with the woman from Venetian security. Or was he still chatting up gamblers at the craps tables trying to find someone who remembered his wife?

And where the hell in all those lights were Bob and his cherry Camaro?

What answers, if any, were sitting in a Kinko's box in my office?

My impulse was to charge downtown and find out.

I reminded myself that what Bob had written was part of a novel.

Fiction.

Stuff he'd made up.

Stuff I was supposed to wait to read.

35

Diane, in rare moments of candid self-doubt, would express astonishment that she'd ended up with Raoul. 'Why me? Look at me. Look at him. Why on earth did he choose me?'

Raoul was an olive-skinned Spaniard with piercing eyes, a prodigious intellect, an entrepreneurial instinct for innovation, and a bloodhound's nose for money. He had a smile as sweet as honey, and his thick hair looked black until the sun hit it just so and lit it up like golden floss. He could give charm lessons to George Clooney, put on continental airs when he felt the situation demanded, or pull on faded jeans and cowboy boots and slide right into a farmhouse discussion of southern Colorado water rights as though it had been his family that had cut the first irrigation canals into the dusty San Luis Valley.

In much the same way that the progeny of Holocaust survivors have been indelibly scarred by Germany's twentieth-century embrace of the Nazis, Raoul had been bruised deeply – down to the place where tissue ends and the soul takes up corporeal space – by Spain's fifty-year flirtation with fascism. Memories of long-absent relatives, and nightmared imaginings of what had happened to them at the hands of Franco's Falangists, flowed through his blood like perpetual antibodies to authority.

The result? Raoul had wide shoulders, and a chip on them that was sometimes big enough to obscure his handsome head.

My impatience to hear an update finally compelled me to dial Raoul's cell number before I climbed into bed. He answered after three rings.

'Yeah?' he said to the accompaniment of Las Vegas background

183

sounds. Music, traffic. Something else – hissing, muted explosions. I wasn't sure what it was.

The single word he'd spoken as he answered had carried a boat-load of hope; every time his phone rang he was praying that the caller was Diane. To me, ironically, his hope meant that he hadn't found her. My own hope, which was hovering like a flat stone skipping on a smooth lake, sank instantly to the muddy bottom.

'It's me, Raoul. You didn't find her.'

He said something in Catalonian. It sounded like *'bandarras.'* From the spitting tone he employed, I guessed it had been a pro-fanity and that it didn't really require translation, although I was always more than a little eager to add to my knowledge of the pro-fane spectrum of his native tongue.

'Were you able to talk with that woman from hotel security?' I found myself shouting to be heard above the din.

'Marlina has a story,' he said. 'Unfortunately, it takes her a while to tell it.'

'Yeah?' I didn't get whatever he was saying.

'She's from Mexico. What's on her mind is about her brother and something that happened to him on the way from Chihuahua to Tucson. She needs to talk. With some women, it has to first be about them. She is one of those women. *Fer un solo de flauta.* Trust me, it's the only way.'

Raoul spoke about women the way he spoke about IPOs and RAM. With authority. Again, I considered asking him for a transla-tion of the Catalonian, but I didn't.

'You haven't learned anything?' I asked.

'Not yet.'

He sounded fried – Raoul's anxiety seemed to be swelling with every conversation we had. The appearance of my voice, and not his wife's, on the line had robbed him of whatever buoyancy had been keeping him afloat. I could feel the deflation in his spirits as hope leaked away; whatever vessel he was in was taking on water and he was getting tired of bailing.

'Did you find anyone playing at the craps tables who remem-bered Diane?'

'I set up a half-million-dollar credit line. I assumed that would give me a little bit of latitude in the casino.'

I couldn't imagine. 'Yeah? How much were you betting?'

'Five or ten. Sometimes twenty.'

Thousand. 'You win anything?' I asked.

'I did all right,' he said. Raoul, I knew, would take no joy in a big pile of craps winnings. In his various tech businesses, he played for stakes that would make a huge pile of casino chips seem paltry by comparison. But given the events of the last twenty-four hours, Raoul would take some pleasure in the fact that he had taken the money – if it were a large enough pile – from the coffers of the Venetian.

'How good?

'I'm up eighty or so. The only luck I'm having in this town is at a craps table.'

I whistled. 'Thousand?'

'Minus four. I tipped a couple of dealers. I'm hoping they're appreciative, might let me buy them a drink.'

Two craps dealers were each a couple of grand richer than they'd been before they'd gone to work that day and met Raoul. With that kind of incentive they might be inclined to have a drink with him after their shifts were over.

I asked, 'When are they off?'

'Three hours or so. We'll see what happens. My expectations are low. I gave a woman some money to pass each of them a note that said I wanted to talk with them. She says she did it, but who knows? Their bosses may have warned them off.'

'A frustrating day?'

'They're the house. They have the cards; they have the odds. My only advantage is that I'm more motivated than they are. They don't understand that yet. One guy at the craps table slipped me his business card when he heard me ask the woman next to him about Diane. He's a VP for some shopping-center developer. They do malls.'

'A gambler?'

'In his heart, that kind of gambler. I waited until he left the table and then I called his mobile number after about twenty minutes. I told him I was the guy from the craps table. He said, "Not now." I asked, "When?" And he said, "I have your number now. I'll call you." Then he hung up.

'*Pastanaga.* I think he was playing with me.'

'He hasn't called?'

185

'In Vegas terms the night is young, right? Me? I'm twenty years older than I was at this time yesterday. A week more of this and I'll be ready to trade in the craps table for some pinochle.'

I could almost feel his despair. I was on the portable phone, wandering between the mostly dark kitchen and the mostly dark living room, where I stopped and found myself, once again, searching for Twelfth Street in Boulder's dark grid. Looking for the Millers' house, and for Doyle's.

The noise in my ear was Sinatra and percussion. Traffic, too. A siren.

'Are you in a club?'

'I'm at the Bellagio. Outside, watching the fountains. I like them. I know they're garish, but I like them. Have you ever seen them?'

'Only on TV.'

'Someday then.'

'Yes.' *Maybe.* 'With Diane.'

'With Diane, *sí*. Alain?'

I was a bit taken aback. He hadn't used the French pronunciation of my name for a long time.

'Yes.'

'If there were a man involved – with my wife – you would tell me?'

'What? You mean a—'

'Yes. *Un autre.* We're grown-ups here, right?'

That Raoul was susceptible to whatever affective tides the prospect of infidelity caused in other people surprised me. Where romance was concerned, Raoul lacked confidence the way Spider-Man lacks grip.

I said, 'To the best of my knowledge, this has nothing to do with another man. Nothing.'

'Thank you. I had to ask.'

'Raoul? The Rachel you're looking for? It's Mallory Miller's mother. That's who Diane went to Vegas to try to find.'

He was silent. I hadn't lost him; I could still hear the Sinatra and the fountains and the impatience of the traffic on the Strip, but Raoul wasn't speaking. As the interlude grew longer, I immediately flashed back to the night before and Diane's abrupt disappearance from the conversation I was having with her in the casino. My heart

186

accelerated like a teenage driver with a lead foot chasing after a pretty girl.

'Raoul? You there?'

'I'm here.'

'I was afraid I lost you.'

'You didn't lose me; I'm thinking. Diane went to see the missing girl's mother?'

'If you've followed Mallory's story in the news, you may also know that Rachel Miller suffers from mental illness. That might be important for you to know when you finally find her.'

'I don't read that kind of thing. Diane tells me, but she didn't tell me that. What kind of mental illness?'

I wasn't sure what the tabloids had reported. 'I know the answer to your question, Raoul, but I shouldn't say. It's something serious. Let's leave it at that.'

'Is she dangerous?'

'Rachel? Unlikely, highly unlikely.'

'Why did Diane want to see her?'

'I found a way to rationalize telling you who Rachel is. Giving you the why part is much harder. I'm sorry. And I'm not sure it will help you to know the answer. If I think it will, I'll tell you, I promise.'

The fact that Mallory's mother lived in Vegas, even the fact that she lived in Vegas and suffered from a severe mental illness, had been reported in the news media. I wasn't telling Raoul anything new by telling him that. If a patient tells a psychologist that the sun came up that morning, the news isn't necessarily confidential. The psychologist can share the revelation with others.

Raoul asked, 'Is Diane mixed up with whatever happened to Mallory Miller?'

'I can't' – I fumbled for a word that seemed to fit – 'address that.'

'You could if your answer was no.'

To myself, I said, *Thank you*. Raoul was absolutely right. I could tell him if the answer was no. But the answer wasn't no, and he knew exactly what that meant. 'I can't argue with your conclusion, Raoul.'

'This mess – whatever this mess is – it started with Hannah's death, didn't it?'

I thought for a moment about what I could say in reply. 'Hannah's death started a lot of balls rolling.'

He responded with, *'Si ma mare fos Espanya, jo seria un fill de puta.'* From the cadence and tone, I assumed it was profane, and from the reference to *Espanya* I guessed that a Spaniard wouldn't be thrilled to hear the phrase cross Raoul's Catalonian lips.

36

I hadn't been on the University of Colorado campus for a while. January wasn't my favorite time for a visit, and the Duane Physical Laboratories wasn't my ideal destination. But when my 11:15 appointment canceled on Thursday, I recognized that if I added the newly freed time to my midday lunch break, I had a seventy-five minute hole in my day. I decided to make the short trip from my office to the university.

The physics building is a large, angular, modern complex on the east side of the Boulder campus, segregated by roadways and by design from the cluster of lovely brick or flagstone structures that form the Mediterranean architectural core of the original university. The newer academic buildings surrounding Duane were, like Duane itself, looming, cast-concrete forms faced with just enough flagstone and roofed with just enough red tile to pay wink-wink homage to the Tuscan soul of the place.

I'd been aware of Duane for years; the tallest structure on campus, situated right across Colorado Avenue from the Muenzinger Psychology Building, it was hard to miss. But, given my arm's-length relationship with the physical sciences, or at least my arm's-length relationship with the study of the physical sciences, I'd never had reason to go inside Duane. Once I did make my way into the building looking for Bob, my initial impression was that Duane was state-university big and anonymous and that the notices on the bulletin boards were mostly about things I didn't understand and, more to the point, until that moment didn't even know that I didn't understand. A professor was looking for a research assistant to study femtosecond optical frequency combs. Another lab needed help developing microcalorimeters and bolometers based on superconducting thin-films cooled to 0.1 K.

189

I didn't know what any of it meant, not even close, but I was almost one hundred percent confident that I wasn't their man. The students wandering the flavorless hallways – students who likely deserved my respect because, unlike me, they might have a prayer of being able to translate the bulletin boards – seemed a bit more serious than those I was accustomed to running into in my usual haunts on campus.

A big, anonymous building full of serious students? I suspected that Bob had gravitated to the physics department by unconscious design and had ended up burrowing into an environment where he could survive – thriving for Bob wasn't really an option – for the many years he'd been putting in his time waiting for whatever would come next.

After a few false starts going to the wrong offices, I learned that Bob was actually a clerk/secretary in the office/lab where plasma physicists did their incomprehensible things. It turned out that Bob's boss, a middle-aged woman named Nora Santangelo who was shaped like a chunk of water main, was as curious as I was about Bob's whereabouts, and had a terrific intuitive sense of the parameters of Bob's peculiarities.

When I introduced myself I omitted the doctor part. I told Ms. Santangelo – she didn't strike me as the type of supervisor that a subordinate, or a visitor like myself, should call 'Nora' – that I was a friend of Bob's and that he had missed a rendezvous we'd planned for the previous evening and wasn't answering his phone.

She responded suspiciously, 'You're his friend? I didn't know he had any.'

Point, Ms. Santangelo.

It had taken some effort on my part to refocus her on the fact that I didn't know where Bob was. 'I called here this morning. The person who answered his phone told me he was out sick. But he's not at home, either. I'm concerned.'

'Well, to be honest, I am too. I hadn't called his home – that's not the sort of thing that Bob . . . appreciates. He missed a day of work back during the spring blizzard in 2003, but that's the only other time I can remember.'

Bob's previous absence was undoubtedly excused: The infamous March 2003 blizzard had dropped almost four feet of snow on Boulder. 'He didn't call in today?'

She shook her head. 'Or yesterday. Bob usually eats lunch at his desk. Puts his nose in a book or plays games online. Scrabble. Sometimes chess. He never hangs with the rest of the staff. Never. But Monday? Around eleven in the morning he told me he was going out for lunch. Came right up to my office, walked right up to my desk, and said, "Mrs. Santangelo, I'm going out to lunch." I was so surprised – and so pleased, really – that I told him to enjoy himself, to take a whole hour.'

'Did he?'

'Sure as heck did. He never came back at all. Didn't call in. I still don't know where he is.'

'Well,' I said, while I digested the news that Bob's vanishing act had started even earlier in the week than I'd suspected.

Ms. Santangelo and I were standing in her office and I was finding myself increasingly distracted by the tubular shape of her. I would swear that her thighs, hips, waist, bosom, and shoulders were all the exact same measurement. She wasn't particularly heavy; she just looked like she'd been forced to spend her formative years hibernating in a sausage casing.

'Listen,' she said. 'Bob is . . . different. Different – different. I inherited him when I came over here from Hellems – the history department? I used to think those folks in history were peculiar, but these physicists? Don't get me started; they're something else. And Bob, he's the oddest ball in the rack. Excuse my honesty, but if you know him then you know that already. He likes to keep his distance. He can be difficult for people to deal with, people who aren't sensitive to his . . . shall we say, tendencies. But he does his job. No more, mind you, not a scintilla more. Bob does just his job. And I've finally found him a desk in a lab where everybody seems to get along with him okay. What I'm saying is that he's not on a short leash like some of the people here. I'm not going to fire Bob for whatever . . . this is.' I watched her expression as her imagination took her someplace she hadn't previously considered. 'Within reason, of course.'

'Ms. Santangelo, it sounds like you know him well. Do you have any idea where I might look for him?'

She thought for a moment and shook her head. 'Sorry,' she said, as she took a step toward the door. 'But you'll call me if you hear anything? I am concerned. Bob grows on you.'

Like a mushroom, I thought. *Or a truffle.* Something parasitic.

'Of course.' I scrawled my pager number on a Post-it that I spotted on the desk behind me and handed it to her. 'Will you do the same?'

She said she would and I headed out the door. Before I'd cleared the threshold I stopped and turned back to her. 'Did Bob take his begonia with him? You know the one I'm talking about?'

She smiled at me. 'Of course I do. You do know him well. But I don't know the answer to your question. Why don't you and I go down to his desk and see about that darn Christmas begonia.'

As she led me down the hall toward the administrative area that included Bob's desk, I allowed myself the suspicion that Ms. Santangelo had quite a mouth on her when she was younger, but that a lot of ambition and some determined self-discipline had turned her from a damn-and-hell young woman to a darn-and-heck middle-aged one.

The Christmas begonia was sitting in what his boss said was its usual place on the corner of Bob's desk. The plant's presence told me one thing, but it told Ms. Santangelo two. She explained to me that if Bob anticipated being away from the office for an extended period – anything more than a long weekend constituted an extended period – he would carefully transport the begonia home with him. The transport was an elaborate process involving a beer-case flat and tented brown grocery bags. She also explained that if he anticipated being out of the office for a period even as long as a full day but not longer than three, he would move the plant and its pebble tray from the corner of his desk to the top of a waist-high bookshelf that sat beside a southeast facing window at the far end of the room.

'Always?' I asked.

'Always,' she confirmed, without hesitation. 'He never puts the begonia in direct sun. And he always watered it from below, you know, from the pebble tray. He knows what he's doing with it. Bob manages to keep the thing in bloom like that from Thanksgiving until spring break some years. People always comment on it, always.'

I'd already noted that the begonia was healthy, its blossoms prodigious. I stated the obvious: 'Bob didn't expect to be gone for this long, did he?'

Ms. Santangelo reached down and caressed the petals of one of the delicate begonia flowers. 'No, he didn't. I wonder if I should move it over to the bookcase so it can get some light while he's gone. Bob would. I know he would. I just don't know if he would want me to.'

I'd followed her hands to the desktop and was scouring the surface for a clue that might tell me something about Bob's destination when he'd left work to go out to lunch on Monday. Other than the Christmas begonia, though, his desktop was devoid of anything personal. I asked, 'When Bob plays games, does he use this computer?' I was pointing at the less-than-state-of-the-art machine that filled a third of his desk.

'No, he doesn't. He has a laptop, he brings it with him to work every day. He asked me a long time ago if it's okay with me for him to hook it up to the university's network over lunch to play his games. I told him to have at it. Bob doesn't cheat. If he's unsure about a rule, he asks.'

Her response deflated me a little. 'He took his laptop with him to lunch?'

'I don't know, heck,' she said, and started rummaging in the drawers of Bob's desk. From my vantage the drawers appeared to have been arranged by a demonic closet organizer.

'Don't see it,' she said. 'He must have taken it.'

'Do you know anything at all that might help me find him?'

'I wish I did,' she said. 'I really wish to heck that I did.' She made her hands into fists and lifted them so that they came together just below her chin. 'A few of my people here are totally reliable, you know what I mean? But some of the rest? Flakes. If they were gone for the amount of time that Bob's been gone – a couple of days – I wouldn't give it a second thought. Par for the darn course is what I'd think. Par for the darn course. But Bob? He's not part of either group. He's not regular, he's not a flake. He's . . .

'You know what? I'll just say it: I don't really like Bob, but I . . . like him. Do you understand? I do hope he's okay.'

I understood.

I crammed in a quick stop at Mustard's Last Stand on Broadway, inhaled my hot dogs with only a small side of guilt over the indulgence, and made it back to my office with just a few minutes to spare before my next appointment.

37

Was the after-work plan I cobbled together a good idea? Probably not. But once my workday was done I realized that I was fresh out of good ideas, so I was left to settle for questionable ones.

I assumed that it would take me a day or so to get an appointment arranged to see the inside of Doyle's house, but I was wrong. When I phoned the listing agent asking if she could meet me for a showing, her eyes apparently began flashing dollar signs at the prospect of mining a buyer for a house for which she was already representing the seller. She asked me what time I got off work. I told her I was done at six. Without a moment's hesitation she asked if 6:15 would work for me. 'You won't believe the water features in the backyard,' she exclaimed. 'They are worth the purchase price all by themselves. Trust me, they're . . .'

I didn't tell her that I already knew.

When I called Viv, our part-time nanny, she informed me that Lauren would be late getting home, too. Viv promised me that she was happy to stay with Grace a little longer. In my head I added a small bonus to her monthly check. I also left Lauren a voice mail at her office that I would pick up some Thai takeout for dinner.

The woman I was meeting was named Virginia Danna. She pulled up in front of Doyle's house in a silver Lexus SUV, the big version, the fancy Land Cruiser clone that was all shoulders and hips. I was parked a couple of doors farther north and walked the short distance from my car in time to meet up with her near the front porch.

'Dr. Gregory?' she beamed when she spotted me coming. 'You're going to absolutely love this place. The bathrooms need a little work, but oh, oh, the potential with the . . .' She was a tall, thin – the word *svelte* actually came to mind – elegantly dressed woman with just a hint of an accent, as though she'd emigrated to the United States from someplace when she was quite young. Despite her last name, for some reason I was guessing she was from Brazil. Her wardrobe made few concessions to winter. She wore no coat and she balanced effortlessly on high heels. All in all, very not-Boulder.

'Ms. Danna?'

'Yes, yes. I'm so sorry. My manners sometimes escape me when I'm excited. And this house, it . . .' She reached out to shake my hand. 'Will you excuse me for just a moment?' She pressed a speed-dial button on her cell. 'Yes, yes. Dr. Gregory is here. We're going in now. Fine, fine. Yes, I'm sure. *Doctor* Gregory. That's right, on Twelfth. Thanks!' Ms. Danna turned back to me. 'With what's happened to some poor agents in Denver – I'm sure you heard – we're required to check into the office before all private showings. I hope you understand, it's . . .'

'Of course.'

She was in the lockbox in seconds, retrieved the front door key, and held the door open so I could precede her inside. 'I don't really like to show houses when they're unfurnished like this one is, but . . .' She sighed. 'I tried to get the owner to rent some things, you know, just for . . . The right furniture makes everything seems so much brighter and . . .'

Ms. Danna had an obvious penchant for uncompleted thoughts. Regardless, I was grateful for the opening she'd just offered about Doyle. Offhandedly I asked, 'Is the owner in town? Did he move to a larger house?'

She was easing me out of the cramped entryway into an adjacent living room with scratched red-oak floors, the original single-pane metal casement windows, and an undistinguished fireplace. 'In town? No, no. Not exactly. But we're in constant touch, constant. I promise I can get a response to an offer in a heartbeat. A day at the outside. He's motivated, he is – he's already dropped the price once. Don't get me wrong; I mean that in all the right ways. Do you live here in Boulder?'

The last question was ripe with raw hope that my answer would be yes and that I might offer her the opportunity for a real estate trifecta: a buyer who purchases a home from a listing agent and then agrees to enlist the same agent to sell his existing home. Three commissions – seller, buyer, seller – and a veritable cascade of closings.

'I do. In Spanish Hills. But I work downtown near the Mall, on Walnut, and with the traffic lately, the drive is getting . . .' I tried to find the right word before I settled on 'tiresome.'

Her excitement at my disclosure was palpable. A Spanish Hills listing? Although naming one of a few other even more precious local neighborhoods might have earned me an almost orgasmic response, in Boulder it didn't get a whole lot better for local real estate purveyors than Spanish Hills. 'Inventory' in Spanish Hills usually meant that there was a single home for sale. With my pronouncement that I lived on one of the rare parcels across the valley, I felt an instantaneous change in the electrical charge in the room.

But Ms. Danna knew that she had to sell me on the house at hand and couldn't risk my getting too sentimental about leaving my current home. She played her hand well. 'Don't I know?' she said. 'That's the beauty of living right here on the Hill. Everything is so close: Chautauqua, downtown, the greenbelt, the mountains, the turnpike, shopping. The location is so . . .'

Perfect?

I caught her staring down at my left hand and accurately predicted her next question. 'You're married?'

'Yes.'

'Children?'

'One.'

'Spanish Hills?' she mused. 'It's so pretty up there. I have clients who have waited for years to . . . the views are so . . .'

Expansive? And the houses so . . . expensive. I didn't have the heart to tell her that I lived in one of the few modest homes – modest by Boulder standards – in the whole neighborhood. She'd be so disappointed.

'Yes, it is lovely,' I said, but I was allowing my eyes to wander the recesses of the bland living room and was beginning to wonder what I'd hoped to gain by traipsing through Doyle's empty house. I moved through an opening from the living room into an equally bland dining room. Ms. Danna followed right behind me.

'Good size, don't you think?' she said. 'Plenty of room in here for a . . .'

Table? Family gathering?

The kitchen had been recently renovated and had a nice little built-in breakfast nook with a large window facing the yard. A compact laundry room was stuffed into what had probably once been a butler's pantry. The quality of the remodel wasn't congruous with the asking price for the house; the new cabinetry and appliances were the kind of warehouse stuff you might expect to find in a Boulder rental.

Ms. Danna apparently shared my impression. 'Some new countertops in here, maybe stone, or even cast concrete, and you'd need to do something with that . . .'

What? I couldn't tell. 'Yes,' I said. I was beginning to recognize her real estate dilemma. She was trying to sell a house in Boulder in winter that's main selling point was its yard. And yards don't show too well when they've been stripped of all their green, and elaborate water features don't show too well when they've been drained of all their H_2O.

We made it through a quick tour of the two upstairs bedrooms and two adjacent cramped bathrooms. She had been correct in her earlier appraisal: The bathrooms were in need of a sledgehammer and a good designer. The master bath was lined with chest-high plastic tile in a color that resembled one of the fluids that Grace emitted from her nose when she had a sinus infection.

As my enthusiasm for the house failed to swell, Ms. Danna's enthusiasm about her prospects seemed to go into decline, but she tenaciously held on to some hope for the finale. 'The two highlights of this property are the media room in the basement, and that wonderful backyard. Which would you like to see first?'

She didn't wait for my reply. She hit two switches on the wall near the back door and instantly the yard lit up like a resort. My eyes were drawn to the granite waterfall that I'd seen in the dark the night before.

'That's nice,' I said.

'Nice? Imagine the water splashing over those rocks, the sound of that stream. Fish in the pond. The birds, the flowers. In spring, I think you'll find that it's . . .'

Breathtaking?

'The basement?' I asked. 'Where are the stairs?'

The lower level wasn't the same size as the upper level. The media room was big enough – I pegged it at fifteen by twenty feet – but the whole basement wasn't even twice that size. A bland powder room, a mechanical room, and a long, narrow storage room completed the downstairs floor plan. On the top third of the storage room wall was a wide opening with a hinged lid.

'More storage?' I asked.

'Crawl space,' Ms. Danna said.

'May I?' I asked, touching the handle on the door.

'Of course.'

I opened the awning-style lid and peered into a neat crawl space about three feet high. The floor of the entire space was lined with thick-mil plastic.

'Radon?' I asked, trying to act like someone who was actually interested.

She nodded. 'Nothing to worry about. It's under control. Completely. I have all the reports. It's been mitigated to levels that the neighbors would love to have. Really, it's . . .'

Whatever. I closed the lid on the crawl space.

'Did you see that projector in the media room?' she asked. 'It's a top-of-the-line Runco. And, yes . . . yes, it's included. All the theater electronics are included. Audio, video. All of them. Denon, B&O. The furniture, too. I don't have to tell you that those chairs are all recliners, and they're not La-Z-Boys. Custom. Crème de la crème. Electronics, finishes, everything. He spared no expense down here. The owner loved his home theater, he . . .'

I didn't know what she was talking about component-wise, and I didn't really care. I was one of those people who couldn't imagine going down into the basement to watch a DVD so I could pretend I was sitting in a theater. I'd just as soon curl up with my wife and daughter and my dogs and watch a video on the old VCR in the bedroom.

'Wow,' I said, trying to sound enthusiastic.

'Oh, I forgot, the screen . . .' She took my hand and led me out to the far wall of the theater. A big white movie screen was hung within an ornately carved frame of polished wood. I was guessing mahogany. 'Now, don't you touch it – fingerprints, fingerprints. I forgot who makes it – somebody good, no, somebody great. I have it in my notes. It's the same screen that Spielberg has in his private screening room at his place in . . . The same exact one. It's like . . . the best. I promise I have the name back in the office. I'll get it for you. I will. First . . .'

Thing? 'Wow.' It looked exactly like a movie screen. Spielberg knew what he was doing.

After what I hoped was a suitable amount of time spent staring at the blank screen, I led Ms. Danna up the stairs and as we walked out the front door I gave her my appraisal of the property. 'It's a little small for us, I'm afraid.'

She was ready for that argument. 'Oh, I know, I know, but the potential? You get a good architect to find a way to cantilever the upstairs a little bit and you could expand that second story in a heartbeat. Think of the covered porch down below and the views from your new master suite upstairs. Just think! You could have a deck that faces the Flatirons! And closets? Oh, I don't have to tell you, do I? You're a man with . . .'

Vision?

The night was cold and a bitter wind was blowing down from the north with the sharp bite of Saskatchewan.

As Ms. Danna replaced the keys in the lockbox she made it clear that she was eager to show me a couple of other 'things,' though 'the price points are up a notch or two from here.' I declined, although I admit that I was curious exactly how many digits constituted a 'notch' in Boulder's hyperinflated housing market. Resigned, she gave me her card and asked for one of mine.

'I'm sorry,' I said. 'I don't have any with me.'

It was partly true. I didn't have any with me.

But I wasn't sorry.

I walked her down the serpentine front walk to her big Lexus and shook her hand, thanking her for her time. Over her left shoulder – at the upstairs window of Mallory Miller's house – I spotted what I thought was the same silhouette I'd seen the night before while I'd been trespassing in the backyard with Sam.

Ms. Danna saw me looking. 'Such a tragedy,' she said. 'That girl's father must feel . . .'

Awful.

38

'Finding reality here is like looking for condoms in a convent. There might be some around, but they're not going to be easy to locate.'

Raoul was talking to me about Las Vegas, and about how he'd spent his day. His voice was as tired as my toddler's when she was up past her bedtime. Raoul was an optimist by nature, an entrepreneur by character. Watching him treading water in a sea of despair was so unexpected that it felt surreal.

The Las Vegas cops remained uninterested in Raoul's missing wife. He had pressed them to try to ascertain at what point Diane would be considered 'missing.' One detective told him that, 'Given the circumstances, it would certainly take more than a long weekend. And so far, Mr. Estevez, that's all she's been gone. One long weekend.' The hospitals continued to have no inpatients matching Diane's name or description. As a sign of his desperation, Raoul had hired a local private investigator who was apparently chewing up money much faster than he was uncovering clues about Diane's whereabouts. All he'd learned so far was Rachel's address. When he checked for her there, no one answered.

Marlina, the woman from Venetian security, enticed Raoul to buy her breakfast at a place near downtown that was filled mostly with locals. They spoke Spanish while they ate. Raoul learned that Mar-lina's brother was in INS detention in Arizona, learned how he got there – or at least Marlina's version of how he got there – and learned in excruciating detail how Marlina felt about the whole affair, but he didn't learn anything about what the casino surveillance tapes revealed.

After the frustrating breakfast, Raoul moved on to an alternative avenue of investigation: The Love In Las Vegas Wedding Chapel. As he told me about it, my impression was that relating the story of what happened there seemed to relax him.

According to Raoul's tale, the minister of the Love In Las Vegas Wedding Chapel was the Rev. Howard J. Horton. By training he was an actor who had enjoyed some success as a young man on Broadway, even once landing the role as understudy for the lead of some Tommy Tune extravaganza. After a move to California to find fortune on the Left Coast, Horton had actually defied the odds and made a living in Hollywood until his thirty-seventh birthday doing bit parts on sitcoms and lawyer and cop shows and getting occasional throwaway lines on big-budget features. In successive years in his late twenties he had been filmed making cocktails for Sean Connery, being pistol-whipped by Al Pacino, and flirting shamelessly with Sharon Stone just before being pummeled into submission by her leading man.

Raoul didn't think he had caught any of those particular movies.

The bit parts hadn't been enough to provide the foundation for Horton's hoped-for long-term career as a distinguished character actor, and as his face matured the parts he was being offered didn't. To pay the bills he'd eventually gravitated to dinner theater and later on made his way to Vegas, where he did some emceeing at shows on the Strip, fell in love with heroin, heroically managed to 'divorce the damn bitch,' and eventually ended up winning a thirty-nine percent stake in the Love In Las Vegas Wedding Chapel in a poker game with some locals that had started one cocktail hour on a Wednesday and ended late in the morning or early in the afternoon – Horton didn't quite remember; it had been that kind of game – the following day.

Horton was forty-seven years old and had been the minister of the moment at the Love In Las Vegas for almost seven years. On bad days he consoled himself that it paid the bills.

The British accent and aristocratic demeanor that Horton employed for the tourists who came to Vegas for matrimony were pure shtick, and the slick Vestimenta suit he wore in the relentless Nevada heat nothing but costume. He'd won the suit from a gay guy from Atlanta in another poker game – that table populated, with the exception of Horton, entirely by out-of-towners – and he told Raoul a hilarious story about them both stripping down to their undies to exchange clothes after the game. Howard had given up his favorite pair of cargo shorts and a well-worn Tommy Bahama silk shirt.

Raoul promised me that he'd get around to telling me the part about the protracted negotiation for the Atlanta man's thong another time.

'You promise?' I said.

'Absolutely,' Raoul assured me.

In a city where visitors were primed to expect spectacle, Horton's wedding show at the Love In Las Vegas was a whisper of sophisticated, or faux-sophisticated, understatement. At the Love In Las Vegas, tourists who were so inclined could be married, not by an Elvis impersonator or a cross-dressing reject from Cirque, but by an ex-patriot British lord who seemed intent on bringing his interpretation of a little bit of the best of the Church of England, whatever that was, to the Nevada desert.

While Raoul waited to get a few minutes alone with the Rev. Horton so he could ask some questions about Diane and Rachel Miller, he had to choose between frying outside in the parking lot in the he-was-told unusual-for-January ninety-three-degree heat or sitting in the air-conditioned comfort of the chapel and observing the nuptials of a young couple that had driven all the way from Spraberry, Texas – that's just outside Midland and not too far from Odessa – to tie the knot in Las Vegas.

The engaged had written their own marriage vows and brought a cassette of the music they wanted played during the ceremony. Her vows ran onto three legal-sized yellow tablet pages.

His didn't.

The bride wore white – an ill-fitting empire-style dress with a long train that her second cousin had scored at the Filene's Basement annual everything-for-$299 wedding dress running-of-the-bulls in Boston. The bride was twenty-two, but didn't look it. She was as innocent as the prairie, and her face was full of the wonder that every woman's face should have before she weds for the first time.

On the final stretch of Highway 95 into Vegas she'd made a valiant attempt to memorize all the vows that she had penned onto the yellow legal pad on the haul from Spraberry to El Paso on Interstate 10, but during the actual ceremony she'd had to consult her notes every few seconds during her long recital of eternal love.

In his retelling, Raoul generously wrote it off to nerves.

Her betrothed was twenty-six years old and was dressed in a tuxedo jacket he'd borrowed from his sister's husband, a ruffled-front tux shirt sans tie, and clean – and pressed – Wranglers. His hair, greasy from all the road time, was combed into a mullet that was as sleek and shiny as the skin of an under-refrigerated fish. This was his third marriage and his second wedding in Las Vegas – he was once widowed and once divorced – and by demeanor and practice he was a love-honor-and-obey-till-death-do-us-part kind of groom. By history he apparently wasn't exactly a love-honor-and-obey-till-death-do-us-part kind of husband, but he'd promised his fiancée repeatedly – including once during the ceremony – that all that rutting was behind him.

The groom's self-written vows were an obviously plagiarized, parsed version of the popular standard. Raoul's impression was that the guy would have been better off just allowing Rev. Horton to do his almost-Anglican-cleric thing. But, Raoul noted, the bride didn't seem to be at all offended by her husband-to-be's lack of vow-writing prowess.

The wedding music, which was played over and over and over again in a toxic loop, consisted of a single upbeat song by Shania Twain with a lot of *uh, uh, oh* s in the lyrics. Raoul couldn't quite figure out the romantic relevance of the tune, but the cumulative weight of the pure repetition of the *uh, uh, oh* s eventually rendered him willing to accept the silky voiced singer's implied warning about whatever the hell it was. By the time the ceremony was over and the newlyweds had kissed and kissed again and walked hand-in-hand down the aisle toward the desert inferno that awaited them outside, Raoul knew just about all he wanted to know about the couple from Spraberry whose wedding he had just helped celebrate, and he also knew he never wanted to hear the damn *uh, uh, oh* song again in his life.

Ever.

'He may have divorced "the bitch" but Reverend Howie still sleeps with her cousin,' Raoul said to me. 'He drinks a bit, and then he drinks a bit more. We spent most of the afternoon at the kind of saloon the Vegas Chamber of Commerce doesn't want tourists to see. That's when I heard his life story and got all that fascinating background on the happy couple from west Texas. Have to give the guy credit, though – Howie knew I was paying but he got the same crappy well-scotch he drinks in that bar every day. He didn't ask the bartender to dust off the single malts just because I was running the tab.'

'Did you learn anything?'

It was late in Colorado – almost eleven at night – and I was exhausted. Although it was an hour earlier in Nevada, Raoul's voice told me that his long day and long story had left him every bit as tired as I was. Maybe more. But something about his day had at least temporarily softened the edge of his despair.

'He wouldn't talk to me about this Rachel woman. I could tell from his little act that he knew who she was, but he wouldn't answer any of my questions, wouldn't even admit that she hung out at his chapel. When I showed him Diane's photograph he wouldn't admit that he'd ever seen her before. I knew he was lying; wasn't sure exactly about what, or why, but I knew he was lying. I was beginning to think I was going to have to just stake out the damn wedding chapel and wait for Rachel to show up again and lead me to Diane.'

'I'm sorry.'

'No, no. That's when it hit me. I lowered my voice to a whisper, pulled a little pile of thousand-dollar chips from the Venetian out of my pocket, stacked them up in front of me, and asked Howie exactly how much he was being paid.'

'Paid for what?' I said.

'That's just what he said to me. All offended and everything. Reverend Howie's a smart guy. He's on the edge, but he has some pride. I don't think he's too dishonest. At the chapel he makes a living providing a service, as screwy as the service is. He supplements his income by taking people's money, or whatever else they might want to bet, in high-stakes poker games. But he plays those games fair. His MO? He sets people up by being a better actor than they give him credit for, and then he takes their money by being a better poker player than they give him credit for. This time? I already know he's a good enough actor, and I wouldn't think about sitting down to a hand of Texas Hold 'Em with the guy.'

'Yeah?' I had one ear focused on Raoul's Las Vegas story, the other tuned to Grace's room. She was making the kinds of nighttime noises that often precede one of those restless nights that end up with one of her parents dozing nearby on the rocker in her room until dawn. I said a silent prayer that my little daughter was merely enduring a troublesome dream.

Raoul said, 'Eventually, he told me. I had to make it clear I wasn't going away, but he finally said, "Fifty."'

'I'm sorry, Raoul. I'm too tired. I don't get it.'

'I didn't get it at first, either. See, my brainstorm was that I thought that Rachel Miller must be paying him. That that was why he let her attend all the weddings. I figured she might be slipping him five bucks, maybe ten, per ceremony. But he was trying to convince me that she was paying him fifty bucks a pop – fifty – to sit in this tacky chapel while Reverend Howie did his pretentious I-now-declare-you-husband-and-wife song and dance.' Raoul paused. 'Do you know how many people get married in Las Vegas on an average day? One hundred and fifty-three. That's what Reverend Howie told me.'

'If it's people, wouldn't it have to be a hundred and fifty-two or a hundred and fifty-four?' I asked. 'Maybe you mean couples; the number can't really be odd.'

Raoul sighed. 'Alain, your point?'

I did the math. Five weddings a week: two hundred and fifty dollars. Ten weddings a week: five hundred dollars. Five weddings a day, with one day off each week: fifteen hundred dollars. That meant that for Rachel Miller to attend weddings to her heart's content would cost somewhere between two thousand and six thousand dollars a month, or between twenty-four and seventy-plus thousand dollars a year.

Plus gifts. Holy moly. Where the hell would a schizophrenic woman living on the streets of Las Vegas get that kind of money?

I asked Raoul, 'Do you believe him?'

'At first, I thought he might be inflating the numbers to see how the negotiations would go with me, that I might be sitting in that saloon watching him drink scotch so that I could try to outbid Rachel for some crazy reason. You know, offer him more than fifty to turn her away.'

'He's making pretty good money by allowing her to stick around for weddings.'

'That part seems clear. Tell me, how sick is Rachel? No details – I'm not asking for anything confidential – just rate it for me. Do it in a way I can understand.'

I couldn't tell him anything specific about Rachel's mental health mostly because I really didn't know anything specific about Rachel's current mental health. 'With the kind of disease that someone like Rachel has, with the kind of chronicity she's endured – she could have very visible symptoms. If you were to measure the disease of a person like that on the figurative ten-scale, say, on a bad day – a day when she's not taking appropriate medicine – she could be approaching double digits.'

'On that ten-scale?' Raoul asked.

'Yes.'

He emitted a high-pitched whistle. 'See, that's what I thought. That kind of sick is scary to people like me. Which means that Rachel is ill enough to be a serious liability at a place like the Love In Las Vegas. What bride wants somebody that disturbed camped out in the front row of her wedding?

'Reverend Howie's fee is insurance: He makes Rachel pay to attend the weddings. Who knows, he may even limit the weddings he lets her attend. Maybe he picks them himself. Makes a judgment about which ones are safe for her to be at, which ones she might create a distraction, cost him some business.'

'Raoul, if Rachel were attending all the weddings she wanted and if she were paying that much, it would cost a fortune. Where would she get that kind of money?'

Before the words were out of my mouth, I heard a prolonged whimper from Grace's room. *Damn*.

'This town?' he said. 'Too many bad ways to answer that question. Way too many.'

I shuddered at the thought of what perverse advantage some people might gain over someone as ill as Rachel Miller. 'What did Howie finally admit to you?'

'Just that she gives him money so he'll allow her to attend the ceremonies. And this is the funny part – she doesn't pay him herself – the money comes from someone else, someone who makes Reverend

Howie very nervous. He wouldn't give me the person's name. He said, "You can buy me scotch all day and all night and I'm not going to give you a name." I even pushed one of the thousand-dollar chips from the Venetian across the table and left it right in front of him. I said, "Name and phone number, Howard, and it's yours." He picked it up, flipped it, ran his fingers over the surface, and pushed it back onto my side of the table.

'I added two more and made it a nice little pile. He pushed them all right back to me. I added two more. He did the same thing.'

Howie had turned down five grand. I was thinking, *Wow*. 'So what are you going to do, Raoul?' I asked.

'I took four chips off the pile and slid the one that remained back across the table. I said, "Different question. Man or woman?"

'"Yeah?" Howie asked me. "For a grand? That's all you want to know?" I said that was the deal and he actually had to think about it. He is so wary of this person that gives him money so Rachel can attend weddings that he actually considered turning down a thousand dollars rather than reveal to me the person's *gender*. Eventually, he picked up the chip and slipped it into his shirt pocket like it was a pack of matches. He said, "It's a man. Not a man you want to fuck with."'

'That was it?' I said. 'That's all you got for a thousand dollars?'

'In business you don't always get value at the front end of a relationship. At the start you form a bond, establish platforms, ensure access. What I got for my thousand dollars is I got Howie on my payroll. And I reduced the possible suspects by half.'

'How do you find the man you're looking for?'

Raoul sighed. 'You remember a guy in Denver named Norm Clarke? Use to write for the *Rocky*.'

I remembered him. 'The gossip columnist with the patch on his eye?'

'*Sí*. Well, I know him – he did a story on me back in the tech boom times. He lives in Vegas now, knows everybody. I'm meeting him downstairs a little later for a drink. I'm hoping he can help me find the man Howie was talking about.'

Grace's unsettled whimper suddenly blossomed into a wail that was so powerful I could have sworn her lungs had been temporarily replaced by air compressors.

Raoul didn't need to be told our conversation was over. I sprinted in Grace's direction, praying that I could quiet her before Lauren's sleep was shattered.

39

After getting all of four hours' sleep I got all of four hours' warning before the next shoe dropped. I spent most of those four hours wondering whether having any warning at all was a good thing or a bad thing.

I never quite decided.

Patients, when they call my office number, are given a voice-mail instruction to call my pager directly in the case of an emergency. How often do my patients take advantage of the opportunity to reach me on my beeper? Once or twice in a bad month, infrequently enough that the mere sight of an unfamiliar phone number on my pager makes me anxious. So, on Thursday morning, while I was idling at the intersection of Broadway and Baseline on the way to work and my beeper vibrated and displayed an unfamiliar (303) 443-number, I was wary.

The 443 prefix meant the call came from a Boulder address. That's all I knew.

I returned the page as soon as I stepped into my office.

'This is Alan Gregory,' I said. 'I'm returning a page to this number.' I don't use the 'Doctor' appellation in those circumstances because I don't know if the person who called me will answer the phone or if someone else will. If it's someone else, discretion might dictate that my profession remain secret.

'Thanks for calling back so soon,' the man on the line said. 'This is Bill Miller.' And then, as if I might not know, he added, 'I'm Mallory's dad.'

What a sad thing, I mused, that he could use his daughter's unfortunate notoriety as a quick social identifier. And an even sadder thing that he would.

'Mr. Miller,' I said, buying some time while I hurriedly chewed and swallowed the ramifications of the simple fact that he had called me. 'What can I do for you?'

'Can you squeeze me in for an appointment? It's . . . important.'

'Umm,' I managed. My eloquence, given the circumstances, was profound.

'Today, if possible,' Bill Miller said.

I wondered whether he was asking me to get my tongue untied sometime 'today,' or whether he was asking for an appointment with me sometime 'today.'

If you asked me to write an ethics problem for a psychologists' licensing exam, or to dream up a delicious ethical conundrum for clinical psychology graduate students' comprehensive exams, I don't think I could have come up with something as devious as the dilemma I was facing at that moment.

'Do you have some time available?' he said, kindly pretending not to notice how flummoxed I was. 'I'll be as flexible as I need to be.'

The problem freezing my communication skills wasn't my schedule. My practice calendar that day was no more or less constricted than usual. On most days, if I was willing to give up a meal or stay late at the office, I could squeeze in an emergency.

The problem I was struggling with was that I didn't know if I could see Bill Miller professionally at all. The issue that was complicating what should have been a simple matter of logistics was a problem of professional ethics.

My initial impulse about the ethical maze? I didn't think that I could see Bill Miller as a clinician. But I wasn't at all sure I was correct in that snap assessment. The circumstances were complex. I quickly decided that I'd never confronted another set of facts quite as complex in my entire career.

The arguments for agreeing to see Bill Miller for therapy? They were easy. He had once, albeit briefly, been my patient. His present circumstances – or at least the ones I knew about – were so public and so tragic that they might cause someone to seek professional help. Empathy and compassion both argued for me to make myself available to him.

The arguments for refusing to see Bill Miller for therapy? This is where things got messy. Psychologists are under an ethical obligation to avoid what the profession calls 'dual relationships.' At its heart, this is a conflict-of-interest clause, intended to ensure that a clinician is free to act in the best interest of his or her patient, uncomplicated by competing forces. In practice, the dictum requires that a clinician not wear two different hats in a patient's life.

In simple English, it means I shouldn't do psychotherapy with the woman who cuts my hair. I shouldn't join a book group run by one of my therapy patients.

Simple, right?

Usually, yes. But try to apply those simple guidelines to my relationship with Bill Miller. That's what I had been trying to do for the hours between his morning phone call and the midday appointment time I'd eventually offered him.

I hadn't gotten very far.

Did the fact that I was a good friend of a Boulder cop who was involved with the investigation of Bill Miller's daughter's Christmas Day disappearance qualify as a dual relationship?

I wasn't sure, but the degrees of separation seemed to be sufficient insulation.

Did the fact that my practice partner was covering the clinical work of a therapist who had died, and possibly been murdered, weeks after seeing Bill Miller's daughter for a single therapy session qualify as a dual relationship?

Once again, blank spaces seemed to separate Bill Miller's place on the board from the space that I was occupying.

Did the fact that I was seeing a patient who parked his car in the garage of the house of the man who lived right next door to the Millers qualify as a dual relationship?

Maybe, maybe not. In isolation, I would lean in the direction of 'not.' My patient had spoken with Bill Miller's daughter, considered her a friend. That was all I knew about Bob's relationship to the Millers. It wasn't much of a tie.

Did the fact that my partner and good friend had disappeared while on a trip to Las Vegas to try to arrange a meeting with Bill's estranged wife constitute a dual relationship?

I knew of absolutely nothing that tied Bill Miller to any of those events.

Did the fact that my friend and partner's husband, someone else whom I enthusiastically considered a friend, was busy looking for Bill Miller's estranged wife qualify as a dual relationship?

Probably not, for all of the same reasons.

But I wasn't totally sure. I didn't know if I should be contemplating additive effects. If a wasn't greater than z, and b wasn't greater than z, and c wasn't greater than z, did I have to be concerned whether $a + b + c$ was greater than z?

Ethical algebra hadn't been covered in graduate school.

I interrupted my obsessing over the Bill Miller conundrum to address a practical problem: Diane was still missing, and Thursday was the day she was supposed to be back in her office seeing patients. Although Diane and I shared space, our practices were separate businesses: I didn't know how many patients she was scheduled to see, nor did I know any of their names.

My problem was that I had to figure out some innocuous yet compassionate way to notify Diane's patients that their doctor would not be in the office that day. My solution was to post a note on the front door, the patient entrance to our little building. It read:

> To Anyone With An Appointment With Dr. Diane Estevez:
> Dr. Estevez is unexpectedly away from the office to deal with an urgent situation.
> She is unable to cancel her appointments personally, but will not be in today.
> She will contact each of you individually upon her return, and she appreciates your understanding, and your patience.
> Dr. Alan Gregory

At the bottom of the note, I belatedly scrawled a handwritten offer that anyone with a clinical emergency should call me, and I left my pager number.

When I'd returned Bill Miller's call, the offer for an appointment that I eventually made to him wasn't any more straightforward than was the prevaricating note I had left for Diane's patients. 'I'm not sure I can see you, Bill. I may have an ethical conflict.'

'How?' he said. 'We haven't spoken in, well, years.'

'It's complicated,' I said, lamely. 'It's not even clear to me that I actually have a conflict. I'm just concerned that I might.'

'Well, how about this,' he said. 'Let's schedule a time. In the interval between now and then you can think about your ethical problem. We'll talk, I'll run my concerns past you, and you can decide if you're able to help.'

He sounded eminently reasonable. I was reminded that even during the session with his wife so many years before, Bill Miller had always seemed levelheaded and reasonable. Almost, I also reminded myself, to a fault.

'How about eleven forty-five?' I asked.

Bill Miller was close to ten minutes late for his appointment. Since I was meeting with him over the brief window in my day that would have constituted my lunch hour, I'd greedily used the free time to devour an energy bar from the emergency stash in my desk.

'Déjà vu, huh?' he said as he settled onto the chair across from me. 'It feels odd to be here without Rachel. That was one day that I will never ever forget.'

My natural human instinct was to offer condolences to Bill, to be sympathetic about whatever had happened with Mallory, to reflect on the sad outcome of the situation with Rachel. But I didn't. Instead I contemplated the fact that after so many years between visits with me his first association in my presence was to his long-estranged wife, and not to the tragedy of his recently absent daughter.

Ironically, one of the most difficult things about the psychotherapeutic relationship is the necessity for the therapist to, at times, put brakes on reflexive human kindness. Were I to presuppose to start this interaction with Bill Miller with expressions of compassion, or even overt sorrow, at his plight – or by giving him a big hug, a pat on the back, and a hearty 'hey, big guy' – I might unwittingly interfere with whatever motivation he'd had for picking up the phone.

So I waited. The truth was that most of the time, when I reached over my shoulder into my therapeutic quiver I ended up drawing out the dullest arrow, the one that was marked SHUT UP AND WAIT.

'I bet you'd like to know why I'm here,' Bill said.

'Yes,' I said evenly. 'I would. That's a good place to start.'

Bill was dressed in wool flannel trousers, good leather loafers, and a crisp blue dress shirt that was the color of his eyes. His sportcoat wasn't new, but it looked like cashmere, and hung on him with the drape of good tailoring. He wore no tie; few men in Boulder did.

'What's your ethical problem?' he asked. The question was

213

neighborly. He could have been inquiring about a problem I said I'd been having with my gutters.

'Explaining the circumstances would lead to a whole different ethical dilemma for me. It's something I'm going to have to deal with on my own. When I reach a determination, I'll let you know.'

'But you've obviously dealt with it enough to have this meeting?'

'I'm hoping to get a better understanding about why you've come to see me. That might make my concerns moot, or it might clarify things so I'll have a clearer sense of what I should do.' That was the plan, anyway.

Bill closed his eyes for a moment, a long moment that grew into seconds. Five, then ten. Finally he opened his eyes, looked right at me, and with pain etched in his brow, he said, 'You've been at my house twice over the past two days. Why?'

40

In the same way that a boxer who has just absorbed a right uppercut has many options as he's lying on the canvas staring straight up at the klieg lights listening to a referee count 'eight, nine,' at that moment I had many options.

I could have reached back into my quiver for the safety of my SHUT UP AND WAIT arrow.

Or I could have said something classically therapeutic, and classically arrogant, like, 'This isn't about me, Bill. This is about you.'

Or, of course, I could have out-and-out lied: *'I don't know what you're talking about.'*

Instead, almost purely instinctively, I chose an alternative that I hoped might buy me a moment to think while at the same time it reinforced the separation that existed between, and needed to continue to exist between, my chair and that of my patient. What I said in reply to Bill's question about why I was at his house was, 'And that's why you're here, Bill?'

'Well, I don't think it's a coincidence.'

'Excuse me?' I was honestly perplexed by his quick reply. Bill Miller was implying that my appearance at his neighbor's house was coincident with what, exactly? I really wanted to know. 'What kind of coincidence are you talking about?'

'Why would you be at my next-door neighbor's house twice in two days with two different people?'

He apparently wasn't eager to answer my question; I was certainly not about to answer his. Discussing with Bill Miller that I'd been at his neighbor's house because I'd been concerned about the apparent disappearance of another one of my patients, and the disappearance of my partner and friend, wasn't about to happen.

'Is this meeting' – I waved my hand between us – 'a professional meeting? Did you come to see me for psychotherapy, or for something else?'

He hesitated long enough that I knew he had hesitated, which told me that he'd had to think about how to answer my question.

I said, 'The distinction is important. If we're going to work together, the distinction is important.'

'Yes, yes, of course it's professional,' he said. 'I need your help, Dr. Gregory. But I'm also concerned why you've been . . . so close to my home in the past few days.'

Was that a reasonable concern for him to have? I could have argued yes, I could have argued no. But was reasonableness the point? 'Go back three days please, Bill. Were you considering calling me for psychotherapy then?'

'What do you mean?' he stammered.

'You said that you've seen me at your neighbor's house twice in the past couple of days. I'm wondering whether that is the reason that we're talking today, or whether you had been considering asking me for help prior to that.'

Shit. By babbling on, I'd just given him a road map for how to respond.

No surprise, Bill consulted the map before he replied. 'I'd been considering it. Seeing you next door brought everything closer to the surface, a lot of old memories, unresolved, you know, feelings about . . . what's happened, so I decided to call and set something up. But I feel I deserve an explanation as to why you've been in my neighborhood so much. I do.'

Did he deserve an explanation? It was an interesting question. Were I truly interested in buying Doyle's house, that would potentially make me Bill Miller's next-door neighbor. If he and I were neighbors, the dual-relationships ethical restriction would definitely kick in: Preexisting therapeutic relationship or no preexisting therapeutic relationship, missing daughter or no missing daughter, I certainly could not provide psychotherapy to my next-door neighbor.

I decided to provide just enough of an explanation to allay his concerns.

'Bill, I can assure you that my presence at your next-door neighbor's house had nothing to do with you or your family.'

216

Was that really true? I actually wasn't sure.

'Are you thinking of buying that house?' Bill asked.

An easy question, finally. 'No, I'm not.'

'You were there with the woman who is listing that house.'

'I'll repeat what I said. I'm not considering buying the house.'

'Then why were you with her?'

'My presence had no direct relevance to you or your family.' Did it have indirect relevance? The question of indirect relevance had to do with Bob Brandt and the conversations he'd had with Mallory through the fence. The answer to the question of indirect relevance was either all chronicled in the pages in the Kinko's box Bob had given me, or it wasn't. My money was still riding on 'wasn't.' Barely.

I went on. 'Assuming for a moment that we each decide that we are comfortable working together . . .'

'Yes,' Bill said.

'How can I be of help?' A quick glance at the clock told me we had precious little time remaining until my twelve thirty showed up in the waiting room.

'I'm under a lot of stress.'

I can only imagine.

'I'm not sleeping. I'm losing weight; I don't have any appetite at all.'

Likely culprits for that constellation of symptoms? Depression, anxiety, post-traumatic stress. Given the circumstances of Bill's life, there were no surprises on that list. The most natural thing for me to do at that moment would have been to presuppose the source of Bill Miller's symptoms. I cautioned myself not to do it.

I pressed him, wondering aloud what he thought was going on. He responded with generalities about 'events' and 'the kids' and 'work.' I tried for some clarification. He eluded me.

Was I observing resistance – that psychotherapeutic Great Wall that separates so many patients from the issues that are most tender to them? Possibly. I decided to challenge the resistance a little. 'How was she feeling, Bill?'

'My daughter?'

Not Mallory. *My daughter.* I nodded.

'The holidays are hard for her. Always. This year, too. They haven't been fun for her since . . .'

217

I filled in the blanks with *her mother left*.

'Hard how?' I asked.

'She gets nervous. Withdrawn, irritable. She's definitely a teenager.'

Bill had grown anxious and withdrawn, too. As I considered the fact that the media had failed to report any details of Mallory's troubled holiday mood, and as the final moments of our appointment time dripped away, I decided not to test the flexibility of Bill's resistance any further. We made tentative plans to meet again the following Monday. I told him that I'd call him if I ultimately decided that my ethical concerns were so grave that I couldn't proceed.

Bill Miller left my office that day without having once spoken aloud his daughter's name.

Was it too painful for him?

I didn't know.

41

To my relief, my note on the door worked and none of Diane's patients camped out in the waiting room.

Until four o'clock.

At four o'clock, I walked out to retrieve my scheduled patient but was greeted not by one person eager to see me, but by two.

The unexpected person was the woman with the cheddar-colored hair who had been so insistent on seeing her therapist on the day that Hannah Grant died. I recalled that Diane had told me that she had begun seeing the woman for psychotherapy. Was she there for her appointment?

I told the young man whom I was scheduled to see at that hour that I would be back with him in just a moment, and invited the Cheetos lady to come down the hall. We walked halfway to my office, far enough to be out of earshot of the waiting room, before I asked, 'Did you see my note on the door about Dr. Estevez? She can't be here today.'

'I saw your stupid note. I have a right to know what's going on.'

In the weeks since Hannah's death this woman had not shed any of her petulance. 'She's unfortunately away unexpectedly,' I said, stumbling over the adverbs I was stringing together.

'What does that mean?'

'She'll call you when she's back in the office.'

'That's what you said about Hannah.'

She was right. That is what I'd said about Hannah.

'I'm sorry.' I was sorry. 'I don't know what else to say. I'm sure, given what tragically happened with Ms. Grant, that this is especially difficult for you.'

I didn't know what else to say. I was also running out of big adverbs.

'How long has she been gone?'

'I'm afraid I'm not in a position to answer that question.'

'Then change your damn position.'

The top of her frizzy head reached just about to the level of my chin. Her hair had a scent that I associated with bad Indian restaurants. 'I'm available for—'

'I don't care what you're available for. Have you checked Diane's office?'

Diane, not Dr. Estevez. 'There's no need to check her office.'

'Then you know where she is. Tell me what the hell is going on.'

'I'm sorry that Dr. Estevez isn't here for your appointment. She'll call you as soon as she is free to do so. I have someone I have to see now. Please excuse me.'

I led her back toward the waiting room.

'This isn't going to stop here,' the woman said before she left.

Before I retrieved my patient, I rushed back down the hall, grabbed my keys, and opened Diane's office door. I was so relieved that it was empty.

'Jay?' I said to my four o'clock after I'd recovered my composure and returned to the waiting room. 'Why don't you come on back? I'm sorry for the late start.'

My last appointment of the day was scheduled to begin at five o'clock. I took a deep breath, reassured myself that the finish line of my day's therapy marathon was only forty-five minutes away, and made the stroll down the hallway. Once again, though, I found two people, not one, waiting for me.

One was my five o'clock. She was a thirty-eight-year-old woman whom I'd successfully helped with depression a year before, but who was back in my care to try to stave off a recurrence of her profound melancholy after a recent diagnosis of breast cancer. She had a PIC line in her upper arm and was in the interlude between her first and second rounds of chemo. She was sitting in the waiting room with her hands folded in her lap, her eyes closed, meditating, I supposed, on some aspect of life's caprice.

At that moment my empathy for her was even more acute than usual.

The other person in my waiting room was my friend, Sam

Purdy. He was dressed in his work clothes – in winter that meant a pair of aging wool trousers, a long-sleeved shirt, a tie that was loose at the collar, and a sport coat that Goodwill would have tossed into a rag pile had he tried to donate it. The jackets he wore were usually ill-fitting, but with his recent weight loss this coat was to his body what a bad slipcover was to a couch. That day, Sam's trousers were of recent vintage, as was his tie. For years Sam had owned so few neckties that I actually recognized them by their stains, but this one was new, and tasteful, and most surprising, appeared to be made of silk.

I suspected that Sam's new girlfriend had taken him shopping over New Year's. I also bet that he had a pair of silk boxers at home he didn't quite know what to do with.

Sam was reading the *New Yorker,* chuckling at a cartoon. When he looked up at me I made a querulous face at him. He shook his head just a little, flattened his mouth so that his lips disappeared under the umbrella of his mustache, and made a little 'everything's cool' gesture with his hand. The gesture closely resembled an insincere 'safe' call by a baseball umpire.

I made another querulous face.

He tapped his wristwatch.

I shrugged my shoulders and led the woman back to my office.

Forty-five minutes later my patient departed and I retraced my steps to the waiting room. Sam was asleep on his chair. A half-dozen magazines were in a heap at his feet.

'Hey, Sam,' I said.

He didn't reply.

'Sam,' I tried, a little louder.

He still didn't say anything.

An image of Hannah Grant's dead body splayed over the leather cube flashed into my mind with Technicolor brilliance. I said, 'Oh shit,' and rushed across the room.

'Got you,' he said with a sudden smile. The stubble of his beard told me it had been many hours since he'd scraped his face with a razor. He was probably as tired as I was.

'You ass,' I said. 'What are you doing here?'

'I come by sometimes just to catch up on my magazine reading.

You guys have good stuff. Not like my dentist's office. You should see the crap he keeps around.'

I made a skeptical face.

He stood up. 'I'm buying you dinner,' he said. 'Come on.'

'Sam, Lauren's expecting me to—'

'No, she's not. I already cleared it with her. You have a free go-out-with-the-boys pass for the evening.'

'Yeah?' I was suspicious.

'Yeah.'

'We walking or driving?'

'We be walking.'

Although it was a cold night for a stroll, we hiked to the far side of the Pearl Street Mall toward the Sunflower Restaurant. Before Sam's heart attack I doubted that he'd ever set foot inside the organic oasis that was the Sunflower, and I was more than a little suspicious that he'd chosen it for a meal for the two of us, but I kept my apprehension to myself. Things definitely weren't what they seemed, so an out-of-the-ordinary restaurant fit right in. We spent the few-block hike catching up on kid talk. Sam was moaning that Simon was making both his parents nuts trying to juggle his hockey and snowboarding schedules, but I could tell that Sam was actually pretty happy about the logistical craziness his son's activities were precipitating.

He declined the hostess's first offer of a table, which was prime territory smack in the middle of the dining room, and instead asked for a booth in the distant corner. Once we were led to his preferred suburban outpost, he took the bench that was facing the big room; I was left with a view of a brick wall that was adorned with a large, quasi-erotic photograph of young eggplants and ripe figs. For some reason I found myself thinking of D. H. Lawrence and Alan Bates.

Then I got it: My association was to the cinematic version of *Women in Love*. I smiled at the memory, and stole another gratuitous glance at the figs. 'What is this, really?' I asked.

'Sherry has Simon. I wanted to spend some quality time with you.'

'Yeah? At the Sunflower? You really expect me to believe that?'

'I'm hurt,' he said, investing all of his energy in the menu. 'Can't even do a nice gesture for a friend. What are you hungry for? Look' – he pointed at the entrée list – 'everything here's free range and wild and shit. Has to make you happy.'

'How's Carmen?' I asked, temporarily giving up on my quest to discover the purpose of the meeting. I wasn't in a hurry; I knew we'd get there eventually. 'She buy you that tie?'

Sam looked up and flicked a quick glance at the dining room. I thought I saw him nod his head just the smallest amount.

I had to resist turning and taking a look for myself. Suddenly, Darrell Olson was at my side. Two seconds later, Jaris Slocum was standing right behind him.

42

'Hi, guys,' Sam said to the two detectives. He didn't feign surprise. I had to give him credit for that.

I glared at Sam. He made the same little hey-everything's-copacetic face and did the same hey-everything's-cool hand gesture that he'd thrown at me back in my waiting room while I was trying to figure out why he was camping out reading magazines.

'Make some room,' he said to me.

I slid over and was immediately pinned against the wall, with no chance of escape, by Darrell Olson.

Sam and Jaris Slocum – their chests and shoulders were much broader than mine and Darrell's – totally filled the space on the other side of the table. A waitress came by and took our drink order. Apparently sensing the tension at the table, she skipped any flirtation and kept her smile under wraps. We all ordered beer. Four different brands. Just another way of shouting out that we weren't a bunch of buddies sharing a pitcher.

'You guys hungry?' Sam asked.

'You bet,' Darrell said. 'I love this place.'

One mystery solved: Darrell had chosen the restaurant. I slid my menu toward him. My own appetite was wavering. While glaring at Sam, I asked, 'What's this about? You should check with my attorney if you want another interview, Detective Slocum. We shouldn't even—'

He snapped back. 'I know exactly what—'

Sam interrupted Slocum's interruption. He said, 'Call him Jaris, Alan. We're all friends here.'

What?

Slocum tried again. 'I'm perfectly aware that I need to go through your attorney to discuss . . . that other matter. I'm always eager for a

224

chance to chat with Mr. Maitlin. But Darrell and I aren't here to talk about Hannah Grant.'

I might have been offended by the gratuitous sarcasm about Cozy if I wasn't still stuck on Sam's announcement that 'We're all friends here.' *Since when? And if we're not here to talk about Hannah, what the hell are we here to talk about?* At that moment I thought of Bob Brandt, and to no one in particular said, 'It's your move.'

'Hey, allow me,' Sam said. 'This little party was my idea.'

I thought my narrowed eyes and tight brow aptly communicated to Sam that I didn't approve of any of the choreography he'd put into his soiree so far.

'A little background to start,' he said, sticking to the charade that we were all just friends having a beer and sharing some crispy tofu triangles. 'Jaris and Darrell had a piece of the Mallory Miller investigation. Lucy and I were doing time line. They were assigned to follow up a couple of potentially promising leads: one being the empty house next door – the one that's for sale – and two being the possibility that the girl somehow ended up with her mother.'

'This is all about Mallory, then?' I asked. Despite my skepticism, I knew my question was evidence of capitulation on my part. I should have been throwing money on the table for my beer and walking full speed away from the three Boulder cops.

'A little patience, maybe?' Sam said. The drinks arrived. Sam waited until the waitress was gone again before he continued. 'I was thinking about the conversations you and I had, you know, about the guy with the car, that classic Camaro, and about the house next door to the Millers' with the waterfalls and shit, and about your friend, Dr. Estevez, and what happened to her in Las Vegas.'

Darrell said, 'Sam came to us. We heard his thoughts and started wondering whether there might be some connection, something that tied things together.'

'Some connection?' I asked, even more skeptically than before. I already feared a connection among Bob and Mallory and Diane, and I was beyond skeptical that I was hearing about this from Darrell Olson and Jaris Slocum.

'Yeah,' said Slocum.

As far as I was concerned he was nothing more than a punk with a shield. 'I'm uncomfortable with this,' I said, trying hard not to sound petulant. Sam's expression told me that I hadn't quite succeeded. I felt as though all the confidential information that I'd been trying to guard about my patients was in a balloon hovering above the table, and that each of the three detectives was dimpling the latex with the point of a saber.

The worst part? I knew I'd gotten myself into this one by trying to finesse the confidentiality rules with Sam.

'Hear us out,' Sam said.

Slocum's mug of beer was almost gone. He'd either been real thirsty, or he was real anxious. He looked toward our waitress and raised the mug and his eyebrows. He wanted a refill.

Darrell said, 'We didn't know about the guy with the car. The one who rents the garage next door to the Millers. That was news to us. It could be an important piece of information. We should have picked up on it, but it slipped through the cracks.'

I glared at Sam. 'Slipped through the cracks, huh?'

Slocum picked up from there. 'And the fact that your friend disappeared in Las Vegas? That's curious to us, too.'

'Curious?'

'Well, worrisome, of course, but curious, too. Given the circumstances.'

'What circumstances are those?' I asked.

'Everything,' Slocum replied.

'Everything?'

'Yeah.'

I found that I liked him almost as much now that we were all friends having beers and I was calling him 'Jaris' as I had when he was ordering me around outside Hannah Grant's office and I was calling him 'Detective.' I said, 'For old times' sake, Jaris, treat me like you treated me at Hannah's office. You know, like an idiot citizen. Tell me what "everything" means.'

'Alan,' Sam said.

I remained unconvinced about the announced agenda for this impromptu meeting. 'We're not talking in code about Hannah Grant right now? You're all sure about that? If we are, my lawyer's probably not going to be too happy about it. Come to think about it, neither will my wife.' I don't know why I threw in the part about Lauren. It was petty, but then so was my state of mind.

Darrell held up a hand to shush Sam. He said, 'Let me, Sam, please.' Darrell was using the conciliator's voice that I'd heard him try on with Slocum and later with Cozy Maitlin the night that we found Hannah's body. I suspected that Darrell had been a conciliator at least as long as he'd known how to ride a two-wheeler, and that his initial mediating role had been to intervene before his argumentative parents ripped the flesh from each other's throats.

'Alan – we didn't get off to a good start with you and Dr. Estevez last month – Jaris and I didn't. Water under the bridge, right? Is that okay? Because based on what Sam's been able to tell us, it sounds like both you and her might have something to do with another situation we're working.' He lowered his voice here, and leaned closer to me. 'Yes, I'm talking about Mallory. Now, it may just all be coincidence. That's always possible. But it's also possible that everything's related.'

I couldn't resist a jab. 'If it turns out that everything's related, it sounds like you and Detective Slocum – Jaris – might have missed some important details during your initial investigations.'

Sam said, 'I'm not sure that's helpful, Alan.'

I turned on him. My tone was level. My words? Not as much. 'And you're the best judge of that, Sam? Of what's helpful? Please. He' – I pointed at Slocum – 'roughed up Diane last month for no reason other than that he'd had a bad day or his feelings were hurt or God knows what else, and now he wants to have a nice dinner with me and down a few beers and he thinks I'll just bow down and help him cover up his mistakes on the' – I caught myself and lowered my voice to a coarse whisper – 'Mallory Miller fiasco. Because what I think this is about is ass-covering.'

Slocum's face was red. He raised his glass and drained the dregs from the bottom of his first beer – a version of counting to ten to calm himself down, I thought – before he said, 'I'm guessing you need help finding her. Not to mention the guy with the old Camaro. Him, too. I don't expect you to like me – to be honest, I don't give a shit – but I'm willing to try to find these people. You want to work something out, or not? Your choice. I don't have time for your sissy-ass games.'

Sissy-ass games? I supposed that meant that Jaris and I were no longer friends. 'What can you do to help? Last time I looked, Las Vegas was in Nevada.'

Sam sighed loudly. I thought he was expressing relief that most of the cards were finally on the table.

The waitress chose that moment to return with Jaris's second beer. She dropped it off in record time and withdrew as though she'd just remembered she'd left the water running in her bathtub.

'If we reach out from here,' Darrell said as she retreated, 'the Las Vegas police maybe show a little more interest in trying to find out what happened to her. I suspect that could make a significant difference. The current situation – an out-of-state husband who can't find his wife for a couple of days – probably isn't creating a lot of investigative curiosity in Sin City.'

Of course he was right. I asked, 'And the other guy? The one with the Camaro? How are you going to help with him?'

'One phone call – and one BOLO later – every cop in the state will have an eye peeled for that car,' Jaris said.

I hadn't touched my beer. I picked it up and took a long, slow sip. 'On what pretense?' I asked.

Across the table, Slocum had already finished half of his second mug. Sam spied Jaris getting ready to jump back into the fray and decided to run interference. He said, 'That's our problem. We'll come up with one. It's not as hard as you might think. By the way, BOLO is be-on-the-look—'

'I know what a BOLO is,' I snapped, almost spitting my beer. 'So what do you want from me, Jaris?'

Sam wasn't done orchestrating. 'What do you say let's order first, okay? I don't know about the rest of you, but I'm starving here. Darrell, what's good? Think I'd like the tempeh cutlets?'

Sam's tempeh question was theater-of-the-absurd offered purely for my benefit. Tempeh was so far outside the boundaries of Sam's comfort universe that Hubble couldn't have spotted it.

Sam was thinking that he'd won, and he was pretty darn proud of himself.

43

We'd almost completed a totally silent trek from the Sunflower back up the Mall to my office when he said, 'You wouldn't have come out with me if I'd told you what I was up to.'

'Damn right,' I said.

A few more steps of silence followed. Then, without the slightest bit of animosity in his voice, Sam added, 'You should get off your high horse, see what the world looks like from down here with the rest of us.'

'And what the hell is that supposed to mean?' I wasn't as careful as Sam was about keeping the animosity out of my voice.

'Your cherished position in life – you know, psych-o-therapist, guardian of all the world's secrets – it's not as special as you think it is. You're just a damn guy doing a damn job. You have trusts to keep. Well, surprise, surprise, other people do, too. Other people take their responsibilities as seriously as you do.

'Me? Tonight? It turns out I saw a way to get Diane some help for whatever mess she's in. I saw a way to get some serious eyeballs out looking for the guy in the Camaro. You wanted me to find a hook for all this. Well, I found one. The way I see it, call me naive, but no blood gets spilled by my strategy. A few people have to swallow some pride – yeah, you included – but so the fuck what? You think this was an easy meeting for Jaris? The guy has his hands full; trust me on that.'

I was inclined to say that I didn't give a ferret fart whether or not it had been a pleasant meeting for Jaris, but I didn't.

Sam had his hands in his pockets and was looking down at the sidewalk as we talked. At Ninth he led us off the curb without looking for traffic in both directions. In half a second a guy heading north on a bike almost creamed him. If the man hadn't screamed a profanity in warning, I'm not sure Sam would have ever noticed.

Even with the profanity, he seemed unfazed. He muttered, 'Too cold for a bike.'

We started up Walnut toward my office. As we passed the building that was the second or third incarnation of one of Boulder's legendary breakfast houses, Sam said, 'I miss Nancy's. Those herb cheese omelettes? They were something. Lucile's is great, but I miss Nancy's.'

'Me, too.' After three or four more steps, I added, 'You're right, Sam.'

'About Nancy's? Course I am.'

I hadn't been talking about Nancy's, but he was right about that, too. 'Wonderful biscuits. Remember those biscuits? But I meant that you're right about what you said.'

'I know that, too.' He exhaled audibly. 'The fact that you admit it doesn't change anything, doesn't mean that what happens next is going to be what you want to happen next, or even that what happens next is what I want to happen next. All that's different now is that some people who care about the jobs they do are going to try to find some of these missing people.' He pulled his right hand from his pocket and yanked at the knot on his tie. 'How bad a thing can that be?'

He was right.

'I'm sorry,' I said.

'For what?'

'For being an asshole.'

'You mean a sissy-ass?'

I laughed. 'That, too.'

'Hey,' he said.

And that was that.

Almost a block later he climbed into the cradle of the driver's seat of his Cherokee. 'Carmen likes to buy me clothes,' he said.

It took me a moment to realize that Sam was revisiting the conversation we'd been having in the restaurant at the precise moment when Slocum and Olson ambushed me. I had just asked him about his tie. 'I figured,' I said.

'What do you think?'

'About the new threads?' I asked. 'Or about the fact that Carmen likes to buy them for you?'

Sam shook his head gently, and I could hear the throaty tang of a little chuckle come out of the darkness. 'See, that's the thing. I don't know one other guy who would ask me that question. Not one. And that's why I'm okay with the fact that you're an asshole sometimes.'

'Goodnight, Sam. Thanks.'

I was halfway home before I realized that I'd spaced out telling Sam about my visit to Doyle's house with the Realtor the previous night.

44

My girls were sleeping in separate beds when I got home. The dogs were squirrelly though, and I had to spend ten minutes outside with them before I could get them settled. Emily detected the scent of a critter of some kind while we were walking the lane and once we were back in the door she strolled the entire perimeter of the interior of the upstairs of the house checking to see if an unseen enemy had succeeded in breaching our defenses. Ultimately confident that all of our flanks were protected, she plopped at my feet with a satisfied sigh.

The entire house shook when she landed.

I was thinking about calling Sam to get his inevitable rage over my visit to Doyle's house out of the way, when the phone rang.

I pounced on it: Raoul.

'I'm starting to get somewhere. Couple of pieces,' Raoul said.

His tone told me that he hadn't found Diane, so I didn't ask. His words told me that he wanted to confront the practical, so I refrained from asking the question that was second on my list: *How are you doing with all this?* Instead, I said, 'What do you have?'

Raoul started with bad news, not, in my mind, a good sign. 'Marlina's a dead end. The woman from Venetian security? One more meal with her tomorrow, and I'm done. I know exactly why the woman's been divorced twice though I still haven't figured out how she got married twice. She's playing me.'

'Okay, then what pieces do you have?'

'Two. The guy from the craps table? The shopping center developer who was playing craps at the same table as Diane? He finally called me this morning, told me he'd been drunk when I phoned him and he'd forgotten to call me back. He was cleaning out the memory on his mobile and saw my number. Anyway, he said that Diane was his luck at the craps table that night and when she cashed out, he decided to do the same. He said he was right behind her as she was walking through the casino.'

'Sounds kind of creepy.'

'*Sí*. He says as Diane's walking across the casino, two guys walk up to her, say hello. Pretty well dressed. Both of them forty to fifty. One tall, one average. One of them whispered something to her. She seemed happy to hear it and the three of them walked on together, talking. She had her phone in her hand, dropped it trying to shake hands with one of the guys. He picked it up and she stuffed it in her purse. One of the two reached around behind Diane, took the phone right back out of her bag, and tossed it on the floor by a row of slot machines. He said the guy was smooth; he picked Diane like a pro. Until the man dumped her phone, the guy from the craps table thought one of the two guys was Diane's husband, or boyfriend.'

'Fits with what I remember, Raoul.' I paused before I added, 'The guy from the craps table was going to hit on her, wasn't he? That's why he was following her?'

'Yes,' said Raoul without any animosity. He understood these things.

'So that was it? He never reported this to anyone?'

'He said that Diane didn't seem to be in any distress. The phone thing was odd, but she went with them voluntarily.'

'But he doesn't know where they went?'

'They were walking in the direction of the lobby, but he didn't follow them out of the casino. He went up to his room.'

'What are you thinking?' I asked.

'I'm thinking what he said to her had something to do with Rachel Miller. That's why she went with them – she thought she was going to get a chance to talk with Rachel.'

'That's what I'm thinking, too.' I paused for a moment. 'Somebody must have picked the phone up off the floor and put it in the tray of the slot machine where that drunk woman found it.'

'It also explains why Venetian security isn't too eager to let me see the surveillance tape. Probably looks a lot like a rendezvous to them. You know, something between . . . adults.'

'But they must have a picture of these two guys, right?'

'Right. You can't walk out of a casino without a camera seeing you. No way.'

'You said you have a couple of pieces of news. What's the other one?'

'Norm Clarke came through. I should've called him the first day I got here. I can be such a putz.'

I was surprised – no, shocked – at the Yiddish. I didn't know it was part of Raoul's language repertoire. I grabbed a beer from the kitchen so I could sit down and listen to his story about Norm Clarke.

Any good big-city daily newspaper that doesn't take itself too seriously has one, though few are fortunate enough to have that special one that becomes a silk thread in the urban fabric. San Francisco had Herb Caen. Denver has had Bill Husted for as long as I can remember.

What's their role? Gossip columnist? Man about town? If they're good, the phrases don't do them justice. These guys, and a few gals, take the pulse on their city. They tell the rest of us what happens behind closed doors, what happens after the bars close, what's new, what's old, what's coming next. They invite us to the city's water cooler for the latest gossip on the movers and shakers, and they whisper the latest dish over the city's backyard fence. They're the ones who know what local boy has done good, and what local girl has gone bad. What famous visitor has been spotted where, doing what, with whom.

Las Vegas's version was Norm Clarke.

Norm had briefly gone head-to-head with Husted back in Colorado, scrounging the usually dull Front Range of the Rockies for paltry scoops, but years before he'd moved on to ply his trade at the *ReviewJournal in the much more fertile gossip terrain of Las Vegas. By all the reports that made their way back across the Great Basin and the Rocky Mountains to Denver, Norm soon owned his adopted town.*

He knew everybody in Vegas, had spies everywhere, had eaten at every now table, could get backstage at any show, and was escorted to the front of the line and past the velvet rope at any trendy club.

After a few years in the desert Norm had, literally, written the book on Las Vegas, and was always busy taking notes for the next edition. His mug, and his column, graced the front page of the paper every weekend.

Celebrities weren't really in Vegas until Norm said they were in Vegas. Some begged him for ink. A few had managers and publicists call and beg him to please, please, please forget what he had seen or heard.

Back in his days at the *Rocky Mountain News*, Norm had done a feature on Raoul, and on Raoul's golden touch incubating Boulder tech companies during the heady days of the early 1990s. Raoul, who generally despised publicity, thought the piece was on the money, and he and Norm had become casual friends. They'd stayed in touch over the years even as each of their lives grew more complicated.

When Raoul called Norm asking for help in finding Diane, he was asking Norm to do something that Norm wasn't often asked to do: He was asking him to keep a secret.

Raoul's first sit-down with Norm had taken place almost twenty-four hours before in one of the many bars that dot the expansive, expensive acreage on the main floor of the Venetian. After some pleasantries Raoul had told Norm that he had a personal favor to ask, and asked Norm if he could speak off the record. Raoul proceeded to provide only the Vegas pieces of the puzzle: that Diane was in town to talk to a patient's mother, which was as good an excuse as she needed to spend some time playing a little middling-stakes craps. On Monday evening Diane had been talking to a friend on her cell while walking through the Venetian casino, and hadn't been heard from since. She'd disappeared. Hadn't returned to her hotel room. Hadn't called anyone. Nothing.

Earlier in the day she disappeared, Diane had tried to track down the patient's mother and had ended up at the Love In Las Vegas Wedding Chapel out on Las Vegas Boulevard, where she'd apparently located someone named Rachel Miller – yeah, Raoul told Norm, *that* Rachel Miller – but Raoul hadn't been successful finding her. Raoul also told Norm about his conversation with Reverend Howie at the Love In Las Vegas and about Howie's suggestion that Rachel could possibly be tracked down through an intermediary – a man, someone who apparently made Howie shake in his Savile Row boots. Somebody scary.

Norm admitted to Raoul that he didn't have a clue about the intermediary's identity, but that he suspected the man didn't inhabit the part of Las Vegas that typically interested his column's readers.

'But . . .' Raoul had said, sensing something.

'But,' Norm had added quickly, 'I think I know somebody who might be able to help.'

The way Raoul told it to me later, he and Norm met again at almost exactly the same time that I was finishing my meal with Sam, Darrell, and my new buddy Jaris at the Sunflower in downtown Boulder.

Norm was on the clock getting ready to chronicle for his column which of-the-moment celebrities were really going to show up at some cocktail-hour charity-do at one of the trendiest of the city's many trendoid restaurants, this one high in the newest tower of the Mandalay Bay. A setup crew was bustling around the still-vacant space, frantically arranging the tiers of a gorgeous raw bar, and test-fitting the blown-glass platters that would soon be heaped with gleaming shellfish, sushi, sashimi, and maki.

Raoul joined Norm at a corner table that had a stunning view of the Strip's neon at dusk. The table in front of Norm was naked except for his ubiquitous mobile phone, a longneck Coors Light that was almost full, and a couple of paper cocktail napkins on which Norm was scribbling notes with a felt-tip pen.

Norm looked up and said, 'Raoul, hi. Any luck?'

Raoul shook his head as he sat down.

Norm asked, 'You want a drink?'

'No, thank you.'

Norm slid the beer aside and leaned forward. 'I didn't think you'd have good news. Especially given what I found out about the guy you're looking for. You ready? His name is Ulysses Paul North. That's U – P – North. Or . . . Up, North. On the street they call him Canada.'

Raoul took a second to pull it all together, then he couldn't help himself: He smiled. 'Up North? Canada? Really?'

Norm smiled, too. He held up his hand like a Boy Scout taking an oath. 'I'm good, but I couldn't make that up.' Norm's grin caused his cheekbones to levitate – just a tiny bit – and that motion caused the distinctive black, flat crescent patch that always covered his right eye to rise.

Raoul said, 'There's more, yes?'

'There's more. Canada's a facilitator, apparently. A street facilitator of some kind.' Norm sipped from his beer. 'If this place were Hollywood' – he gazed down at the flashing neon skyline of ersatz New York, and the ejaculating fountains at the Bellagio, and the distant faux icons of Egypt and Paris and Venice – 'and if Canada's people were movie stars, he'd probably be called a manager. But this is definitely not Hollywood, and Canada's clients are, well, definitely not movie stars, so there's not exactly a name I know of for exactly what he does.'

'He's not a pimp?'

'No. He probably counts some pimps and prostitutes among his . . . clients.'

'He's not muscle, protection?'

'Not in any conventional sense. But should the need arise, he has all the muscle he might want. That's what I'm told.'

'I assume he gets a percentage of—'

'He does. I was told he advises his . . . clients – I'm sorry, I keep stumbling over that word – on business matters, helps them formulate strategic plans. I swear; that's the party line. He intervenes only when necessary. Tries to keep turf fights in his territory to a minimum. Settles occasional disputes. For those services, he is paid a percentage of his clients' . . . proceeds.'

'The clients are crooks?'

Norm took a moment before he decided how to reply. 'Let's say they don't report their income to the IRS.'

'And Canada's a scary enough man to do this . . . job?'

'He is known to be ruthless when necessary. And sometimes more, when he needs to make a point.'

'Your source knows him?'

'Of him.'

Raoul sat back. 'You have contacts everywhere.' He intended it as a compliment, and as a question. Norm read it both ways.

'Everywhere I can. To do my job for the paper, I need all the eyes I can find.' He gestured over his shoulder. 'When nobody knew where Jacko was after his indictment, I found him. When Britney got married for ten minutes, I knew about it before her mother did. Roy Horn after the tiger mauled him? I knew things his nurses didn't know about how he was doing.

'Tonight? One of the busboys here is going to tell me exactly who shows up for this shindig. Sometimes it's a host who helps me, occasionally a chef. Some of my best sources are people on the fringes of the A-list. They get invited to the hot parties, then tell me who else is there. Rule number one in this business: Everybody knows somebody.'

'And one of them knows how I can find this Canada?'

'You won't find Canada. He doesn't like to be found by people outside his orbit. But if you would like, the man who's talking to me will pass the word along on the street that you would like to speak with him. That's how it works, apparently.' Norm shrugged, a gesture that at once apologized for the melodrama and acknowledged that the show was totally out of his control.

Raoul sat back. 'Canada is what? Nevada's answer to Osama? I get a canvas bag on my head and get driven out to a cave somewhere in the desert?'

Norm's face remained impassive. 'I'm a reporter; I don't make this stuff up. I'd never heard of this guy before today. Odds are I'll never hear about him again after today. This is North Vegas stuff. It's way off my beat.'

'But you trust your guy? Your source?'

Norm took a long pull from his Coors Light. 'I work hard to write my column. It's not a party. To do this right, I have to have great instincts, I have to hustle, and I have to have a good bullshit detector, or I end up becoming a joke. I don't get them all right, Raoul, but I get almost all of them right. My gut says I have this one right.

'I grew up in a middle-of-nowhere town in Montana. Small-world time: Turns out a guy I went to high school with is part of the North Vegas street life. I tracked him down after his photo showed up in the paper one day with a story on the homeless. He's my source on this. He has no reason to lie to me, and it was pretty clear to me that he's honestly afraid of this guy Canada. He would much rather have been telling me that he knew where I could get serviced by the pope's favorite hooker.'

Raoul pondered for a few seconds. 'This man you know? Did he tell you anything about Rachel?'

Norm shook his head.

'Diane?'

'No. I'm sorry.'

Norm's cell phone rang. He excused himself to Raoul. 'Sorry, I have to get this. I'm waiting for a confirmation about an item for to-morrow's column. That thing at The Palms.' He opened the phone. 'Hello.'

Raoul didn't know about the thing at The Palms, and preferred it that way. He'd read it fresh in Norm's column the next morning.

Norm listened for a moment, stood up from the table, faced the window, and said, 'Of course, yes.' He listened for a longer period, almost a full minute, before he said, 'He's with me right now.' Beat. 'Okay, you know that . . . You want me to ask him?'

Norm set the phone on the table between himself and Raoul. He nodded at it and with an extended thumb and pinky held up to his face, he mimed that the telephone conversation was continuing.

'It's one of Canada's . . . people. If you agree to leave the police out of this, totally out of this, Canada will talk with you.'

In a heartbeat Raoul said, 'Agreed. Is my wife safe? Can he tell me that? Please?'

Norm shrugged. He didn't know the answer. He picked up the phone and placed it against his ear. 'You heard?' he said. Norm listened some more, nodding, and finally added, 'It shouldn't be a problem. He'll be there.' Norm folded his phone shut.

'I'll be where?' Raoul asked.

'The tram platform at the Luxor at seven o'clock. That's only twenty minutes from now.'

'Is it far?'

'If we could get a real good running start, and if we could jump out those windows over there, we could probably land on it. But from way up here, without flying? It'll take us most of that twenty minutes to get over there.'

'You know the way?'

Norm stood up. 'Of course.'

Raoul threw twenty dollars on the table and they ran.

'We had to hustle,' Raoul said to me. 'Down the elevator, all the way across the casino, which is like the size of Luxembourg, over to the monorail station. Wait for the train, get onto the train, ride it over to the Luxor. It's a turtle. The thing moves so slowly, you wonder why they bothered to build it. My mother has a cane; she walks faster than the damn tram moves. We finally made it to the platform with only a couple of minutes to spare.'

He stopped.

'And?' I asked.

'And nothing. We stood there for half an hour. Nothing. Nobody. Trains came, trains left. Nothing.'

'Nobody met you?'

'No.'

'Now what?'

'I don't know,' Raoul said. 'I suppose I'll continue to try to reach out to Canada some other way.'

I'd grown increasingly discomfited listening to Raoul's recanting of his meeting with Norm Clarke, especially the parts about the man called Canada. I stood up and began to pace in front of the big windows that faced the mountains. My movement caused Emily to stir. She was so exhausted that it appeared as though the simple act of lifting her big head to see what I was up to required a monumental effort.

'When I got back here a little bit ago?' Raoul said.

'Yes.'

'Marlina had dropped off an envelope. A single grainy screen shot from the casino security tape. Diane with the two guys who walked her out of the casino. They're all in profile.'

'How does she look?'

'Fine.'

'Any idea who they are?'

'No.'

'It's something, right?'

'It's something.'

'Raoul, I have some news that I originally thought was good news, but may now be bad news.'

240

'What?'

'The Boulder police are involved. They're asking the Las Vegas police to take Diane's disappearance seriously.'

In my ear, I heard one of the familiar Catalonian profanities. Then he said, 'I'll have to call Norm, so he can tell Canada.'

45

What if this is why she died? . . . What if somebody killed Hannah because she met with Mallory that one time?

As my head hit the pillow and I tried to find the sanctuary of sleep, Diane's original conspiracy theory about Hannah Grant's death – a hypothesis I recalled I'd dismissed out of hand at the time – bounced back and forth inside my skull like the digitized ball in a game of Pong.

What if this is why she died? . . . What if somebody killed Hannah because she met with Mallory that one time?

It didn't take long for my sleep-depriving musing to move on to cover fresh ground: If Diane had been right, and Hannah had been murdered because of something she'd learned from Mallory, could Diane and Bob somehow have suffered the same fate, too?

I shuddered at the thought.

The links were there. Diane had consulted with Hannah about Mallory; Bob had talked to Mallory across the backyard fence.

It was a far-fetched stretch, but could everything – Hannah's death, Mallory's disappearance, Diane's disappearance, and Bob's disappearance – really be related? Could some immense ball have started rolling the December afternoon that Mallory decided she just had to see Hannah Grant?

But why?

And how?

I gave up on sleeping and stumbled back out to the living room in search of a common denominator.

If Diane's theory was true, there had to be a secret in the Miller household. Something that Mallory had revealed during her single session with Hannah. Or at least something that someone thought she'd revealed.

What was it?

During that week after Christmas, the week after Mallory disappeared, Diane had said, *'She said her father was "up to something," remember?'*

So what had Bill Miller been up to?

Had he been up to something at home? At work? Planning a career change? Planning a major change in his parenting?

And why, I wondered, was Bill Miller so curious as to why I had been at Doyle's house?

Yeah, why?

During the psychotherapy session I'd had with Bill Miller earlier that day, I'd been so busy feeling guilty about being caught snooping around at Doyle's house that I'd missed the obvious: Why had Bill Miller been so damn curious about the fact that I'd been looking at the house that was for sale next door?

46

I woke Sam. He wasn't happy that I woke him. Once we managed to blunder past his unhappiness I began to explain to him why I'd interrupted his sleep. I tried to ease into it but his impatience forced me to admit earlier in the conversation than I wanted to that I had been inside Doyle's house. 'I pretended I was interested in buying the house; I got the agent to show it to me last night after work.'

'You woke me up to talk real estate?'

For a long moment he'd fooled me; I'd thought he'd sounded genuinely befuddled. 'Sam, please. That house is at the center of something. It is.'

He wasn't done poking at me. 'You liked it? I found it overpriced, personally. Kitchen's hardly bigger than mine. I don't think Lauren would go for it, anyway. She'd be fretting about Grace and all that water in the backyard. And that bridge? With a toddler? Alan, you'd never have a moment's peace.'

'Come on, Sam.'

'Okay, okay. Just remember that you're the one who woke me up. So why did you feel this compelling need to sneak into the house next door to the Millers? It's an empty friggin' house. We've been in there.'

'Given all that's happened, it seemed important to see it. I have this feeling that the Millers' neighbor is key to all this.'

'All what?'

'Everything. Mallory, Diane, the guy Bob with the Camaro. The BOLO? Why are all these people missing, Sam? Three people are missing. Don't you wonder about that? I mean, even—' I almost said, 'Even Hannah Grant,' but I caught myself. The only link I could make to Hannah in all this was through Diane, and that wasn't my privilege to abrogate.

244

'Three people are missing? Could be two. Could be one. Could be zero. But assuming I buy your premise that three people are missing, what does the neighbor's house have to do with Diane?' Sam asked.

Sam wasn't easily tricked. My obfuscation-by-shotgun-blast hadn't fooled him for long. I stammered, 'I don't know. That part is once removed. But there's a connection, there is. I can feel it.'

'Once removed? What the hell does that mean?'

'I can't say.'

He sighed. 'You were about to say something else. You said, "even" and you stopped. Even what?'

'Everything.' Lame, but it was the best that I could do. 'I was talking about everything.'

Sam yawned. 'You know something else, right? Don't you? Something you can't tell me?'

I didn't hesitate. I said, 'I do.'

'Fuck,' he muttered. 'What's the point in talking to you about stuff like this? It's all riddles. It's like trying to get a politician to tell you what he really thinks.' I took some solace that Sam's profanity had been mumbled and dull, and not sharply carved and poison-tipped. 'I can't start an investigation because you have some confidentiality bee in your butt, Alan. You know that. You do. We've been here before.'

'What about the snow thing?'

'Dear Lord, not the snow thing again.'

'Have you guys thought about those lines that you can string between trees and stuff? What are they called? What if they strung those between Mallory's house and Doyle's? What if they did that? What if that's how she got out of her house without leaving any footprints?'

'A patient feed you this? She slid down one of those lines? That's your latest theory? Are you nuts?'

Hearing it out loud, it sounded silly. All I was able to say was, 'No. Maybe.' Sam had no way to know I'd answered his questions in order, skipping the second one and the final one.

'Why?' Sam asked.

'Why what?'

'If she's running away, why would she care if she got out of the house without leaving any footprints? Why go to all that trouble? She didn't know when the snow was going to start and stop; she didn't know Fox was going to have a helicopter overhead. She's a kid. If she runs, she runs. Everything else is crap and you know it.'

I hadn't thought of questioning what motivation Mallory might have for trying to leave no trail behind – it was definitely an oversight in my thinking – but I found myself relieved that Sam was using the present tense to describe Mallory.

Sam wasn't done. 'Before, you said, "They"? Who's "they"?'

'The neighbor and . . .'

'Mallory? Come on? They were in this together? Now you're talking some conspiracy, right? Alan, I'll forgive you for calling. It's late. I know you're upset about your friend.'

'Sam—'

'We searched the house. We talked to the neighbor. Nothing came of it. Let it go.'

'Remember when we were in the yard and someone was watching us from the upstairs window?'

'Yeah?'

'Well, why? Why was he watching us?'

'He?'

Sam was sharper three minutes after being woken from a sound sleep than I was at the end of a long day. 'Has to be a he, right? It's only Bill and his son who live there.'

'The Millers aren't allowed to have guests? I didn't know that. Boulder and its laws? Wouldn't want to be a cop here – be arresting people for farting on the wrong side of the street.'

We'd moved from amused incredulity to aggravated sarcasm. Where Sam was concerned, that wasn't a healthy progression. With some defensiveness creeping into my voice, I said, 'I think it was a he.'

'Then what did you mean when you asked "why?" What's the big deal about somebody watching you from his own bedroom window? Maybe it was a neighborhood watch thing and Bill Miller's the block captain. Who the hell knows? It's not a crime to spy on your neighbor's yard. We'd have to arrest half the old ladies in town if it was.'

'Did you talk to the neighbor yourself, Sam? You or Lucy?'

He forced patience into his voice. It was a tight fit. 'Lucy and I were doing other things. You know that.'

'It was Slocum, wasn't it?'

'Your point?'

'Talk to the neighbor yourself, please. I don't trust Slocum.'

'I thought Jaris behaved himself tonight.'

'Barely. He was nervous. And you and Darrell were watching everything he did. I still don't trust him.'

The silence that ensued suggested to me that Sam was considering saying something else about Jaris Slocum. He didn't. He said, 'You talk about this Camaro guy as though he's a victim. You considered that he may be mixed up in all this, like criminally?'

'It doesn't fit,' I said. 'Psychologically.'

'And in your world people never act out of character?'

Sam actually asked that question with only the slightest hint of sarcasm. 'Talk to the neighbor, Sam.'

'On what pretense do I do that?' he asked.

'You're looking for that Camaro. You wanted a hook? That's your hook. Now that the BOLO is out, you want to tie up a loose end. Slocum himself said he didn't know about the Camaro during the first interview. You just have to make a call, one call, maybe go have a chat with the guy who owns the house and the garage.'

Ten minutes later I crawled into bed and sprawled on my side, facing my wife. Silently, Lauren backed toward me until I could feel the warmth from her nighttime flesh on the front of my naked thighs. I'd almost drifted off to sleep when a fresh thought forced me to snap open my eyes in the dark.

Maybe the secret has to do with Rachel Miller, not with Mallory.

Maybe this is all about Rachel.

That's why Diane disappeared.

She knew something about Rachel. Or she was about to learn something about Rachel.

I climbed back out of bed, pulled on a pair of sweats, and used the kitchen phone to warn Raoul that when he'd walked into the Love In Las Vegas Wedding Chapel and met Reverend Howie he may have inadvertently walked into something that was extremely dangerous.

But Raoul didn't answer his hotel room phone at the Venetian.

He didn't answer his cell, either.

My next thought? Sam was going to kill me when I tried to explain Canada to him.

47

All I told Bill Miller on the phone was that I had some further questions that I needed to address before I could make a commitment to
see him for ongoing psychotherapy. He readily agreed to come in on
Friday morning. I never quite decided how surprised I was that Bill
was so accommodating about meeting with me again on such short
notice. My indecision, I was sure, was a product of the fact that more
than twelve hours had passed and I still hadn't been able to track
down Raoul in Las Vegas.

Lauren shared my dismay about Raoul's silence. The look she'd
given me that morning when I slowed her down on the way to the
bathroom to let her know Raoul wasn't answering his phone was like
the look I might expect after I'd told her I'd not only lost my car keys
but also managed to misplace the spare set, too. 'Diane *and* Raoul?'
she'd said, finally. Before shutting the bathroom door behind her,
she'd added, 'Find him, honey. Today would be good.'

Bill settled into the chair across from me and without any visible
indications of concern, said, 'Shoot. I'm ready. Ask your questions. I'd
love to get this whole thing settled.'

In typical shrink form, my question wasn't really just a question.
'Thanks for being so flexible,' I said. 'I'd like to know more about
your current relationship with your – is it ex-wife? – Rachel.'

'Well,' he said, sitting back on the chair. 'I didn't expect that one.'
He wasted a moment picking at the crease on his perfectly pressed
trousers.

I, of course, grew curious about what question he had expected.
But I didn't ask him that. I waited.

'Rachel and I are separated, not . . . divorced. For some reason,

I thought you knew that. I feel like I don't have any secrets anymore. We never went through the whole legal process. It just never felt . . . necessary to me. Or even appropriate. Given her difficulties, I couldn't just . . . You know the circumstances back then as well as anyone.'

Actually, not as well as Mary Black, I thought. 'Are you legally separated?'

Bill struggled to find the right word before he settled on 'Rachel is my wife.'

'And the nature of your current relationship?'

He shifted on his chair, crossing his legs, left ankle over right knee. He took a moment to make certain that his cuff was adequately shading the top of his sock. I wasn't sure he was going to answer my question at all, but he finally said, 'Rachel's in Las Vegas, still attending weddings, still delusional, still . . . psychotic. Sadly, that hasn't changed.' He paused. 'She moved there for the weddings. I'm sure you could have guessed that even if you hadn't heard about it. She still feels compelled to . . . There's no shortage of weddings in Las Vegas, that's for sure.'

Yes, I know. I know a lot about Reverend Howie and the Love In Las Vegas Wedding Chapel.

'And she's still suffering, that hasn't changed. She's still struggling with her illness, and . . . and with the medicines. She hates the medicines. She hates the new ones as much as she hated the old ones. Sometimes she takes them, more often she doesn't. They help when she takes them, but they don't solve anything. They're not a cure, not for her.' He exhaled through pursed lips. 'I hope you don't mind if I ask, but why is this important?'

I went into a matter-of-fact spiel about a psychologist's ethical burden to avoid dual relationships, and explained that it would be difficult for me, as a psychotherapist, to avoid them if I didn't even know they existed. My explanation was intentionally convoluted, but Bill seemed to buy it. I'd figured he would.

I'd counted on the fact that he would. My voice as level as a freshly plumbed door, I said, 'Bill, you still haven't told me about your current relationship with Rachel. That's the part that most concerns me.'

I thought his eyes narrowed at my use of the word 'concerns.' Maybe not. I wished I'd said 'interests.'

'Well,' he said, 'that's not exactly true, I said that . . .'

Bill's apparent predilection was to argue the point with me, but he changed his mind and seemed to decide that my statement was, in fact, accurate enough that he'd leave it alone.

'We're in touch,' he said. 'If you can call it that.'

No problem, I'll call it that. 'Go on,' I said.

'We talk about once a week. That's not true. I call Rachel once a week, but we probably only talk about twice a month.' He exhaled hard and grimaced. 'She doesn't call me . . . often. Sometimes I leave messages. And the truth is that even when I do reach her, I do most of the talking. I fill her in on what's going on here, with the family.

'She's, um . . . I still think that . . . You know, hope's not really the right word. But I have . . . I pray for . . .'

I watched fascinated as Bill's usual unshakable composure disintegrated before my eyes.

'Yes,' I said, nudging him on.

'Rachel always asks about the kids. Almost always, anyway. So often she's off in a different . . . you know. Her mind is in other places. The weddings. The brides, the grooms. Their families. It's always like she knows them, and that I know them, too. But usually she gets around to asking how the kids are doing, seems interested in what's going on with them. They don't get any older for her. They don't age. I don't know what else . . . to say.'

Although I would have preferred that Bill keep talking on his own without any prompting from me, I decided to go ahead and ask the money question – literally and figuratively. 'Do you still support her, Bill? I mean financially? How does she make ends meet? Given what you're describing right now, I can't see how she would be able to make a living, or even survive on public assistance.'

'Well . . .' he said, flustered by my latest query. 'I didn't think we were going to talk about this today. I don't see how it has much to do with your . . . ethical concerns.'

I waited. Why? I couldn't think of a thing to say.

'I pay the bills,' he said, sounding defiant. 'I pay the bills. It's something I want to do, I choose to do. I feel a . . . responsibility to her. On our wedding day, I said "till death do us part" and I meant it. My love for Rachel didn't end when she got sick. It didn't end when she decided she needed to live someplace where she could be closer to more weddings. I take my vows seriously. So, yes, I support her.'

Was there a little self-righteousness in his tone? Yes, there was. But the reality was that what Bill had been doing for his wife for almost a decade was extraordinary. Not too many men in the same circumstances would have done it. I was touched by his compassion and commitment.

'That must be a difficult burden for you,' I said.

'I don't look at it that way. Not financially, anyway. Emotionally, yes – it's hard. I miss . . . having my wife. There's been a hole in my heart since she left me. But financially? I look at it that . . . it's our money, Rachel's and mine, and that she needs some of it to live. That's all. Truth be told, I spend more of it than she does. I don't love her any less because she's ill. I tell myself that it could be worse.'

She could have cancer, I thought, ironically. *Hoho.*

Again, I waited.

'You can't tell anybody about this, right? I've never . . . admitted to anyone that I still support Rachel. I'm not sure people would understand.'

Understand? What, that you're a saint? Why is that such a secret?

'I can't divulge what you've told me, Bill. I won't tell anyone that you support Rachel.'

'Good.'

'Do the kids know?'

He hesitated before he said, 'No. They know I love their mother. That's all they need to know.'

I considered the hesitation. *What was that about?* Why would he lie about that?

I couldn't rationalize my follow-up question therapeutically. I knew I couldn't, so I didn't even try. But I asked it anyway. 'How expensive is it? To support someone in Rachel's circumstances? It must be a severe burden.'

He didn't stumble over the question. 'Of course it is. It helps a lot that she's still on my health insurance. Frankly, that's one reason why I would never – even if I felt differently – why I'd never go ahead with a divorce. If we were divorced, Rachel would have to rely on public health. That would be a . . . tragedy for her. The medicine alone . . . The occasional hospitalizations . . . The ER visits?'

251

Bill looked to me for an acknowledgment. I said, 'I can only imagine.'

He sighed. 'She has an apartment in Vegas, a small one, but it's a nice place in a decent neighborhood. I pay . . . a caretaker . . . to look in on her, make sure she has food, has decent clothes, is clean, you know. And I provide what she needs for . . . the weddings. Dresses, gifts. She's generous – you know that. I don't want her to be living in filth or out on the street. I want my wife to be comfortable, and to be safe.'

I almost said, 'A caretaker?' but I didn't. I was wondering if Canada was Bill's idea of a caretaker for his schizophrenic wife. Instead, I refocused on the budgetary arithmetic. I said, 'It must add up.'

'It does,' he said. I thought he was going to say something else, but he stopped.

While I waited for him to resume, I revisited the math. Supporting Rachel the way that Bill described must be costing him two, three, maybe even four thousand dollars a month, depending on housing, medical, and pharmacy costs. I figured twenty-five to fifty thousand dollars a year. A lot of money.

If I added that amount to the amount that Reverend Howie told Raoul that Canada was paying him so that Rachel could attend weddings – I figured it was probably a similar amount, actually, another twenty-five to fifty thousand dollars a year – we were talking big money. Potentially very big money, since Canada was probably keeping an additional cut for his services. My gut instinct said that the total, fifty to a hundred thousand dollars annually, had to be more than someone in Bill Miller's circumstances could afford.

Especially since we were talking after-tax dollars.

Bill tried to explain how he handled his generous allowance to his wife. 'I make a good living. The company's been good to me over the years. My career's gone well. It would be better if I could make this living in Nevada, but I can't. I consider myself fortunate. The kids and I cut some corners. We live simply. We manage. My car's a lot older than yours.'

Bill had noticed my car? That gave me a little chill.

'Rachel's not in treatment?' I asked.

'She's not interested.'

'And you don't use a home health care agency?'

'We've tried, but Rachel can be . . . difficult to deal with. Over the years, I've pieced something together, some . . . services that seem to work out. They meet her needs.' He smiled at me, just a little sheepish grin. 'Is that it? Is that all that you needed to know?'

'No,' I said. 'I have one more question. It's similar to the first one I asked.'

'Shoot.'

'What is the nature of your relationship with the man who owns the house next door to yours?'

He nodded. 'Doyle?'

I immediately knew that he'd been ready for that question; it was the one he'd been expecting from me all along. It wasn't too surprising; Bill had twice spied me loitering on Doyle's property. But I didn't want to divulge the fact that I knew the name of the house's owner, so I asked, 'He owns the house to the north of yours?'

'Yeah, that's Doyle. I barely know him.'

'Barely?'

'We were neighbors for . . . almost four years. But we weren't close. He's a loner, a single guy. He kept to himself. He'd be outside working; we'd say hi. That sort of thing. He invited me over once to look at his new waterfall, and his pond. Impressive. That's probably the most time we ever spent together. He moved away before Thanksgiving, maybe even before Halloween. The house is vacant. But you know that.'

I noted the dig, but didn't bite. 'When's the last time you spoke with him?'

'I'm having trouble understanding why that is any of your business.'

Although I knew that the reason Bill Miller was having trouble understanding why it was any of my business was because it wasn't any of my business, I reiterated my dual-relationship concerns. Not too surprisingly, Bill seemed less satisfied by my explanation than he had been the first time.

He crossed his arms over his chest. His voice grew wary. 'So you have some . . . professional relationship with Doyle? And if I'm his friend, you can't have a professional relationship with me? That's the deal?'

'I can't divulge the nature of my current professional relationships. I'm sure you respect that. You asked me for my help with something. Before I'm able to agree to that request, it's my responsibility to be certain that there aren't any impediments.'

'Impediments?'

It was a stupid word, born of my anxiety over what I was doing, the tightrope I was trying to cross. But I was stuck with it. 'Yes, impediments.'

Bill looked at me as though my subterfuge was as transparent as glass. He said, 'Last fall sometime. He told me he was going to list the house. That was the last time I talked to Doyle.'

A pad of graph paper. A pencil with a fresh eraser. A whole lot of conjecture.

The meeting with Bill Miller was over and I was busy trying to compute how much it would take to raise two adolescent kids in an overpriced neighborhood in an overpriced town in an overpriced world. I had one small child in a similarly overpriced neighborhood in the same overpriced town, so I could fathom a guess as to what it was costing Bill Miller to support his family in Boulder. Mortgage, property taxes, food, health insurance, car payments, some amount of recreation, teenage whims . . . hell, I hadn't even considered any additional funds that Bill might try to set aside to fund his eventual retirement.

To the sum at the bottom of my sheet of graph paper, I added the approximate costs I'd already computed that it would take to maintain a schizophrenic wife in a gambling and resort town in another state, and somehow simultaneously support her extravagant serial wedding habit.

Total all those amounts, do some rough reverse income-tax calculations, and I would have a guess, admittedly shoddy, as to exactly how many pretax dollars Bill Miller would have to earn to possibly meet all his financial commitments. My conclusion? I was guessing that Bill Miller would need to earn three hundred thousand dollars a year, minimum.

One of the things therapists do every day is listen to people talk about personal things, things like their money. Over the years, hearing various patients discuss their salary ranges for this job and that job, I'd developed a pretty good sense of what kind of living people made doing what kind of work in Boulder County.

There was no way Bill Miller made three hundred grand a year as a district manager of a chain of retail drugstores. What did I think Bill Miller was paid? Low end? Eighty to a hundred thousand dollars. High end? One fifty. One eighty, tops.

Tops.

That was not enough to provide for the two households Bill was supporting, let alone enough to have anything left over for Rachel's nuptial peculiarities, and certainly not at the rates that Reverend Howie charged.

Family money? It was possible that some trust fund somewhere or some generous recently dead relative had come to the rescue to cushion the Millers' financial burdens. But Bill hadn't alluded to anything about any family money softening his financial plight.

So where, I continued to wonder, was Bill Miller getting the money to support two households, not to mention to make all the payments to Canada and Reverend Howie, and to otherwise endow Rachel's sundry bizarre wedding imperatives?

I didn't know. But I was beginning to think that the answer was crucial.

Mallory says her dad is up to something.

I tossed my pencil onto the desk and watched it skitter across the oak and tumble to the floor.

With some sadness and a lot of resignation, I admitted to myself that I'd just crossed a serious ethical line. The meeting that I'd just completed with Bill Miller hadn't been psychotherapy. I hadn't met with him for his clinical benefit.

I'd met with him for my own purposes, whatever those really were.

48

Grace was usually all mine on Friday mornings, my day off. That morning Lauren was in a trial and Viv had a chemistry class from ten until noon. Viv had kindly agreed to watch Grace while I saw Bill Miller but I had to rush back home to pick up my daughter so Viv could get to class on time.

Grace and I often used our Friday time for outings or errands, but on cold winter mornings we sometimes tossed 'usually' out into the snow and snuggled up inside with hot cider, good dogs, and a warm fire. And books.

The temperature had dropped into the single digits overnight and snuggling seemed like a marvelous plan. But my discomfort over Diane and Bob and Rachel and Mallory wouldn't allow me that kind of leisure, so I covered my daughter in multiple layers of cotton, fleece, and Fiberfill, shuttled her out to the Audi, powered up the seat heater, and began motoring west around 9:30. Grace was a good traveler; she seemed cool with our inclement adventure.

In front of us the vertical planes of the Flatirons were draped in a thin fog, as though a designer had decided that a gauzy covering was just what the foothills needed that morning. As we angled closer to the hogbacks north of the city, tiny glistening crystals descended from the frozen mist. 'Look, Gracie, it's raining diamonds,' I said.

Gracie laughed. On Friday mornings, until she needed a nap, I was almost always funny.

I spent the next mile or so trying to explain the concept of triplets to my daughter. For a moment, I actually thought she got it. But when she started squealing, 'Three me, three me,' I was pretty sure that she was still in need of a hands-on demonstration.

* * *

I hadn't called Mary Black to tell her we were coming by, mostly because I thought she would tell me not to bother, but partly because I was ninety-nine percent certain I would find her at home and that announcing my visit in advance would give her time to get her thoughts in order, which was something that wasn't necessarily in my best interest. The reason I was so certain I would find her home was that, considering the energy it took to get one small person out of the house in near-zero January temperatures, I thought it was a safe bet that Mary would need a damn good reason to layer up her three bundles of six-week-old joy to lug them outside.

Mary, her husband Gordon, an anesthesiologist, and their triplets lived in a sprawling contemporary ranch in a tony enclave off the Foothills Highway just south of the mouth of Lefthand Canyon. The house hadn't been built for a family with three infants, and its out-of-town, almost-in-the-mountains location wasn't the most convenient for schlepping multiple kids to pediatricians, preschool, and soccer. I wasn't at all surprised to see a FOR SALE sign out front. Babies change things. They just do.

Triplets change everything.

Before I left the car I tried to check my voice mail for word from Raoul but I couldn't get a cell signal in the mountain shadows. Yet another reason for parents of triplets to move closer to town.

I was relieved the Chinooks that the weather people had been forecasting hadn't yet started blowing. Chinooks are fierce winter downslope winds, cousins of California's fabled devil winds, the Santa Anas. Chinooks warm as they descend from the tallest peaks of the Continental Divide, the gusts compressing and accelerating as they squeeze through mountain canyons before they ultimately rupture out of the foothills onto the communities of Colorado's Front Range in fifty- to one-hundred-mile-an-hour bursts.

A wise man once said that there is definitely a place not to stand when an elephant has gas. In a similar vein, the mouth of Lefthand Canyon was one of the places not to linger in Boulder County during a serious joust with Chinooks.

It took Mary a moment to respond to the doorbell, but my guess was right – she was home.

'Alan, what a surprise.'

She looked surprised. That much was clear. Pleased? That would have been a stretch. Mary had a well-rounded son curled in each arm and the third member of the newly born trio was screaming somewhere in one of the back rooms of the house. Mary seemed inured to the wail.

'Hi, Mary, this is Grace. Gracie, this is Dr. Mary Black.'

'Hello,' Grace said.

'The babies are lovely, Mary,' I said.

Mary sighed and forced a smile. 'They are. Thanks for reminding me. Come in,' she said wistfully as she led us into a living room that had been transformed by necessity into a day nursery. The grown-up furniture – a lot of leather and stone and glass – had been shoved to one end of the long room and most of the remaining space was consumed with infant paraphernalia, including three immense boxes of Huggies from a warehouse store and two matching, side-by-side changing tables.

The memorable aroma of stale diaper pail lingered in the air.

'Let me hand these guys off to the nanny. Hold on a second. Grace? Would you like to come back with me and see all the babies?'

Grace was thrilled. She looked to me for permission – I nodded – before she took Mary's hand and followed her toward the back of the house.

'Sometimes I'm convinced that no one is ever going to come, ever,' Mary said when she returned to the living room.

'Do you know why I'm here?'

She shook her head, but I thought her expression said otherwise. Was I misreading? I thought Mary looked beat up. Her hair was ragged, her face hadn't seen makeup in a long while, and the fleece clothing she wore was spotted with some of the fluids that were either intended to go into infants or with some of the fluids that naturally and copiously came back out. Sleep? Not recently, I suspected.

'Triplets are a handful, I take it.'

'A handful? A puppy is a handful, Alan. A baby changes everything. You know that. Three? You wouldn't believe what it's like. Entire weeks pass and I don't even notice. Christmas was a blur.'

'You know why I'm here?' I asked again.

'No, not at all.'

I thought her response was wary, and just a little defensive. 'Believe it or not, I'm here for a consultation.'

She gave me a you've-got-to-be-kidding look. 'I'm really on . . . an extended leave from my practice. I was originally thinking six months, but that no longer feels like a maximum. I have no idea how long it's going to take for life to feel under control again. My consultation is that you go talk to somebody else.'

I no longer had any doubt: She was chary. I wondered for a third time if she'd somehow expected my visit and knew what was coming.

Mary and I were colleagues, not friends. We'd already exchanged condolences at Hannah's funeral, and I decided that I didn't need to squander any more time on social niceties. She hadn't exactly concurred with my desire for a consultation, but she hadn't overtly refused, either. I said, 'Mary, do you know that Hannah saw Mallory Miller for an intake session not long before she died?'

From the flash in her eyes, I knew instantly that Mary had not known. Her 'No' was absolutely superfluous. 'You're sure?' she added.

'She consulted with Diane about it right after the session. Diane didn't know who the kid was at the time, but she's put things together since. It was Mallory.'

Mary's brain was full of infants and infant things and she seemed to be struggling to shift gears to contemplate the weight of my news. 'Anything that relates to what happened to her?' she asked.

'No, not directly.'

She changed her expression. 'About what happened to Hannah?'

'Diane suspected there was. She went to Las Vegas last weekend to talk to Rachel Miller about Mallory. Diane thought that Rachel might be able to fill in some pieces.' I paused. 'You knew Rachel was living in Las Vegas?'

'Of course. Why didn't Diane just talk to Bill?'

Not 'Mallory's father.' Not 'Bill Miller.' *Bill*. 'Let's say that because of what Hannah told Diane about the session with Mallory, it wasn't an option.'

That got her attention. 'I'm not sure what you're trying to say, Alan.'

I didn't want to give Mary any more information than I had to. 'Diane disappeared on Monday evening in a casino and nobody's heard from her since.'

'What?'

'She walked out of the casino with two men and she . . . vanished.'

'Diane went to Las Vegas because of a discussion she had with Hannah about a single intake session with Mallory?'

'Within two weeks of that intake, Hannah was dead and Mallory was missing. Diane felt she had a responsibility to try to figure out what had happened. You know Diane.'

'God.' Mary turned her head as though she couldn't bear looking at me. 'What do you think I might know that would be . . . pertinent?'

'What *do* you know, Mary?'

She walked away and began folding a pile of recently laundered sleepers and impossibly small T-shirts. 'I wish it were that easy, Alan. I wish it were that easy.' She looked back at me. 'You know the rules we play by. Did Diane ever find Rachel? I wonder how she's doing sometimes. She was so resistant to treatment.'

'Diane tracked her down, yes. At a wedding chapel in Vegas, not surprisingly. Had she talked with her? I'm not sure about that.'

The triplets were quiet. Grace was singing them a Raffi song – 'Down by the Bay.' From which parent she'd inherited the ability to carry a tune wasn't at all clear. It was a recessive gene, though. Guaranteed.

'What do you want from me?' Mary asked. The question wasn't particularly provocative; Mary seemed sincerely curious.

'I'd like to know what Bill Miller was up to. His daughter told Hannah that he was up to something. I'm worried that Diane has gotten herself in the middle of whatever that was.'

'The police?'

'In Las Vegas? No help.'

'Up to?' she said. Her breathing had changed. 'What do you mean, what Bill was "up to"?'

'I'm not sure. Bill seems to have access to money he shouldn't have. He's spending a fortune to support Rachel in Las Vegas. I'd like to know where it comes from.'

She reacted physically to my words: She stepped back. 'Alan, I—'

'Do they have family money?'

'No. They don't. I shouldn't be talking to you about this.'

She was right; she shouldn't be talking with me.

It was her problem, one I didn't want to give her time to

contemplate. 'What do you know about a guy named Canada?'

'Oh God,' she said. 'You know about Canada? How do you know about Canada?'

'Raoul is in Vegas looking for Diane. He found Canada.'

I wasn't about to tell Mary that I was treating Bill Miller. But I found it interesting that Mary knew about Canada, too. Was that good or bad? I couldn't decide.

Was Canada good or bad? I didn't know that either.

'What do you know about him?' I asked.

'Bill asked for some advice about him once. About trusting him. His motives. That's all I know.'

'When?'

'Years ago. Not too long after Rachel moved.'

'What did you tell him?'

'I told him that, given what he knew about the man's background, it would be hard to predict how reliable a ... Canada would be. Whether he could be trusted with Rachel's welfare. I told him I could argue it either way, psychologically speaking.'

'Background? What do you mean?'

'Canada grew up with a schizophrenic mother. She left him when he was young, like eleven. Took off with a guy she met in a bar. He's haunted by it.'

'Makes sense.' But in my business, hindsight almost always makes sense. Foresight is the more valuable, but much rarer, commodity. 'Which way did you end up arguing it with Bill?'

'Alan, please.'

'Help me find Diane, Mary.'

'I argued against it. I suggested that Bill use social services to help him with Rachel if he couldn't afford a home health care agency.'

I changed tactics. 'Do you know why Hannah was in your office the morning she died? Not in her own office?'

'No.'

She'd answered quickly, maybe too quickly. It's not that I didn't believe her reply; it was that I wasn't sure if I believed her reply.

'But you've wondered?'

'Of course I've wondered.'

'Is there any reason Hannah would have been in your office?'

'I didn't think she'd ever been in there without me. Ever.'

'But she had a key?'

'Yes, we each had a key to the other's office.'

Diane and I had keys to each other's office, too. 'Why would she have left her purse in the middle of her office floor?'

Mary opened her eyes wide and shook her head at that question. 'She left her purse on the floor?'

'Yes. Right in the middle of her office. That's where it was when Diane and I got there.'

'That's too strange. The police didn't tell me that. It's so not Hannah. She kept it in the back of a drawer in her file cabinet.'

'Are your records in your office? I didn't see them the day that I found Hannah.'

'What records?'

'Practice files. Specifically, your case file for Rachel Miller.'

'I have cabinets built into the back wall. They look like wainscoting.'

I'd been distracted by other things that day. The image of Hannah splayed over the leather cube, hitchhiking her way into death, continued to intrude on my thoughts with some regularity.

'Rachel's chart is there?'

'I assume it is. Why would Hannah's death have anything to do with the Millers, Alan? I still don't see the connection.'

I could have told her that I didn't see the connection either. Instead, I tried the truth. 'Hannah met with Mallory a couple of weeks before Christmas. Before too long, one of them was dead, the other one was missing.'

She pondered for a moment before she said dispassionately, 'Correlation doesn't imply causality, Alan.'

Ah yes, science.

'I think we both know it doesn't rule it out either, Mary.'

49

We agreed to take two cars into town. The nanny would watch the
triplets for an hour or two. Grace would stay with me. I ended up
parking in the spot behind the small building where Hannah's pristine
Passat had been parked the night that Diane and I had found
Hannah's body.

Mary's car, a Honda minivan with temporary plates – her new
triplet-mobile, I assumed – was already in the other parking slot.

The back door of the old house was unlocked. Gracie and I found
Mary standing in the hallway, her hands hanging limp by her upper
thighs. The narrow passage was dimly lit and she was silhouetted by
the distant front windows. I thought she seemed disoriented. As Grace
and I approached she said, 'I don't like being here anymore. It's so
strange. I never thought I'd feel that way. I used to love being in this
space,' she said. 'Hannah and I were perfect together here. Perfect.'

'I can only imagine what it's like for you,' I said. 'Mary, I need to
get Grace settled with a book or something. I'll be right back.'

I showed Grace where I'd be talking with Mary, and then led her
to the waiting room where I made space on the coffee table for her
books and for some paper and crayons. She chose to sit on the same
location on the green velvet sofa that the Cheetos lady had chosen on
the day that Hannah died. Grace settled right in, picking the crayons
and paper over the books. Her cooperation didn't surprise me; I was
already confident that one of my daughter's enduring skills in life
would be her capacity to ride whatever wave rolled her way.

Mary had unlocked her office door and was standing a couple of
feet inside. I squeezed in behind her. The leather cube was gone from
the room, as was the stained dhurrie. The pine floors looked naked
and ancient. The room appeared as cold as it felt.

I spotted the recessed handles for the lateral files that had been built into the rear wall. The three long file cabinets did indeed appear to be part of the beadboard wainscoting.

'I've only been back once, with the police and my attorney. The detectives wanted to know if anything was missing. I looked around and told them I didn't think so. Nothing appeared disturbed to me at the time, but I didn't do an inventory.'

I recalled how hard it was to return to my own office years before after Diane had been attacked by a patient's husband. I touched Mary on the arm. She put her hand on my fingers.

'You know where . . . her body was, don't you? I mean, exactly?' she asked.

'Yes, I do. Do you want me to . . .'

'No. Not yet. I'll tell you if I do.' She stepped away.

'Okay,' I said. 'She was wearing a blouse that day, Mary. Button-front, collar, silk, I think. A basic thing.'

'So?'

'The front tail on the left side was tucked up underneath her bra when I found her, exposing her abdomen. I've never seen a woman do that before.'

'The police didn't tell me that. You're sure?'

'I am.'

'That's interesting. Hannah was a Type 1 diabetic – she was insulin dependent. She usually injected into her abdomen. Rather than unbuttoning her shirt, she had this habit of just tucking it up under the front of her bra to get it out of the way. Did the police find a syringe close by? Had she just taken insulin?'

'I didn't see a syringe, but I suppose it could have been beneath her body.'

'Have you seen the results of the autopsy? How was her sugar?' Mary asked.

'I assume it was within normal limits; nobody mentioned it as an anomaly.'

'If her shirt was tucked under her bra, then she was preparing to take insulin. There's no other explanation.'

'But in your office?'

'That part doesn't make any sense. She kept the insulin in back, in the kitchen. She would load the syringe back there. But she injected herself in her own office. Hannah was modest, and she was very private about her illness.'

'Always?'

'Always.'

After a poignant pause – I suspected she was still debating whether or not she really wanted to know precisely where Hannah had died – Mary stepped toward the built-ins. 'The file is in here.'

The key was secreted on the shelves above the cabinets in a ceramic jar, something small and celadon. Mary retrieved the key and unlocked the middle cabinet. She chose a pillow from the sofa and threw it on the floor before she kneeled down, slid out the top drawer, and began searching for the file. She fingered the brightly colored tabs sequentially, her middle, ring, and index fingers running after each other as though they were skipping over hurdles. After one time through the area that marked the center of the alphabet, she retraced her work.

That's when she found it.

In a calm voice she announced, 'It's here. I almost missed it, but it's here.' She pulled the dusky red folder and held it up for me to see.

My voice every bit as level as hers – we were both therapists, after all – I suggested, 'Why don't you take a few minutes and make sure that it hasn't been . . . I don't know, tampered with.'

She crossed her legs and sat on the pillow on the floor. Slowly, she made her way through the inch-and-a-half-thick pile of pages of scrawled notes and medication records and hospital admission papers and discharge summaries.

'It all seems to be here, Alan. I can't be a hundred percent sure, but everything seems to be here. It looks just the way I left it.'

I sighed involuntarily. Relief? Disappointment? I wasn't sure.

She gazed up at me. 'You thought someone stole it, didn't you? That someone was in my office that day, that Hannah heard them in here, came in to see what was going on. And that's why she was killed.'

'It was one thought. It all depended on what was in that file.'

She closed the file and stood. 'I can't tell you what's in it. You know how this works.'

'If it's a consultation you can.'

'What good will that do? You can't tell anyone what I tell you. It won't help.'

'I've been looking for Diane all week. I already know other things. Every piece helps. If I can put it all together, I may be able to find her. I'm terrified that time is running out.'

'You won't divulge what I tell you?'

I said, 'No,' and I hoped that I wasn't lying. Was I willing to be lying if it would help Diane?

Yes. Mary had to know that.

'I wouldn't treat her the same way today. Probably wouldn't even diagnose her the same,' Mary said remorsefully, while giving Rachel's file a little shake. 'We know so much more now, don't we? Take me out for coffee, Alan. I'm dying to sit down with an adult for coffee.'

I made an apologetic face. 'Grace will be coming with us.' Grace would be thrilled to go out for coffee; she thought a petite espresso cup full of steamed milk foam with shaved chocolate on top was as good as life got.

Mary deflated, took a step, and slumped down on a nearby chair. 'I forgot. She's a sweet kid, but she's not an adult.'

'Not the last time I looked, no.'

A strong wind exploded out of Sunshine Canyon ten blocks to the west. Had the Chinooks arrived? The *whoosh* shook the house, the naked tree branches squinted together and bent to the east. Debris and dust filled the air.

I excused myself and stepped out into the waiting room to check on Grace. She seemed oblivious to the gales; in fact she was so busy coloring that she didn't notice my arrival in the room. A second blast put the first to shame – the century-old glass began to hum in the window at the front of the house. After one more selfish moment observing my daughter's concentration, I returned down the hallway to Mary's office.

She'd moved to the couch, pulled her legs up under her, and tugged a pillow to her chest. She asked, 'Did Bill Miller ever mention to you that he'd done something he wasn't proud of? Something that was eating at him?'

'No, doesn't ring a bell. Should it?'

'I'm thinking maybe it might be important. He never really explained it all to me, but it had something to do with a traffic accident he witnessed. A young woman died. He was torn up about it.'

I surprised myself by remembering. 'She was an orthodontist,' I said.

The winds had quieted. Strange.

Mary said, 'Yes.'

50

Mary had to get back to the demands of the triplets, and the clock said it was almost time to get Grace home for some lunch and a nap. But something Mary had said convinced me to risk squeezing one more errand into our outing. I didn't even try to explain to Grace exactly what business was conducted at the office of the Boulder County coroner; all I told her was that Daddy had another short meeting.

Years before, during my brief stint as a coroner's investigator, my supervisor was a good man named Scott Truscott. I'd always liked Scott and had felt that once I wasn't working for him he'd grown fond of me, too. Grace and I tracked him down at his desk in the Justice Center on Canyon Boulevard. I introduced him to Grace and he and I spent a moment catching up before he asked, 'So what's up?'

'I'm hoping I can help you a little with the Hannah Grant thing.'

'Yeah?' He seemed interested, but just the slightest bit skeptical. 'I'd love to get that one out of the "undetermined" column.'

The words he used – genteelly chosen without overt reference to death or murder – told me that he was happy to edit his part of the conversation for Grace's tender ears.

He added, 'Why me and not the detectives handling the case?'

I could've finessed my answer, but with Scott it wasn't necessary. 'I have issues with Jaris Slocum.'

'Gotcha.' Scott wasn't surprised, obviously.

'Will you answer some questions for me, too?' I asked.

'Depends what they are.'

That was fair. I said, 'Hannah was a diabetic. Type 1. We both know that. How was her blood sugar when, you know?'

'Blood doesn't actually tell us anything about sugar level during a post; natural autolysis renders the numbers meaningless. But because we knew she was insulin dependent, the coroner checked the vitreous fluid.'

'From her eye?' I asked, a shiver shooting up my spine. I didn't know what autolysis was, natural or otherwise, but feared that asking would either tug Scott down a blind alley, or leave my daughter with nightmares.

'It's the only way to get a reliable post mortem sugar. I don't have it memorized, but she was within normal limits.' His hand reached for his computer mouse. 'You want me to check for the exact number, I can pull the labs.'

'It's okay. Did the detectives recover a syringe that night?'

'You mean with insulin in it? No. They found fresh supplies in the kitchen. Nothing already prepared for injection though, and nothing recently used.'

'Did you hear anything about an open roll of LifeSavers in her coat pocket?'

His shoulders dropped, and he frowned. 'No, nobody mentioned LifeSavers to me. It wasn't in any of the reports.'

'It was there; I saw it. The package was open, the wrapper was curly-cueing out of her pocket.'

Scott appeared perplexed. 'She must have thought her sugar was low. Considering her normal levels, though, that's odd.'

'It is odd. Did you collect her . . . that night?' I skipped a word intentionally. The omitted word could have been 'body' or 'remains.'

He filled in the blank and said that he had. One of the tasks of coroner's investigators is to visit death scenes to begin collecting data, and to prepare bodies for transport to the morgue.

I said, 'Her shirttail was tucked up under the front of her bra when I found her.'

'When I got there, too. Same.'

'Ever run across that before at a death scene?'

'Never,' he said.

'A good friend of hers just told me that Hannah did that when she was preparing to do an insulin injection in her abdomen. To get her shirt up out of the way.'

Scott crossed his arms and sat back. 'I didn't consider that, but I should have. Slocum was already thinking homicide when I arrived.'

He made a sound with his tongue and the roof of his mouth. 'You'll make a statement about the LifeSavers?'

'Of course; I bet the crime-scene photos will show that wrapper.'

'I'll take a look. Will her friend give a statement about the shirt tail?'

'Can't see why not. Why would a diabetic be eating sugar one minute and preparing to take insulin the next?'

'It makes no sense to me. That's one of the things I'm going to have to think about.'

We said good-bye. I bundled Grace back up. On the way out to the car she asked, 'What are LifeSavers?'

We stopped at a convenience store on the way home and I bought her a roll. I guessed she was a Butter Rum kid.

It turned out that I guessed right.

When we finally weaved across the valley Viv was almost done cooking up a pot of macaroni and cheese. As the three of us were finishing lunch, Virginia Danna, the Realtor whom I'd tricked into showing me the interior of Doyle's house, phoned me on my cell.

After reintroducing herself she proceeded without any further niceties, her tone full of conspiracy. 'The rules have changed. They always seem to in situations like this, don't they? With Mr. Chandler dead, buyers are going to come out of the hills looking for a fire sale. Act fast and you might be able to get that house for a . . .'

Song? What house?

I walked out of the kitchen. 'Mr. Chandler is dead?' I said.

'Yes! Can you believe it? This world! Sometimes . . .' She sighed. 'A detective called me today to find out when I'd last spoken with him. You could have knocked me over with a feather when he told me Mr. Chandler was dead, maybe even murdered. Who knows what happened to him? The poor man! Murdered? It gives me gooseflesh, right up my thighs. Now, I will admit that I'm not privy to the estate situation in this particular circumstance, but sometimes people – heirs – at times like this are truly eager to settle things after a . . . especially after a . . . So if I could persuade you to make . . .'

An offer?

She went on. 'Even a lowball offer would be . . .'

Acceptable? Delectable?

I asked, 'Ms. Danna, who exactly is Mr. Chandler?'

'What? The owner of the house I showed you on Twelfth. The one with the water features and that yummy media center downstairs? I'm sorry, I thought you knew.'

'Doyle?'

'Yes, Doyle Chandler.'

'He's dead?'

She was growing impatient with me. 'Mm-hmmm,' was all she said in reply to my last question. Then she waited while I caught up.

'What detective phoned you?' I asked. I was thinking *Sam*.

'I don't recall exactly. Mr. Chandler's body was found up near Allenspark. Maybe it was an Allenspark detective.'

Allenspark is a small town in the mountains about thirty minutes from Boulder by car, not far from the eastern boundaries of Rocky Mountain National Park. When not swollen with summer tourists, Allenspark's population typically hovered – guessing – somewhere around two hundred people. The village was as likely to have its own homicide detective as it was to have its own traffic helicopter. Any investigator involved in a homicide inquiry in Allenspark would be part of the County Sheriff's department, on loan from a bigger city, like Boulder, or someone assigned from the Colorado Bureau of Investigation.

Rather than argue the point, I said, 'I'll talk it over with my wife and get back to you. The house is still a little small for us.'

'One word: cantilever. My mobile number is on the card I gave you. Call any time. When news gets out about this . . . situation, there will be other offers, certainly by close of business tomorrow. You can count on it. There have been four showings of that property this week alone and I don't have to tell you how slow the beginning of January usually is. And that screen in the basement? Remember? Of course you do. I checked. It's a Stewart Filmscreen. I told you, the best. Think hard – a house like that, a location like that, circumstances like . . .'

These.

'I understand,' I said. But, of course, I didn't.

I called Lauren. She didn't return my call until midafternoon during a break in her trial. She'd already heard through the law enforcement grapevine about the discovery of the body of an unidentified male in a shallow grave not far from a trail that meandered off Highway 7 in northern Boulder County. She said she thought the location was east of Allenspark, actually closer to Lyons and Hygiene. I asked her to get me whatever information she could and to call me right back.

'Why are you interested in this?' she asked, of course. The tone of her question made it clear she wasn't sure she wanted to hear my reply.

'It might be related to Diane,' I said.

'Two minutes,' she said.

It took her four. 'We don't have much yet. Pending a post, it appears to be a homicide. Animals had gotten to the body. ID found at the scene indicates it may be a man named—'

'Doyle Chandler.'

'How did you know? Is he one of your patients?'

I could have said, probably should have said, 'You know I can't answer that.' Instead, I said, 'No.' Were the answer yes I would have answered with stony silence. Lauren and I both knew that the silent yes would have been just as declarative as the spoken no had been.

'One of Diane's patients?'

Well, that was a thought. What if Diane had treated Doyle? I didn't think so. I said, 'No.'

'But you know him?' she asked.

'Personally, I don't. Doyle Chandler owned the house that's next door to Mallory Miller's house on the Hill. When she disappeared he'd already moved away and put the place on the market.'

'I don't think the police mentioned that this afternoon. Are you sure?'

'Yes.'

'Is this related to Mallory's disappearance?'

'I don't know. You have to wonder.'

'Diane's disappearance?'

'I don't know that either.'

'But you have reasons to be suspicious?'

'Yes.'

'Then this might be important to you: Sam's up there. He asked the sheriff for permission.'

'He's up where they found the body?'

'Yes.'

'I'll call him.'

'Have you heard from Raoul?' Lauren asked.

'No. I'm still worried.'

'Keep me informed, okay?'

After we hung up, I sent Sam a text message on his pager: 'I know about D. Call me. A.'

While I was waiting for Sam to get back to me, I took a call from Scott Truscott at the coroner's office. 'Try something on for me?' he said.

'Sure.'

'We know that Ms. Grant hit her head when she tripped that morning at Rallysport, right? On the tile floor in the locker room? That's confirmed?'

Hannah Grant, okay. I fought to change gears. 'Yes,' I said. 'The witnesses apparently agree on that much.'

'She tells the women in the locker room she's fine, and she drives straight to her office.'

'We think.'

'Okay, we think. On the way, or shortly after she gets there, though, she begins to feel that something's not quite right – maybe she has a headache, maybe she's a little confused, lightheaded – but she doesn't put two and two together, doesn't consider that she's just bumped her head and that she might have a concussion, or worse. Instead she decides that after all the exercise she'd done that her sugar's too low. She's in her car by then, she doesn't have any orange juice, so she sucks on a couple of LifeSavers. With me?'

'So far.'

'When she gets to her office she's still not herself, not feeling right. The candy didn't help – she's not feeling better yet. How do we know? Easy: She puts her purse in the middle of the floor. All her friends say she's a compulsive person, OCD, truly anal, so the purse? On the floor? That's not like her. Totally out of character. At this point I think she's feeling even worse, not better. Maybe much worse.'

'Why much worse, Scott?'

'Post showed two subdural hematomas, remember? One of those two certainly came from a blunt surface – the tile floor – at the health club, during that initial fall.'

273

'Yes.'

'So we know she has a subdural from that earlier trauma. My theory is she actually already has both subdurals – one from the impact with the floor, and one from something with a sharper edge, maybe the locker room bench – and she's actively bleeding into one or both of those hematomas. Ms. Grant was on aspirin therapy – you might not know that. Family history of heart disease.'

'I didn't.'

'Doesn't matter. Pressure's slowly increasing on her brain, and she's gradually getting more symptomatic. Half an hour passes, then an hour, and she's more and more confused, lethargic, maybe vertiginous. Anxious, probably. Not too surprisingly, her thinking's impaired. All she can come up with is that her diabetes is way out of whack, she has a problem with her sugar. The LifeSavers were there, Alan; in her pocket, like you said. I confirmed that with the crime-scene photos. But if she ate them, they didn't help, so she goes in the other direction, decides maybe she needs insulin.

'But her confusion is severe; she's disoriented – she can't even get her routine quite right. Instead of retrieving her kit from the kitchen to check her sugar, she tucks her shirt up under her bra the way she always does just prior to her injection.'

I saw where he was heading. 'And instead of going to the kitchen for the insulin, she's lost and she goes to the office across the hall?'

'Exactly. Maybe once she's there she begins to recognize her confusion, and she sits. Maybe not. But that's where she collapses, in that other office. Eventually, she loses consciousness. She's still bleeding into one of those subdurals. Eventually, Ms. Grant dies from the intracranial pressure.'

'Go on,' I said.

'That's where you find her. Her shirt is tucked up under her bra like she's going to do an injection, but there's no syringe around, no insulin. It's definitely possible she's eaten some candy. No weapon is ever recovered that matches the second trauma to her head. What am I missing?'

I couldn't think of a single thing left unexplained. 'Nothing, Scott. I think maybe you nailed it. No intruders, no assault, no murderer. No second blow to the head.'

'And no more "undetermined." Hannah Grant's death was accidental.'

'I can't tell you how relieved this makes me.'

'Do me a favor?'

'What?'

'Sit on this until I can run it by the coroner.'

'Of course.'

What was I thinking? I couldn't wait to give the news to Diane. She'd be so happy.

It took Sam a couple of hours to reply to my message about Doyle's body, but he did.

'How'd you hear?' Sam asked. Actually, it was more like a demand than a question.

'The real estate lady. She thought I might spot a housing opportunity in the ashes of the tragedy that was unfolding.'

'Shit. Who'd you tell?'

'Lauren. How come you guys didn't let the DA know that Doyle Chandler lived next door to Mallory?'

'I've been busy.'

Right. 'You still near Allenspark?'

'They just wrapped things up. I'm on my way back to Boulder now.'

'How long has your guy been dead?'

'My guy?' Sam laughed, turning my question into the melodic refrain of the Mary Wells ditty. 'My guy has been dead a while. But it's frigging cold up here, so the body's been pretty well refrigerated. In the meantime, wild animals have been busy doing their wild animal thing. What they nibble on first? Let me tell you, it takes away much of my faith in the natural kingdom. ME's going to have his hands full on this one.'

'Homicide?'

'If it's a suicide, he was considerate enough to bury himself first. If it was an accident, he conveniently died by tripping and falling into a shallow grave.'

'Why'd you go up there?'

The signal faded and wavered. When it was strong enough to carry Sam's voice again, I heard, '. . . and somebody convinced me that I should be asking this Doyle Chandler about the guy who used his garage in Boulder to store a classic old Camaro. The agent thought that since he moved away from his house in Boulder, Chandler was living out this way. I'd called the sheriff to give them a heads-up that I would be chatting with him as a follow-up to the Mallory Miller thing. When the sheriff learned that some snowshoers found what appeared to be his body, they gave me a courtesy jingle.

'For what it's worth, this body shouldn't have been discovered, not during the winter anyway. Most years it would've stayed hidden till spring, at least. You'll like this – want to know how it was found? A woman on a snowshoe outing with some girlfriends had gone off by herself to answer nature's call and was finishing taking a crap when she saw part of a hand sticking out from below this log she was crouching behind. Poor crime-scene techs had to collect it as evidence.'

'Collect what?'

'Her . . . you know.'

I knew. 'What's next?'

'I got twenty minutes to get from here to pick up Simon from hockey practice.'

'You want me to get him? Meet you at your house? I'm happy to.'

'Nice of you, but I think I'm cool. I'll make it in time. Any word on Diane?'

'Nothing. Anything on the BOLO?'

'Nope. Go home, Alan. Stop playing cop.'

With that, the signal faded for good and the call dropped off into the great mobile phone ether.

I wasn't ready to stop playing cop. The day's events had shaken me and I was ready to do what I'd been thinking about doing for most of a week. I drove downtown to my office, opened the dark-blue Kinko's box, and prepared to read Bob Brandt's opus, *My Little Runaway*.

A run, run, run, run runaway.

51

The manuscript was, guessing, about a hundred pages long, but the sheets weren't numbered so I didn't have an exact count.

Bob's story started with a single provocative phrase that constituted an entire sentence, an entire paragraph, an entire page, and an entire chapter.

It moved from there into a series of short, essay-like digressions, one having to do with Del Shannon's childhood, another having to do with the mechanics of installing low-maintenance water features.

A page-turner it was not.

More than half of the sheets of paper in the box were blank.

But that solitary phrase on page one was evocative enough that the manuscript lived up to its billing in the most important area: Bob's story did indeed contain a version of what had happened to Mallory on Christmas night, and proposed a fascinating theory about how she'd managed to make it out of her house without leaving any marks in the fresh snow.

I reminded myself at least five times while I read and reread the few words on the first page that Bob had told me that the work was fiction.

Fiction. Right.

Once I'd completed an initial pass at the manuscript, and after I'd come up with a plan on what to do next, I had some time to kill before I made my next move. I ended up driving home after stopping on the way to buy my girls some of their favorite takeout from Chez Thuy, a little Vietnamese place that Viv – part of Boulder County's Hmong community – had turned us on to. Grace was in a terrific mood while we ate and seemed totally enamored with the way that her rice noodles stuck together.

Over sublime catfish and green onions in a sauce that had more flavors than the sky had stars, I went so far as to tell Lauren that I had some significant news that might impact the investigation of the body that had been discovered that afternoon near Allenspark. She asked for some clarifications that I couldn't provide. But she was kind enough to phone somebody in the DA's office to confirm my suspicion about what would happen next: The Boulder police had indeed already applied for a warrant to search Doyle Chandler's Twelfth Street home.

'How long will it take to get the warrant?' I asked.

'They'll have it soon,' Lauren said. 'Judge Heller has the request; I have no doubt she'll comply. This one's a no-brainer. Likely homicide? The police need to search the vic's house.'

'I'm going to have to go over there and see Sam in person. Tell him what I know.'

'You can't just call?'

'I want to help him find something at Doyle's that I think he might otherwise miss. If I don't tell him what I'm expecting to find there, and then if it turns out that I'm wrong, I won't end up having to breach privilege.'

'And you can't tell me how you know what's inside this man's house?'

'I have a hunch based on something – a story a patient . . . told me. I wish I could tell you more. If I'm right, you'll know all about it tomorrow.'

I arrived on Doyle's block around 9:30. In order to execute the search warrant the police department was out in force – I counted five law enforcement vehicles, mostly unmarked, in front of the house. Doyle's neighbors were curious about the commotion; despite the cold night they were congregated in small groups on nearby sidewalks and on front porches watching events unfold. I chose to park around the corner. If it was possible, I preferred not to be spotted by Bill Miller while running this errand.

I dialed Sam's cell phone from my car.

'I thought I told you to go home,' he said.

'Yeah, well. You get Simon on time?'

'Barely.'

'Who's watching him now?'

Impatiently, he asked, 'What's up, Alan? I'm kind of busy.'

'I have something to show you.'

'I'm working. Maybe tomorrow.'

I could tell he was trying hard to be nice, but that his decorum was on its last legs. 'I know you're working, Sam. That's why I asked who was watching Simon. I'm right outside. I have something to show you.'

'It can't wait?'

He sounded both perplexed and annoyed. I said, 'No, it can't. What I want to show you is inside Doyle's house. You'll want to see it. Trust me.'

'What? You're outside this house? That's what you meant?'

'Right around the corner.'

'I can't bring you in here.'

'Sure you can.'

'This better be good,' Sam said. We were standing in the cramped entryway of Doyle's house. With one deep inhale Sam could have filled the space by himself.

'It'll either be very good, or it won't.'

'That second possibility won't leave me feeling great about bringing you in here in front of God and everybody.' He gestured toward the interior of the house. 'Where do we go to find your treasure?'

'Basement. Where's Lucy?'

Lucy was Sam's longtime detective partner.

'Cabo San Lucas. Cancun. Ixtapa. Someplace like that. Some place I should be, but I'm not.'

I led the way down the hall and through the kitchen to the basement stairs. 'An empty house like this makes executing your warrant pretty easy, doesn't it? Don't really have to toss anything.'

'We don't "toss anything." We're careful.'

Sam had apparently forgotten that my own home had once been the target of a law enforcement search. I was in a position to make an educated argument about the actual neatness of police searches; I decided not to choose that moment to remind him.

'What did you specify on the warrant?' I asked.

Before he followed me down the stairs and into the basement

storeroom he smiled wryly at my question but didn't respond. I hadn't really expected him to. I read his smile to mean, 'Nice try.'

Sam had latex gloves on his hands; I didn't. 'You have any more of those?' I asked, pointing to his gloves.

'I don't want you to be tempted to touch anything. Just keep your hands in your pockets; it's a good place for them.'

'Then open that door.' I pointed at the awning door that led from the basement to the adjacent crawl space.

'Sorry. We haven't been in there yet. I can't go in there until it's been photographed. You certainly can't.'

'My fingerprints are already on that handle. I opened it when I was here last time. You know, with the real estate agent.'

'Terrific. I'll pass that on. Let's hope your prints aren't flagged by NCIC. It'd make for a long night.'

I shrugged. 'I'll just wait until the photographers are free.'

Sam had an alternative in mind. 'Or you could simply tell me what we're looking for. I really don't have time for your games.'

'If what I think is here isn't here, I don't want to blow confidentiality. If it is here, I'll find it, and you'll know.'

He thought for a moment about my plan. 'If you're wrong about all this you're going to end up making me look like an idiot.'

'No, Sam, I'm going to end up making us both look like idiots.'

'I don't give a fuck if you look like an idiot. I do care if I look like an idiot.' With pronounced reluctance, he called upstairs and redirected a photographer from the top floor of the house into the crawl space.

He parked me on one of the recliners in the fancy theater where Doyle had allowed Bob to watch movies.

'Sit here and don't move,' Sam ordered. 'I have to go back upstairs for a while. I'll tell you when the photographer's done doing what she needs to do. Then you can go into the crawl space and uncover your amazing secret.' Sam stopped at the door. 'I mean it. Stay right here, wait for me to come back. Don't even think about going into that crawl space without me.'

I smiled at him. 'Do you mind if I put on a DVD? I hear that projector there' – I pointed – 'is a top-of-the-line Runco. And the screen is the same one that Spielberg has in his very own personal screening room. It's a Stewart, Sam. An actual Stewart Filmscreen.'

Sam gave me the finger and walked upstairs.

It took me about five minutes to get bored. I'd already played with all the levers and buttons on Doyle's fancy leather recliner. In addition to thirty-seven different reclining positions, the thing had a seat heater and a couple of recessed cup holders. All that was missing was a coin slot for a vibrator.

I checked out the vaunted Runco projector that was mounted to the ceiling near the back of the room. Since I didn't even know what I was looking at, that chore managed to use up no more than another twenty seconds.

The recessed speakers? They were only good for ten. There wasn't much to admire in a recessed speaker with the sound turned off.

Doyle's theater was actually rather spartan considering the big bucks that had been invested in its creation. No popcorn maker. No Old West saloon and mahogany bar to belly-up to on the back wall. No Xbox or souped-up Nintendo setup. The fancy Spielberg screen was all that was left for me to examine. I ambled to the front of the theater and gave it a thorough once-over. My impression of the screen was the same the second time as it had been the first: It looked suspiciously like a movie screen.

I returned to my designated recliner. *Where is the remote control?* I bet myself that Doyle had one of those fancy programmable remotes that operated everything electronic on the whole block, including his neighbors' toasters and microwave ovens. That would be an interesting find, right? That would capture my attention for at least a few minutes. Maybe there was a hockey game on TV. Sam would let me watch hockey.

I couldn't find the device. I checked the other recliners for hidden compartments and secret drawers. Didn't spot a single cubby that was spacious enough to stash a fancy remote control.

I began searching the perimeter of the room for a panel that might disguise a hidden cupboard. I used my elbow to put pressure on the wall every twelve to eighteen inches, suspecting that the room might have the kind of panel that you have to press on to free the latch.

Nothing budged. Most of the wall panels were padded and fabric-covered. Whatever was beneath them felt rock solid.

Where is the remote? What good are all these electronics without a remote control?

I was about to conclude that someone had pilfered the thing during one of the showings of Doyle's house when I guessed that the storage cabinet I'd been searching for might be secreted behind the Spielberg movie screen. I returned to the front of the room. Careful to use only my fingernails, I pulled on one side of the mahogany molding.

It didn't budge.

I moved to the other side of the screen and did the same.

That side didn't move either.

I tried the hidden latch trick and used my elbow to put pressure on the right vertical section of the frame.

The mahogany slid backward half a centimeter and clicked.

Bingo.

I released the pressure and the screen swung forward from a recessed hinge on the opposite side of the frame.

My mouth dropped open.

Well, I thought, *this part of the book isn't fiction.*

I pulled myself into the opening behind the screen, used my fingernail to flick on a light switch, and stared, trying to drink in every detail before I was banished from the house, because I knew that it was almost certain that I was about to be banished from the house.

I spent about a minute sitting there – examining, figuring, memorizing – before I hopped back down into the theater, flicked off the light switch, swung the screen back into place, and found Sam in the kitchen. He was engaged in a dialogue with a woman dressed in street clothes. I figured she was a detective or a crime-scene tech. I manufactured some fresh surprise for my voice as I interrupted them. 'Excuse me. Something to show you in the theater downstairs, Detective Purdy.'

The woman with Sam gave me a who-the-hell-are-you look. Sam glared at me, too, and seemed prepared to launch into some low-velocity attack on my character either because I'd interrupted something important or because I'd ignored his instructions to stay put downstairs.

Or both. Most likely, both.

'Now,' I said. 'It's important.'

'Give me a minute,' Sam said. He said it not to me, but to the woman in the street clothes.

52

Earlier that evening, back in my office, I had lifted a dozen or so sheets from the top of the stack inside the blue Kinko's box and placed them in my lap. I'd turned the pages one by one, lingering for a long moment over the handwritten sheet that Bob Brandt had written warning me not to read any further.

Ultimately, I turned that one, too. Considering the transgression I'd committed by arranging the fake-psychotherapy session with Bill Miller that afternoon, breaking my promise to Bob Brandt not to read his manuscript until he gave me permission seemed, by comparison, like a paltry professional sin. Right or wrong, I'd already rationalized that Bob's apparent disappearance was a sufficiently emergent circumstance to void the previous arrangement, anyway.

I was beginning to feel so adept at rationalization that I was considering running for Congress.

The next sheet in the box was the first page of actual text of Bob's book, written in that tiny font he preferred.

No one had considered the possibility of a tunnel.

Talk about starting your joke with the punch line.
A *tunnel?* 'No one had considered the possibility of a tunnel.'
Holy moly.

53

Doyle's excavation was a work of thoughtful engineering.

The length of the subterranean construction wasn't exactly mind-boggling; the distance between the south side of Doyle's basement and the north side of the Miller home was only about fifteen feet. And this wasn't a highway tunnel; the diameter of the mostly round bore ranged from a maximum of about thirty inches a few feet from where it began behind the Spielberg movie screen to as narrow as twenty-four inches or so near the Millers' house. Parallel tracks of angle iron were embedded in the flat floor of the tunnel all the way from one end to the other. A long string of outdoor holiday lights – white only – were stretched along the entire distance to provide illumination.

The slope of the tunnel – it ran downhill at a steeper angle than I would have expected – was curious to me, but my initial impression was that the slope was deliberate. It appeared that the floor of the tunnel dropped about six or seven feet over its short length. A husky winch was bolted to the outside of Doyle's foundation wall and a sturdy stretch of conduit connected it to the house's electrical system. The stout cable from the winch was hooked to one end of an ingenious contraption that was constructed of four sets of skateboard wheels topped with two narrow, interconnected sections of thick plywood, loosely hinged in the middle. The wheels of the makeshift sled fit perfectly into the angle iron tracks that had been set in the tunnel floor.

A flimsy remote-control unit jerry-rigged from a garage-door opener would have allowed Doyle to operate the winch from any location in the tunnel. By climbing prone onto the sled, hanging on, and pressing the remote-control button, Doyle could either slowly extend or retract the cable on the winch, which would either lower the sled farther into the tunnel toward the Millers' house or pull it back up the slope toward his own house.

Simple. Elegant.

Building the tunnel would have been tedious, no doubt. But if Doyle had managed only six inches of fresh digging a day, he could have completed the excavation in a little over a month. A foot a day and he'd have been done in a fortnight. The dirt that he'd removed from the tunnel was undoubtedly part of the weaving contours and berms of Doyle's personal backyard water park.

And the snow thing?

Mystery solved.

54

'You should close that door,' I said, after Sam had followed me back downstairs into Doyle's theater.

He hesitated, his bushy brows burdened more with aggravation than curiosity. But he complied. The chatter from the rest of the house disappeared as the door settled against soundproofing gaskets in the jamb.

I stepped across the room. Without fanfare I raised my elbow and pressed on the edge of the movie screen. The frame swung open on its long hinge, revealing Doyle's portal.

Sam stepped closer and leaned inside. He said, 'Holy shit.'

'Yeah.'

Sam did what I had done, although he pulled on fresh latex first. He lifted himself up into the opening behind the movie screen, flicked on the light switch, and stared. I watched his eyes move from the dirt cave, to the angle iron tracks, to the string of holiday lights, to the winch, to the sled.

I couldn't be sure, of course, but I thought that he was adding things up the same way I had. He didn't say a word at first; he just shook his head slowly. Admiration? Frustration? Amazement? I couldn't tell.

After a couple of minutes silently going over the specific elements and the implications of Doyle's tunnel, he hopped back down from the opening and stood next to me. 'This is what you were looking for?' Sam's voice was only a few decibels above a whisper.

'A tunnel, yeah.'

'But you thought it was in the crawl space?'

'That was my guess. I figured that was most likely. I thought we'd find the opening underneath the plastic in there.'

'You going to tell me how you knew?' he asked.

'No.'

'How did you find it?'

'Boredom. Luck.'

'Tell me how you knew about it.'

'I probably shouldn't have disclosed the tunnel to you, Sam. I absolutely can't rationalize disclosing how I know about it.'

For the time being he appeared to accept that. He put his hand on my shoulder, the act of a friend, and said, 'Come on. We need to clear out. It's hurry-up-and-wait time.'

'Why?' I didn't want to leave; if he'd let me, I was planning to stay and watch the photographers and crime-scene techs do their thing on whatever they discovered in Doyle's tunnel.

'This isn't exactly covered by the search-warrant request we made. I have to amend it and go back to Judge Heller.' He paused, filling his ample cheeks with air and exhaling loudly before he spoke again. 'And now I'm going to need a fresh warrant for the Millers' house to see how this thing looks from the other end.'

He sounded weary. 'I thought you'd be excited about this,' I said.

'You're thinking Mallory, right?' He looked back up at the opening in the theater wall. 'This is how she got out of her house that night? This is the answer to the snow puzzle?'

'Sure. You have to admit that it adds a whole new dimension.'

'I've told you before: The fact that the kid didn't leave any footprints in the snow the night she disappeared doesn't mean anything. What's important about this tunnel isn't that now we know how Mallory got out of the Miller house. That's not why the tunnel's here. What's important about this tunnel is that now we know how Doyle got into the Miller house.

'What we still don't know is why. Why did the guy living next door want this kind of access?'

Sam had a point. 'He certainly went to a lot of trouble, didn't he?'

'This is the sort of thing bank robbers used to dig to get into a vault full of cash. But if Doyle Chandler wanted to bust into the Millers' house to steal, why do all this? People bust into houses all the time. And they get away with it, neighbors even. They pick locks, break windows. But this tunnel wasn't built for some onetime burglary. This was built for long-term access. Bill Miller never reported

287

a burglary at that house. If Doyle wasn't stealing from them, why did he want in so badly?'

'Mallory?' I said in reply to Sam's question.

'Yeah, maybe it's that simple, maybe he was a perv. Time will tell.'

'What if your underlying assumption is wrong, Sam? What if she didn't run? What if Doyle took Mallory out through the tunnel? What if that's why he wanted access to the Millers' house?'

Sam closed his eyes and his body stilled as though he were narcoleptic and he'd suddenly started sleeping standing up. For a moment even the act of breathing wasn't apparent. Finally, he opened his eyes and said, 'Again, why? There are easier ways, and there's a lot we don't know.'

'Like?'

'Like . . . where does this thing come out in the Millers' house? Why didn't we spot it last month? That house got more attention than the new girl at a titty bar.'

'You weren't looking for a tunnel. I wouldn't have found this if I didn't suspect it was here.' I actually didn't feel like admitting to Sam that what I'd been looking for when I stumbled on the tunnel was Doyle's fancy remote control. 'Who would have guessed that somebody had dug a tunnel into his neighbor's house? Who does things like that?'

Sam eyed me suspiciously. 'You didn't go down there, did you? To the other end? Tell me you didn't mess with this evidence.'

'I went no farther in than you did.'

I waited in the vacant living room while Sam went through the house ordering all the search personnel to pack up their equipment and immediately leave Doyle Chandler's home. While he was upstairs I ambled over to the southern window in the living room and checked to see if I could spot the familiar silhouette in the front upstairs window of the Millers' house. I couldn't.

Sam was the last to clear out.

'Not a word,' he said to me as we approached the front door.

'What do you mean?'

'I don't want Bill Miller to know we're heading over there. All I've told the team is that I'm modifying the affidavit. They don't know about the tunnel yet.'

I made a zip-it motion over my lips.

Sam clarified. 'Not even Lauren.'

'She's probably asleep. I'll tell her in the morning.'

'That's fine. You can tell her in the morning. But you can't tell your source. Your patient, whatever.'

I looked at him quizzically. 'Because I know you aren't clairvoyant, I also know that somebody told you about the existence of this tunnel. It wasn't Doyle Chandler since I don't think he's done much chatting to anybody over the last few days. So it was someone else. Maybe the Camaro guy, maybe not. Doesn't matter. Keep the discovery of the tunnel to yourself.'

'I understand.'

'Wait.' He glared at me. 'You weren't seeing the kid for therapy, were you?'

'Mallory? No.'

The glare degraded into a face that was merely suspicious. 'Was Diane?'

I shook my head. I was glad I wasn't hooked up to a polygraph.

'No bullshit?'

'No bullshit.'

'And your guy's still missing, right?'

'Who?'

'The Camaro guy? You haven't talked to him.'

For the moment, I'd almost forgotten about Bob's plight. 'Yes, he's still missing, and no, I haven't talked to him.'

Sam kept his eyes on mine for a few seconds after I answered his question. He was trying, I thought, to decide whether or not he believed me.

'There's something else to wonder about, too,' he said.

'What?'

'Say the Camaro guy knew about the tunnel. What's his part in all this? You're afraid he's a victim. Not me. I'm seeing his name on our list of suspects. Everything's in play again, Alan. Everything from Christmas Day on.' He opened his eyes wide in amazement. 'And I'm right in the f-ing middle of it.'

It was at that moment that I stopped waiting for Sam to thank me for my help in discovering the tunnel. It was apparent he wasn't too happy about being right in the f-ing middle of whatever the tunnel represented.

'Sam, Mallory could be alone somewhere. If you guys have been wrong all along – if she didn't run, if she was abducted by Doyle . . . well, Doyle's dead. She could be locked in some crappy cabin up in the mountains all by herself. She may not have food or water. It's freezing outside. She may need help.'

'I know all that.'

'Did you guys find out where Doyle's been living since he moved out of here?'

Sam just shook his head. 'We have a cell number, that's all. He was pretty intent on keeping his profile low.'

'Why?' I asked.

'We don't know.'

'You don't know or you won't tell me?'

'We don't know,' Sam admitted.

'Did you find his car?'

'Truck, but no.'

Finally, he opened the front door and allowed me to walk out in front of him. 'Go home. We can do this,' he said.

I thought he was trying to convince himself, but I kept that thought to myself.

55

I took advantage of the cover provided by the cluster of crime-scene techs still huddled outside the front door of Doyle's house and immediately cut across the neighbor's front lawn toward my car. I was hoping that Bill Miller hadn't spotted me either arriving or leaving, but I didn't turn around to check for his silhouette at the window.

The night had turned cold, bitter cold, so cold that the snow on the ground squeaked beneath my feet with each step. I raised the collar on my jacket and stuffed my hands as deeply into my pockets as I could. A breeze was blowing down from the north and I lowered my face to retard the harsh chill of the Canadian air. Each fresh gust cut at my skin like a shard of glass.

'I thought that was you over there.'

Someone was leaning against the hood of my Audi wagon, bundled in a ski parka, a wool cap pulled all the way down past the ears. It took me a moment to process the available data – first, that the person was a man, and second, that the man was probably Bill Miller.

'Good evening,' I said. I thought I'd managed a pretty fair attempt at disguising my fluster.

'We need to talk,' he said.

Politely, I said, 'Well, we have a time set up, I think. I don't have my calendar with me.' I didn't really expect my parry to work, but mounting it seemed like a necessity.

It didn't work.

'No, now. You're back in my neighborhood. And you're here with a whole shitload of police. That means we talk tonight. Is that too much to ask?'

Shitload? That wasn't a Bill Miller word.

I was starting to shiver from the cold. I was dressed to travel short distances between warm houses and cars with seat heaters. I wasn't dressed warmly enough to linger on a Boulder sidewalk in January in the face of a north wind.

'It's not appropriate for me to see you here, Bill. This isn't the place for a professional meeting.'

'You want to come over to my house?'

The tone of the question was appropriately sarcastic. When I didn't reply, he added, 'Or I could follow you over to your office. That would be fine with me, too.'

My fingers clumsy, I fumbled for the tiny button on the key that would unlock the doors on the Audi. 'Let's get out of the cold. At least tell me what's on your mind.'

Bill's ski parka was noisy. The nylon or Gore-Tex or whatever the sleek fabric was rustled and crackled as he settled into the front seat of my car. I waited patiently for the crinkling to diminish, and I used the time to put the key in the ignition, start the engine, and flick on the seat heaters. Truth be told, the seat heaters were half the reason I'd bought the Audi. I never knew it before I tried seat heaters for the first time, but it turned out that if my butt was warm, I was warm.

What an epiphany.

I tried to guess what was coming next from Bill Miller. On that front, I was drawing a blank.

Bill pulled his cap back so that it sat high on the crown of his head like a kid's beanie. He stared at me. In another circumstance I would have found the portrait humorous, and might have laughed. Not that day, though. Not those circumstances.

'Yes?' I said.

Bill turned his whole body on the seat, locking his eyes on mine. His parka erupted in fresh crackles and I concluded that the fabric wasn't Gore-Tex. It would be quieter. He said, 'In Las Vegas? Where Rachel is? There's this guy named Canada.'

Holy moly, I thought. *Holy moly.*

56

I had no way knowing it, of course, and wouldn't learn about it until much later when he told me the story, but at that moment Raoul was in circumstances similar to my own.

Similar, not identical.

The weather, he told me, was warm in Las Vegas, the air in Nevada's southern desert hovering in the low seventies. Needless to say, no one was wearing a ski parka or a wool cap. And no one in his right mind was flicking on an electric seat heater.

But, like me, Raoul was thinking about Canada.

The man sitting in the driver's seat of the car in which Raoul was a passenger was wearing a cap, but Raoul wasn't totally certain what the cap was made of. Not wool. The stuff seemed to be part of the stretchy family of fabrics ideally suited to follow the curves dictated by women's swimwear. The cap hugged the contours of the man's shaved skull and was a dark enough charcoal to be mistaken for black. His shirt wasn't Gore-Tex; it was a sleeveless, well-ventilated version of the kind of shell that boogie boarders use to retard board rash. Raoul thought the random vertical ventilation slits in the garment had been fashioned with a razor blade. All the man had on his feet were fluorescent orange flip-flops with rubber soles that had been worn almost all the way through at the heels.

'You carrying?' he asked Raoul. 'I'm gonna be checking later. Tell me now be better.'

Raoul said, 'No, nothing.'

'Cell phone?'

'The cabbie who dropped me off took it. I'd love to have it back.'

'I'll look into it,' he said. They pulled to a stop at a red light. 'U.P.

doesn't fuck around. You have to know that. Just go back home wherever that is, you don't know that. Don't even.'

The car was an old VW bug, similar to the first car Raoul purchased in America decades earlier after ignoring the expiration of his student visa. From dashboard clues Raoul guessed that it was a late '60s vintage, one of the models that came just before what Raoul considered to be the particularly ill-advised bumper design change in '68. The Beetle still had the original beige paint, and the original radio. From the scratchy sound of the hip-hop that was playing, the car had its original speaker, too.

Raoul liked the car. It brought back memories of uncomplicated times.

The man's ethnic background and racial makeup were a puzzle, even to Raoul, who prided himself on his ability to distinguish a Montenegran from a Serb or an Egyptian from an Iraqi across a crowded café. The driver definitely had some Asian blood – Raoul was guessing Tibet – and some African American blood as well, but something else was mixed into his DNA cocktail, too, something Raoul couldn't quite put his finger on.

'U.P. is Canada? Just want to be clear,' he asked.

The man nodded. 'Don't go talking to him that way. People call him that, but people don't *call* him that. You dig?' He shifted through the car's four gears as though it were as natural as breathing, moving the stick with the middle finger of his right hand or with the webbing at the base of his thumb, never allowing the engine's RPMs to climb into the whining range.

'Thank you for that advice,' Raoul said. 'How would you suggest I address him?'

The man seemed honestly perplexed by the question.

'What do you call him?' Raoul asked.

'Boss.'

'That doesn't sound appropriate. How about Mr. North?'

He thought for a moment. 'That'll work.'

'What's your name?'

'Tico.'

'Thank you, Tico.'

'Hey.'

* * *

After a few days tracking his wife, Raoul knew enough about Las Vegas to know that the VW was traveling away from whatever version of civilization the Strip represented on the other side of downtown. He also knew he'd never been in that particular neighborhood before. Literally, or figuratively.

After Raoul had called Norm Clarke late on Thursday to ask him to warn Canada that the Vegas cops were going to start seriously looking for Diane, Raoul had spent some restless hours waiting to hear back. Norm had finally called Raoul and told him that another meeting was arranged with Canada, and that he should wait in a specific spot outside the meeting-room entrance of the Venetian at 11:30 that night. The man who picked him up had been an oldblond guy driving a Vegas cab that was even crappier than the typically crappy Vegas cab. The driver had what appeared to be corn silk growing out of his ears, and he smoked like a crematorium during the Plague. For the short drive down the Strip the taxi was thick with a fetid Marlboro cloud.

Raoul spent much of the next twenty or so hours in a vintage – as in 'old,' not in 'classic' – sixteen-foot Airstream that had been left forlorn in one of the trailer-park slums that stain the arid fields on Tropicana Boulevard just a few blocks from the faux munificence of the Strip. The not-so-mobile villages – anachronistic oases of transiency, poverty, and despair – consumed conspicuously undesirable real estate within spitting distance of the end of the runways at McCarran International. Raoul's Airstream hovel appeared to have been in the same spot in that park so long that it looked like the rest of the place was choreographed around it.

Raoul had been alone in the trailer since he'd been dropped off. He'd killed off the long hours counting takeoffs and landings, studying a couple of blackjack manuals printed in the late '60s, and watching local Vegas news for nuggets about his wife. The TV was a tiny black-and-white with rabbit ears that reached all the way to the concave ceiling of the Airstream. The view out the filthy awning window at the rear of the trailer was of the blunt end of an old Winnebago. The plates on the RV were long gone, the aluminum skin pitted, the paint faded to nothing, and the bumper stickers so sun-bleached that Raoul could only make out the one that was once a lure for Crater Lake. Raoul tried to get lost in imagining cool, deep water and high country air. Couldn't.

He was trying hard not to think about whatever was happening with Diane. Couldn't do that, either.

Before he'd assured Raoul that someone would come soon to pick him up and take him to see Canada, the cabbie had instructed him not to wander outside the trailer.

'What about food?' Raoul asked.

'Help yourself to whatever's there,' the guy had said.

The only food in the Airstream cupboards, it turned out, was a yellow box of cornstarch, a rusty can without a label, and an old margarine tub that was half full of something that resembled ground chilis.

The water from the faucet smelled like a rat had peed in it.

Raoul had decided it was a good day to start a cleansing fast.

Despite his hunger and his impatience and a lot of apprehension, Raoul eventually got it. The last piece of Tico's heritage puzzle?

Pacific islands. Maybe even Hawaii. Raoul smiled to himself, momentarily savoring the unknowable hows and the whys of the lives that had intersected and the passions that had collided and ultimately melded together in the startling mitotic process that had eventually created this Tibetan/Pacific Islander/African American who was driving a classic old German car out into the scruffy desert beyond the urban boundaries of Las Vegas, Nevada.

But, right then, in Tico's VW bug, Raoul was – like me – thinking mostly about Diane, and about Canada.

Canada was never far from his mind.

57

'I don't understand what you're saying, Bill.'

I'd actually already made a guess. Bill was continuing the conversation we'd had earlier that day in my office, the one about all he did to support Rachel in her home away from home in Nevada.

'The caretaker for Rachel in Vegas? It's a guy. Canada's a guy. Canada – it's his name. Street name, I don't know. He's, um, kind of adopted Rachel. He looks after her. Keeps her safe. I owe him a lot for what he's done over the years. I'm . . . grateful to him.'

Kind of adopted? What does that mean?

Bill's sentences came out in a series of discrete bursts. Each succeeding sentence was tagged on as though it were a complete afterthought to what had come before. The choppy cadence was something I'd never heard before from him, which told me that he was feeling something right then that he hadn't felt before in my presence. What was that? What was he feeling?

Anxious was the best descriptor I could conjure. As an explanation though, it felt insufficient.

I said, 'Okay.' I didn't feel anything remotely resembling okay, but that's what I said.

'You know about him already?' he asked me.

'About who?' I stammered.

'Canada?'

'I don't know what you're talking about.'

It was a lie. Was it a smooth lie? Probably not. I lie like I ski. Not as well as most people I know, and my form tends to leave a lot to be desired.

'Canada's help doesn't come cheap. These things are expensive.'

These things? Was Bill telling me that he had financial issues

297

about Rachel's care after all? I had the good sense to stay quiet while I waited to find out.

But he changed gears. He said, 'We've been together, what, three times? You haven't asked me a thing about Mallory. Do you know how weird that is after what I've been through for the last few weeks?'

I thought: *Well, Bill, we've been together, what, three times? You haven't really mentioned a thing about Mallory, either. Do you know how weird that is after what you've been through the last few weeks?*

I didn't say that. I said something else that was just as true, though not quite as honest. 'It's not my call. I thought you would get there when you were ready.'

'Ready? What the hell does that mean? Ready? You've got to be kidding. Hell, what's wrong with you?'

He grew quiet again. I decided to try being a therapist. I said, 'You mentioned a man – Canada? – someone you said looks after your wife. And then you obliquely referred to your daughter's situation. Is it possible that there might be a connection of some kind between the two?' I feared that I'd been way too obvious with my question.

'What are you saying?'

'I'm not saying anything. My job as a therapist is to follow closely behind you, see where you're going, look over your shoulder. Hopefully, I can point out things that you don't see or aren't prepared to see.'

'And that's what exactly? What are you implying I'm not prepared to see?'

Bill wasn't curious to hear my response, not in any sincere way. He was challenging me, provoking me, poking a finger into my chest, trying to get me to back off of . . . something.

'You also mentioned money,' I added. I added it because I guessed that money was what Bill didn't want to talk about.

'No, you're the one who mentioned money.'

'This afternoon, I did. Tonight, you did.'

'All I said is that it's expensive.'

I was too tired for verbal sparring. I wanted to go home, hug my wife, hold my daughter, play with my dogs. Eat something hot. Drink something with alcohol in it. I wanted to spend a couple of hours without anyone doing any inferring or any implying or any alluding. My impulse to flee felt selfish and cowardly, at least partly because I was certain that I was missing something that a more contemplative person would see, but I tried for an out anyway. 'Bill, these are important things for you, obviously. But I don't see any reason that they can't wait until our scheduled appointment time.'

Something about my suggestion seemed to shake him free, allow him to change tracks again. Not exactly what I had hoped for, but at least momentarily I felt the air between us settle.

'What was going on next door?' he asked. 'Why all the cops? Nobody will talk to me. I can't reach my lawyer.'

'I can't say. The police asked for my help with something.'

'Is it about my daughter?'

'I'm sorry. I've promised them that I wouldn't discuss it.'

'Is it?'

'Bill, I'm sorry. I can't say what it is. I can't say what it's not. I've been told not to discuss it.'

'Doyle gave them permission to go into his house?'

Doyle's dead, Bill. His giving-permission days are behind him, I thought as I replayed Bill's question in my head, tasting for disingenuousness. I was wondering if Bill already knew that Doyle was dead.

'I'm sorry.'

'This is bullshit.' Bill's voice suddenly became a hoarse whisper and the anger in it was unmistakable. 'If this is the way it's going to be, I'm not sure I can continue seeing you.'

If that was a threat, it was lame, like holding a rubber knife to my throat. 'That's certainly your choice, Bill. I'll be happy to make a referral, if you would like.'

'Yeah,' he scoffed. 'That worked out well last time.'

And what does that mean? Mary Black bent over backward to help Rachel.

'Mallory saw a therapist. Did you know that?' he asked.

I was startled. I managed a flustered, 'What?'

'The woman who died. Mallory went to see her a couple of weeks before Christmas. She didn't tell me; she left a note about it in her journal.'

I had a thousand questions. One of them was: *Have you told the*

299

police about that journal? I chose a different one: 'Why did she see a therapist?'

'I don't know that exactly.'

'Do the police know? The therapist may have left some . . . records behind.'

He didn't answer my question. He cracked open the door of the car and prepared to climb out, but stopped. 'Do you know anything about her? Are you keeping something from me? You wouldn't do that, would you?'

Now those were tough questions. I didn't have an immediate answer for any of them.

'I'm talking father to father right now, Alan. Father to father.'

'I wish I knew something that could help you find your daughter. I'd tell you if I did.'

He considered my words, tasting them for the sweetness of truth. 'You're a father. You have a daughter, too. Imagine losing her. You have to understand the vulnerability I'm feeling.'

I swallowed. I didn't want to be reminded of that vulnerability.

Bill went on. 'A father would do anything to protect his family. Anything. You know that. The things that can happen to kids? Daughters. You wouldn't wish that on me, would you? I wouldn't wish it on you.'

I immediately began pondering the question of how truthful my answer had been. Surprisingly, I decided that, other than the existence of the tunnel, and the fact that I knew she'd seen Hannah for a single therapy session, I didn't actually know anything substantive about Mallory. I really didn't. How odd.

'You wouldn't divulge our conversations to the police, would you?'

'Of course not,' I said. I wondered how much Bill really knew about Mallory's situation. 'What do you think happened to Mallory? Did she run? Was she abducted?'

'Those are the only options?' he said.

What? Was he taunting me? 'I'm not sure what you're saying.'

'Why would she run?' Bill asked.

'Kids aren't always rational, Bill. Especially when they're distraught.'

'She was distraught. Christmas was always hard for her,' Bill said. 'Always. But I thought we were doing okay this year.'

300

That's what Bob had said, too – that Christmas was hard for Mallory. *Huh.* I reminded myself that Rachel had deserted her family during the holidays years before, and that it wouldn't be surprising that Mallory was suffering an anniversary reaction.

'You were doing okay, you and she?' I asked.

'What are you asking?'

'Nothing. I'm fishing.'

'Fishing?'

Bill hovered, half-in, half-out of my car for a long three-count before he stood. I sat frozen in place, still troubled by Bill's admission that he possessed a diary from his daughter that he hadn't shared with the police. 'Let's do this in the morning, Bill. At my office. Is ten okay?'

He held up his gloved right hand and extended two fingers. 'Can't do ten. I'll be there at two,' he said before he slammed the door.

The bitter air had frosted the hairs inside my nose.

But I did notice that my ass was nice and warm.

58

The same night, at almost the same time, Raoul was still thinking about Diane and Canada.

He told me later that he was surprised to see how Las Vegas bleeds out into the northern desert. There is no natural demarcation, no river, no ridge, no rail at the craps table. There is no single line in the dirt and sand where a visitor would say, well, this here is Las Vegas, and that there isn't. At some point you know you've left town, but even if someone offered you to-die-for odds, you couldn't go back and find the precise spot where it happened.

Raoul looked back over his shoulder at the profile of the distant Strip that stained the near horizon with artificial vertical interruptions and radiating flashes of neon. He guessed that he and Tico were about five miles outside of town. It could have been seven, could have been three, but he was guessing five.

Tico had yanked the VW through a lot of turns to get where they were, many more than Raoul thought should be necessary to get from point A to point B across a landscape of flat, mostly barren land. But the turns had accomplished what Tico had intended: Other than being some number of miles out in the desert north of Las Vegas, Raoul didn't know where he was.

Wide expanses of scruffy land separated the houses. In some other place, somewhere where the soil was arable, such distances between homes might make sense, but in the desert outside Vegas it seemed to Raoul that people lived as far apart as possible simply so that they could feel some separation. In Colorado's mountains, a ridge or an outcropping of rock or a thick stand of lodgepole pine was enough to leave neighbors feeling distinct from one another. Out in this endless desert, though, the geography made no natural allowances for privacy, and separation apparently meant space.

Tico doused the headlights on the VW a few hundred yards before he pulled to a stop at an expensive wrought iron gate in an even more expensive high stucco wall. There wasn't much of a moon and the desert was dark. Raoul couldn't tell where Tico had taken him, but he was guessing the building was a residence. Tico waved casually toward a security camera mounted on the stucco wall, and seconds later the gates clanked loudly and started to swing inward.

The place wasn't much to look at. It was a sprawling, low-slung ranch with long overhanging rooflines designed to protect inhabitants from the relentless Nevada sun. Raoul dated the construction from the '60s or '70s. Somebody had once tried to do some landscaping, but the effort had been abandoned a long time before. Tall, vaguely Greek planting urns sat forlorn and empty at intervals around the property. Adjacent to the crumbling concrete driveway a swimming pool shaped like a spade was a third filled with murky water. The front of the separate pool house was almost totally obscured by junk. The shadowed symmetry of the red tile roof on the shack was interrupted by broken and absent tiles and what looked to be an abandoned array of solar panels.

Raoul said, 'That fence we went through is worth more than the house.'

'Boss isn't picky about stuff. Everything's temporary but people. That's what he says, says it all the time.'

'I take it he doesn't swim.'

'Don't go there, man.' Tico smiled. 'Don't go there. Uh, uh. No swimming jokes, you dig?'

'Yes,' Raoul said. 'Thanks. Does he live here?' He didn't expect to get an answer and was surprised when Tico decided to give him one.

'Stays here sometimes. Other places, too. A lot. He lives where he happens to be. At some point soon enough this place will get sold. They be another, and another after that. Like that. He gets 'em. Gets rid of 'em. We move on.'

'The Airstream?'

Tico smiled. 'Had that one for a while. May be gone now, too.' He killed the tiny engine on the bug. For a moment the clatter of the valves was the loudest sound in Raoul's ears.

Raoul said, 'Your boss and me have that in common. Buying and selling. I'm a bit of a speculator, too.' Initially Raoul thought Tico had been considering saying something in reply, but had thought better of it. 'You have some advice for me?'

'Advice?' Tico adjusted the fabric that clung to his shaved skull, pulling it tighter toward his ears, tight enough that a phrenologist could have done a comprehensive exam without removing the cap. 'Whatever you think is about to happen here, bro, you wrong. That's my advice for you. If you think you here 'cause you want to talk to U.P., you wrong. Want to know why you here? You here 'cause U.P. want to talk to you. No other damn reason.' He opened the door and hopped out of the car. 'I need to pat you down now. No offense.'

Raoul joined him on the driveway and lifted his arms. 'None taken. I apologize for the smell. The shower in the Airstream wasn't working.'

59

A frosty halo was framing what was visible of the moon as I turned east on Baseline toward my house. Most days, late rush-hour traffic would have dictated that I take South Boulder Road across the valley, but that night, because of the hour, I took Baseline. I was stopped at the traffic signal at the Foothills Parkway when my cell chirped in my pocket. I fished it out, managed to hit a tiny button with my almost frozen fingers, and said, 'I'll be home soon, I promise. I'm on my way. I'm sorry.'

But it wasn't Lauren. It was Sam.

'Sweet,' he said. 'Total capitulation. I find that so attractive in a man. Where are you?'

'Baseline. Across from Safeway.'

'Good, you're close. Come on over to the department. I want to show you something.'

'Now?'

'You'll want to see this.'

The signal arrow turned green. I checked my mirrors and cut across two lanes of the intersection to make one of the more illegal left turns in Boulder history, and accelerated back toward Arapahoe.

'Tell me,' I said.

He of little patience said, 'Patience.'

I arrived at the Public Safety Building on Thirty-third Street within minutes and parked on the deserted street out front. Sam was pacing in the public lobby, eating the last few bites of a Chipotle burrito that I knew had originally been almost the size of a loaf of Wonder Bread. My stomach growled at the tantalizing smell.

'Chicken?'

'Carnitas. Not too much fat. Niman Ranch pork. No hormones

or shit. I get them with no sour cream, no cheese. Living in Boulder is finally starting to rub off on me.' He stuffed a final chunk of burrito into his mouth. 'Probably too much salt, though. Whatever, it's a treat. A year ago I probably would have been sucking that white shit out of the middle of a Twinkie.'

'Got any more?' I asked.

'Ha. Come on,' he said, balling up the tinfoil and dropping it into a trash can by the reception counter. He wiped his mustache with a napkin and tossed that away, too.

'You already revise your warrant?' I asked.

'Just waiting on Judge Heller and then we head back to the Hill for round two.'

I followed him down the central corridor to a detective's work area that was set up with a video monitor. The detritus of a few other investigations and the refuse of a few other recent fast-food meals littered the surface of three laminated tables that had been pushed into a clumsy U-shape.

Detectives cleaned up crimes; they apparently didn't clean up after themselves.

'Make yourself comfortable,' he said, pointing to a chair that didn't scream 'comfort.'

'I'd be more comfortable home in bed.'

'Yeah,' he said wistfully, but without any empathy whatsoever.

I sat. 'What is it you wanted me to see?'

He gestured at the AV setup. 'You tell me.'

He flicked on the monitor and used a remote control to start a VCR. After a moment's whirring the familiar logo of the local Fox news affiliate filled the screen.

'We recorded this off the air. TiVo. Somebody upstairs transferred it to tape for me to play with. VCRs I can handle, barely. TiVo? Sorry, I don't TiVo.' He chuckled at something. 'Department has frigging TiVo. When I got here we had yellow squad cars.'

I ignored the fact that the allusion made no particular sense and smiled at the memory of the banana-colored patrol cars that Boulder's cops had driven around town for a while as part of a short-lived, amusing experiment in community-friendly policing.

I expected I was about to watch tape of the local Fox affiliate's coverage of the discovery of Doyle Chandler's body near Allenspark that afternoon. Why? Sam would tell me when he was ready. Not before. But Sam surprised me, as he often did.

'Christmas night,' Sam said as the screen showed Fox's infamous Mallory Miller money shot: the helicopter footage of the Hill on Christmas night, the tape that purportedly showed no footprints or tire tracks leaving the Millers' home after the snow started falling in earnest.

'You oriented?' he asked.

'Yes.' I'd seen the footage often enough to know what was what. If you lived in Colorado in the days after Mallory's disappearance and had turned on your TV set, you had seen this film as many times as you'd seen the other little Boulder girl dancing around at beauty pageants.

Sam paused the screen, picked up a laser pointer, and let the red dot settle. 'Harts' house.'

'Got it.' The holiday lights were unmistakable.

'Millers' house and Doyle Chandler's house are over here.' He made a dot appear on the wall behind the monitor.

'Right where they've always been.'

'Fox has been kind enough to superimpose the time line on the bottom of the screen.' He started the tape again. 'Here's where the controversy starts: nine-sixteen.'

The footage was the enhanced version that Fox had promoted and promoted and promoted a few days after Christmas. It was the clip that started at 9:16 on Christmas night and stopped a couple of minutes later with the famous few seconds that showed no footprints or tire tracks leaving the Millers' home.

'I've seen this,' I said.

'Yeah, but have you *seen* it? Start with your eyes at the lower-right corner of the screen – here, Doyle Chandler's garage.' He paused the footage momentarily. The Harts' house was in the center of the screen; Doyle's house, but not the Millers' house, was visible on the lower edge.

I'd never noticed that Doyle's house showed up in the early moments of the Fox footage. Sam said, 'That's smooth snow around the garage, right?'

'Yes.'

'Fresh? You're sure.'

307

'Yes.'

'Well, keep your eye on the garage as the chopper moves around. With the distraction of the Christmas lights and the shadows it's kind of hard to follow, but try.'

Sam aided me with his laser pointer; he was remarkably adept at keeping the red dot targeted on the dark mass of Doyle's garage. As the angle of the shot varied with the helicopter's movement the garage would frequently shift totally out of the frame; one long absence lasted for a good half minute, another for almost as long.

I stated the obvious. 'Can't see it most of the time, Sam. It goes off the screen.'

'I know. It's important that you can't see it. The last few seconds are coming – watch carefully.'

Fox hadn't enhanced the area on the footage that included Doyle's garage – they'd focused all their technological wizardry efforts on the Millers' property – and it wasn't easy to discern much detail in other parts of the frame, especially with the startling bright lights that stayed mostly centered on the screen, lights that were emanating from the garish Christmas display at the Harts' house on the next block.

The Very Hart of Christmas.

'There,' Sam said. He paused the tape and allowed the red dot to linger on the short driveway that led from Doyle's garage to the alley. 'What do you see now?'

I stood up and moved closer to the monitor. The closer I got, the larger the pixels on the screen appeared. At first I wasn't sure what I was seeing, or even if I was seeing anything at all. Then I was.

I turned and faced Sam. 'Are those . . . tire tracks leaving Doyle's garage?' I asked. 'Those weren't there at the beginning.'

'Yeah, that's what I see, too,' Sam said. His tone was understated and self-satisfied.

Bob, I thought. Bob had pulled his Camaro out of Doyle's garage during the second extended period that the garage was out of the frame.

The tunnel. The damn tunnel.

The damn movie in the damn theater in the damn basement.

Did Bob really have something to do with Mallory's disappearance?

I was shocked. 'Did he help her leave, Sam? Or did he take her?'

308

I didn't have to say who 'he' was. He knew I was talking about Bob.

'You don't know where he is, do you?' Sam asked.

'No, I told you I didn't. I don't.'

'This isn't some therapist nice-nice secret-secret bullshit?'

'I don't know where he is.'

'You know where to look for him?'

I hesitated for a split second. 'No.'

Sam made a guttural noise – okay, he growled at me – and mouthed a dry 'f' sound. It didn't take much lip-reading skill to know what exactly he'd thought about saying.

'I really don't, Sam. If I did, I'd tell you. Given what already happened to Doyle, Bob could be in danger, too. I would tell you if I knew.'

He wasn't satisfied. 'You know something, don't you? You know something that could help me? Something you're not telling me?'

'Sam . . .'

'Man . . .' He stood up quickly, almost knocking his chair over.

Five minutes later Sam walked me back to my car. He seemed impervious to the cold. I bet he didn't even care that his Cherokee didn't have seat heaters.

'Chinooks tomorrow,' Sam said.

'They thought they were coming today, too. They're wrong a lot,' I replied, wondering why we were talking about the weather. 'If the Chinooks do start to blow, at least it will warm things up a little. It's too cold.'

'The media isn't going to know what to do with those winds,' Sam said. 'Should be fun.'

'What?'

'They'll be back tomorrow. You know they will. With word of the tunnel and the Doyle Chandler situation? All the trucks and all the cameras – they'll all be back outside the Millers' house doing their stupid live shots. The idiot lawyers on cable will all be saying we blew it again. Us, the Boulder cops. "It's just like Christmas eight years ago," that's what they'll say. But then the Chinooks will start blowing late morning and they'll blow the goddamn experts all the goddamn way to Denver, maybe farther. It'll be too windy to raise the antennas on their trucks. I wish I could be there; it'll be fun to watch.'

I checked his expression. He was truly sorry he was going to miss it.

'I'm going to tell Lauren about all this, Sam. The tunnel, Doyle, Bob,' I said. 'I need some advice from her.'

'Tell her to sit on it till morning. Our bases will be pretty well covered in the next couple of hours. Get some sleep for me tonight.' He stuffed his hands in his pockets. 'I don't think I'll be getting much.'

'How did you put this together?' I asked as I clicked open the wagon doors with the key remote. 'The Camaro? Why did you decide to go back and look at that tape?'

'This is far from together. The tunnel changes everything. One of the things it changes is which house we should be paying attention to. Where Mallory's disappearance is concerned, we've had our eyes on the Miller house, not on Doyle Chandler's house. On the way back here to amend the warrant app I remembered that you had asked me if there was a car in Doyle's garage when we searched the house the day after Mallory disappeared. I told you I didn't think so, but it's been something I've been meaning to ask your patient Bob about if we ever caught up with him.'

'But you decided to check the Fox footage instead? Smart, Sammy. So do you have a theory to explain all this? Does tonight – the tunnel and this video – does it change your thinking about her disappearance? You still sure she's a runaway?'

'I have a few theories,' he said. 'How many do you have?'

He waited for me to answer.

When I didn't, he added, 'Thought so. I'll show you mine if you'll show me yours.'

I left the show-and-tell right there. 'You still want to run in the morning? I'm happy to bag it if you're too busy.'

'I want to run,' he said. 'No excuses. Since it's Saturday, I'll let you sleep in. Come outside at seven-thirty – I don't want to ring the bell.'

60

I finally made it home from the police station, took the dogs out for a last time, climbed into bed, and rubbed Lauren's back until she awakened. Although I left a few names and a few details out of my story, I told her enough of what I knew that she understood the magnitude of my dilemma. I finished by asking for her advice.

Her counsel was succinct. 'Higher, on my neck. Right there.'

'That's it?'

'No, that's not it. On one hand you know a lot. On the other hand you don't know much. You need to leverage what you have. Save Diane no matter what it takes, screw the rest.'

'It's all that clear to you? I could get censured, lose my license.'

She rolled over and faced me. My eyes were adjusting to the dark and I could see the shimmer of her irises. She said, 'You'd have to sleep with a patient, kill her, and then have sacrilegious sex with her dead body before that spineless state board would yank your license, and you know it. But what if they do? You and me and Grace? We'll make it if you have to change careers. We will. Will you make it if you knew you could have done something that might have helped Diane and you didn't do it? I don't think so. You're pussyfooting around this, Alan. The rules need to be broken sometimes. This is one of those times. Break the damn rules, save your friend, suffer the consequences. You won't be able to live with any other choice, you know that.'

'Just like that?'

'Just like that.'

She reached a warm arm out from under the comforter, put her fingers on the side of my neck, and lowered her voice to a late-night whisper. 'There's some things I know about you, sweetie: You're a better cook when you're not too hungry. You're a better dad when you're not feeling too protective. And you're a better lover when you're not too horny.'

'You have a point?'

'You want this to be right too much, and it's clouding your judgment. Step back. Take off your therapist hat. Be a friend, first. You'll know what to do.'

I didn't have to think long to know that her advice was sound.

'What?' she said, sensing something.

'I'm a better lover when I'm not too horny? Really?'

She smiled and shrugged. She dropped her hand so that it slid down my bare chest. 'You want to prove otherwise?'

The truth was, I didn't. Not right then.

61

The way he told it to me later, Raoul's evening, like mine, ended with just the slightest ray of hope.

More quarry tile than he had seen in a long, long time. Big tiles – eighteen-inch squares. Brick-red, uneven surfaces, with dirty grout lines as fat as a grown man's finger. The tile extended through every doorway, down every hall. This house was apparently where the awful quarry tile from that dubious '70s design burp had gone to die.

Raoul had expected to find a posse surrounding Canada, a jury of pathetic hangers-on. He'd expected to have to weed through a motley assortment of tougher-than-shit Cristal and Courvoisier-and-Coke-drinking parasites.

Instead he found a fit, barefoot man wearing crinkled linen slacks and a faded polo shirt that was the color of the flesh of a ripe mango. The man was sitting on one of two big armchairs that shared a large, mismatched ottoman and faced floor-to-ceiling sliding glass doors in the living room. His legs were crossed at the ankles. One toenail on his left foot had turned the brown-black of just-roasted coffee beans. It was the toe next to the pinky.

Canada was alone.

'Sit,' he said to Raoul.

Tico loitered across the room near the back door where the parking lot of quarry tile started, or ended. He said, 'You cool, Boss?'

'Yeah, get yourself something to eat.'

Tico saluted with a motion of two fingers flying out from his right nipple. Raoul figured it meant, 'Yes, sir.' Or something in that vicinity. Tico spun. His flip-flops squealed once before they began a percussive *smack-smack* against the hard floor as he made his way toward the kitchen.

'I can't find her,' Canada said. 'Come on, sit.' He pointed at the chair beside him. 'You want something to drink?'

Raoul did, but it could wait. *You can't find whom?* That's what he wanted to know. That couldn't wait. He said, 'No, thank you.'

He was thinking that U.P. North was late thirties, maybe forty. The man was fair-skinned with a full head of curly jet-black hair, and he apparently went to some trouble to avoid the desert sun. He was strong. Not I-live-in-the-weight-room strong, but I've-got-a-personal-trainer and I-play-a-heck-of-a-lot-of-tennis strong.

Raoul fought an instinct that was telling him that he knew the man, or at least knew his type. Sometimes in Boulder he met the smug, self-assured, I've-got-shit-going-on-you-don't-even-know-about types at parties. At first impression, U.P. North could be one of them, just another Boulder trust-fund baby. But Raoul cautioned himself that North probably wasn't one of them. Not by a long shot.

Intimidating? Not to Raoul, not yet.

Blood? Northeast U.S., sure. Whatever that means anymore. Some French ancestry, and maybe something else. Could North have some Eastern European blood, maybe Jewish? Raoul wasn't certain. Didn't know if he had enough clues.

Raoul sat. 'You can't find her? My wife?'

Three sets of sliding glass doors were open to the night air. The pattern meant that every other panel was glass, every other panel was screen. The prodigious sweat that Raoul had developed while doing time inside the Airstream and then compounded in the cramped front seat of Tico's bug wasn't evaporating at all. No breeze was blowing across the wide desert that night.

'I like the heat,' the man said as though he'd anticipated Raoul's thoughts. 'Hate AC.'

Raoul duly noted that his question hadn't been answered and decided not to press it. North wasn't actually talking to Raoul, he was talking to Raoul's reflection in the glass. Raoul adjusted his gaze, found the mirrored image of his host against the black hollow, and did the same. He said, 'I changed my mind. I'd love a beer, thank you.'

Canada called out, 'Tico? A brew for our guest.'

Tico came and went. He left behind a long-necked Bud that was sweating even more than Raoul. The bottle immediately left a round tattoo on the table.

'You like the desert?' Canada asked.

'I grew up on the Mediterranean,' Raoul said as a way of answering. 'Live in the mountains now.'

'I grew up on Long Island, not far from Jones Beach. I like the desert better.'

'Taste,' Raoul said. 'It's a personal thing.'

North chewed on that for a moment. 'There's some shit we do that has nothing to do with taste. It has to do with cycles. Ebb and flow. Moon and tides. Sunrise, sunset. You play golf?'

'Some. I suck,' Raoul said.

North laughed. 'Bastard game. In golf . . . in business . . . with women . . . dear Lord, with women . . . all the time, I'm big on mulligans. I . . . treasure the living that happens in the echoes. Like to think I do some of my best work in the echoes.'

'The echoes?'

'The opportunities that come back around. The do-overs. A man has to learn in life. He has to. In golf, it's not really that satisfying. It's hard to learn enough from one tee shot to the next. If you do better on your mulligan than you did on your first drive, could be dumb luck. Probably is dumb luck. In life, though, the do-overs tend to come around less often. That gives the wise man time to adjust, to be grateful for the opportunity, to make the most of the blessing of the second chance. You're a successful man. You must know about the echoes. Every successful man I've ever met knows about playing the echoes.'

Raoul drank enough of the Bud that when he pulled the bottle back down from his lips the beer leveled off at a line about two thirds of the way down the label. He said, 'If I'm understanding you right, I think maybe I do know about the echoes.'

'Rachel's one of my echoes.' Canada's eyes locked on Raoul's in the black mirror of the glass. He held Raoul's gaze like a strong man holds a handshake – a few beats too long, just to prove that he can do it. 'She's a paranoid schizophrenic. You know about that?'

Raoul decided the time was right to once again interject Diane into the conversation. 'My wife's a psychologist. I learn some things from her.'

North nodded. Raoul translated the nod to mean, 'Whatever.'

'My mother was one, too. A paranoid schiz. I watched her do her crazy thing most of the time I was growing up. Nobody helped her out. Not really. People laughed, the ones who didn't avoid us took advantage. She ended up running away with some loser she met in a biker bar. Came home with him, grabbed some things, said she'd be back soon. I never saw her again. I still don't like to think about what happened to her next.'

Raoul felt the rhythm of the melody that was developing and decided to skip right to the chorus. 'But for Rachel, you're what happened next?'

'There's the echo. When they come back around, you get another chance. Not all the time, but sometimes. When you do, it's important to get it right. The gods count on it. They keep score.'

'You take care of her?'

'I watch out for her. Difference. Nobody can protect her from being crazy. I learned that lesson as a kid. Paranoid schizes have the kind of crazy that comes from someplace else. Someplace where the tiniest wires are jumbled, someplace you and I don't ever get to visit. All I do – all I can do – is I protect her from people who prey. That's all. I let them know if they fuck with her, they have to fuck with me. People in town have learned to leave well enough alone; people new to town need lessons. It's what I wished I could have done for my mother.'

Raoul lost the visual connection in the pane of glass as Canada shifted the range of focus from Raoul's eyes to the infinity of the desert night. From inside to out.

'That's generous of you,' Raoul said, already wondering whether his empathy was being misapplied.

'Is it?'

Raoul didn't want to argue the point. A linguistic chameleon, he adopted his host's vernacular. 'Has someone fucked with her lately?'

'People have been coming in from out of town. It's not been welcome. We've had to deal with it.'

Raoul felt the reverberation: Diane had come in from out of town. He put his cards on the table. 'My wife flew to Las Vegas looking for Rachel. She had some questions about her daughter – Rachel's missing daughter. I'm sure you know that. Before she was able to meet with Rachel, Diane disappeared off the casino floor at the Venetian. That was Monday night. I'm worried about her, very worried. I'd like to know where she is. I'm happy to tell you what I know.'

With just the slightest spice of menace added to his tone – a verbal dash of cayenne – North said, 'Doesn't make any difference to me whether or not you're happy. But you will tell me what you know. One thing, though, Raoul. May I call you Raoul?'

'Of course. What's that?'

'It's not all about your wife.'

Raoul felt some intimidation then. He shrank a little at the words, had to remind himself not to cower, and had to remind himself that Canada held all the good cards. 'Okay,' he said.

'Now, like I said, I can't find her – Rachel. You feel the echo there? Yes, me, too.' He exhaled through pursed lips. 'I'm not happy I can't find her. Are we in the same boat, Raoul? You and me? The not-happy-I-can't-find-her boat?'

'Are we?' Raoul asked.

'I think so. I think we are.'

Raoul dove so far into his host's eyes that he was almost submerged. Sensing something there, he took a last look at his cards and went all-in. 'Diane was led out of the Venetian casino on Monday evening by two men. They weren't yours?' He pulled the grainy screen shot that Marlina had given him from his pocket, unfolded it, and handed it to Canada.

'You think they were mine?' Canada asked after a quick glance at the photograph of three people walking through the casino at the Venetian.

Totally cognizant of how provocative his words were, Raoul said, 'I did.'

'If they were mine, you'd be a dead man. You feel like a dead man?'

'I admit I've felt better.'

Canada laughed. A stretch of silence consumed half a minute before he added, 'They're not mine.' He raised the photograph, grasping it between his thumb and index finger, and rotated it so that it faced Raoul. 'You don't recognize the tall guy? I'm surprised; you seem like an observant man.'

Raoul leaned over and squinted at the taller of the two men. 'Should I?'

317

'I hear you call him "Reverend Howie."'

'What? *Mierda*. His hair . . .'

'That's not his hair. Probably won it in a poker game.'

Raoul had participated in a thousand negotiations, some of them involving tens of millions of dollars. In every deal, instinct was his guide. He relied on that intuition and felt around in the dark for whatever direction he was going to get. 'Howie didn't take Diane for you?'

Canada hesitated before he shook his head.

'Do you recognize the other man?' Raoul asked.

Canada took another fleeting glance at the paper. 'If I admit I do, what happens then?'

Raoul jumped at the bait. 'If Diane's okay, I swear I'll—'

Canada held his left hand out. A stop sign. 'No, my friend. No . . . No. The ifs are all mine. You don't get any ifs. These two people weren't working for me. I don't know what they've done, or to whom. That means there are no ifs left over for you. We clear?'

No, Raoul thought. He said, 'Yes.'

'Good. I repeat, if I admit I do recognize him, what happens then?'

'I will be grateful for your assistance,' Raoul said.

'How grateful?'

Raoul wondered momentarily if Canada was trying to extort some money. He recalled Tico's admonition in the car – *Everything's temporary but people. That's what he says, says it all the time* – and decided that it wasn't likely that Canada was squeezing a reward from him. Raoul said, 'I will be completely grateful. So grateful you won't be playing any echoes about this.'

'Ever?'

'Ever.'

'And if you happen to run across Rachel?'

'Goes without saying. You'll know first.'

Canada poked at the photograph. 'This guy? The one with Howard? Showed up in town a day or so before your wife, went to Rachel's apartment looking for her, failed, then started asking around about how to find her. Howard alerted us that the guy came to the chapel. Howard, it now appears, was playing both ends against the middle. Well, that's a tougher game than Hold 'Em – and soon enough, if he isn't already, Howard will regret he anteed in. We started keeping an eye on the new man. Lost him for a while. Found him again. Eventually he had a traffic accident. Sad thing.'

'Serious accident?' Raoul asked.

Canada feigned a sympathetic face. 'Misjudged a curve in the mountains. His car had Colorado plates. Tico?' he called.

Tico hustled in carrying a half-eaten piece of cold pizza. His mouth was full. Canada pointed at the photo. 'You know where?'

Tico glanced at the picture, then at Raoul, swallowed, and said, 'I could probably find it.'

'Show our friend.'

'Not sure I can do it in the dark, Boss. You tell me to try, though, I will.'

Canada tapped his manicured fingernails on the arm of the chair. 'Find Raoul a bed for the night, some clean towels, and offer him some food. You can take him out in the morning. And Raoul?'

'Yes.'

'You don't mind that I hold on to this?' He lifted the photograph. 'I'd like to show it to Howard.'

62

I was wide-eyed and body-weary long before Sam's arrival for our Saturday run, but the winter sky was too black for daybreak and the bedroom too cold to consider popping right out of bed. I waited for the growl of the paper guy's Power Wagon to come and go and for the first unmistakable illuminations of dawn before I rolled reluctantly into the day.

Even the dogs thought I was crazy. Emily sighed at me, but she didn't bother to get up to see what I had planned. Anvil, whose ears were beginning to fail him, didn't acknowledge that I'd moved.

I forced myself to drink some water and I downed a banana after mindlessly trying to peel a plantain that Lauren or Viv had stuck in the fruit bowl. The plantain wasn't ripe and wasn't at all eager to be peeled. I totally mangled the thing before I figured out that I wasn't wrestling with a mutant Chiquita.

New errand: Replace the damn plantain.

I thought I heard a car on the lane and peeked out the front door at 7:25. No Sam. I was hoping he'd spaced out the run or that he'd overslept. Jogging on a fifteen-degree morning didn't sound any more appetizing to me than had eating an under-ripe plantain.

Seven-thirty. No Sam. Out loud, I prayed, 'Give it a rest, Sammy. Take a day off.' That, of course, is when he drove up the lane. He climbed out of the Cherokee in his fancy running duds and a brand-new pair of trainers. His frosty breath was visible in long, slow rolls. Lauren's advice from the night before felt as sage to me as it had then, but I still hadn't decided exactly what I knew that I could tell Sam that might help Diane. He rescued me from my temporary paralysis by saying, 'Let's stretch a minute. I want to tell you about the tunnel search.'

The tunnel. The opening that had been excavated from Doyle's basement was cut at a steep enough angle that it actually descended all the way down below the spread footing of the foundation of the Millers' house. At that point the track-and-trolley system terminated and a vertical shaft about two feet in diameter rose straight up into the Millers' crawl space. The top of the shaft was covered by a fitted piece of one-inch-thick plywood upholstered with an ample amount of dirt that had been glued to the wood with some kind of industrial-strength adhesive.

Were someone to venture into the crawl space, any evidence of the construction project was hidden from view by the thick-milled black-plastic sheeting that stretched from foundation wall to foundation wall over the entire expanse. The plastic was installed to collect the natural radon that was common in soil in Colorado, so the gases could be vented to the outdoors and the lungs of the home's inhabitants could be protected from the toxic consequences of long-term radiation exposure.

Access from the tunnel into the Miller home was ingenious. False sills had been attached to the tops of the foundation walls in the corner closest to the tunnel shaft. The plastic sheeting had been removed from the original sills and reattached to the false sills, where it could be easily lifted and folded back to reveal the opening of the shaft. After an intruder was ready to return to Doyle's house next door, he had only to lock the false sills back in place – which would return the plastic to its normal location – and then slide the plywood lid back over the shaft.

A cursory examination of the crawl space by someone in the Miller home would reveal no evidence of the tunnel. Once Sam was down in the crawl space, it had taken him a few minutes to figure out exactly how it all worked, despite the fact that he knew almost precisely where the tunnel should be entering the house. The only clue to the location, he said, was a slight interruption in the dust pattern on top of the plastic sheeting.

Bill Miller professed shock and ignorance at the discovery of the tunnel. Although the revised warrant that Sam delivered to Bill's door gave him no choice about the matter, he was totally cooperative with the police about access to his crawl space.

He also rapidly put two and two together and got four. 'Where is Doyle?' Bill had demanded. 'Have you guys talked to him? Is he under arrest? Somebody tell me something! Does he know where Mallory is?'

Sam made a tactical decision to allow Bill to hover close by during the search – he wanted to observe him – but he wasn't buying Bill's act. 'He knew it was there,' Sam told me. 'Might even have known Doyle was dead.'

'He knew about the tunnel? What makes you think that?'

'You interview enough people you get to know when they're lying. Meryl Streep could lie to me and get away with it, maybe Al Pacino. Definitely what's-his-face, Anthony Hopkins. But Bill Miller? He couldn't even get a bit part with the Flatirons Players. Must be the same for you, you know, in your business.'

The truth was that my patients often lied to me with absolute impunity. I rationalized my often embarrassing credulity by trying to convince myself that when my patients lied to me they were lying to themselves as well, and that was why I was so inept at spotting their mistruths.

But the simple reality is that I am gullible. In reply to Sam, I said, 'Yeah.'

He chuckled. 'Exactly what I'm talking about. Exactly.'

I asked, 'Speaking of being fooled – Jaris Slocum blew it, didn't he? His piece of the investigation.'

Sam nodded. I'd expected him to mount a defense of Slocum, but he didn't. He said, 'I'll deny this if it's ever repeated, but Slocum didn't ever lay eyes on the Millers' neighbor. After the initial search of Chandler's house was negative, Slocum did the follow-up interview by phone – by frigging phone – not in person.' Sam paused and grimaced like he had a bad tooth. 'And he never ran him.'

I was incredulous at the last bit. Sam was admitting that the Boulder Police had never put Doyle Chandler's particulars through the NCIC – National Crime Information Center – database.

'He never ran him? If he'd simply run him, you guys might have focused on Doyle a day or two after Christmas?'

'Something like that.'

'Would have changed everything. Everything. For Mallory, maybe for Diane,' I said. I'm a master of understatement.

'Woulda, coulda.'

Sam didn't seem particularly contrite about his support for Jaris Slocum. Did I want him to be? I guess I did. It seemed to me that a whole gaggle of Sam's colleagues had been complicit in covering for Jaris. 'Well?' I asked. Sam wasn't looking at me; he was staring at his right hamstring, which was the size of a pork tenderloin.

'Jaris is meeting with the bosses now. They're trying to find a way out of this that doesn't smell too bad for the department. But no matter what, it's not going to turn out too good for Jaris.'

I considered what I'd witnessed at dinner at the Sunflower. 'Alcohol?'

'That's part of it.' Finally, he looked up from his leg.

'You knew?' I said.

'His wife left him a year ago, got his kids after a nasty custody eval. As you might expect, Jaris had developed a little animosity toward mental health professionals and lawyers after that little fiasco. He should never have been sent out to Hannah Grant's office that night, but that's hindsight – who knew that he'd be spending his evening hanging out with shrinks and lawyers?'

'Sounds like his superiors should have known enough to rein him in. You did. Darrell Olson did.'

'This all started right after Sherry left me. Despite the fact that I'd never really liked him, I had sympathy for the guy. I thought he just needed some room, some time to sort through all that was going on. We covered for him, all of us did. Could've been me, Alan. Could just as well have been me. Or you. You done chewing on him? I have other stuff I want to tell you.'

'He was still drinking the other night at dinner, Sam.'

'Couple of beers.'

'That he downed like Gatorade after a marathon.'

'And?' he said. He said it provocatively.

'And what?'

'You're doing it again, Alan.'

'I'm doing what?'

'Cops are people. Guess what? We have problems. Sometimes we handle them, sometimes we don't. Same as shrinks. Same as teachers. Everybody. Jaris Slocum screwed up. Happens. People cut him some slack. Nice people like Darrell Olson do that. Slocum hung himself with it. Happens. Get over it. Nobody knew he fudged his investigation of Doyle Chandler. And nobody guessed what was going to come of it.'

Sam offered me nothing but a stony face that was more punctuation than anything else. I read the punctuation to be a period.

I said, 'Okay, I'm done.'

'Wise. The partials we found in the search last night? One of them is Bob Brandt's right index finger.'

'Oh shit,' I said.

'Yeah,' Sam said. 'Oh shit. We have his fingerprint in the basement theater and we have his car leaving the garage of the house at the other end of the tunnel during the window when Mallory disappeared from her home. Circumstantially speaking, it doesn't look too good.'

'But nothing on the BOLO?'

'It's a rare car. It shouldn't be as hard to find as it's turning out to be. I'm thinking it's parked inside someplace. I don't think he's using it; we'd have it by now. We're going back into his place on Spruce later, this time with a warrant. We're going to test that blood.'

'Pine.'

'Pine then.'

'Say hi to Jenifer for me.'

'Jenifer?'

'The cute kid? The one who wants to go to Clemson?'

'I'll be sure to send your regards,' Sam said sarcastically.

63

Sam wasn't talkative as we ran, nor was I. My lungs were trying to recover from their shock at being forced to process enough oxygen for cardiovascular exercise in Colorado's best impression of a deep freeze. After his initial, 'Let's go,' we covered a good quarter-mile before Sam grunted anything more. He had been running on my heels, but pulled up astride me and said, 'News.'

I thought it was a question, that Sam was asking me what I'd heard about Diane. Tapping my pocket I replied, 'Nothing. Got my phone with me in case Raoul calls.'

'No, I have more news for you. About the neighbor.'

'Doyle?'

'You'll hear this soon enough: Doyle Chandler's not Doyle Chandler. It's a stolen identity. We don't know who he is. Was.'

'You're kidding.' I knew he wasn't kidding.

'The Doyle Chandler whose social security number matches that of the guy we found murdered yesterday died in a car crash with his parents, Renee and Dennis, in 1967 in Roanoke, Virginia. He was six years old at the time. The man who lived next door to the Millers filched the kid's identity. He's been using it for sixteen years.'

'So whose body was it?' I suddenly didn't even know what to call Doyle.

'We don't know, and we may not ever know. AFIS doesn't pull a match on the index print he gave for his Colorado driver's license. NCIC has bupkis.' Sam paused to allow his breathing to catch up with his talking and running. 'Animals had chewed off almost all of the fingertips and most of the face before the body was discovered. We're not going to get usable prints from what's left. We have his teeth, of course, but the guy hadn't seen a dentist in a while.'

'What about the house? There must be prints there.'

'The techs aren't hopeful – the place had been professionally cleaned after he moved out. Need to match them with something, anyway.'

'This case,' I said.

'Tell me about it,' he agreed, and fell back into position on my heels.

Five minutes later, from the ridge top above the neighborhood, I watched a sedan without headlights approach the junction of dirt lanes that leads toward our house. It wasn't a car I recognized. Light in color, GM in ancestry, its boxy shape dated it back a decade or more. Our neighbor Adrienne's latest nanny? Possibly. I kept an eye on the car as it took the turn onto our lane, but our route carried us down the other side of the ridge and I couldn't see the car's ultimate destination.

Sam passed me on the downhill and increased the pace for the final mile. I was exhausted after the run. He, too, seemed unnaturally winded. We both knew it wasn't just the jog. 'Coming in?' I asked. 'I'll make you breakfast.'

I'd already looked around for the GM sedan. It wasn't at my house or at Adrienne's.

'Have to get to work,' Sam said. 'Simon's with Sherry.'

I was perseverating on Sam's news that Doyle wasn't Doyle. But I had no easy way to digest that news, so I refocused on Sam's implication that Bob might be deeply involved in Mallory's disappearance, but couldn't get anywhere with that either. Bob was a schizoid personality. He was as schizoid as anyone I'd ever met. Bob kidnapping Mallory – or anyone else – made no more sense to me than a pedophile breaking into an old folks' home.

'You no longer consider Mallory a runaway, do you?'

Sam said, 'I go back and forth. If she is, it looks like she had help getting out of the house. If she isn't, we have a different problem. What was the neighbor's role in all this? Did he take her? Did he help her? What was Camaro Bob's? Did he have something to do with it? Looks like he did. What's what exactly, I haven't decided. I still want to know why Doyle dug that tunnel in the first place. Why did he want into the Millers' house so badly?'

The obvious was to me, well, obvious. 'He lived next door. People prey on kids, Sam. He could've become obsessed with her.'

'A voyeur? That's all you got?'

'I'm thinking worse.'

He scowled. 'Why dig a tunnel?'

'To do his thing. Access.'

'Risky as shit. Three people live in that house. He's bound to get caught wandering around in there trying to get at the girl. Doesn't work. You live next door, there're much easier ways to spy on a kid.'

'Maybe he went in at night when they were asleep.'

'There are pervs who like to watch girls sleep?' Sam asked.

After all his years as a cop, Sam's residual naiveté still ambushed me sometimes.

'There are pervs who like just about everything.'

He held up his hand. 'I don't want to hear it.'

I thought about the theater in Doyle's basement. All the top-end electronics. 'Did Doyle wire their house? Hide video cameras in Mallory's room? The bathroom? Anything like that?'

'We checked. Fixtures are all clean, attic's clean. No holes drilled where they shouldn't be drilled. There's nothing there, not a single extra cable in the Millers' house, not a single cable coming back through the tunnel to Doyle's. No transmitters. If he put surveillance in, he took it back out when he moved away.'

I thought for a moment, forcing myself to go back to basics. Psychology basics. The best predictor of someone's future behavior – maybe the only predictor – is his past behavior. I said, 'Car thieves steal cars, right? Bank robbers rob banks?'

Sam looked at me as though he'd just realized I was mentally challenged. 'Yeah, and psychologists ask stupid questions.'

'What do we really know about Doyle Chandler?'

'Not much,' Sam admitted. 'Did I tell you he was shot?'

'No, you didn't.'

'He was shot. Behind the ear, slight upward angle. Shooter wasn't real close, no burns on his skin. Slug looks like a .38. Second and third shots to his back. But they were just insurance. He was already dead with the first slug.'

'Suspects?'

'Camaro Bob's on the list.'

I didn't want to hear that. I went back to Doyle. 'You know one more thing about Doyle for sure, Sam: He steals identities,' I said.

'Yeah?'

He knew where I was going. I said, 'You were wondering about the motive for the tunnel. There it is.'

'Doyle went into the Millers' house to build a new identity?' Sam said.

I noted – with some relief – that his question was almost entirely devoid of skepticism.

'What better place? Say Doyle went in during the daytime when Bill was at work and the kids were at school. He'd have the run of the house. Personal records, financial records, work stuff that Bill left laying around. Computer files, his e-mails, maybe even passwords. Be like Wal-Mart for an identity thief. With a tunnel he could take all the time he needed to fill in every last blank.'

'"Lying" around. Bill would leave stuff "lying" around. Not "lay-ing" around.'

I smiled. 'Does the gratis English lesson mean you think I got the rest right?'

'Maybe,' Sam said. Even though he'd already caught his breath, he put his hands on his hips the way exhausted athletes do, stared at me, and momentarily left any parsimony behind. 'We blew it the first time. Eight years ago? We did. I don't care about the public face we tried to put on it, the damn truth is that we fucking blew it. Guess what? I don't want to be the guy who blows it this time. If you have something that'll help me find that girl, I need to hear it. Second chances don't come around too often in life. I have one. We need to redeem ourselves.'

In the years since the other little girl's death, I'd never heard Sam be so brutal in his appraisal of law enforcement's role. 'Okay, yeah,' I said.

'Yeah, you have something? Or, yeah, you understand?'

Did I have something? If I did, I wasn't sure what it looked like. I said, 'Yeah, I understand.'

He stepped toward the Cherokee. 'I don't need your understand-ing.'

64

I tried to stretch out my calves a little more as I pondered Sam's challenge and watched him disappear down the dusty lane. I was just about to go back inside when the square front end of an approaching car came my way. It stopped a hundred yards or so down the road, in a little turnout on the soft shoulder.

The car was the GM sedan I'd seen earlier. The sun had crested the eastern horizon and was reflecting off the windshield. From my vantage point I could tell the car was pale yellow. The hood ornament clued me in that it was a Cadillac.

I stuck my hands in my armpits to warm my fingers, and I waited.

A man climbed out of the driver's seat, stuffed his hands in his pockets, and began walking toward me.

Bob Brandt.

Even at a hundred yards I recognized the denim jacket. My thought? *Thank God you're alive.*

'Somebody's been in my house,' he said when he got within fifty feet. His voice was pressured. He didn't say hello.

So what else is new?

'I know,' I said. I'd come to the conclusion that it was Doyle who had trashed Bob's place, but I kept the guess to myself.

'Did you read my stuff?' he asked.

That's why Bob was at my house: to chastise me for breaking his trust and spilling his secrets. That was fair – I had broken his trust and spilled his secrets. 'Hi, Bob,' I said, reframing things, at least for a moment. 'I've been worried about you.'

'Why?'

Bob's 'why' was a classic schizoid question, but perfectly sincere.

329

His disorder left him with only the most rudimentary concept of 'concern,' at least the person-to-person variety.

'I hadn't heard from you, thought you might be in . . . danger.'

'Oh.' He played with the notion for a moment before he added, 'I went somewhere. Do you know what's going on? Who was in my place?'

'Are you okay?'

'Tired. Drove all night.'

'Are you here by yourself?'

He turned his head and looked back at the Cadillac, as though he needed to check to be sure. 'Yes. What's going on? Did you read my stuff? I told you not to. You must have seen my note.'

'Like I said, I got worried. Anyway, I think you wanted me to read it. Otherwise you wouldn't have given it to me. We can talk about it.' It was shrink talk, but it also happened to be true.

'I was just getting started. It's just a story.'

'The tunnel part is real.'

He swallowed, and his eyes started their disconcerting shimmying. He spit a solitary word: 'So?'

Bob's retort was schoolyard bravado, nothing more.

'How can I be of help right now?' I said, trying to sound therapeutic.

He seemed surprised by my offer. After a moment, he said, 'That's a good question.'

He stepped back, literally and – I feared – figuratively. Instinctively, I sought safer ground for him. 'Is that your car?'

His eyes found the Caddy and lingered there. 'It's my mother's.'

Your mother's? Was Bob being sardonic? I couldn't say. 'You like it?'

He'd returned his attention my way, but was looking past me toward the distant turnpike. Finally, he said, 'Lots of power. Good cruiser. Cushy. Only fourteen K on it.'

'Not as cherry as your Camaro,' I said.

'Close,' he said. 'Pretty close.' He made an unfamiliar popping sound with his lips. 'Maybe you can help somebody . . . I know.'

'A friend?' I asked. *Please tell me Mallory's okay.*

Emily chose that moment to erupt; she'd apparently just realized that her homeland security had been violated and that a stranger was on her doorstep. Her fierce barking – even though it came from inside the house – caused Bob to retreat a few steps.

'She's fine,' I said.

'I don't like dogs. You know that.'

I didn't think I knew that. 'She'll stay inside. Bob?' I waited until I thought I had his attention. 'The police are looking for you. They want to talk with you about Mallory. I think you should get a lawyer and go see them. I can put you in touch with someone.'

'Sheesh,' he said, and did his little half head-shake thing.

I experienced an odd sense of relief that I'd finally lit on something I could share with Sam. I said, 'You should know that whatever you decide to do, I'm going to tell the police you were here.'

He was puzzled. 'Is that some . . . rule? You have to tell?'

'No. It might even be breaking some rule. It's what I think is the right thing to do.'

He nodded. 'That's what I did, too. What I thought was the right thing.'

'You could be in danger. Doyle's dead.'

'No, he's not.'

Okay. I didn't see a point in arguing. 'The police need to talk with you.'

'I didn't do anything wrong.'

'It'll be fine then. Let me put you in touch with an attorney.'

My phone rang. I pulled it from my pocket and checked the screen: Sam. I said to Bob, 'Excuse me. This will take just a second.' I turned away, putting a dozen feet between us. 'Yes,' I whispered into the phone.

'I passed that DeVille on the way out of your neighborhood – the one we saw during our jog. Had a funny feeling, so I ran it. Expired tags, but it's registered to somebody named Verna Brandt in—'

'I know.'

'He's there?'

'Yes.'

'A deputy is on the way. I'll be right behind them.'

I turned around. Bob was almost all the way back to the Cadillac. 'Don't,' I yelled.

He jumped in the car, spun the sedan in the dirt as though he practiced the maneuver on weekends, and was gone within seconds.

A huge gust of wind whooshed from the west. I didn't sense it coming and the blunt force of the gale almost blew me over. When I finally caught my balance I looked toward the mountains the way somebody might look to check the identity of somebody who just sucker punched him. My conclusion? The forecast Chinooks had definitely arrived; the slopes of the Front Range were already haloed in snow that was being whipped off the glacial ice of the distant Divide.

I braced my feet and tried Sam on his cell, but didn't get an answer. I waited until the sheriff's deputy and Sam drove up, told Sam what had happened, and wished I could start the day all over again.

Lauren was planning to hang out with Grace on Saturday morning and then the two of them were going to do some clothes shopping at Flatiron. Later in the day, winds permitting, they were planning a mother-daughter 'tablecloth restaurant' visit someplace Gracie kept insisting was a big secret. I spent the morning hoping to hear from Raoul or Sam. Didn't. I filled the time writing a couple of reports that were long overdue, and did a few chores around the house before I cleaned up, hopped in my car, drove the few miles west to my office, and prepared to see Bill Miller.

I wasn't looking forward to the visit, and half hoped he would bag the session because of the Chinooks.

65

Bill was waiting for me.

His car was parked where Diane usually left her Saab, not too far from the doors that led from our offices to the backyard. He was standing between the taillights, leaning back against the trunk, his arms folded over his chest. The January sun was already low over the southwest mountains and the fierce wind gusts were blowing anything that wasn't bolted down from the west side of town to the east. Some day soon, one of these Chinook events was going to propel our rickety garage from our side of downtown to the other.

I stopped my wagon parallel to his car – but a few feet farther from the rickety garage than usual – and stepped out. I didn't like that his car was parked in back. I didn't like that he wasn't waiting for me by the front door.

He greeted me with, 'You knew.'

I chose defensiveness. Wise? Probably not. 'I'd given my word to the police, Bill. I also knew you'd find out what happened soon enough. I'm sorry I couldn't tell you. It would have made things easier for both of us.'

He nodded; he'd probably traversed that territory himself. 'What's your role in all this?' he asked. 'Why were you at Doyle's last night? And those other times?'

His voice seemed to carry better in the wind than mine did; mine felt like it was being swallowed up like spit in the ocean. 'It has to do with what was making me concerned about the dual-relationship problem I talked about.'

Bill nodded as though he understood. But I wondered how he could even hear, let alone understand. The nod must have meant something else.

'When we talked last night did you know that Doyle was dead?' he asked. I had the sense that he was methodically going down a list of questions. I also had the sense that he didn't really expect to learn anything novel in my responses.

'Same situation, Bill; I couldn't talk about it with you. I knew you would find out this morning anyway.'

He turned his head momentarily so he was gazing west toward the mountains, frankly into the wind. His hair flew back behind him like he was a character in the cartoons. 'Do you know where my daughter is?' he asked.

I half heard him, half read his lips. 'No, I don't. I wish I did,' I said.

'You're sure?'

'I am.' Almost reflexively, I asked him the same question. 'Do you know where she is, Bill?'

'No.'

'What's the third option? The other night you suggested the possibility that running and kidnapping weren't the only options.'

'Hiding.'

'Hiding? From what?'

He surprised me by taking a quick step closer to me, closer than I liked. 'Life. Yes, hiding. I have a story to tell you.'

In retrospect, that was the point when I should have stopped him. Walked away. Told him therapy was over, or that it had never really begun. Handed him my license and let him use it for a coaster. Given him the phone number of the state board that censures wayward psychologists, like me. Something.

But I didn't. I still had a scintilla of hope that Bill knew something that would help me find Diane.

'One day last spring,' he began, 'I came home from work and found Doyle Chandler inside my house, sitting at my kitchen table drinking a beer. My beer. My records – my files, my bills, my checkbook, you name it – were spread out all over the table in front of him.'

'Bill, I—' I tried to interrupt him. Why? Something visceral was still telling me to get him to stop.

'I'm not done.' He raised both eyebrows and through a hissing exhale said, 'Give me this. I deserve this.' I stepped back involuntarily.

He immediately closed the distance between us. 'Doyle knew everything about me. Said he'd spent almost a month going through my things. Paperwork, letters, tax returns, computer files. Passwords. Everything. He knew about Rachel, her . . . problems. He knew the kids' grades, their teachers' names. Knew I have a swollen prostate, that my LDL's too high. Everything that makes our family different from the Crandalls across the street, everything that makes us who we are, he knew.'

I had an incongruous impulse to comfort, to tell Bill the truth about Doyle Chandler, his neighbor, and the truth about Doyle Chandler, the boy who'd died in a car accident in Roanoke with his parents back in 1967. I wanted to try to placate Bill with the fact that he'd been had by a damn good con man.

A blast of wind sandblasted my skin. The impulse passed.

Bill went on. 'I was irate. I asked him what he was doing in my house. He just laughed. I demanded that he get out, that the kids were coming home any minute. He stood up and walked over to the refrigerator and pointed at our family calendar. He said, "No, they're not. Reese is at hockey practice till seven. Coach usually keeps them late, you know that. And it's Kyle's mom's turn to drive, anyway. Last time she stopped and got the kids dinner at Pizza Hut, remember? She'll probably do something like that again – Frannie's like that, such a sweetheart. And Mallory is studying at Kara's. Cute kids, Mallory and Kara. Really cute kids.'

'He knew it all. Everything. Take a minute, try to imagine it. Go ahead, try. What that would be like. He knew every secret. Every intimacy. Every dirty detail. When you think you know how bad it feels, double it. Then double that. That's what it was like.'

I tried to digest what that kind of intrusion would feel like to a father. Surreal.

A huge piece of Styrofoam jumped the fence to the west and crashed into the side of Bill's car. I ducked; he continued to seem oblivious to the fierce gales. I forced myself to observe him, to try to read what I could about his affect. I wasn't getting a clear sense of where he was at that moment. It was apparent that he had no trouble summoning the rage he felt at Doyle Chandler. But there was something else present in the mix, some other emotional component that I couldn't put a finger on.

'Doyle had already gone through every last thing I owned and decided that simply stealing my identity wasn't enough of a payoff for all his effort. He wanted money, of course,' Bill said. 'Lots of it.'

'Why didn't—'

'—I go to the police? Because I have things to hide. He knew by then that I couldn't go to the police. Same reason I couldn't turn over Mallory's diary when I found it after she disappeared.'

'Things to hide?'

'Everybody has something they don't want the world to know. Everybody. For some people, it's something embarrassing. Maybe even humiliating. For some, it's something . . . worse. To save my family, I did some desperate things years ago. I made hard choices. For me it was something worse.'

'Rachel and Canada?' I said, guessing that Bill's secret had to do with money. Instantly, I wished I hadn't guessed, at least not out loud.

'Do you know? I'm not sure . . . doesn't matter. I'll tell you.'

'Bill, it's not—'

'Shhhh. I'm not done.'

For a fleeting second, right then, I felt menace from him. The scent of peril was fleeting, like a waft of perfume as a lovely woman waltzes by. I allowed myself the luxury of believing that I'd misread him, and I somehow convinced myself that it was okay to dismiss the menace as an illusion, to allow it to be carried away on the wings of the Chinooks. In retrospect, that was a bit of a mistake.

'Rachel's illness almost buried us financially. When we came to see you way back when it was already bad, but after? That year after? Lord. The medicine, the doctors, the hospitals. Not to mention all the damn weddings. There were always more and more damn weddings, always. Rachel was better when she went to weddings, much better. The voices weren't as frequent, not as scary. So I fed the beast, paying for the outfits, the gifts, everything. I was in so far over my head. Mortgaged to the hilt, credit cards maxed out. Every month I was borrowing from a new Peter to pay an old Paul.

'I was about to declare bankruptcy. I didn't know what else to do. Then the voices began telling Rachel – demanding – that she had to move to Las Vegas or . . .' He took a moment to reflect on some ugly, ugly room in his wife's private hell. 'And that meant she would need even more money. I begged her not to go, but the voices were too frightening. I thought I was going to lose everything then. The house, the kids, Rachel.

'Then I got handed a way out. My boss had just been promoted to western regional manager – a big deal for him. His wife threw him a surprise party up at the Flagstaff House just before Christmas. Late, close to two in the morning, I was driving behind him down Baseline and . . .' Bill shook his head, disbelieving. 'He was distracted, I guess. I don't know what it was, but a pedestrian was walking from the Hill over to Chautauqua, right across Baseline. I saw her clearly from a block and a half away – she had her hands in her pockets, her head down against the cold. Walter just mowed her down.

'She must have flown a hundred feet in the air. Turned out she was a young mother, an orthodontist. He never even touched his brakes; he just plowed into her. I still see her body flying. Sometimes, I feel the impact when I'm asleep.

'He killed her, of course. She was dead at the scene.'

He paused, and I reminded him that he'd told me about the accident years before when he'd stopped by to thank me for my help with Rachel.

'I didn't tell you the next part. Walter was in shock. Kept saying, "What happened, Bill? What happened?" I saw an opportunity. I told him to shut up and listen to me. As out-of-it as he was, he did. When the cops came, I told them what I saw. A white van was coming up Baseline in the other direction. The woman walked out from behind it. My boss couldn't have seen the woman. I told them I was right behind him and I didn't see her until she was in the air. It wasn't Walter's fault at all. That was my story.'

'You made up the van?' I asked.

'It was two in the morning. I figured I was the only witness. My boss matched his story to mine. It worked. Why wouldn't it? Turned out his blood alcohol was just a hair below the legal limit so he wasn't even arrested. He was never charged with anything. He didn't go to prison. His promotion was secure. His family . . . was safe.'

'You saved his ass?'

'I did it for me, not for him. I was saving my family. I told you I was desperate. I don't even like Walter. He's a prick.'

'I don't understand,' I said. But I did. Before I'd left her office, Mary Black had suggested enough that I could guess the rest.

'I knew Walter would be grateful.' Bill suddenly seemed out of breath.

'The promotion you got,' I said, filling in a blank for him. 'The one you told me about years ago?'

'Yes, that promotion. My salary went way up, and then it went up again. I began getting regular Christmas bonuses. That was eight years ago. I had a good job, better than I deserved. I was making enough money to make ends meet here and enough to keep Rachel safe in Vegas, barely.'

'Until Doyle Chandler showed up at your kitchen table?'

'I'd kept a record about everything that happened in case Walter ever turned on me. When Doyle starting coming into my house he did it simply to steal my identity, but then . . . then he ended up finding every last thing I'd kept about Walter and the orthodontist. Newspaper clippings. Notes. Everything. Once he understood what I'd done, and how vulnerable I was, he changed his plans. Doyle wanted a cut.'

'How much?'

'He asked for ten thousand a month. We settled on five at first. But I knew I couldn't do five for long. Canada was demanding more and more money to keep doing what he was doing for Rachel in Las Vegas. As she got sicker he had to pay more people more money so that she would be . . . left alone. What choice did I have? What could I do? I was in so deep.

'When Doyle moved out in the fall and put his house on the market, I thought he might have realized that the till was empty, you know? Hell, he knew my finances as well as I did. Better, maybe. I thought – God, I was naive – I thought things might be over. But that's when Doyle went to Walter and started blackmailing him, too. Walter and I realized he'd moved away so that we couldn't find him. My boss wasn't happy. He's not a pleasant man when he's not happy.'

The sky was getting dark and, despite the warming winds, I felt winter and January all the way to my bones. It wasn't just the temperature, though; I knew that.

'Bill, would you like to come inside?' I said. 'Sit down?'

He looked around as though he'd needed to remind himself we

were indeed outside, nodded, and followed me to the back door of my office. Once we were in I flicked on some lights and sat across from him as though we were doctor and patient.

Were we? Partly yes, partly no. Mostly no. All the ethical guidelines I'd always held so dear were designed to keep therapists from feeling the ambiguity of roles I was feeling right then, were designed to keep patients from suffering the conflict-of-interest vulnerabilities Bill was floating in right then. What a mess I'd made.

The thing was, I wasn't too upset about it.

Bill crossed his legs, uncrossed them, stood suddenly, and moved to the southern windows. His back was to me, and he seemed to be focused on the advancing sunset that was visible through the skeleton of the ash trees. My sense was that he wasn't sure how to resume his narrative. I could have drawn the shut-up-and-wait arrow from my quiver. I didn't. To help him find a way to restart his story I chose an option that I thought was a gimme: 'That's when you found out he'd dug a tunnel? The day Doyle showed up in your kitchen.'

'No, I had no idea that's how he'd gotten in. Learning about the tunnel last night was a complete surprise to me. A tunnel? Never crossed my mind, not for a second. I thought Doyle had a key to our house, that he'd discovered where we hid our spare, or had somehow gotten hold of one of the kids' keys. That's what he'd led me to believe. He had told me not to get an alarm, not to change the locks. Told me I'd regret doing any of those things. When he'd threaten me with what I was going to regret if I didn't cooperate, he'd always mention the kids.'

'He threatened them?'

'He tried. I threatened him right back. I told him if he came into my house when the kids were home, I'd kill him. If he so much as talked to them, I'd kill him. I think he believed me.'

She was scared. That's what Bob had said about Mallory. *She was scared.*

Was that why she was scared?

'What did Mallory know about all this?' I asked.

'Mallory,' he said in a long exhale. His breath temporarily clouded the window glass in front of his mouth. 'Mallory.'

I thought he was about to cry.

66

'She hasn't had a good Christmas since she was six.' Bill said into the glass. 'That's eight years, most of her life. She hates Christmas.'

She misses her mom. Diane had told me that Mallory missed her mom. The year that Mallory was six was the year that Rachel abandoned her family for the lure of Las Vegas weddings.

Psychotherapy 101: Christmas for Mallory was irrevocably linked to loss.

Finally, I thought I understood why Mallory had felt so compelled to see Hannah Grant for psychotherapy: Mallory hadn't had a good Christmas since she was six. She went to see Hannah because she didn't want to have another bad Christmas, another Christmas when her primary emotion involved desperately missing her mother.

'She'd get so scared,' Bill said. 'Every year, right after Thanksgiving she'd start to get scared.'

Scared? That's what Bob had said about Mallory, too. *She was scared.* Why scared?

'Scared?' I asked. I would have suspected that Mallory would show signs of anxiety or depression on the anniversary of her mother's abandonment. But fear?

Bill wiped at his eyes with his fingertips. 'She thought it was going to happen again. She couldn't be comforted. No matter what I tried to do over the years to help her deal with it, nothing worked.'

Rachel had deserted her family eight years before. Was Mallory afraid that her father was going to leave, too? Was that the vulnerability she felt? 'What, Bill? Mallory thought what was going to happen again?'

He turned back from the window. His face was pink and bright. 'What happened eight years ago on Christmas? Mallory thought she'd be next. Every year since that year, she's been afraid that she'd be next. That the same man was coming to get her.'

Oh my God, what an idiot I am. Mallory was scared because of the murder of her friend. 'They were friends? When they were little?'

'Classmates. A sleep-over or two. You know what it's like for girls when they're that age. That Christmas, Mallory was already so vulnerable because of . . . what was going on with her mom. What happened that night scared her so much. She used to cry and cry every time she saw the pictures on TV. And those pictures were everywhere.

'She was so determined to confront her fears about Christmas, to grow out of it. She desperately wanted to get past all this, to feel safe.'

'The police know all this?'

'Of course; it's why they think she ran. They think she got spooked and left to go find her mom and that something – you know – happened to her on the way.'

'Did she know about Doyle? About the blackmail?'

'She knew something was up with me, that I wasn't myself. She'd mentioned it. It's in her journal.'

'Did she know about the tunnel?'

'I know what you're thinking – that that's how she got out of the house. But how could she know about it? I didn't know about it until last night. She was terrified of the basement. The basement is where her friend's body was found eight years ago. She never went down there. Never.'

'Doyle?'

'Doyle could have shown it to her, I guess. But why? He had too much to lose if he exposed what he was doing. And I think he knew I meant that I'd kill him if he went near the kids.'

I thought, *Bob.* That's how she could know. Bob's fingerprint was in the basement. Bob was taking care of Doyle's empty house. Bob knew all about the theater – he had told me that he thought it was a great place to watch movies. And Bob certainly knew about the tunnel.

Bob and Mallory had talked.

Had Bob actually been there on Christmas night, holed up in Doyle's theater watching movies?

Mallory's friend – the other little girl, the tiny blond beauty queen – had died eight years before as Christmas Day became the day after.

She was scared, Bob had said about Mallory.

She thought it was going to happen again, her father had said about Mallory. She feared that someone was going to come into her house and do to her what someone had done to her little friend. She feared that someone was going to bust in and leave her head crushed and her neck garroted, that someone was going to abandon her alone and dead in her grungy basement on Christmas night.

Doyle? Bob? The man loitering outside?

Who?

I'm a gullible guy. But I'm aware that I'm a gullible guy, so aware that sometimes I catch myself and pause long enough to question what I'm hearing. Right then, I stopped, and I questioned. *Do I believe what Bill is telling me?*

Yes, kind of.

Is he telling me the truth? No, probably not completely.

I replayed some of the earlier conversation I'd had with Bill Miller. '*When Doyle moved out in the fall and put his house on the market, I thought he might have realized that the till was empty, you know? He knew my finances as well as I did. Better, maybe. I thought – God, I was naive – I thought things might be over. But that's when Doyle went to Walter and started blackmailing him, too. Walter and I realized he'd moved away so that we couldn't find him. My boss wasn't happy. He's not a pleasant man when he's not happy.*'

'What,' I asked, 'did your boss do when Doyle started blackmailing him?'

'Same as me. He paid him off, bought some time. After so many years you don't expect to get caught.'

Content is the aphrodisiac of psychotherapy. For a therapist, it's so tempting to get caught on the wave of the story, to get lost in the facts and the promise and the details of the narrative. What suffers when the therapist succumbs to that seductive lure?

Process. And process – what is going on in the room – is almost always where the truth hides. I forced myself to be a therapist. I returned my attention to the process.

'Why did you decide to tell me all this, Bill?'

'I didn't know what you'd already figured out. I actually thought you might know too much. That would be a whole new problem for us.'

'Us?'

'Me and Walter.'

'I don't quite understand,' I said. But I did.

Bill's voice was almost apologetic as he said, 'I've just tied your hands, Alan. You can't tell anyone what I told you. It's confidential, now. I can't afford to have anyone know what I've done. Walter can't either. So, just in case – for some insurance – I've sealed your lips.'

Was Bill right?

In his reading of the law, and of my professional responsibilities, yes.

In his reading of me, no. He had no way to know, but I was more than ready to say 'screw it.' Was I angry? A little. Less than I would have anticipated. 'Doyle knew everything,' I said. 'He may have—'

'Doyle's dead, remember?'

'Did you—'

'Kill him? No. God, no. I would have liked to, I might even have been willing to, but . . . no.'

'Did your boss?'

'He's probably capable of it. Walter's in Vegas now trying to find Rachel. To see if Mallory's with her. We have to keep her under control. He and I are in the same boat on this one. Our families are both at risk.'

'Rachel knows about the orthodontist?'

'She's my wife; of course she knows. I don't have secrets from Rachel.'

I stated the obvious. 'You're desperate, then. You and . . . Walter?'

'Yes, we are.'

'Why did he go to Vegas?'

'One of us had to get to Rachel. I couldn't – the press might have spotted me. They're everywhere.'

I'd noticed. 'Do you think Mallory's there?'

'I hope she is.' His despair about his daughter was palpable. 'The alternatives are so horrifying that I can't even . . .'

My cell phone rang. I checked the screen: Raoul. Thank God. 'I need to get this,' I said. 'It's an emergency. There may even be some news that affects Mallory.'

'Go ahead then,' Bill said.

'Raoul?' I said. 'Any news?'

'I'm at the hospital with her. She's okay.'

Diane? 'Hold on a second; I'm with someone.' I covered the phone and turned to Bill. 'Could you please go out to the waiting room while I take this?'

Reluctantly, I thought, he walked out of my office and down the hall. I kept my hand on the phone until I heard the waiting room door open and close.

67

'She's really okay?' I said.

'She's safe. She held my hand. We talked. She had a little food. Now she's sleeping.'

'Where has she been? What happened?'

'I was sure Canada had Diane, or he could lead me to her. I had it all wrong.'

'What do you mean?'

'None of Canada's people have seen Rachel since Tuesday. Turns out Canada's had me on a leash since I got to Vegas. He's been watching me, concerned I'd be causing him more trouble with Rachel, later on hoping that I'd lead him to her.'

'I don't understand. How did you find Diane?'

That's when he took a deep breath and slowed his voice and began relaying the long story about the ratty cab and doing dead time in the Airstream and about the old VW bug and Tico, and about playing the echoes with Canada.

Before dawn on the morning after Raoul met with Canada in the walled house in the scruffy desert outside of the city, Tico fired up the VW and drove Raoul into the desolate mountains west of Las Vegas. Raoul recalled seeing a sign for Blue Diamond near their destination – so wherever that is, that wasn't too far from where they ended up. Just as it was beginning to get light Tico stopped the bug on a mountain curve, and asked Raoul if he was up for a little hike.

'This is where the accident was?' Raoul asked him, recalling Canada's story the night before.

'The guy's driving too fast,' Tico said, pointing down the road. 'Way too fast, and he comes around the curve – that one – and sees

345

a guy standing in the road with a .45 pointed at his windshield.' He held up both hands. 'This is what I hear. The man in the road fires a shot – you know, to warn the guy – a little bit over the top of the truck. Driver doesn't handle it good. Freaks.' Tico then pantomimed a dive off a cliff before he kicked off his flip-flops and began pulling an ancient pair of orange high-top Keds onto his bare feet.

A moment later Raoul followed him down a scruffy hillside covered with nothing but scree and big boulders. They went down a hundred feet or more into a narrow wash that had been invisible from the road above. A battered, crushed, bronze Silverado with Colorado plates rested upside down on a rock that was half the size of Tico's VW. Inside was the body of a man. The stink was horrific.

Tico said, 'That's the guy, the guy in the picture with Howard, the guy who met your wife in the Venetian. You want me to check for ID?' Raoul wasn't able to come up with an answer for him, but Tico pulled on some work gloves and crawled into the overturned truck. A minute later he handed Raoul a Colorado driver's license.

The name meant nothing to Raoul. 'What's farther up the hill? Where was he going?' Raoul asked.

'A couple of old cabins. Might be important. To you, anyway.'

'But not to you?'

'This . . . accident? It happened before Rachel lost touch with the boss. We weren't too interested in what was up there. Not our business, you dig. We stay out of things that aren't our business. That's one of the boss's rules.'

'Can we look?' Raoul asked him. 'At those two cabins? Now?'

Tico said, 'I got a little time.'

The second cabin they checked, the last one on the road, was where they found Diane. Raoul went in alone and found her cuffed to an iron bed. She'd been there a long time. She was delirious, almost unconscious.

Tico used his mobile phone to call somebody down in Vegas, asked them to send help. Then he told Raoul, 'I gotta go before, you know . . . And my man? The police don't need to know about the Silverado. That'd be better for everybody.'

Raoul told him he understood and he promised to come up with a story for the police.

Fifteen minutes later people started showing up to help Raoul save his wife.

I briefly relayed to Raoul most of what I'd told Lauren the night before. I told him about the tunnel and the car that had left Doyle's garage right around the time Mallory disappeared. I told him that Doyle Chandler wasn't Doyle Chandler, and that whoever he really was, he was dead.

'Are you coming home?' I asked.

'As soon as they clear her to travel,' he said.

'Can you tell me who the guy in the Silverado was?'

'Does it make a difference?' he asked. 'I promised I'd be discreet. The cops didn't find it. It needs to stay that way.'

'I think I know.'

'Who?'

The irony didn't escape me: Raoul was protecting secrets, too. I gave him the name he already had: 'Guy named Walter.'

His voice grew tight. 'You've known about him for how long?'

'This afternoon. Just now.'

'He was a bad guy?'

'He had something important to hide. He was afraid Diane might have learned what it was from Hannah.'

'When I get back we'll have a beer, you'll tell me how you know all this.'

'I'm looking forward to that, Raoul. Listen, I'm with a . . . patient. Call me back when I can talk with Diane, okay? Please?'

We said good-bye after Raoul asked me if I had any idea how to thank someone for saving his wife's life. 'Canada?' I wondered.

'No, Norm Clarke,' he said.

I thought I'd read somewhere that Norm had a weakness for foie gras, but I promised Raoul I'd think more about it and stepped back out to the waiting room to get Bill Miller.

The front door was wide open. The coffee table was tipped over, magazines scattered on the floor.

Bill was gone. *Damn.* Immediately, I regretted leaving him alone for such a long time.

The winds seemed to have stopped.

68

Huh. What did Bill's hasty exit mean? Why the overturned table and the open door? Had something happened while I was talking with Raoul, or was Bill making a statement about his frustration with me, or about his annoyance that I'd interrupted our meeting to take a phone call?

My relief that Diane was okay was so strong at that moment that I wasn't particularly upset about whatever had prompted Bill's departure, but I was perplexed. Why had he taken off so suddenly?

I was becoming more and more convinced that Mallory's Christmas night disappearance had been accomplished with Bob's help. What had happened next? I was guessing that she'd talked Bob into driving her somewhere and I was hoping that she'd somehow made it to Vegas to visit her mother. Where were mother and daughter right then? I didn't know. Raoul's story satisfied me that Bill's boss, the by-then-dead Walter, hadn't been successful in tracking them down in Vegas.

But where was Bob? If Sam had caught up with him, I was sure he would have called and let me know.

I straightened up the waiting room, walked back to my office, and phoned Bill Miller at his home. No answer. I left a message, and asked him to call me back on my pager. Then I called home. The girls were still out on their excursion. I left Lauren a message that I was going to run a few errands and that I'd be home in time for dinner.

As cold as it can be in Colorado in January, there are always respites, warm days in the high fifties or low sixties when the sun defies its low angle in the southern sky and the blue above is just a little bluer. I was surprised when I stepped outside to discover that the Chinooks had

348

abated and left the day so much warmer than it had been earlier. The seat heaters in the Audi seemed superfluous. I flicked them off and drove east to begin my errands.

I felt the vibration of my pager while I was waiting in line to buy some fish for dinner at Whole Foods. Had Lauren asked for ono or opah? I couldn't remember. I pulled the beeper off my belt and read Bill Miller's familiar number. My turn at the fish counter had arrived, so I mentally flipped a coin and chose a good-sized piece of opah before I meandered over to the relative quiet of the dairy department to return Bill's call.

'We need to talk,' he said.

'I went back out to the waiting room and—'

'I just got a call about Mallory.'

'From whom?'

'The Colorado State Patrol. They found a body, a girl, in a ditch near I-70 west of Grand Junction.'

'Oh my God,' I said. 'What can I do?'

'I want to talk to you before whatever happens next. I need to make sure I'm thinking straight.'

'Bill, you just admitted that you're using the therapy to shut me up. I don't think I'm the right person to—'

'Fire me tomorrow. Tonight I need some help.' He sounded genuinely frantic. I couldn't imagine his terror. I looked at my watch. 'My office. Ten minutes,' I said.

'I have to be here, at home, if they call back. I can't leave. Can you come over?'

'I'll be right there,' I said. I tossed the opah on top of a display of organic butter in the dairy case, and sprinted to my car.

349

69

Maybe it was the time of day, just past dusk. Or maybe, as Sam predicted, the fierce assault of the Chinook blitzkrieg had scared everyone off. But the media encampment outside the Millers' home was deserted, the street peaceful. Doyle's house was dark.

Bill met me at the front door. I didn't even have to knock.

'Thank you for coming,' he said as he ushered me inside. 'Can I get you something? Some tea? I make good hot chocolate. That's what the kids tell me, anyway.'

'No, thank you.'

His cordial greeting left me off-balance as he led me to the back of the house and a battered oak claw-foot table with some mismatched pressed-back chairs. 'Sit, please.' He pointed me to a seat that faced the service porch and the rear yard. 'Thank you,' he repeated.

'What can I do to help, Bill?' I wanted to get down to business, whatever it was. I wanted to get home. I wanted to convince myself that I hadn't made a big mistake by agreeing to this impromptu house call.

'You being here helps.'

It wasn't what I wanted to hear from him. 'Bill, I'm glad you find my presence comforting. But my advice to you is simple: Tell the police everything you know. The journal, everything. If you have new information, they need to know it. Mallory's welfare is more important than anything else.'

'I appreciate your counsel. You were absolutely right about Rachel years ago. But I'm not sure you really understand the dilemma I'm in. Calling the police isn't an option.'

'Mallory's safety is the most important thing. Your legal situation is secondary.'

'I'm her father. She needs me. Both kids do.'

'I'm sure that's true, but—'

'But nothing. If someone had your daughter, or your wife, or both, you would do anything to get them back, wouldn't you? Anything?'

Once I had. Once when a madman was trying to break into my house I'd closed my eyes and pulled a trigger to protect my pregnant wife. I'd do it again if I had to. And again after that.

Bill had continued talking through my silent reverie; I wasn't sure if I'd missed anything. When I tuned back in he was saying, 'Like right now, if you didn't know where your family was, I bet you would do anything to find them, to make sure they were safe. Right?'

'Of course.'

'Do you?'

'Do I what?'

'Do you know where your wife and daughter are right now?'

What? 'What do you mean?' I was trying to keep my voice level. I was certain I was failing.

'Your family? Do you know where they are right now?'

No, I didn't know where they were. 'Right now? What are you saying, Bill?'

'Nothing. I'm just trying to describe my situation in a way that might make sense to another father. The desperation I'm feeling. Do you understand the desperation?'

'Are you threatening my family, Bill?'

'What on earth are you talking about?'

'Have you done something to my wife or daughter?'

'See? That's exactly what I'm talking about. Right now? I think you're beginning to get it. My desperation. That's good.'

'Answer my question.' I stood up. 'Have you done something to my family?'

A creaking sound pierced through the house. The floor? A door? Had I caused that?

'Did you hear that?' Bill asked. He stood, too.

'Yes. Is someone else here?'

'No. Maybe it was nothing. Old houses, you know.'

Was he unconcerned, or merely cavalier? I couldn't tell.

Another creak disturbed the quiet.

351

'Then again,' Bill said. 'I'm going to check around a little. You want to call your wife and daughter, ease your mind, you go right ahead.'

Bill stood and left the kitchen. Immediately, I pulled out my cell and phoned home. No answer. I tried Lauren's cell. No answer. I placed the phone in front of me on the table. My heart was pounding. Bill came back into the room.

'See anything?'

'No.' He spotted the phone on the table. 'Don't worry, I'm sure they're fine,' he said, as though he knew I hadn't reached Lauren.

Any pretense of patience gone from my voice, I asked, 'What can I do to help, Bill? You said this was about Mallory. Tell me what's going on or I'm leaving.'

Certain sounds are as clear as photographs. Glass breaking is one of those sounds. The stark retort of shattering glass filled the house.

'Shit,' Bill said. He stood.

I stood, too. 'Where?' I whispered.

'Sounded like the basement.'

I wasn't so sure, but it wasn't my house.

He moved toward the stairs. 'I'm going down. Probably just some neighbor kid trying to scare me. It's been like that around here.'

'I'll call nine-one-one.'

'No, this is my home. No police. I'll handle it. Stay here.'

He flicked on a light and disappeared down the basement stairs. I spotted a rack of knives on the kitchen counter and shuffled a little closer to them.

Before I reached the counter, all the lights in the house flashed off, at once.

70

I stumbled back toward the table to grab my phone and as I reached out I managed to push it over the edge onto the floor. The phone clattered and slid away into the darkness. I dropped down to my hands and knees to try to locate it.

'Alan!' Bill stage-whispered from the basement. 'Down here, please, hurry.'

'I'm calling for help.'

'Please, it's Mallory!'

The tunnel? I scrambled to my feet and felt my way toward the basement stairs, found them, and slowly started descending. A solitary step into the basement I ran into someone. The shock of the collision took my breath away.

'It's me,' Bill whispered. I could feel his breath on my face. 'Come on.'

He took my wrist and led me across a room and through a doorway. 'This is where the glass broke, I think.'

I couldn't see broken glass. But then, I couldn't see much. 'You said it was Mallory. Where is she?'

'What are you talking about?'

What? 'Where's the tunnel?' I asked.

'In the crawl space.'

Somewhere nearby, a door closed in the house. Bill released my arm and stepped away from me, back toward the door we'd just come through.

I moved in the same direction.

'Shhh,' he said.

'Is there a phone down here?' I whispered.

'Quiet. I need to listen.'

The door at the far side of the room we were in opened slowly. A figure paused in the doorway – a black silhouette against an almost black background. Burnt food on a cast-iron skillet.

Mallory? No. Too large, too masculine.

Bob? Maybe.

I was about to call Bob's name when the person's right arm began to rise and a brilliant flash blinded me and a deafening roar blasted my ears. Before I could even process the first explosion, another one erupted. Then, I thought, another. The figure's knees began to buckle and he grasped at the door frame with both hands.

The support did him no good. A second later he heaved forward and collapsed to the floor.

My hearing temporarily gone, my eyes useless in a basement dark as a moonless night, I was most aware of the smell of the burnt powder from the gun. I was trying to figure out what had just happened. Bill touched my arm and forced a flashlight into my hand. I flicked it on and saw the gun he was holding. It was a revolver. A big thing.

'Over here,' Bill said. I pointed the light in the direction of his voice. He'd stepped away from me and was standing in front of a gray electrical panel. With the benefit of the illumination he reached up and pulled hard at the main power circuit.

Instantly the lights in the house came back on.

With great relief I realized that I didn't recognize the man in the heap at the foot of the stairs. It definitely wasn't Bob.

The butt of a pistol had come to rest two inches from the man's nose. Had the man been holding it? I didn't remember hearing it clatter to the floor. I said, 'Who is it? Do you know him?'

Bill moved closer. 'It's Doyle.'

He didn't sound surprised.

71

I was.

'Doyle's already dead, Bill.'

'That must have been somebody else they found in the mountains. That's Doyle, right there.'

I used the toe of my shoe to move the pistol away, knelt, and placed my quivering fingers on the side of the man's neck. I couldn't find a pulse. I thought of Hannah a month before, the same fingers, the same result.

'Who was it that they found near Allenspark?' I asked.

'I don't know. I don't care. Doyle's dead for sure, now. For me, that's nothing but good news.'

Bill wasn't upset.

'Why . . . did you shoot him?'

'He broke into my house. You saw that.'

'He's been in your house a dozen times. Why did you shoot him?'

'You saw what happened. A broken window. An intruder in the dark. He was going to shoot me. Us.'

He stressed the words 'intruder' and 'dark.' I thought his explanation sounded rehearsed and I immediately questioned whether Bill knew that Doyle was going to be in his house, in his basement. 'Did you know he was coming over?'

Bill didn't answer me. 'Did you? Did you know he was coming over?'

He still didn't reply. I thought, *Damn, make my day.*

You set this up, you bastard.

Car thieves steal cars. Bank robbers rob banks. For Bill, this was the white van and the orthodontist all over again.

I started up the stairs to get my phone to call 911. When I was about halfway up I heard a woman's voice. 'Willy? You down there? What was that noise?'

72

Willy?
  Rachel.
  'Rachel? Baby?' Bill said.
  This time he sounded surprised.

73

Sam didn't arrive first – some patrol cops did – but he was there within fifteen minutes.

He wasn't happy to find me in Bill Miller's house. He wasn't happy to hear Bill Miller claiming that he and I had been having a psychotherapy session when we heard the glass break. He wasn't happy to hear me concur with Bill that what he had told me prior to the shooting had to stay confidential.

What was Sam happy about?

I think he was reasonably pleased that Rachel Miller was there, and that she was insisting that her daughter, Mallory, was fine. 'She'll be here any minute. Any minute,' Rachel kept saying. 'Don't worry, don't worry.'

Before he and I were separated by the cops, Bill readily admitted shooting the intruder in his house, whom he continued to insist was the man he knew as his next-door neighbor, Doyle Chandler.

Sam parked me in the Millers' living room. 'You okay?' he asked.

I said I was.

'Good. What about Rachel?' he said to me. 'How did she look to you? As a shrink.'

'From what little I saw, not too bad. I suspect she's on her meds. I'd have to evaluate her to be sure, but she looks much better than I would have predicted.'

'Do you believe what she's saying about Mallory?'

'I think she believes what she's saying about Mallory. It's either delusional, or it's not. I don't know her well enough to tell you which.'

'Thank you, Dr. Freud.'

'There's a chance she's telling the truth, Sam. That's a good thing. Hope, right? Has she said how she got here?'

'"With Mallory and her friend." I'm thinking Bob, the Camaro guy.'

'You never found him this morning?'

'No.'

'Is Bill claiming the shooting was a "make my day" thing?'

Colorado has a frontier-justice 'Get Out of Jail Free' law that permits citizens to use deadly force to protect personal property. Intrude on a Coloradan's homestead – and raise enough of a ruckus while you're at it – and you had better hope that the home-owner isn't armed, because he or she has every legal right to blow you to smithereens, even if you're not threatening any imminent bodily harm. The law is popularly known as the 'Make My Day' law.

'Yeah,' Sam said. 'He is. Loudly. Was it?'

'I'm not a lawyer, but probably. Glass broke, power went out, suddenly the guy is there in the basement. Bill shot him. Three times, I think.'

'Three?'

'Yeah. I think three. He kept shooting.'

'Was the guy armed?'

'It was dark. After the lights were back on, I saw a gun next to him on the floor.'

'All sounds pretty convenient.'

'Maybe, I don't know. Bill's been through a lot.'

'The broken glass? You see it?' Sam asked.

'No.'

'Wasn't a window. Somebody put a couple of clear vases or some-thing on the sill in the basement window well. Anyone who opened the window would have knocked them off. I find that kind of . . . sus-picious.'

'People put stuff on windowsills all the time.'

'Window was unlocked,' Sam said. 'No sign it was forced.'

'A lot of people have been in and out of this house lately.'

'You sticking up for him?'

I didn't want to go there. 'Bill said the guy he shot was Doyle, Sam. Is that possible?'

'Yeah, I heard. Maybe he has a twin,' he said. 'Only thing I know for certain about this whole mess is that there are way too many

Doyle Chandlers around for my taste.' He stood up. 'Tell me again, why were you here?'

I looked him in the eye and told him it was privileged, which told him almost all he needed to know.

Diane wasn't in danger anymore. I had secrets to keep.

'Figured.' He ran his fingers through his hair while he continued to stare at me. His next sentence surprised me. 'Scott Truscott says you solved the Hannah Grant thing.'

I shrugged. 'I had a thought; I shared it with him. He put it all together; I guess the coroner agreed.'

Sam's raised eyebrows mocked me more than his words did. 'A thought? You had a thought? You seem to have a lot of thoughts.' He paused. 'And a lot of sources.'

I took the comment exactly as Sam intended it – as an accusation.

A patrol cop stuck her head into the room and said, 'Detective? That Cadillac? The BOLO? We got it.'

'Where?'

'CU. Parking lot near the stadium. SWAT's responding.'

He looked at me, waiting to see if I was going to be obstinate. I surprised him, I think. I said, 'Duane Labs. Plasma physics. Fourth floor.'

Sam repeated the location into his radio as he rushed from the room, leaving me alone.

I walked to a beat-up mahogany secretary, picked up the telephone, and called my house. Lauren and Grace were safely home from a wonderful dress-up afternoon, enjoying high tea at the Brown Palace in Denver. Turned out that Gracie loved scones and clotted cream and peppermint tea in china cups, and was absolutely over the moon for cucumber sandwiches. I gave Lauren a concise version of what was going on in Boulder and assured her I'd be fine. After we hung up I dialed a second number from memory.

'Cozy?' I said. 'Hate to ruin your Saturday, but someone I know needs a lawyer.'

74

Bob had indeed told Mallory about the tunnel.

She'd used it on Christmas night to get away from the bad guy she had convinced herself was waiting to do to her what had been done eight years before to her young friend. She'd discovered Bob watching movies in Doyle's theater, and had asked him for help in getting away.

Bob had complied.

Mallory had stayed in Bob's flat for the first few days after she'd left home. Once she'd recovered from her Christmas night fright, she ended up mostly terrified about the ruckus she'd caused by running away, and fearful of the repercussions she was sure she would face when she surfaced. She never was quite sure what to make of the fact that the therapist from whom she'd sought help had died.

Out of boredom as much as anything, she finally cajoled Bob into a road trip to see 'our mothers.'

Their first stop was Las Vegas, where they picked up Rachel. The second stop was the assisted-living facility in southern Colorado where the trio paid a brief visit to Bob's mother. That's where Bob switched the Camaro – it had developed a problem with its clutch – for his mother's pale-yellow '88 DeVille, which was almost, but not quite, as cherry as Bob's '60s muscle car.

After the real fake Doyle was killed by Bill Miller in his basement, the police didn't have too much difficulty piecing together the identity of the fake fake Doyle.

The man whose body had been discovered in the shallow grave near Allenspark turned out to be a homeless man named Eric Brewster whom Doyle had apparently hired to be an unidentifiable corpse rotting in the woods. That probably wasn't the job description he'd offered Brewster when he'd recruited him off the streets of Cheyenne, but that was the job the poor man got. Doyle was ready for the Doyle Chandler identity to die, and he'd picked Brewster carefully, choosing a man about his size and coloring. He gave Brewster some of his own clothes before he led him out into the woods and shot him in the head. Doyle planted his ID on the body, reasonably figuring that a winter and spring in the elements would destroy any clues, except DNA, as to who the dead man really was. Without a sample for matching, he knew the DNA wouldn't do law enforcement any good.

Doyle Chandler would be dead for at least the second time.

Raoul brought Diane home on a medical jet charter on Monday, the day after he rescued her. Medically she was going to be okay. Psychologically? We held our breaths; time would tell. She'd have love and support, all she needed. Would it be enough? I hoped it would. Diane was tough.

She used Scott Truscott's assessment that Hannah Grant's death was a tragic accident as a crutch to help herself get back on her feet. I wasn't too surprised that Diane was back to work within a week. The first patient she saw on her initial day back?

Fittingly, it was the Cheetos lady. We passed each other in the hall as Diane led the woman from the waiting room to her office. She smiled at me as though we were buddies.

All, apparently, was forgiven.

With Diane safe, and Bob safe, and Mallory safe, I went back to keeping secrets. I was well aware that had Raoul found Diane even half a day later, I probably would have spilled all the beans I had on Bill Miller. With my friend out of harm's way, though, I knew that revealing what I'd learned from my patients would have been nothing more than a self-destructive act of reprisal.

Still, believe me, I had considered it.

I didn't reveal what I knew about Bill and Walter and the ortho-dontist. I'd initially learned all those things in my role as a psychologist, and couldn't rationalize revealing them. Did I feel good about keeping those secrets? No, I didn't.

Deep down, I'm quite fond of the idea of justice. But, as fond as I am of justice, it's not the business that I'm in.

Walter's family soon reported him missing, but I kept my mouth shut about the location of his body. Raoul did, too. I wouldn't have known anything about Walter if I hadn't been treating Bill, so I considered that information privileged. Was I haunted by the fact that I had knowledge that could help end a family's fruitless search for a missing husband and father?

Yes, I was.

Nor did I ever publicly share my suspicions that Bill had enticed Doyle back to his house so he could murder him, once and for all, or that I thought he'd arranged for me to be there as his hapless witness. I couldn't prove any of it, but I believed it all to be true. I think Sam did, too. He told me that the police had some phone records that provided circumstantial support to the theory.

But Sam didn't think he could prove it either. Lauren admitted that when the DA reviewed the evidence, she'd concurred.

The Millers became a family again: Mallory was home, Reese came back from his sabbatical with out-of-state relatives, and Rachel moved back into the house. Would the familial bliss last? I had my doubts. Mary Black, still consumed with her triplets, referred Rachel to a psychiatrist in Denver who was having success treating people with symptoms like Rachel's with some innovative pharmaceutical cocktails.

Miracles happen sometimes. Rachel needed one, probably deserved one.

Bill?

As the dust was starting to settle I phoned him, and asked politely for one last session.

He declined.

I rephrased my request, turning it into something a little less polite and a little stronger than an invitation. He relented, as I knew he would, and when he came to my office to see me I didn't bother to waste any time on therapeutic niceties. I told him I wanted both of his kids in therapy, and gave him the names of the carefully chosen therapists I wanted each of them to see. I made it clear that I wasn't making a suggestion; the consequences of not heeding my advice would be harsh.

'Yeah?' he said, cocky as shit. His attitude was, 'What the hell can you do to me now?'

I had placed my walnut-framed Colorado psychologist's license upside down on the table between us.

'Yeah,' I said, failing to match his cockiness.

He crossed his arms. 'I don't think so, although I appreciate your concern.'

It was readily apparent that he didn't actually appreciate my concern. I reached down to the table and flipped the frame right-side up. In case he didn't recognize the parchment document, I said, 'That's my psychology license.'

He looked down at it. 'So?'

'I'm willing to lose it.'

He eyed me suspiciously. Disbelieving my resolve, I think.

I added, 'What are you willing to lose, Bill?'

'You wouldn't.'

I handed him a copy of a letter that I'd mailed the day before. 'Read this. All it lacks is a name. Your name, actually.'

He took a moment to read the letter.

'You release my name like this, you'll never work again.'

'Maybe. My colleagues on the state ethics board have always proven themselves to be rather lenient, even to a fault. Regardless, I'm willing to take the risk. If it does come to losing my license, I think I can find work, but something tells me it won't come to that. Why? Because I don't think you really want your role in this whole thing examined by a panel of skeptical strangers with Ph.D.'s.'

Was I blackmailing him?

Yes.

Bill knew plenty about blackmail. He'd seen it from both sides.

Ultimately, he accepted my prescription about his children because he didn't have much choice. How did I know he followed through? Both therapists called and thanked me for referring the kids. I felt some consolation that Reese and Mallory were getting the best mental health care possible. Would it be enough to save them?

In truth, probably not. I wasn't even sure what saving them would look like. But I held out hope for them anyway.

75

The letter that I'd mailed the day before I met with Bill Miller?

The head of the Ethics Committee of the Colorado Psychological Association didn't know exactly what to do with it.

Psychologists don't usually turn themselves in for ethical violations.

But I did; I turned myself in for multiple violations of the ethical code of the American Psychological Association.

There's a psychological phenomenon, an ego defense if you will, called undoing, or sometimes, doing-undoing. A husband sends flowers to his wife the day after he flirts shamelessly with his secretary. A mother makes a special dessert for her daughter after she sentences the kid to death row for not putting the cap back on a tube of toothpaste. It's unconscious psychological misdirection – the substitution of an act that is acceptable to the ego for something that was not. In the world of psychological defenses, it's the great cosmic chalkboard eraser.

Turning myself in for unethical conduct was my own twisted version of doing-undoing.

What I'd prepared and submitted to the ethics board was a detailed account of my multiple professional transgressions in the clinical care of both Bill Miller and Bob Brandt. Although I had to withhold plenty of specifics – including my patients' names – I put in sufficient evidence of misjudgment to make my myriad ethical lapses crystal clear to my colleagues.

I'd also sought written permission from both Bob and Bill to release their names to the ethics investigators, but both, not surprisingly, chose anonymity and declined to participate in the inquiry. Neither was eager to prolong public scrutiny of their behavior.

Without the cooperation of the patients involved the board had little to go on other than my self-damning appraisal of my own professional conduct.

The head of the board phoned and asked me, mildly exasperated, what I thought they should do with me.

I suggested a sanction: a full year's monitored supervision of my practice by a senior, respected psychologist.

The board greedily concurred, content to have the matter behind them.

I felt a little better, but not much. As an ego balm, doing-undoing is a notoriously ineffective palliative. And when you know you're doing it – and employ it without the insulation of unconscious motivation – as I was, undoing amounts to little more than a half-hearted *mea culpa*.

76

Bob?

Our regular Tuesday at 4:15 came around slightly less than forty-eight hours after he and Mallory had been picked up by the police in the plasma physics reception area in the Duane Building at CU. Mallory was watching Bob deadhead his Christmas begonia when the first few SWAT officers burst into the room and scared the crap out of both of them.

Head down, as usual, he walked into my office for his appointment at the regular time. He plopped his backpack onto the floor and sat across from me without a word of greeting.

We'd been there, literally, a hundred times before.

Bob had spent one night stewing in police custody while Cozy Maitlin convinced the authorities that his client was guilty of nothing more than piss-poor judgment. Mallory had repeatedly denied that Bob had ever coerced her to do anything, denied that he encouraged her to run away, vigorously maintained that the road trip had been her idea, and asserted that he'd never placed a hand on her during their entire time together. Mallory's only actual complaints about Bob were that he wasn't very friendly and hardly ever said a word that wasn't about cars or board games.

Rachel Miller confirmed that Bob had been a well-behaved, if boring, companion to her and her daughter.

The police discovered no evidence to the contrary. None.

I waited only a moment for him to settle onto his chair before I said, 'Hello.'

He was staring at his hands. I supposed that Bob knew that I had

367

arranged for Cozy to represent him. Although Bob Brandt and Cozier Maitlin were probably the oddest client-attorney pairing since Michael Jackson and anybody, I suspected that Cozy would have told Bob how lucky he was to have him for a lawyer. I doubted Bob would mention it to me, and I wondered if I should bring it up if he didn't.

'Am I going to be charged?' he said, finally breaking the silence, and interrupting my reverie long before I'd reached anything approximating a decision.

With kidnapping? Didn't look like it, but that was definitely a question that should be directed to Cozy, not to me. It was my turn, though, so I said, 'Charged for what?'

'For last week.'

Oh. 'The session you missed? No, I won't bill you for that.'

Bob acknowledged me with a nod, but he didn't thank me. Did I expect him to? No, not really.

When he finally raised his face enough so that I could see it, I spotted a cold sore the size of a lug nut on his lower lip. The rounded wound was fresh and blistered. Had to hurt. I thought, *Stress.* He didn't speak again for a while. Then, 'I almost lost my job. It was stupid.'

'What was stupid?' I could have asked. But the recent idiocy options were numerous. Too numerous. Plenty by him, plenty by me.

More by him.

I waited. The Kinko's box sat beside me on the small table next to my chair. Had Bob seen it when he walked in? I hadn't noticed him even glancing in my direction.

'She asked. I didn't kidnap her. Sheesh.'

No half head-shake, just the 'sheesh.'

Although technically it was my turn to speak, Bob said, 'I shouldn't have shown her the tunnel in the first place.'

I could have argued with him at that point, suggesting that maybe what he shouldn't have done was drive a minor who was the subject of a national manhunt across state lines, but time was on my side. An entire year of Tuesdays littered the calendar ahead. Bob and I would get there eventually.

'She was scared after that therapist died,' he said. 'I thought she should know how to get out of her house.'

His tone, I thought, was defensive, which wasn't too surprising. But was Mallory's fear really the way Bob was going to try to rationalize his decision to help her stay hidden when the whole world was frantically looking for her? I suspected not.

Why? Pulling off that argument would require that Bob convince me that he'd suddenly developed a capacity for empathy. Sadly, the events of the previous couple of weeks would no more leave Bob with empathy than they would leave Bill Miller with a well-functioning superego. 'Go on,' I said.

He sighed before he turned away, reached down, and rooted around in his rucksack. He lifted out an electronic device about the size of a paperback book and held it up for me to see.

I couldn't help but smile. It was a fancy, programmable remote control. The one from Doyle's basement, no doubt.

'Perhaps you should give that to your attorney,' I suggested.

He stuffed the remote back into the daypack and gazed out the window. The southern sky warned of dusk. He said, 'She doesn't look fourteen.'

My spleen didn't spasm. I allowed the force of gravity to press me solidly against my chair.

'Tell me,' I said.

I thought I'd try to be a therapist for a while.

Acknowledgments

As usual, I got a lot of help.

My gratitude to the kind, talented people at Dutton, especially Carole Baron and Brian Tart, and to my agent, Lynn Nesbit.

Jane Davis, Elyse Morgan, and Al Silverman continue to support me in ways that are personal as well as professional. I've said thanks. I'll say it again, knowing it's not enough. Nancy Hall, once more, brought her critical eye to the process.

If I wore one, I'd tip my hat to Virginia Danna and Darrell C. R. Olson, Sr. Call it courage, call it blind faith, but they paid good money to charity to have their names used for characters in this book. I think I'll just call it generosity. Norm Clarke, on the other hand, was a draftee. His gracious, one-of-a-kind introduction to Las Vegas and his willingness to let me give him an important role in the story were much appreciated.

Robert Greer, who does more things well than anyone I've ever met (other than perhaps his late wife, Phyllis), provided some consultation about one of his many specialties. And although I've long been indebted to them for pushing the swing, the Limericks – Jeffrey and Patricia – deserve some fresh credit for one of this book's small secrets.

Xan, Rose, and my mother, Sara White Kellas, continue not to be surprised that I'm able to do this. They believe, and what is better than that?